Gaelen Foley is the *New York Time*
bold historical romances set in the g
England and the Napoleonic Wars. Her books are available in twelve languages around the world, and have won numerous awards, including the Romantic Times Reviewers' Choice Award for Best Historical Adventure.

Gaelen holds a BA in English literature with a minor in philosophy and it was while studying the Romantic poets, such as Wordsworth, Byron and Keats that she first fell in love with the Regency period in which her novels are set. After college, she dedicated herself completely to her artistic pursuits, spending five and a half years moonlighting as a waitress to keep her days free for writing and honing her craft.

Gaelen lives near Pittsburgh with her college-sweetheart husband, Eric, and a mischievous bichon frise called Bingley. She is hard at work on her next book.

To find out more about Gaelen's books visit her website at www.gaelenfoley.com

Also by Gaelen Foley

The Knight Miscellany Series:

The Duke
Lord of Fire
Lord of Ice
Lady of Desire
One Night of Sin
His Wicked Kiss

Inferno Club Series:

My Wicked Marquess
My Dangerous Duke

The Spice Trilogy:

Her Only Desire
Her Secret Fantasy
Her Every Pleasure

Devil Takes a Bride

Gaelen Foley

piatkus

PIATKUS

First published in the US in 2004 by The Random House Publishing Group,
First published in Great Britain in 2006 by Piatkus Books Ltd
This paperback edition published in 2011 by Piatkus

All characters and events in this publication, other than those clearly in the public domain, are fictitious and any resemblance to real persons, living or dead, is purely coincidental.

A CIP catalogue record for this book is available from the British Library.

ISBN 978-0-7499-5620-2

Typeset in Sabon by Hewer Text UK Ltd, Edinburgh
Printed and bound in Great Britain by CPI Mackays, Chatham ME5 8TD

Piatkus
An imprint of
Little, Brown Book Group
100 Victoria Embankment
London EC4Y 0DY

An Hachette UK Company
www.hachette.co.uk

www.piatkus.co.uk

Dedicated with love and many fond memories to all my wonderful cousins on both sides—

The never-a-dull-moment Kenny clan, who made Sundays at Mimi and Pap's house so much fun, and the wild-and-wacky Foley bunch who throw great family reunions complete with ghost stories around the campfire.

Blessings and much joy to you, your spouses, and adorable children.

Special thanks to Dan, the brother I never had, and to Tim, who tells people everywhere he goes to read his little cousin's books.

Love you, and thanks for bringing so much joy and laughter into my life . . .

Prologue

England, 1805

Moonlight flashed on three black racing-drags tearing up the Oxford Road, a heedless cavalcade – whips cracking, snorting blood-horses wild eyed and flecked with foam. The drivers were roués of notorious reputation in Town, their hardened young faces flushed with speed, taut with desperation. There was murder in their eyes, for each had everything to lose if they failed to overtake the stagecoach traveling some miles ahead. The autumn wind sent an eddy of dead brown leaves swirling across their path; the leader plunged through it, wheels whirring.

They barreled on.

A few miles up the road, the stagecoach bound for Holyhead rolled to a halt in the courtyard of The Golden Bull Inn and disgorged its weary travelers. 'You may rest for two hours before we're under way again,' the cheerful driver instructed, helping a lady passenger down from the coach.

'Thank you,' she murmured from behind her light lace veil. She stole a swift glance into the darkness behind them. *No sign of them yet*. 'Come, Johnny.' She took the hand of the frightened lad who climbed out of the coach behind her and firmly led him into the quaint, thatched-roof inn with its wooden galleries and neat black shutters.

As she strode into the hotel's lobby, the coppery ends of her waist-length red hair showed beneath the edges of the veil that concealed her famous face – and the black eye her protector had given her.

'Do you have a room open?' she asked, her hand shaking slightly as she signed the guest register, not under the name by which she was known throughout London – not her stage name – but under her real name: Mary Virginia Harris. The name they still called her at her village back in Ireland, where she was fleeing to now. Johnny clung beside her, all his thirteen-year-old's bravado gone, his thin, pubescent body shivering more with fear at their brash escape than with the chill of the November night.

'Aye, ma'am.' The aproned landlord tried to get a look at her through the pale barrier of lace, but her frosty stare rebuked him. Soon, he led her and her 'son' out of the lobby and away from the nearby public room, where numerous local men were drinking and playing darts, up to the second-floor gallery, where he showed them to their room.

As Johnny and she stood in the corridor, waiting for the landlord to unlock the chamber door for them, a little girl of about four poked her curly head out of the next room and giggled, playing peekaboo with them. Startled and decidedly charmed, Mary gazed at the wee thing for a second, until a woman's voice chided from inside the other chamber: 'Sarah, pet, come back in this room.'

The child grinned and disappeared again. Mary nodded her thanks to the landlord and pressed a coin into his palm as she followed Johnny into their room.

Little Sarah peeked out the door again a moment later, but the pretty veiled lady had closed her own door. She skipped across the chamber past her parents and climbed up carefully onto the chair to peer out the window. She breathed on the glass, then drew a happy face in the steam with her fingertip, just the way her big brother, Devlin, had shown her. She could hardly wait to see him, for they were on their way to fetch him home from school. It wasn't even Christmas yet, and he was allowed to come home! Yet for some mysterious reason, this wonderful news had set Mummy and Daddy to arguing.

'Now, Katie Rose,' Daddy was saying as he cleaned his spectacles with a handkerchief. 'There's no need to go flying up into the boughs. I'm sure the lad can explain himself.'

'Explain himself? Stephen, your son punched a truancy officer in the nose! We've sent him to the best university in England, and this is how he behaves? Skipping classes to go drinking and playing billiards with his friends?'

'He's seventeen, Katie. All boys get into a bit of roguery at school. It's a natural part of growing up. Besides, Devlin is still making some of the highest marks in his class.'

'I know it, blast him. He doesn't even have to try.' She folded her arms across her chest with a huff. 'Our son is lucky that he got his brains from you.'

'And his fighting spirit from you,' he said fondly, capturing her chin. 'Not to mention his big, blue eyes. Now smile for me, Lady Strathmore, or I will kiss that frown off your lips.'

She smiled at him in spite of herself. 'Save your charm for the dean, husband. After your son's antics, a large donation to the college is probably the only way we can contrive to get him merely suspended instead of expelled. Oh, I do hope Devlin's all right.'

'No doubt he was just showing off, as boys are wont to do.'

She nodded. 'I'm not sure whether I'll want to strangle him when I see him or give him the biggest hug in all the world.'

'You're his mother,' he said gently. 'Letting you down is, for Devlin, punishment enough. I opt for the hug.'

'I love you Stephen,' she sighed, resting her head on his

chest. 'What would I do without you? You're so patient and kind and good—'

'Horsies!' Sarah exclaimed, cupping her hands around her eyes and squinting out the window at the three noisy black carriages that came clattering into the courtyard below.

As the lead racing-drag shuddered to a halt behind the stagecoach, the first of the young men jumped out. Quentin, Lord Randall, was a great, towering brute in his mid-twenties, fearfully known as Damage Randall in the fashionable boxing studios of London. He was hazel eyed and thick featured, with a shock of brown hair and a square, rugged face ending in a cleft chin.

Quint stalked into The Golden Bull without waiting for Carstairs and Staines to catch up. Seeing the stagecoach parked in the courtyard had told him all he needed to know: Ginny was somewhere inside. He knew she had fled on the Holyhead stage, intent on taking the packet boat to Ireland, but Quint had no intention of letting her go.

She was his.

He plowed through the lobby, glancing into the nearby taproom for her, then marching over to grab the guest book out of the landlord's hands.

'May I 'elp you, sir?'

Quint merely growled, scanning the names until he saw the one that looked familiar. Mary Harris. Ginny had told him her real name once. He was surprised he had remembered it, for he usually chose not to dwell on her common origins. He preferred her stage name instead – Ginny Highgate. The glamorous actress, wanted by all, but he had got her through sheer bloody-minded persistence.

His mistress, his beauty, his prize.

Without explaining himself to the landlord or to anyone else, the big Yorkshire baron began a search of the premises, bellowing for her now and then.

'*Ginny!*'

'That damned fool. Has he never heard of discretion?' Carstairs mumbled under his breath, exchanging a taut glance with Staines as they strode into The Golden Bull two minutes behind their larger, more hotheaded companion.

The elegant and impeccably dressed Julian, Earl Carstairs, was flaxen haired and fine featured, with ice-blue eyes; by contrast, the dead-shot duelist, Sir Torquil 'Blood' Staines, had piercing black eyes and a dark satanic beard that came to a point.

'Let's try and do this quietly, shall we?' Carstairs murmured.

Staines nodded; then they split up to help Quint find the Irish bitch, who had dared to take it upon herself to rescue Johnny from *him*. Ah, well, Carstairs thought with an inward sneer, he'd get the boy back before anyone learned a thing.

In the upstairs hallway, Quint was throwing open doors of guest chambers and looking inside, not caring whom he disturbed in his search for his fled mistress. There were indignant exclamations, occasional shrieks at his brief intrusions, but the other guests, seeing the size of him and the ruthlessness in his eyes, did not protest.

He continued down the corridor in this fashion until he suddenly came to a door that was locked. He gripped the doorknob and put his ear to the planks. 'Ginny?'

No answer. He closed his eyes, trying to feel her, sense her through the door, for he believed they were that closely bonded. God, he smelled her perfume on the air.

'Ginny!' He rattled the door until he heard a low sob of fright from within. 'Come out, Ginny! Now! We're going home! Damn it, you know I love you!' He kicked the door in with three massive blows, his black Hessian boot nearly shooting through the wood as the door splintered off its hinges. Ripping it aside, he prowled into the guest chamber, his barrel chest heaving.

'Ginny.' He struggled for patience.

She was cowering in the corner with Carstairs's little servant boy clinging to her.

Quint saw how her eye had blackened, but he refused to feel guilty. By God, she had brought it on herself.

'Come on,' he repeated, holding out his hand to her. 'You're coming with me.'

'No,' she uttered.

'Leave her alone!' Little Johnny stepped in front of her, facing down the giant.

Quint muttered a curse and backhanded the boy, who fell with a yelp.

'What on earth is going on over there?' Lady Strathmore exclaimed in the next room, turning to her husband with her hands planted on her waist.

Stephen's narrowed stare was fixed on the partitioning wall as he listened. 'I think I'd better go and see if I can help. Stay with Mama, sweetie.' Patting his daughter's curly head, the tall, athletic viscount left the room and walked down the corridor, just missing young Johnny, who had fled the neighboring chamber a moment ago to run for help.

Bolting down the stairs in terror, Johnny flung around the corner so fast that he crashed into someone coming up. Gloved hands grasped his shoulders – a touch he knew all too well. His heart sank, but deep down, he had known their attempt to escape would never succeed. Not when Carstairs was the one chasing them.

'Johnny! So, there you are.' The earl gripped him harder and bent to peer into his face, his ice-blue eyes sharp with angry reproach. 'How dare you run off on me, you ungrateful little shit?' he whispered harshly, giving him a shake. 'How could you turn on me after all I've done for you?'

'I'm sorry,' Johnny choked out at once for the sake of self-preservation.

'Didn't I take you in, care for you – and you would help that wicked woman send me to the gallows?'

'The gallows?' he echoed, his heart pounding.

'Yes, Johnny. That's what they do to fellows like you and me. That's why we must keep it our secret.' Carstairs held him in a warning stare. 'Who's going to look after you if they hang me, Johnny? Who will send money to your poor mama?'

When Johnny hung his head, suitably chastened, Carstairs was somewhat mollified, though still a bit shaken by his horrifying brush with exposure for his proclivities. He straightened up. 'Come now. I'll take you back out to my carriage.'

With his hand on Johnny's back, he walked the boy outside and made sure he climbed up onto the drag.

'Stay here,' he ordered him. 'I'm going to make sure Quint has sorted things out with Miss Highgate. By tomorrow, we'll forget this ever happened.'

'Yes, sir,' the boy mumbled.

Carstairs's relief was short lived, however, for as he walked back toward the inn, a gunshot ripped through the night.

He paused midstride. *Ah, bloody hell.* So, Quint had finally done it, had finally killed the bitch.

Rushing onto the scene, however, Carstairs discovered the situation was far worse than that.

The whole thing had spiraled out of control.

A little curly-headed tot was crying in the hallway at an unbelievable volume while Ginny and another woman, quite hysterical, were on their knees beside a fallen man. Quint stood stock-still nearby, his pistol sagging in his grip; the hardened insolence on his face was slowly turning to shocked dread at what he had just done.

'Stephen! Stephen! For God's sake, get a surgeon!' the

raven-haired beauty screamed at them as she tried to plug the bullet hole in the man's chest with both her hands, to no avail.

In a state of dazed unreality, Carstairs walked forward and looked down at the ill-fated stranger. It took him a second; then he recognized the man from the House of Lords.

'Jesus Christ, Quint,' he breathed. 'You've shot Strathmore.'

'Stephen!' the viscountess shrieked, trying to wake her husband, who was unresponsive.

Something came over Carstairs, an extraordinary will to survive. It made his mind crystal clear, needle sharp.

Quint suddenly grabbed him. 'I didn't mean to do it. You've got to help me! I can't think, Carstairs—'

'Calm down, damn you! I'm going to get us out of this, Quint. Just – listen carefully.'

Quint's chest heaved with panic, but he bobbed his head, awaiting instructions.

Fighting panic himself, Carstairs steeled himself and took control. 'Go stand out in the hallway and keep guard at the top of the steps. No one leaves this corridor. We must keep this problem contained. You can do that, yes?'

'Yes,' Quint rasped.

'Go.' As the baron ran out to fulfill his duty, Carstairs strode over to Lady Strathmore and crouched down beside her, gripping her arm. 'Try to calm down, my lady. We've already sent for a surgeon,' he lied. 'He's on his way. Staunch the wound till he gets here, just like you're doing. That's good. Concentrate.'

This shut her up, gave her something to do and a straw of hope to grasp on to. Too dazed to realize he was lying, the lady nodded, shaking all over, then suddenly seemed to recall her screaming child. 'My little girl! Will you—?'

'I'll get her,' Ginny murmured, and ran out to collect the crying tot.

Carstairs eyed the actress with hatred as she rushed past him, then turned to Staines. 'If anyone gives you the slightest trouble, finish them.'

Staines gave him a mercenary nod.

Carstairs went to try to handle the rest of the hotel. He schooled his face into a charming, easy smile a moment before he went striding out into the lobby, where several people were looking toward the stairs in alarm, only now just beginning to wonder if something was wrong on the second-floor gallery.

'I apologize, sir, if I disturbed anyone with the report of my pistol,' he said to the landlord, loud enough for everyone to hear. 'I was cleaning my gun in my room when it went off. I'm afraid I gave the lady in the neighboring room a bit of a fright, so I wish to pay for her room to make it up for her.'

'Why, that's very kind of you,' the landlord said cheerfully, looking relieved at his explanation.

He spilled a handful of coins on the desk. 'Again, sorry for the disturbance. A round for the gents in the taproom, eh, landlord?'

'Why, that's a capital fellow,' several people murmured as he strode outside.

Well aware that he had come through that by the skin of his teeth, Carstairs sucked in a deep breath of cool night air, retching slightly. He knew his explanation had been too flimsy to do more than buy them some time, an hour if they were lucky. He wished to God they could simply flee, but too many people had seen them, and the death of a courtesan-actress was worlds away from the murder of a fellow peer. Strathmore was a quiet man, but universally esteemed.

Dry mouthed, the blood pounding in his veins, Carstairs glanced around for some means to make this whole debacle go away. He knew that if he did not cover up Quint's blunder immediately, Strathmore's death would be investigated; Carstairs, being part of it, would also be placed under the microscope, but

God knew he could not afford anyone probing into his personal life. There were still ancient laws on the books that decreed hanging for so-called sodomites, and he was not about to be publicly disgraced and executed on account of his taste for pretty young boys.

He saw Johnny still waiting obediently in his carriage, but as his frantic gaze swept the courtyard, Carstairs spied a delivery wagon parked on the side of the inn, near the entrance to the taproom. It was loaded with barrels, and the painted block letters on the side of the cart read BRANDY AND FINE SPIRITS.

An idea stirred in his mind. He looked at the inn's wooden galleries, dry as tinder; the thatched roof; the black shutters, mostly closed for the night. He glanced again rather evilly at the barrels of highly flammable liquor.

And he knew what he had to do.

A few minutes later, he, Quint, and Staines were working in swift, ruthless silence, each hefting a barrel, pouring and splashing brandy, whiskey, and port all over the perimeter of the building, locking the metal teeth of the window shutters as they went. Johnny looked on from his perch on the carriage.

'What about Ginny?' Staines grunted, bringing the torch. 'Do you want to get her out of there?'

'That bitch can go to hell,' Quint growled. 'This is all her fault.' Then he lit his torch from Staines's and they set the place on fire.

The three racing-drags thundered away from the scene a few minutes later, flames climbing into the black night sky behind them.

'Hold on, Stephen. I'll get you out of here. Darling, try.'

The fire raced through the hotel. The two women had barely noticed it at first in their panic over Lord Strathmore, but now smoke was filtering up through each tiny seam of the floorboards.

Mary held the screaming four-year-old in her arms and tried to urge the child's mother to come with her, but the viscountess would not leave her husband's side. He was still alive, vaguely conscious now, whispering, 'Katie.'

'Come, Stephen. You've got to get up. Lean on me.' The woman struggled to pull the tall, muscular man to his feet. Mary helped, too, but he could barely stand.

'I'm sorry, Katie. Go,' he pleaded. 'Take Sarah—'

'I'll not leave you!' His wife spun to Ginny. 'Get my child out if you can.'

'But, ma'am, you must—'

'Save my daughter!' she cried.

Mary nodded, abashed, for it was her fault the Good Samaritan had been struck down in the first place. Throwing her cape over the little girl to shield her from the smoke and fire, Mary left the woman to her continued efforts to save her husband and carried the bawling child down the stairwell. As she approached the ground floor, the fire roared, the screams growing louder as thick, black smoke choked the air.

The lobby and taproom were ablaze, the guests stampeding, trying to find a way out; a burning beam had crashed down in front of the only door, and every window seemed to be blocked from the outside. Someone broke a window with a chair to get out, but the inrush of air only made the flames explode with renewed fury.

It was like being in Hell.

Mary looked around in sweeping horror, no doubt in her mind that Quint and his evil friends had brought this about. Her heart was pounding, the heat becoming too intense to bear. The ash in the air stung her eyes so she could hardly see where she was going; coughing and choking, she could barely breathe. She knew if she didn't get out quickly, she would lose consciousness, and that would be the end of both her and the little girl.

Driven by her need to save her gallant rescuer's child, she ran from room to room, searching the ground floor for an exit. In the back parlor, everything was on fire, but as she glanced in, one of the burning shutters fell away, leaving a hole that led out into the night. A chance!

The heavy brocade curtains framing the window were on fire, however. Somehow she'd have to get past them. Hurrying to the window, she used part of her cloak to protect her hands while she fought to pry the window open. In terrified fury, she succeeded at last, wasting no time in lowering the little girl out.

'Run, Sarah!'

As Mary struggled to follow her out the window, she was almost in the clear, when the twisting flames that were devouring the curtains brushed her face. She screamed, falling out the window as her whole body jerked away from the pain. Her hair caught; she could not writhe away from the horror; it followed her as she ran. She fell to the ground in agony, and did not know where the water came from as it suddenly drenched her, several buckets full.

When she opened her eyes a moment later, she made out the shapes of several men mulling around, trying to help whomever they could.

'The little girl!' she wrenched out.

'She's right here, ma'am. Don't try to move. The doctor's coming.'

She didn't listen, struggling to stand. One side of her face felt flayed.

At that moment, the burning roof caved in. The Golden Bull collapsed in on itself like a failed soufflé. The screams were lost in the roar of the victorious fire. There could be no survivors now. Unsteady on her feet, Mary gathered the thrashing child in her arms. She knew she was hurt badly, but somehow she was alive – and so was little Sarah. They would not be that way for long, however, if her evil lover and his friends came back.

Blocking out the pain, Mary slipped away in the confusion, taking the child with her. She knew she must hide, must get help for her wounds; as soon as possible, she and the little orphan would flee to Ireland.

The raven-haired lad with sea-colored eyes and a sulky mouth drowsed on the hard bench in the anteroom to the dean's office, where he had wearily been awaiting his punishment for what seemed like ages.

At first, Devlin James Kimball, the seventeen-year-old heir to the Strathmore viscountcy, had been too hungover from his spree to think at all about 'the consequences of his actions,' as several school officials had instructed him to do.

Recovering somewhat later, he had spent a good twelve hours rehearsing pretty speeches with which to meet his mother's certain wrath over his row with the proctor's bulldog, but hang it all, the blackguard shouldn't have made that remark about Admiral Lord Nelson's glorious death and final victory at Trafalgar of a few weeks ago. Dev had considered it a matter of honor to defend his fallen idol's name.

Despite his excuse, though, he knew his tempestuous dam would call him to the carpet. Thankfully, Father was sure to come to his defense. God knew one disappointed glance from his sire weighed more on Dev than all his mother's stormy shouting. He heaved a sigh and thunked his head back against the cool plaster wall, his stomach rumbling with hunger. A chap could starve around here. Where were they, anyway? Why had no one come for him yet?

There was no clock in the detention room, but it felt like he had been in here for days.

Again that cold, creeping feeling inched down his spine – the inexplicable premonition that something was wrong. Hearing footsteps coming down the corridor, he sat up and scowled at the locked door. *Finally*. He quickly ran his fingers through his tousled black hair and did his best to adjust his cravat, bracing himself to face his parents' displeasure.

When the door opened, however, Dev furrowed his brow, for it wasn't Lord and Lady Strathmore, but the dean and the school chaplain, both old buzzards looking grim as death.

'Have a seat, son,' the dean murmured with unprecedented kindness.

Dev obeyed, but glanced through the open door into the hallway and furrowed his brow. 'Have they come?'

The chaplain winced and sat down slowly with him. 'My dear boy, we've sent for your aunt Augusta to come and collect you. I'm afraid there has been some terrible news . . .'

Chapter One

London, 1817

The fanciful cupola-topped pavilion languished in desolation on the frozen marshes south of the Thames, a gaudy ruin, with a gray February sleet blowing against its rusty, fake turrets and boarded-up windows. Some said the place was haunted. Others claimed it was cursed. All that His Lordship's unassuming little man-of-business knew, however, was that if his glamorous patron did not soon arrive, he was sure to catch his death in this weather.

Clutching his umbrella over his head, Charles Beecham, Esquire, stood wrapped in his brown wool greatcoat, his beaver hat pulled low over his receding hairline, and a look of abject misery on his face. He sneezed abruptly into his handkerchief.

'God bless ye.' Mr. Dalloway, standing nearby, slid him a greasy grin.

'Thank you,' Charles clipped out before turning away from the unkempt property agent with a respectable *humph*.

Dalloway was the opposition in this matter, determined to bilk His Lordship out of three thousand pounds for the dubious privilege of owning the god-forsaken place. Charles meant to advise his patron against the purchase in the strongest possible terms, not the least because it would fall to *him* to explain the mad expenditure to old Lady Ironsides. Stealing another discreet glance at his fob watch, he pursed his lips. *Late*.

Alas, his staid life as the Strathmore family's solicitor had become alarmingly interesting since His Lordship's return from his high adventures on the seven seas and elsewhere.

Though barely thirty, the viscount had done the sorts of things Charles preferred to read about from the safety of his favorite armchair. Her Ladyship had oft regaled Charles with tales of her dashing nephew's exploits: battling pirates, chasing down slave ships, living with savages, fending off mountain lions, surveying temples in the wilds of Malaysia, crossing deserts with the nomad caravans of Kandahar. Charles had thought them a lot of cock-and-bull tales until he'd met the man. What on earth could he want with this place? he wondered, then rehearsed a diplomatic warning in his head: *This, my lord, is precisely the sort of rash adventure that drove your uncle into dun territory . . . .*

Ah, but thinking a thing and saying it to Devil Strathmore were two different matters entirely.

Just then, a drumming sound approached from behind the wintry shroud of pewter fog and needling rain, like thunder rumbling in the distance. Barely discernible at first, it swiftly formed into the deep, recognizable rhythm of pounding hoofbeats.

At last. Charles stared in the direction of the pleasure grounds' great iron gates. The ominous cadence grew louder – driving, relentless – reverberating across the marshes, until it shook the earth. Suddenly, a large black coach hurtled out of the indistinguishable gray, barreling up the graveled drive that offered the only safe course through the boggy waste.

The quartet of fine, jet-black horses moved like liquid night, their hooves striking sure over the mud and ice, steam puffing from their nostrils. Stationed fore and aft on the shiny body of the coach, His Lordship's driver, groom, and two footmen stared straight ahead, impervious to the weather. They were clad in traditional Strathmore livery, a sedate dun color with smart black piping, stiff felt tricornes on their heads, and frothy, white lace jabots at their throats.

Charles looked askance at his opponent as Mr. Dalloway ambled down from his shelter atop the flamboyant curved steps of the pavilion. His wily stare was fixed on the approaching vehicle. Noting the gleam of greed in Dalloway's eyes, Charles fretted with the unhappy premonition that his rival would win the day, and then what on earth would he tell Her Ladyship? He could only cork his terror at the thought of the formidable dowager's displeasure by reminding himself of her stern orders seven months ago, upon her nephew's return to London.

'Send all of Devlin's bills to me,' the old dragon had instructed in no uncertain terms. When Charles had tactfully questioned the command, seeking only to protect the elderly woman, Her Ladyship had pooh-poohed his hesitancy. *'It is enough that he has come home at last, Charles. My handsome nephew must cut a dash in Town! You will send his bills to* me.'

And so, obediently, Charles had.

His Lordship's bills, like a flock of ink-smudged doves, had winged their way to the dowager's elegant villa in the Bath countryside: the handsome house on Portman Street and all its elegant furnishings, Aubusson carpets, French damask drapes, Classical paintings and nude marble statues; the wine cellar; the staff's wages; the coach, the drag, the curricle; the horses; the clothes; the boots; the club dues for White's and Brooke's; the opera box, the parties, the jewels for himself and a number of unnamed women; even the IOU's from a few unlucky hands at the gaming tables. Dear old Aunt Augusta had paid them all without a peep. But three thousand quid for an old, abandoned pleasure-ground? It seemed excessive even for *him*.

As his coachman pulled the team to a halt in front of the pavilion, Charles swallowed hard, his heart beating faster. The footmen jumped down from their post in the back of the coach and marched forward like soulless clockwork automata, one opening the carriage door, the other producing an umbrella, which he held at the ready.

Dalloway cast Charles a nervous glance, no longer looking quite so cocky.

'You haven't met His Lordship yet, have you?' Charles murmured under his breath, feeling a trifle smug.

Dalloway did not answer. He looked again at the coach, where the footman knocked down the folding metal steps and then held the door, staring forward in stone-faced efficiency.

The first person to climb out of the coach was the amiable Bennett Freeman, a neatly dressed, young black man from America who served as His Lordship's gentleman's gentleman, had followed him on his journeys around the globe, and attended the viscount in much of his day-to-day business. Behind his wire-rimmed spectacles, Mr. Freeman's intelligent brown eyes scanned the bizarre location with a perplexed glance, but when he saw Charles, he waved affably and dashed toward the pavilion to escape the weather.

Next, a dainty, gloved hand emerged from the carriage, accepting the footman's assistance. Charles sneezed again as His Lordship's latest elegant ladybird stepped down from the coach and minced toward the stairs, teetering over the mud on her high metal pattens. It was not her clothes but her mercenary eyes and wiggly walk that gave away her profession – these days the top courtesans dressed as fine as the ton's best hostesses. She wore a tight spencer of maroon velvet and held up her skirts with one gloved hand, while with the other, she tried to shield her magnificent hat with its clutch of ostrich plumes from the steady drizzle.

Gentleman enough to show chivalry even to her sort, Charles hurried over and gave the high-priced harlot his umbrella.

'Oh, thank you, sir,' she responded in a breathy purr.

Dalloway eagerly assisted the hussy in going up the wet stairs.

Last of all came Devil Strathmore.

The footman with the umbrella had to hold his arm higher in order to shelter his towering master from the weather. His Lordship slid out of the coach with a sinuous motion, then paused to adjust the fur-trimmed greatcoat of luxurious black wool that hung carelessly from his massive shoulders and draped his powerful frame. Small, tinted spectacles shaded his eyes from the flat, gray glare of afternoon; he wore his long, raven hair tied back in a silky queue. A small gold hoop adorned his left earlobe. Eccentricity, after all, ran in his family, as did his Irish good looks. His skin was still coppered from that desert he had crossed months ago, but his lazy grin when he caught sight of his loyal family retainer flashed like the white cliffs of Dover.

There was no helping it. Even to a middle-aged fuddy-duddy like Charles, that smile, when Devil Strathmore doled it out, could make a person stand up taller. He looked every inch the hardened, worldly roué – and he was no man to cross, to be sure – but if he liked you, there was a warmth in him that no one could resist.

'Charles, good to see you.' Lord Strathmore strutted toward him with long-legged, confident strides, the umbrella-holding footman hurrying to keep up.

'My lord.' Charles winced at his hearty handshake and nearly tripped forward when the big man clapped him on the back.

He swept an elegant gesture toward the building. 'Shall we?'

'Yes, of course, my lord. B-but, first I really must say—'

'Problem, Charles?' He took off his tinted spectacles and stared down at him for a moment with pale, wolf-like eyes.

Charles looked into that fathomless gaze and saw traces of the wilderness still lingering there: leafy shadows; blue vistas; deep, dark canyons. He gulped. 'N-no, of course not, my lord, no problem. It's just, well, it's a terrible expense, don't you see.' He faltered, seeing he was having no effect. 'That is to say, I am not entirely sure Her Ladyship would approve.'

Dev paused, studying him.

As an ardent student of human nature, he appreciated the courage, indeed, the loyalty it took his little solicitor to stand up to him. He truly did. All the same, in this matter, he would brook no denial. Explaining his true motives was out of the question, of course. It seemed he was just going to have to brazen it out and insist on having his way because – well, because he was Devil Strathmore and had always done exactly what he liked.

He slipped Charles one of his most charming smiles and tucked his spectacles inside his breast pocket. 'Don't be daft, Charles. Aunt Augusta thinks I hung the moon.' He turned and jogged up the stairs.

'Well, that is true—' Charles hastened to follow. 'But perhaps I could explain it better to her if it would please Your Lordship to inform me wh-why you wish to buy this place?'

Dev laughed. 'Why, for the same reason I do everything: because it amuses me. Come, come, Charles, don't be a killjoy. Let's have a look.'

'But, sir – she'll have my head for this!'

'Charles.' He stopped, turned, and sighed, then affectionately fixed the little man's lapels. 'Dear, dear, Charles. Neat, tidy Charles. Very well, I shall tell you what's afoot, but I am taking you into strictest confidence. Understood?'

'Sir!' His eyes widened at this spectacular show of favor. 'Of course, my lord. You have my word a-as a gentleman.'

'Capital.' Dev grasped his shoulder and pulled him nearer, staring firmly at him. 'Now, then.' He bent his head toward the shorter man and lowered his voice. 'Have you ever heard, Charles, of the Horse and Chariot Driving Club?'

Charles's eyes widened in scandalized innocence. 'Sir!' he breathed.

'Quite,' Dev replied. 'You know how I enjoy the sport of driving.'

'Y-yes, sir. The curricle, the racing drag, your silver stallion—'

'Precisely. Well, there are a few . . . shall we say, requirements for entrée into the club, you see.' He ticked them off on his fingers. 'First, a prospective member must be of good birth, have no morals and a great deal of money.'

'But – you don't, sir.'

Dev laughed without humor. 'Not yet, of course, but it's the same as if I did.'

Indeed, he was counting on his aunt's fortune as critical to his success. Gambling, for example, was how he had gotten close to his targets in the first place, for such sharpers as the boys of the Horse and Chariot Club could always use another deep player to round out the whist table. Curious – the more he lost without complaint, the more the blackguards seemed to enjoy his company. But let them win for now, he thought. Soon, they would lose everything.

Including their lives.

'The second requirement an aspiring member must fulfill is

to show his respect by presenting the brotherhood with a suitable gift. This—' Dev glanced around at the building, then gave Charles a conspiratorial wink. '—will knock 'em off their bloody feet.'

At least it would when he had packed the floor with explosives.

'I've heard there's a third requirement,' he added breezily, 'but so far, I've been unable to find out what it is.'

'Yes, but sir – the Horse and Chariot!' Charles whispered in dread. 'Everyone knows – well, you have been away from Town all these years – perhaps you have not heard—?'

To Dev's amusement, his little lawyer glanced from side to side, as though Damage Randall, Blood Staines, or that elegant pervert, Carstairs, might be lurking nearby.

'They are a very bad sort, sir. Very bad. Duels – unspeakable things! I am quite sure your aunt would not at all approve. Not at all!'

'Well, Charles, you may be right, but as I said, I do love the sport. A true aficionado of the four-in-hand is prepared to overlook such things. Don't you agree? I'm so glad you gave me your word not to mention this to old Lady Ironsides. Shall we?' Dev cast him a silky smile.

'Oh, dear,' Charles said under his breath, hurrying after him as Dev continued up the stairs. 'Very well, but do please take care not to appear too eager in front of this Dalloway creature, my lord. He is a low, sly thing.'

Having traded guns, camels, and spices with the Bedouin caravans in Marrakech, possibly the shrewdest hagglers in the world, he trusted he could manage one ill-groomed Cockney property agent, but Dev hid his amusement and bowed to his solicitor with princely grace. It was the man's loyalty that mattered, after all. 'Thank you, Charles. I stand duly advised.'

Mollified by his acknowledgment, Charles followed him into

the building without further fussing. Introductions were quickly exchanged, and in short order, they embarked with Mr. Dalloway on their tour of the pavilion.

Leaving the octagonal foyer with its red-painted ceiling, tainted mirrors, and touches of chipped gilt, they went through a pair of large, ornately carved doors that looked like the product of some opium eater's fevered fancy. The whole place had an eerie, almost sinister air of intoxication and decay; the lingering odor of stale beer rose up in a fog from the worm-eaten floorboards and mingled with the general musty smell.

As they moved away from the foyer, the gray daylight shaded into darkness, for the windows were all boarded over. Dev's two footmen carried candles for their party, as did Mr. Dalloway. They ventured deeper into the gloom, the floors creaking like tortured ghosts. One could almost hear the phantom echoes of forgotten laughter; spiders went scuttling across the walls. Even inside, the place was cold enough to cloud their breath.

The blonde shrieked and huddled close to Dev when something swooped over their heads. Lifting the candles higher, they soon discovered the colonies of bats and house martins that had entered through one of the chimneys.

In the main corridor, the flickering flames of their candelabra revealed tall columns painted like candy canes, a grimy parquet floor laid out in a dizzying zigzag design. Brightly colored, swirling murals flowed fantastically across the walls. Interior doors led to shadowed galleries and a dozen garish salons. There was even a ballroom with an elevated stand for an orchestra.

'God, it's hideous,' Ben declared, turning to him.

'Deliciously so,' Dev purred too low for Dalloway to hear. He sent his trusty valet and friend a devilish glance. 'It's perfect.' The twisted lads of the Horse and Chariot would love it. The perfect setting in which to lull their senses so he could move closer to the answers he so desperately craved.

Ben frowned, but Dalloway kept up his lively soliloquy, ignoring the rotting floorboards, the decade's worth of cobwebs hanging from the lightless chandelier, and the little cascades trickling down here and there where the tin roof leaked.

Charles wiped a chilly droplet off his forehead, his lips pursed in distaste, but Dev saw that his solicitor had been right about the property agent. Dalloway was as slick as oil and cheerful as a rat atop a garbage pile as he led them through the place, extolling its supposed virtues.

'The main pavilion in which we now stand encompasses eleven thousand square feet, with extensive kitchen facilities suitable for feedin' an army. Mind your step, miss. Here's the stairs. Ye must see the rooms above . . .'

On the upper floor, themed chambers led off the main corridor. One was made like a jungle; the Egypt Chamber had a fake palm tree sprouting up from the center of the room and walls painted with a faded trompe l'oeil of the Pyramids. Another chamber represented Caesar's palace in ancient Rome, with faux-marble nudes in cheap white plaster and sprawling scarlet divans, lately serving as tenement housing for mice. Dev's survey took in the tattered wall hangings and piles of bat guano.

From the corner of his eye, he saw Dalloway creep nearer, watching him like a stray dog sizing up a ham bone that someone had left unguarded on the table. 'What do you think of 'er, sir? If this property does not suit your needs, we 'ave others ye might like to see. What exactly is it you're after, if I may inquire?'

Dev stroked his chin, glancing all around him. 'I need . . .' *Home territory. An environment I can control.* After all, he would be surrounded by enemies. He turned smoothly with a smile, playing the role of dissipated rake to perfection. 'A place where I can entertain my friends.'

The blonde giggled with excitement at the prospect. Dev smiled at her, rather wishing he could remember her name. So far he had gotten by with *darling*.

Last night was a bit of a blur, as well, but he imagined he must have enjoyed himself a great deal, by the look of her. Nevertheless, he had been astonished to wake up and find her still there, especially after he had worked her so hard. It had taken him half the night to come, not that she had seemed to mind. He couldn't help it. He was losing all interest in these hardened professionals with their bag of tricks and their scheming eyes. Now he merely wondered if the chit ever planned on going home.

'Entertaining, sir? Then this could be just the spot!' Dalloway beamed, determined to make the sale. 'This is a capital establishment for private parties! As Your Lordship will 'ave noted, it's convenient to London by a short drive over the bridge, or the guests can be ferried over the river by the watermen. There's plenty o' space and many whimsical outbuildings suitable for all manner o' charmin' entertainments.'

'There is also the matter of privacy. My, er, friends prefer to take their pleasures away from the scrutiny of prying eyes. The bloody gossip-writers follow us everywhere, don't you know, scribbling their little tattletales.' Dev waved his hand in a dismissive gesture. 'I need a place . . . far from any crowds. An isolated place.' *One I can destroy without fear of harming innocent bystanders.*

'Well, sir, you passed the gatehouse when you come in – very sturdy, just needs a coat o' paint. And there's an admirable wrought-iron fence that runs the perimeter o' the premises. The property has only one entrance, straight up the drive. To either side is bog. Very treacherous, them mud flats. The only other way in would be by boat, but then, an intruder would have to catch the river's tide just right or be stranded.'

Dev gave a businesslike nod and feigned indecision, but by the time they returned to the ballroom, his mind was made up. The place would suit his purposes to a tee.

Dalloway turned to him, beaming. 'As I said, sir, all she wants is a little tender lovin' care to be brought back to 'er former glory.'

'That will, ah, cost money,' Charles delicately asserted.

'Hmm,' Dev said in a noncommittal growl. Clasping his hands behind his back, he drifted over to inspect the murals on the walls in all their flowery, faded exuberance, leaving his lawyer to ask Dalloway the appropriate questions.

He gazed at a section of the mural that portrayed the beautiful goddess Flora, wearing nothing but an artfully placed garland of roses.

'Er, my lord?' His solicitor cleared his throat.

'Yes, Charles?' Dev asked in a tone of weary indulgence as he went on studying the picture, but Dalloway interrupted before Charles could speak.

'All the paintin's you see before you are likenesses of the famous beauties of the previous decade, milord. They all performed 'ere when this place was in its prime. We had water spectacles with fireworks, musical extravaganzas, tightrope walkers—'

'Tightrope walkers, really?' he asked with interest.

'Oh, yes, sir.'

'As I was saying—,' Charles tried again, flicking Dalloway an annoyed glance. 'I have doubts, sir. Serious doubts. I – I fear the building is not safe.'

'Life . . . is not safe, Charles.' Dev bent closer to the wall, narrowing his eyes at the figure of Flora as he noticed some marred and faded words etched on the gold ribbon that was painted below the goddess.

Good God. He suddenly raised his arm and snapped his black-gauntleted fingers. 'Candle.'

One of the footmen immediately stepped forward and held up the light. Dev scrutinized the awkward calligraphy by the candle's feeble glow, stunned to make out the name inscribed there: *Miss Ginny Highgate, 1803*. He stared. By God, 'twas an omen.

'What is it?' Ben asked, joining him by the wall.

'Ginny Highgate,' Dev murmured, turning to him in amazement.

They exchanged a shocked, ominous glance.

'Oh, yes, milord,' Dalloway offered, 'Miss Highgate used to sing here every summer. Such a favorite she was with the lads!'

'Who is, ah, Miss Highgate, if I may inquire?' Charles asked.

'A beautiful lady of the theater, sir. Irish, I think,' Dalloway told him. 'Such long red hair as you've never seen. Aye, all the young gents were mad for Ginny Highgate.'

'What happened to her?' the blonde piped up a trifle jealously.

'Nobody knows,' Dalloway said. 'She disappeared.'

Not entirely true, Dev thought, pained by his fairly clear idea of the ugly fate the young beauty had met.

For two years, through various hired agents, he had been covertly investigating the fateful night of the fire that had taken his family from him. He had run from his guilt for a decade, sailing from one end of the globe to the other, but on the ten-year anniversary of his family's deaths, he had resolved himself to examine every last detail of that night, something he had not been able to face as a shattered youth.

It had not taken long before he had begun to notice that many of the facts about the fire did not add up. Since then, he had chased down every lead, had spent a fortune in bribe money, and had collected a trunkload of documents on the case – newspaper obituaries, indeed, full background investigations of every person who had died in the fire, interviews with the intimidated fire official, depositions from a few useful witnesses, logbooks from the stagecoach companies whose vehicles had traveled that stretch of the road that night. Everything he could lay his hands on.

Unraveling the knot thread by meticulous thread, Dev had finally traced his way through the disappearance of Ginny Highgate, aka Mary Harris, to the Horse and Chariot Club, and it was there that he had met a brick wall. It seemed the murdered redhead was the club's best-guarded secret.

To learn it, Dev had spent the past six months infiltrating the group, slowly attempting to gain their trust, even though doing so was akin to playing roulette with his life, for they knew full well who he was.

Why they hadn't killed him already, he was not exactly sure; he could only conclude that, so far, they had bought into his highly convincing facade as a dissipated rogue of the first order. He made them believe he was such a thoughtless pleasure-seeker that it had never crossed his mind that his family's destruction was anything but the tragic accident that it had been ruled.

They surely suspected him, he mused, but he supposed they let him near because it helped them to feel that they were keeping an eye on *him*. The thing required the utmost finesse, but Dev was prepared to chance it, for the prize was the one thing he craved more than anything else in the world: peace.

Answers. There could be no peace until he had answers. Why? How? All he really wanted was for life to make sense, but it didn't and it wouldn't. Not until he had the answers to the question, nay, the furious demand, that had burned in his brain for twelve long years and had turned the heart in him to ashes.

What had really happened on that terrible night his family had been taken from him? Who was to blame? If there was one shred of hope that there was someone, anyone else that he could blame instead of himself, he was willing to go to any lengths to find it.

By God, if it cost him his life and every last penny of his inheritance, he would find the truth, lay hold of the answers – answers that only his enemies could give him. And when he had the truth in his grasp, when he finally knew who had set that blaze, he would wreak vengeance on them in an orgy of violence the likes of which they had never seen.

Rising once more to his full height, he moved restlessly away from the painting of Ginny Highgate and sent Dalloway a brisk nod. 'Right. I'll take it.' Charles looked at him in alarm. 'However, there is the question of price,' he conceded. 'It's much too high. Charles?'

He left his solicitor to negotiate with Mr. Dalloway and sauntered back out to the foyer, where he leaned in the battered doorway and stared out at the frozen swamp, feeling moody and pensive with the return of old memories.

Ben joined him, his large brown eyes full of sensitive intelligence behind his rain-flecked spectacles as he searched Dev's face. 'Are you all right?'

He shrugged, lost in his thoughts. Folding his arms across his chest, Dev cast a jaundiced eye over the ragged gardens. 'I look at this place and see something of myself,' he said, his voice low, edged with bitter irony. 'Sinking into the swamp.' His stare wandered across the lifeless marsh, the stubbled grasses, grayed and stiff with frost. He cast Ben a cynical half-smile. 'They say it's haunted, have you heard? And cursed.'

His friend stared earnestly at him. 'I wish you would not do this, Dev. You can still walk away.'

'No, I can't.' His wry smile faded, the cold hatred darkening his eyes once more, like a cloud shadow moving across the face of a sun-swept hill. 'I pay my debts.'

'Even in blood? Even if it costs you your life?'

'What life?' he whispered.

He walked back to rejoin the others, leaving his loyal valet staring after him in distress. As Dev strolled back into the gaudy ballroom, Charles turned to him brightly.

'Ah, there you are, sir!' he said, looking pleased with himself. 'Mr. Dalloway has agreed to a new price of thirteen hundred pounds. If this is acceptable to Your Lordship, the deal is done.'

'You think it fair?'

He nodded. 'It is reasonable.'

'Well done, Charles.' He snapped his fingers. 'Cheque.'

Immediately, the other footman stepped forth bearing a portable desktop, which he held for him. Dev opened the hinged top and pulled out his draftbook. Dipping his quillpen into the tiny inkbottle, he scratched out the promissory note, chuckling darkly to himself. *Cursed. Haunted. How very apropos.* 'See that the place is properly insured before work begins on it, Charles.' He handed Dalloway the cheque. 'We'll need a reliable contractor to coordinate the repairs. Carpenters, roofers, painters, plasterers.'

'You need the rat-catcher first,' Ben muttered, walking in with a disgusted glance at the ballroom while Charles blanched at the expenditures.

'Right. Summon the exterminator to rid the place of pests. As always, thank you for your time, Charles. Mr. Dalloway, you've been most helpful. Darling.' He beckoned impatiently to the woman and then stalked out, his entourage falling into ranks.

Behind them, Dalloway silently danced a jig over the rotting floorboards.

Upon walking back out into the cold, Dev heard the cadence of galloping hoofbeats and looked over to find someone riding hard up the drive.

'What an ugly horse,' Ben remarked, also watching the rider.

'Fast, though. Good, long stride,' Dev murmured. 'Are we expecting someone?'

'No, my lord,' Charles offered, 'I believe it is an herald.'

And indeed, as the rider came closer, they could see the cockade in his hat and the uniform that marked him as an express messenger. Dev helped the blonde into the coach, and a moment later, the rider reined in nearby, his horse's hooves kicking up a clattery spray of gravel.

'Lord Strathmore?' he called out.

'Yes?'

'Express for you, sir!' The messenger held out the letter.

'Thank you.' He quickly took the letter before the ink ran and nodded to Ben to pay the messenger for the delivery. BATH, read the outer fold of the envelope.

Aunt Augusta?

A twinge of guilt stabbed him. He knew he owed the old girl a visit. More than that, he wanted to see her. The dragon had been like a mother to him. She had even saved his life back when he was twenty-one, half-mad with grief, and destroying himself with the bottle. She had bought him a ship, put him on it, and sent him off to see the world in the care of their gruff Scots gamekeeper, Duncan MacTavish. Hang it, he missed the old girl, he thought as he broke the wax seal, but each time he thought of going to see her, everything in him shied away again like a spooked horse refusing a jump.

He couldn't help it. The love in him was so tied up with loss and pain that he could scarce separate one from the other, and so tended to avoid the whole situation. *Like a coward*, his conscience readily supplied. He ignored it, his lips twisting in broody self-annoyance while Ben counted out the messenger's charge.

Dev opened the neatly folded letter and read. As his gaze skimmed the page, the blood promptly drained from his face:

Express
9 February 1817
Bath

Dear Lord Strathmore,

Though we have never met, I trust you will forgive my presumption in writing to you on a matter of greatest urgency. Necessity compels me to set propriety aside to convey to you a most alarming intelligence.

My name is Miss Elizabeth Carlisle, and since August, I have been serving in the capacity of lady's companion to your esteemed Aunt. It is my sorrowful duty to advise you of a change in the excellent health Her Ladyship has always heretofore enjoyed, and to implore you, if you love her, to come with all due haste . . . before it is too late.

Godspeed,
E. Carlisle

For a moment, Dev could only stand there, his face drained of color.

No. Not yet. *She's all I have left.*

'My lord?' Charles ventured in a worried tone. 'Is aught amiss?'

Without a word, Dev strode over, reached up, pulled the messenger down bodily from his horse, and swung up into the still-warm saddle.

'What the devil—'

'Pay him, Charles. I'll leave this brute in the stable at home. I must to Bath.' His voice sounded odd and tight in his ears. 'I'll take the curricle – it's fastest.' He gathered the reins and wheeled the roan around, glancing over his shoulder. 'Ben, follow with my things.'

'But, Devlin!' the blonde protested, poking her head out the carriage window in that ridiculous feathered hat.

He rolled his eyes, losing patience. 'Would someone *please* take that woman home or wherever it is that she goes?'

She let out an angry gasp, but he was already gone, galloping off, hell-for-leather, down the drive, his stomach knotted with panicked dread and guilt for neglecting his only living kin. The despairing knowledge spiraled through his mind that when Aunt Augusta finally left him – never mind his vast inheritance – he would be left completely and unutterably alone.

Chapter Two

Bath, the next day

Translucent in the light, the delicate porcelain shard was as thin and fragile as a bit of some exotic eggshell as she held it up between her fingers, studying its shape. She tested it here and there on the half-mended vase until she found the spot where the little piece fit; dabbing the jagged edges with a few droplets from her tiny glue brush, she gently pressed the broken fragment back into place. Lizzie Carlisle sat very still, careful not to let her hand waver lest the piece set crookedly.

White winter sunshine streamed through the lace curtains, but the parlor smelled of springtime, of beeswax and lemons, with a graceful hint of lavender from the dried bouquet on the round worktable where she sat. The restful silence of her employer's elegant country villa was broken only by the muffled voices from the next room, where Dr. Bell was quizzing the dowager on her latest symptoms.

Cautiously releasing her hold on the shattered vase, Lizzie glued another piece back into place and cast a skeptical glance upward at the culprit. Pasha, Lady Strathmore's haughty Persian cat, lay luxuriously sprawled atop the Chippendale highboy, his fluffy tail swinging idly over the edge, his gold eyes gleaming with a distinct look of feline amusement at the hapless human whose job it was to smooth out all of life's little disasters. If one of the maids had broken the small, elegant Wedgwood vase – a gift from Her Ladyship's rakehell nephew – the servant would have been summarily sacked, but the dowager's spoiled darling appeared not a whit repentant.

'You, sir, are a menace to society,' she told the cat with a pointed glance.

Pasha's sable-tipped ears merely twitched with a knowing air.

Just then, the parlor doors swung open and Lizzie glanced over, flashing a quick, warm smile as the dowager and her doctor came in from the drawing room. Hastily setting her project aside, she rose to greet them.

Frail but regal, Augusta, the Dowager Viscountess Strathmore, sat in her wheeled Bath chair like on a throne as her handsome young doctor gallantly rolled her in. Her Ladyship still commanded a stately beauty, her wrinkled skin taut across her high cheekbones. Her blue eyes were rheumy, but as bright and shrewd as ever.

'Here we are, then.' Dr. Andrew Bell had a cherubic face, a tousle of blond hair, and big, brown, puppy-dog eyes. In the environs of Bath, he was considered a fine catch, quite making his fortune. He ran a thriving practice and had recently enhanced his medical reputation by inventing the wildly popular Dr. Bell's New Pills for Bilious Complaints. Even the local vicar swore by them.

'So, Dr. Bell, how do you find your patient today?' Lizzie asked with cordial cheer. As an afterthought, she turned and put the lid back on the glue, with a suspicious glance at Pasha.

'Right as rain, I am happy to say,' he declared with an amiable smile.

'Told you so,' Lady Strathmore clipped out, brushing a few

long cat hairs off her black bombazine skirts with an air of brisk nonchalance. 'There's nothing wrong with me.'

'And we are glad to know it,' he agreed, meeting Lizzie's gaze with a twinkle in his eyes at old Ironsides's curmudgeonly manner. 'I vow it must be the excellent care that Miss Carlisle is taking of you that is to account for it, my lady.'

'Bosh,' Lizzie muttered, blushing slightly as she bustled over to poke the hearth fire back to life lest Lady Strathmore catch a chill.

Dr. Bell watched Lizzie with attentive interest; the dowager observed him with a narrow smile. 'Won't you stay for tea, dear boy?' she purred, then gestured to Lizzie to ring the bellpull.

She obeyed, even as Dr. Bell touched his hand to his heart with a fond wince. 'I wish I could, ma'am. Alas, I must look in on the Harris children. The whole brood has come down with the measles.'

'Oh, dear. We shall add them to our prayers.' Lizzie turned to him, fretting at the news. When the weather was fine, their neighbor's rambunctious children sometimes visited, bringing cheer and laughter into the house. 'Do tell Mrs. Harris that if there is anything I can do to help, she need only ask.'

'How thoughtful you are, Miss Carlisle. I am sure she will appreciate your kind offer.' His gently admiring gaze was a little too intent for Lizzie's comfort, but thankfully, Margaret, the maid, appeared just then in answer to the bell.

The skinny, sallow girl dropped a curtsy. ' 'Ow might I be of assignation, milady?' she asked proudly.

All three of them looked at the girl in bafflement for a second; then Lizzie winced with private chagrin at her pupil's blunder.

'What a bizarre question.' The dowager turned to Lizzie, nonplussed. 'Whatever does the silly creature mean? Assignation?'

'Ah, *assistance*, ma'am,' Lizzie soothed, coloring a bit. 'She meant assistance.'

'Pardon my corrigendum, ma'am,' Margaret piped up, undaunted. 'I seem to have misunderspoken myself.'

'Daft gel, have you been in the liquor?' Lady Strathmore demanded.

Margaret gasped. 'No, ma'am! Never!'

'Then cease this gibberish at once and fetch our tea.'

Lizzie sent Margaret a bolstering look, but the crestfallen maid fled. 'Really, my lady, one oughtn't mock her. She is doing her best to learn.'

'I am well aware of your bluestocking proclivities, Miss Carlisle, but I will not have you ruining the lower servants with this nonsense of teaching them to read. You must desist. It can only come to no good.'

'But, ma'am—'

'Servants reading! Unnatural, I say. Really, child, you have the most extraordinary notions.'

'Margaret is surprisingly clever—'

'I prefer her ignorant, the way God intended her to be.'

Stifling a cough of laughter, Dr. Bell sent Lizzie a look of discreet congratulation for her efforts. 'Pardon me, ladies, but I really should be going.'

'Of course, dear boy. We mustn't keep you from your very important work of ministering to the sick of the parish. Would you be so kind, Miss Carlisle, as to show Dr. Bell out, hmm?'

Mischief glinted in Lady Strathmore's sharp blue eyes as she turned to her companion.

'Of course,' Lizzie answered faintly after the barest pause.

Curse the old girl's deuced matchmaking.

Dr. Bell bowed to the dowager and wished her well, then gestured to Lizzie to lead the way.

'I say, the weather has cleared up nicely,' he attempted as they walked out to the spacious entrance hall with its light blue walls, white columns, and Italian marble floor. 'Quite a bluster through the night.'

'Indeed.' The frigid gales and snow of the night before had ceased by afternoon.

'Perhaps we shall see an early spring,' he suggested.

'One can hope.' She forced a smile and looked around at nothing in particular, nervously rearranging the umbrellas in their stand beside the door. Dr. Bell buttoned up his neat blue coat. When Lizzie handed him his top hat, he held her in an earnest gaze for a moment.

'I should very much like to see you ladies at the next Assembly Ball, Miss Carlisle. It would lift Her Ladyship's spirits – and mine.'

'Oh—!' Startled, Lizzie swiftly opted to ignore his cautious overture. 'If she is well enough to venture out, I'm sure we shall try.'

'I will content myself with that hope, then.' He put on his hat. 'If you need me,' he added softly, 'send for me anytime.'

'I thank you, sir,' she said, stiffening slightly.

He tipped his hat, looking mystified but undiscouraged by her stubborn reticence. 'Good day, Miss Carlisle.'

She bowed her head in answer; then he strode out to his waiting carriage, a handsome barouche drawn by a team of fine liver bays. Enjoying the bracing rush of chilly fresh air, Lizzie raised her hand in a courteous salute as he drove away.

As she lingered in the open doorway, her gaze swept the frozen hills. The landscape was dusted in a thin but crisp coat of snow, the broad curve of the road beyond like a dark ribbon on a field of white. There was no sign of Devil Strathmore yet, but with the roads coated with snow and ice from the fierce blow last night, she did not expect him until tomorrow at the earliest.

She closed the front door and went back to the parlor, where Margaret had just brought in the tea tray.

Taking her seat across from her employer, Lizzie smoothed her beige muslin skirts and avoided the dowager's expectant stare.

'Well?' Lady Strathmore toyed with the long strand of jet beads that hung around her neck and eyed Lizzie in knowing amusement. 'What say you, gel? He is very gallant.'

Lizzie shrugged, said nothing, and nodded Margaret's dismissal. The chambermaid scurried out.

'Oh, come, Lizzie, he is a poppet,' the dowager scolded with barely suppressed mirth. 'You do not like him?'

'To be sure, he is an excellent doctor, amiable, competent, and kind.' She focused her attention on the task of pouring out. 'Beyond that, I have no thoughts of him whatever.'

'La, the poor boy will be crushed! I daresay he comes here to see *you* more than me, for I have very little use for his services.'

'Ma'am, really. Dr. Bell's sole interest lies in your good health, as you well know.'

'Oh?' The viscountess shot her an arch look from across her teacup. 'He asked me in confidence if I thought you might be amenable to a drive in his new barouche.'

'He *what*? Good Lord!' Lizzie set the teapot down in astonished indignation. 'Can't the man see that I am on the shelf?'

'Stuff and nonsense, Miss Carlisle. You're barely twenty.'

'I'll be twenty-two this autumn,' she said hotly.

'Tut, tut, the only person who decides when a woman is on the shelf is the woman *elle-même*.'

'Well, if I choose to put myself on the shelf, that is my own affair, surely,' she huffed, much to the dowager's amusement.

'But why, in heaven's name, when there are respectable young gentlemen of pleasing countenance and promising expectations eager to pay suit, despite your efforts to put them off? Ungrateful gel, I daresay you want for a proper feminine vanity.'

'What I lack in vanity, ma'am, I hope to make up for in sense. My passion is for books, not a pair of handsome eyes or a well-turned calf.'

'Extraordinary. Do you claim to be immune to the attentions of a charming young man? Even I am not. Never was.'

'A man is a creature who will say anything to get what he wants,' she replied in a blithely philosophic tone, mollified by her own certainty on this point. She shook out her napkin and laid it on her lap.

'Even the saintly young Bell, trotting from house to house, mending his neighbor's ills of body and mind?'

'New carriage, did he say? Impressive how profitable such altruism can be.'

'Touché, my dear, touché.' Lady Strathmore chuckled, sipping her tea. 'Still, you might at least try getting to know him better.'

'I might also try whale hunting, bullfighting, or getting lost in the Sahara atop a camel. Oh, yes, that would be a grand adventure . . .'

Her employer was laughing. 'Then you'd be like Dev.'

'Mmm.' Lizzie hid her thorough skepticism about Lord Strathmore's supposed exploits, which she considered highly exaggerated at best.

Any man who had seen and done so many incredible things would surely not be wasting his time living like a dissipated rake in London, as Lord Strathmore had been doing since his return to England some months ago. She knew his type – hedonistic, immature. But she supposed a man like that had to seek his thrills somehow.

'Well?' Lady Strathmore prodded.

Lizzie gave her a wry smile. 'If I were to let the oh-so-wonderful Dr. Bell court me, sooner or later, I would notice something base and inevitably *low* in his male nature, and then I would kick myself for wasting my time with him when I could have been here with you, keeping you out of mischief – or trying to.'

'But you must be practical, my dear. The abundant faults of the male species aside, you must have a husband, children to look after you in your old age. You don't want to end up like me.'

'For shame, ma'am, I should be very happy to be like you in any respect, and rest assured, I am not at all concerned for my old age. As it happens, I have already made provisions to support myself when I am a spinster lady of advanced years.'

'How shockingly independent.'

'Thank you,' she replied with a firm nod, though she gathered it wasn't a compliment. 'I shall open a bookshop in Russell Square – I'm sure I've told you all this before.'

'Bookshop!' the dowager snorted. 'A young woman of your caliber has a duty to concern herself with the multiplication of the species, Miss Carlisle. Really,' she continued as Lizzie blinked at the rare compliment from the old dragon, 'I have never in all my days heard a woman speak so cheerfully about spinsterhood. It's altogether morbid.'

'Oh, I don't know,' Lizzie answered with caution. 'I rather like it on the shelf, safely out of harm's way – where certain "cats" of my acquaintance cannot knock one down and shatter one into a hundred bits, like your poor vase.'

Lady Strathmore leaned nearer, sliding her a mischievous smile. 'But on the shelf, my dear, all you get is dusty.'

Lizzie burst out laughing and shook her head at the incorrigible old woman. Nevertheless, she was eager for a change of subject rather than her nonexistent love life. She turned to show Lady Strathmore the progress she had made on repairing her treasured vase, when suddenly a high-pitched shriek pierced the air from somewhere near the entrance hall.

'Good heavens, what now?' her employer exclaimed.

Lizzie was already on her feet, rushing to see what was the

matter. She was halfway across the room when Margaret burst into the doorway with a look of wild excitement.

'Oh, milady, it's Master Dev! He's come! He's riding up the drive!'

'Devlin?' the old woman breathed, her face lighting up with instantaneous joy.

'Aye, ma'am!' Margaret cried, her eyes sparkling. 'He'll be here in a trice!'

'Heaven preserve us!' she whispered. 'He's come!' Radiating shocked amazement and motherly pride, the formidable old dragon did not seem to know what to do with herself all of a sudden. She was breathless, positively fluttering. 'Why, that rascal, he gave no warning! Isn't that just like him? Well, don't just stand there, daft creature! Run and tell Cook to set another place for supper! My nephew will be hungry – he always is! Lusty appetite, that boy – no doubt it's why he's grown into such a fine, strapping figure of a man.'

'Yes, ma'am!' Margaret agreed a bit too eagerly, then dashed out a curtsy and raced off to carry out the divine privilege of feeding Master Dev.

'I don't trust a man who doesn't relish a good meal,' Lady Strathmore went on, quickly wiping away a tear that she thought no one saw, but Lizzie barely paid heed.

She stood frozen with astonishment, her mind in a whirl.

Good God, her ruse had worked!

But how? How on earth had he gotten here so fast? He would have had to have traveled all night through the blizzard at breakneck speed—

'Quickly, child, how do I look?' Lady Strathmore demanded. Busily adjusting the lappets of her black lace house cap, her cheeks were flushed with pleasure, her coloring better than Lizzie had seen it in weeks.

It was miraculous.

Darling Dev had not even shown his face yet, but somehow he had the power to revitalize the old woman with an impact that all Lizzie's patient, cheerful, daily companionship could not begin to approach. And that, she supposed with a lonely pang, was the power of genuine love.

'You look beautiful, ma'am,' she forced out. 'As ever.'

'Well, don't just stand there, Lizzie, go and change that frumpy gown!'

'Ma'am!' she said indignantly.

'I've told you how stylish he is.'

A hint of temper flashed across her brow. 'It's not the Regent come, my lady.'

'Headstrong gel. Take that awful thing off, at least.' Lady Strathmore pointed to her head.

Lizzie frowned, touching her white muslin house cap. 'What's wrong with it?'

'It makes you look *old*.'

'I am old,' she insisted.

'Child, I have gowns in my closet that are older than you. Well, suit yourself, stubborn creature. You always do. But don't blame me if Devlin teases you about your dress. He is always teasing,' she added with lavish doting.

'He wouldn't dare.'

'Oh-ho, dear miss, there is little my nephew would not dare. I cannot wait for you to meet him at last!'

'My lady, I pray you, do not set your hopes too high,' Lizzie warned with an earnest shake of her head. 'I doubt His Lordship will be able to stay long.'

Especially when he realized the truth of her deception.

'Of course he won't stay long, silly chit. One can hardly expect a Corinthian of Devlin's mettle to spend his days squiring his old dragon aunt around Bath. Now, do hurry, Miss Carlisle. It is a grand occasion!' Lady Strathmore gripped the wheels of her Bath chair and rolled herself out of the ground-floor parlor and toward the entrance hall.

Change my gown, indeed. For what? Lizzie scoffed. Glamorous, highborn rakes did not even *see* plain, sensible women like her, she knew from experience. Besides, she had too much self-respect to go prancing about in finery merely to attract the notice of a loose-living scoundrel whose character she doubted and whose manner of living she disparaged.

But despite her employer's urge to hurry, she lingered in the parlor a moment longer, a trifle apprehensive to learn what manner of man she had deceived. Hearing his horse's hoofbeats approaching even now, she sidled over to the window, nudged one of the lace curtains aside, and stole a discreet peek out.

Instantly, her eyes flared with alarm – and a certain measure of confusion.

There must be some mistake. The man she saw did not match her expectations one iota – not a pampered prince, but a fierce-eyed, black-haired warrior-hellion, who yanked his snorting horse to a clattering halt and flung down from the saddle, his sodden greatcoat whirling around his massive frame with the motion. A brooding scowl hardened the ruthless planes and angles of his fiendishly handsome face, sun-coppered, she realized, by his adventures in more sultry climes.

Stalking swiftly toward the house, he was wild and wind tousled, dripping with the elements, his chiseled face flecked with mud and cold with hellbent will. He paid no mind to the groom who dashed out to meet him and captured the pawing horse's bridle. His battle stare was fixed on the front door.

Lizzie's heart stopped for a second in sheer disbelief as she stared at him, fascinated and appalled. It was all too easy, in a flash, to imagine him in flowing desert garb, strapped with a huge, curved sword; too easy to picture him roaring orders at his crew from the storm-lashed rigging of his gun-ship.

Good heavenly Lord. She gulped.

Surely this ruthless-looking giant was not the man she had crossed. Not the decadent London rake she had planned to take to task like a truant schoolboy.

Devil Strathmore could not have been more intimidating if he were clad in black chain mail with a broadsword in his leather-gauntleted hands.

His jet-black mane was a wild tangle that flowed over his shoulders. Her eyes widened to spy the small gold hoop that glinted in his left earlobe, paganlike.

Then he cast a glance over his shoulder at his horse – perhaps making sure he had not killed the animal in his haste – and it was then that Lizzie spotted the scarlet streak of blood that marred his right cheek, beneath the spatters of mud and grime from the road.

With a gasp, she clapped her hand to her mouth. He was bleeding! But why? What had happened? He marched on, and she leaned forward so fast to keep watching him that she bumped her forehead on the wavy glass, but he exited her line of vision, disappearing into the house.

Oh, dear. She winced and rubbed her brow in dazed dismay as she withdrew from the window. *Oh, dear, oh, dear*. For the first time, the possibility occurred to her that she might have made a . . . serious miscalculation. She heard the front door open from a distance through the house, but suddenly did not know what to think. Until this moment, the main evidence on which she had based her admittedly low opinion of the dowager's nephew was the steady stream of his bills that arrived each month on Her Ladyship's desk.

Lizzie knew that she had no business peeking at her employer's correspondence, but once she had begun to suspect how Darling Dev was taking advantage of his aunt's blind love, she had made it her business to keep an eye on those despicable endless bills. Each one had made her a little more resentful than the last, but his gambling debt that had come last week had been the last straw, pushing her past the point of fury into brazen action. For reasons she did not care to examine, Lizzie had been so outraged by his insolent assumption that his rich aunt would pay his gambling debts, no questions asked, that she had dashed out her letter with shaking hands and had sent it to London by the express messenger, bent on teaching the cad a lesson.

If he came every now and then – if he cared – it would be different, but the blackguard could not even be bothered to write his aunt the occasional letter, never mind the old woman thought the sun shone for him and paid all his bills, placing no restraints on him whatsoever. Lady Strathmore might never complain, but as Her Ladyship's caretaker, Lizzie was fed up with it. She could not bear another day of watching the lonely old woman staring out the window for endless hours with her heart slowly breaking, thinking she had been forgotten by her only living kin.

Coldly satisfied with her dispatch, she had thought herself fully prepared for Lord Strathmore's reaction when he arrived. She had imagined a pampered rogue sulking and huffing and stomping about in his overpriced boots, fretting over the fact that he would miss a few nights' revels all for naught, but his ire would not ruffle her calm nature, and her ruse had at least a chance, she had hoped, of teaching him to appreciate his aunt's love.

It had seemed a perfect plan. From the moment she had penned her angry letter, there had been no doubt in her mind that she had done the right thing.

But now the thought of that hard-eyed giant's wrath made her heart pump with trepidation, while guilt began poking at her overactive conscience. Why was he bleeding?

It was unlike her to lie under any circumstances: she had certainly not intended for the man to suffer physical injury because of her deception. Had he taken a spill on the road? Well, it was no wonder, given the weather last night, she mused, then shook her head to herself uneasily. Riding all night through blizzardlike conditions was hardly the sign of a man who did not care.

Normally rock-sure of her judgment, she felt thrown off balance and glanced toward the parlor door, wondering how to proceed. A disturbing suspicion was forming at the back of her mind that she had somehow confused Devil Strathmore with someone else. Some other London rake. Someone whose name had been struck from the book of her mind with a great, black *X* and who, henceforth, would only be referred to as A Certain Person.

And then another thought struck her, one so dire that the color drained from her face. Lady Strathmore was going to be furious.

Good God, it was bad enough that she had dared to deceive a man so far above her station, even if her intentions had been the very best. But if Darling Dev had been injured because of her meddling, why, that could be grounds for dismissal! This might well cost her her job.

A wave of faint nausea washed over her as she remembered anew the bitter reality of her station. Would she never learn? She was not part of the family. The dowager's villa had begun to feel like home, but it was not really her home, and if she displeased, she could be sent packing, like any other employee. Truly scared now, her mouth going dry, Lizzie bunched her fists at her sides, gathered her courage, and forced herself out of the parlor to meet her fate.

Instead of going directly to the entrance hall, however, she glided down the hallway to the closet tucked beneath the stairs, reached in, and took out a nice, clean, folded, white towel. She shut the closet silently, then turned and squared her shoulders. Holding the towel against her chest, she did her best to school her expression into one that she hoped resembled her usual serenity and marched resolutely toward the entrance hall, fairly certain she was about to get the sack. *What then?* she thought. *Where will I go?* She had no home of her own. She never had. All her life she had lived on the fringes of other people's families.

Dragging her feet down the corridor to the entrance hall, Lizzie heard Lady Strathmore's regal voice lifted in joy to greet her nephew while the staff made much of him.

The man, no doubt, was baffled.

She could hear a deep, gentle baritone voice anxiously questioning Her Ladyship. She closed her eyes at the bewildered anguish in his tone. He sounded thoroughly shaken.

'What's happened, Aunt Augusta? Tell me everything at once. Why are you out of bed? Shouldn't you be lying down?'

'Lying down? Devlin, it is the middle of the day.'

'Yes, but—'

'But what?' The dowager sounded bemused.

A pause.

'I thought— That is to say— Do you mean you're . . . all right?'

'Of course, I'm all right.' The dowager laughed unconcernedly. 'Darling, what in the world?'

Lizzie arrived at the far end of the entrance hall and stopped, her presence yet unnoticed. Seeing them, her heart clenched at the unexpected tableau before her: Lady Strathmore was an aged queen on her throne, her nephew on one knee before her like her most devoted knight, mud streaked and bloodied from battle. Dripping with cold and shivering a little, he searched her face with an earnest, upward gaze, the shadow of frantic fear in his light eyes.

'You're sure – there's nothing wrong? You would not lie to me, Aunt Augusta? You are feeling well?'

'I'm fine, Devlin!' The dowager chuckled. 'Dear boy, did you come all this way to ask me that?'

'Yes,' he whispered, and stared at her for a long moment, comprehending at last that she was telling the truth. Then he closed his eyes with a look of utter relief and slowly laid his forehead on her knee.

'Darling, what is the matter?' Lady Strathmore rested her hand on his tousled hair. 'You're beginning to scare me, Devlin. Where is your carriage? You're a mess.'

'I know. Sorry.' He did not lift his head.

'My God, Devlin, is that blood on your cheek? What's happened?' the dowager cried.

'Mishap on the road. It's nothing,' he said, quickly ending her fright.

'What is going on? I demand that you tell me right now—'

'I missed you,' he whispered. 'That's all.'

Staring at him with deepening wonder, thoroughly mystified, Lizzie shivered with some strange, vaguely frightening emotion. Why did he not speak out? He could have exposed her, could have mentioned her letter, but he had not. At least not yet.

'There, there, my sweet boy,' his aunt chided, petting his sleek raven hair for a moment. 'You know I'm always here for you. Tell me what's the matter, Devlin. I shall fret with worry till you do.'

'I . . . had a dream you were sick.'

'Well, I daresay I'm in better shape than you. Put your mind at ease. Dr. Bell was here a short while ago and said I'm as right as rain. Didn't he, Lizzie?'

At the mention of her name, his head snapped up. His eyes narrowed.

Lizzie tensed, awkwardly holding the towel. His gaze fixed

on her, and the coldness that came into his pale, glittering eyes made her gulp.

Oh, yes, it seemed he had figured it out.

Lady Strathmore did not appear to notice the sudden hostile tension that crackled in the air. 'Dev, dear, you have not met my young companion. Allow me to present Miss Elizabeth Carlisle.'

Rising with a smooth motion, he stared at her, for all the world like a big, bristling wolf.

'Lizzie, this is my Devlin.' Beaming, the old lady clung to his gauntleted hand.

He moved in front of his aunt slightly – as if to protect the dowager from Lizzie!

'My lord.' Her heart thumping, she managed a stilted curtsy.

'Miss . . . Carlisle.' The way he held her in an arctic stare, it seemed she was not so invisible, after all; all things considered, she rather wished at the moment that she were. His sea-bright eyes brimmed with dangerous fury and a rich promise that she was in for it.

Still waiting on the very knife edge for him to expose her lie, she swallowed hard and ventured forward with her peace offering. 'Um, towel?'

Chapter Three

What the hell was going on? Raw nerved and jittery with exhaustion, his heart pounding, head reeling with the aftermath of shock and fear, Dev took the towel warily but kept his outraged glare pinned on her as he ran it over his damp hair. His relief upon finding his aunt well was so complete, he could have wept, but his fury grew as the evidence of how he had been duped sank in. A trick! But how? And for God's sake, *why*? He did not know this chit. He had never wronged her. Why would she torture him like this?

'Shall we repair to the parlor, children? I'll have the servants draw you a bath, Dev, dear. It will be but a moment.'

'Thank you, ma'am,' he growled, his gaze still fixed on the young deceiver – this 'Lizzie' person – this stranger who had invaded the only home he'd known in years and seemed to have taken it over.

She dropped her gaze, all cool serenity, turning away from his fiery glower. Veiling her dove-gray eyes beneath the sweep of her dusky lashes, she grasped the handles of his aunt's Bath chair and assisted her without a word, wheeling the dowager into the parlor.

Dev tracked them slowly, keeping a guarded distance. He

was ravenously hungry, soaked to the skin, and did not own a muscle that did not ache, but the day would never come when he was too hungry or fatigued to notice a shapely young female in his sights, especially one that he knew now to be dangerously clever.

Good God, the chit had played him like a harpsichord.

He was in no mood to admire the sheer brazenness of it. At the moment, her mysterious allure only added insult to injury. Inspecting her rudely from behind, he hoped that she could feel his stare and that it unnerved her. Her prim, beige gown, high-necked and long-sleeved, was sprigged with small white flowers, but Dev's practiced eye took in the way the soft, light muslin draped her round bottom and flowed against her hips with her gliding walk. The floppy white house cap that hid her hair was better suited to a spinster twice her age, but a few soft-brown curls escaped the ugly thing to play at her nape, as though beckoning him to tear it off and loose the rest of her tightly suppressed locks.

Upon reaching the parlor, she maneuvered the Bath chair around so that his aunt could face him, then went to the table and brought the old woman her tea. Dev watched her every move. For a moment, he did not hear a word his aunt was saying. Time seemed to slow in his fascination as his gaze drifted down to the young woman's gentle, white hands.

Steady and soft, unerringly capable, they fluffed the pillow behind his aunt's back, then snugged the old woman's shawl more closely around her bony shoulders. The demure simplicity of those hands, and the tiny lace ruffle at her dainty wrists, did something strange to his insides.

His hungry stare traveled up her slender arms until it came to her breasts, round and smooth and tantalizing. Between them dangled a small, plain crucifix on a gold strand. No sign of vanity, this. Not like the glittering whores he slept with in Town.

This was something altogether new . . . and very, very dangerous.

As she bent down to pick up the handkerchief his aunt dropped and handed it back to her with a smile, there was such tender sweetness in her eyes, such dignity and quiet strength in her manner that Dev, exhausted, felt something in him break.

He was so tired and hungry and cold.

Bleary-eyed, he stared at Miss Carlisle as if she might know better what to do with him than he knew what to do with himself.

Slowly, she looked over and met his gaze in guarded uncertainty.

Their eyes locked, and Dev forgot all about her drab clothes.

Elizabeth Carlisle had the flawless complexion of a woman whose daily habits were beyond reproach. Only plenty of sleep, wholesome food, fresh country air, and a stainless conscience could have produced such creamy perfection, naught but a tinge of roses in her cheeks. She had a high forehead, a prominent nose that thrust forth at a decisive angle, straight and true, and finely shaped eyebrows of walnut brown. The left curved slightly higher than the right, giving her a quizzical expression, as though she were perpetually mulling over some intriguing notion. But her mouth was soft and sensitive, her lips plump, silky pink, and Dev had to jerk himself roughly out of her spell.

On your guard, man. The lying little baggage was a menace. His scowl returned just as the sound of clip-clopping hoofbeats approached, grinding carriage wheels clattering up the drive.

'Who can that be?' Aunt Augusta murmured, turning toward the window.

Through the lace curtain, Dev saw his shiny black traveling-coach roll up in front of the house, Ben peering out the carriage window.

He shook his head to himself in disgust. So much for his

haste. The luxurious traveling coach was a larger, slower vehicle, but obviously whatever time Dev had gained by taking his fast, ill-fated curricle had been lost again in sorting out the accident. He wished he had saved himself the trouble and had traveled in comfort, when a familiar voice from the doorway broke into his churning thoughts.

'Excuse me, my lady?' Mrs. Rowland, the housekeeper who had served his aunt for thirty years, popped her head in the doorway with a questioning look. She was a short, stout, ruddy-cheeked woman of sixty in a white house cap and apron. 'Might I trouble you for a moment, ma'am?'

'Yes, Mildred?' Aunt Augusta asked.

Dev gave the housekeeper a weary smile and nod in greeting.

'My lord,' Mrs. Rowland said fondly, sketching a heavy-limbed curtsy, then glanced at her employer again. 'His Lordship's staff has just arrived, and I've a question about their accommodations – as well as this evening's supper,' she added meaningfully.

'Ah, I'm on my way!' The two old women exchanged a conspiratorial look and would no doubt soon be plotting to make his favorite dessert for him – it pleased them to treat him as if he were still nine years old – but that suited Dev quite well.

A moment of privacy with Miss Carlisle was all that he required. He would soon get to the bottom of this.

The girl seemed eager to flee. 'Let me get your chair for you, ma'am.' She started to follow, but Aunt Augusta shooed her off.

'No need, dear. Children, I shall return in a trice.' Gripping the wheels, the dowager rolled her chair easily out of the parlor.

Immediately, Miss Carlisle mumbled some excuse, but Dev grabbed her arm as she tried to dart past him. 'A moment of your time, mademoiselle!' He swung the door partly shut and met his captive's look of alarm with a glower. 'Whoever you are, you had better start talking. What in the hell is going on around here?'

She looked down slowly at his leather-gloved fingers wrapped around her elbow, then flicked a defiant glance back up to his face. 'You are no longer among the heathens, Lord Strathmore. Pray, do not act like one.'

His eyes narrowed. 'Is that all you have to say for yourself?'

'I am not inclined to say anything until you unhand me. Do please try to calm down.'

'Calm down? I wrecked my carriage and nearly broke my neck – for what? My aunt is fine! There's nothing wrong with her!'

'And is that not cause for rejoicing?'

'That is not the point.'

'No, my lord, that is precisely the point. Her Ladyship has more money than time. I care not what you do with the former, but pray, use the latter well.'

'How dare you take the high moral ground with me after sending me such a pack of lies?'

'I did not lie, sir. Not if you read my note closely—'

'Oh, but I did, my dear! Many times – before it dissolved to a pulp in my pocket, thanks to the snowstorm! "Come at once," you said. "If you love her, come at once." Well, I'm here, aren't I?' He threw his hands up at his sides, presenting himself with an insolent glare. 'Now, if it would not be too much trouble, perhaps you would not mind telling me why!'

Lizzie struggled to maintain her famous patience, perfectly willing to hold a civilized conversation with the man, but if he was going to behave like a domineering barbarian, it hardly encouraged her to cooperate. His grip around her elbow had not hurt, but it had offended her; freed now from his grasp, she rubbed her arm while shooting him a look of reproach. Deeming prudence the better part of valor, however, she took a step backwards just to be safe – then drew in her breath when he advanced.

She took another step back, sending him a vexed look of alarm.

'Tell me, my clever Miss Carlisle,' he asked in a rather sinister purr as he pressed his advantage, stalking her aggressively through the room. 'Are you in the habit of deceiving my aunt as you did me?'

'Obviously, you have not heard a word I've said. I see there is no point in trying to reason with you in your present state.' She cleared her throat, determined to bring the situation under control, backing away as he advanced step by slow, tantalizing step. 'Wh-why don't you go upstairs, change out of your wet clothes, and have something to eat? Then perhaps you will be in a more receptive humor—'

'Don't . . . manage me, little miss,' he taunted, just as she found her retreat blocked by the sofa behind her.

She blanched, bending back as he leaned closer, trapping her against the couch. Her heart pounded wildly.

All dressed in black and wickedly handsome, he loomed a foot taller than her, his shoulders so broad, she could no longer see the door behind him. She gasped and froze when he reached out and captured her chin between his black-gauntleted fingers, raising her face to inspect her.

She stared up at him, wide-eyed. A cynical smile full of menace and mockery curled one side of his lips as he studied her at close range, his pale eyes gleaming with dangerous intelligence.

Lizzie felt absurdly faint, a trifle dizzy. He smelled of winter and leather, wet horse and warm, ruthless male. For a moment, she could only watch, transfixed, as an ice crystal melted off of his long, jet lashes with the throbbing heat of his body. Her mesmerized gaze tracked the droplet's trickling course down the scratched side of his sculpted face to the corner of his hard, beautiful mouth. When he licked it away, she caught her breath abruptly, then looked away, jerking her face out of his light hold.

His velvety laughter at her electric reaction to him snapped her back to her senses. 'Well, now that I've met you, I wish I had *not* written to you!' she muttered, looking away with a fierce blush. 'If I had known you'd take such amusement in chasing me around the parlor, I wouldn't have bothered, believe me!'

'Ah, but you did, *chérie* – you summoned me, and here I am. The question is, what are you going to do with me now?'

'You are indecent!' She slipped around the couch, putting the furniture between them. 'I summoned you here for the sake of your aunt. Stop it!' she cried when he began to move around the couch, sauntering toward her again.

Miraculously, he obeyed.

Letting out a weary sigh, Lord Strathmore lowered his chin and clasped his hands behind his back, knitting his raven eyebrows together as he studied the floor. For a long moment, he was silent. 'Your letter, Miss Carlisle, quite scared the hell out of me. No small feat. I confess, at the moment, I do not know what to believe. Is my aunt ill or no? Tell me – and by God, speak the truth.'

Somewhat reassured that the decadent nobleman was done playing with her for the moment, she shook her head earnestly. 'All that ails Her Ladyship is loneliness, my lord. Is that so hard to understand? I do my best to entertain her, but I am not her flesh and blood. You are all she talks about. She misses you desperately – not that she'd ever complain. I'm sure you must realize this, and yet you ignore her.'

'I don't ignore her!' A shadow of some dark emotion tautened his chiseled features. Perhaps it was guilt. 'She is always in my thoughts.'

'I'm afraid that is not good enough,' she told him softly. 'Good intentions cannot replace your spending time with her. If you could see how she sits here – at this table – playing solitaire for hours on end, day after day after day, with nothing to break the monotony but her weekly visits from the doctor – I can't bear it!'

Her pained words hung on the silence as Devil Strathmore studied her in keen perception. 'If my aunt is unhappy, you could have simply said that in your letter. You had no cause to lie to me.'

'I did not lie! Merely – exaggerated slightly – and if I hadn't, you wouldn't have paid any heed!'

'What makes you so sure?' he challenged her. 'You never even gave me a chance.'

'What chance?' she cried, but flushed at the grain of truth in his accusation.

'Men like you don't concern themselves with the health of their aged relatives.'

'Oh-ho, men like me? And what, pray tell, do *you* know about me?'

'More than you realize,' she bit out, her voice turning tight and prim.

'Like what?'

'I know of – of your travels. A-and your preference in tailors. And the fact that you have no head for three-card loo! Really, you must be the worst gambler on the planet!'

'And how, exactly, do you know that?' he asked with the most ominous arching of his eyebrow.

She stared at him in stubborn silence, cursing herself for saying too much.

'Miss Carlisle?' he prodded, folding his arms slowly across

his chest. 'I'm waiting. Or shall I inform my aunt of your deception? A word from me, and she'll throw you out on your sweet derriere, *ma chérie*.'

She bristled at his deliberately lewd threat. 'Very well. You want an explanation, my lord? You shall have one!' Rattled now and dangerously angry, she pivoted with her chin high and marched out of his looming shadow to Her Ladyship's desk. She glanced at the door to make sure they were still alone, reached into the desk with trembling hands, and returned with a stack of his bills. 'Your aunt is the one who should be demanding an explanation, but since she will not, I will do it for her.'

He regarded her in suspicion as she strode back to him with a pile of his shameless bills in her hand.

'Explain these, if you can! Two hundred guineas for a diamond cravat pin?' She flicked the jeweler's bill at him as if she were pitching cards. 'Or this? A thousand guineas to Hoby's for ten pairs of boots. Ten!' The cobbler's bill bounced off his lean stomach and glided across the smooth surface of the nearby worktable. 'Or Tattersall's – fifteen hundred quid for a matched pair of Cleveland bays – never mind the dozen horses already languishing in your stable. Oh, but here is my favorite!' she exclaimed then quoted aloud from his scrawled note. '"IOU – Strathmore agrees to pay Damage Randall twenty-five hundred quid for losses at three-card loo." Explain that, if you dare!'

'You read my aunt's mail?' he asked, staggered.

'A small transgression compared with yours! For shame, sir! You spend her money like there's no tomorrow, but you can't even be bothered to write her a letter now and then, let alone visit of your own free will! The measures I took were extreme, I admit, but a grown man should not need to be given such a jolt to remind him of his duty!'

He stared at her, looking flabbergasted. For a second, he opened his mouth as if to speak, then apparently thought better of it and snapped his jaw shut. 'I am leaving,' he clipped out, 'because I am a gentleman.'

'Ha!' she replied as Devil Strathmore pivoted and stalked out, his greatcoat swirling around him.

The door slammed, startling her. Lizzie blinked, suddenly realizing she had won their argument. Then she grinned. She twirled around on her heel, but the second she faced forward again, her heart racing, the first thing her gaze fixed upon was the trail of large, muddy footprints that Lord Strathmore had tracked across the floor.

Her smile of victory promptly went flat.

The big dark footprints seemed to mock her – the very symbol of the male race that went treading so carelessly over female hearts, not caring what kind of mess they left in their wake. But even more keenly, they vexed her because they brought into focus her own greatest flaw – her automatic impulse to bend down and start cleaning them up. She refused – aye, utterly, from the very depths of her soul.

Never again would she serve as doormat for any beautiful, highborn man. Those days were over.

Eyeing the doorway through which her mighty opponent had made his exit, she suddenly heard the dowager's voice in the hallway. Rushing to gather up the bills she had flung at him, she quickly put them back in the drawer and sped away from the region of the desk mere seconds before Lady Strathmore rolled back into the parlor wearing a breezy smile.

'Devlin's gone to clean himself up for supper, dear. I just saw him in the hall. Tut, tut, the poor thing. We'll dine at half past five. I've arranged with Mrs. Rowland to make a floating island for dessert!' she added in a girlish whisper. 'It's his favorite. Isn't he as handsome as I said?'

Lizzie's eyes shot sparks, but she conceded the obvious in a mutter. 'That he is, ma'am.'

'Is everything all right, dear? I thought I heard arguing coming from this room a moment ago.'

The question startled her, as did the shrewd look in the dowager's blue eyes. Goodness, she had forgotten that Her Ladyship still had excellent hearing.

'No, ma'am. Everything is fine.' She forced a smile, but Lady Strathmore wasn't fooled. She let out a knowing chuckle and clucked her tongue.

'Dear Lizzie, did Devil tease you about your gown?'

'A little,' she agreed. It was as good an excuse as any.

'Well, we shan't give him cause to do so again, shall we?' Lady Strathmore's managing smile broadened. 'You have lots of pretty things from when you lived in London – you just never wear them. Tonight I expect you to dress for dinner, do you understand? And *no* house cap. That is an order.'

'Yes, ma'am.' She kept her chafing gaze down, but maybe her employer was right.

In her former, lifelong post as companion to the sparkling young Lady Jacinda Knight, Lizzie had attended enough Society ballrooms to know how to play the game; she had always simply chosen not to play it. But since she was even more certain of losing her job now that she had trounced Darling Dev – the male ego, after all, could not withstand such defeat without retaliation – why not go down in a blaze of glory?

Meanwhile, Lady Strathmore glanced sardonically at the big, dark footprints. 'Dear me – ring for Margaret, Lizzie. I see my nephew has tracked mud through the house.' She looked up brightly. 'Ah, well, boys will be boys. Mud or no, it's still so nice to have a man around the house, don't you think?'

Lizzie just looked at her.

'My *own* fault?' Dev bellowed as he dressed for dinner a while later in his usual quarters, a handsome bed-chamber done in maroon, dark blue, and gilt. 'What's the matter with you, Ben? I can't believe you're taking her side! My curricle's in splinters, I nearly cracked my head open, and it was all just a – a dirty trick!'

'Well, you really shouldn't have had four horses hitched to a vehicle meant only for two,' Ben chided. 'Especially with snow and ice on the roads. It was rather reckless.'

'Speed!' Dev said in exasperation as he wrenched on a pair of black trousers and angrily buttoned the falls. Elizabeth Carlisle might be in the right, but he sure as hell didn't have to like it. Nor did he like recalling his hasty retreat from the parlor and the chagrin of knowing that a mere slip of a girl had kicked his arse. It was even worse than recalling the debacle of the accident.

At some point in the middle of the night, he had taken a curve too fast and hit a patch of ice. His light curricle had rolled. If he had not jumped clear of the crash at that precise moment, he probably would have been killed. After ascertaining that he was still alive with no broken bones, only a few cuts and scrapes from an ill-tempered bramble bush, he had had to work alone in the blackness of a winter night, pushing his battered curricle back up onto its broken wheels. Then he'd had to recapture the horses, who had fled in terror, dragging the broken whiffletree behind them. He had walked the team to the nearest livery stable, where he had been forced to answer a great many questions about the mishap and to pay a large sum for the supposed damage to the horses.

After dispatching a few hirelings to see to his broken-down curricle, he'd had to buy a mount to ride the rest of the way to his aunt's house because the livery owner refused to rent him another horse – he was obviously too 'careless' to be trusted.

Just another flaw to add to the roster of his faults that Lizzie Carlisle had so kindly endeavored to list for him.

'Smug, self-righteous little conniver—'

'If you're so angry at the girl, why didn't you speak out when you had the chance to inform your aunt of her deceit?' Ben asked, collecting the shaving accoutrements from the side of the nickel-plated bathing-tub which Dev had just left and placed them back in the square, leather *necessaire*. He took Dev's cologne out of the traveling box and handed it to him. 'Could it be because, deep down, you know the girl is right?'

'Aunt Augusta has never complained of my treatment of her,' Dev huffed, but his cheeks flushed, for in truth, his anger at himself for neglecting his aunt equaled if not exceeded his indignation at having been so ill-used. He pulled the stopper out of the small, silver-braced bottle and slapped on some of the cleanly pungent clove-and-rosemary water.

'True, Her Ladyship has always let you slide by on minimal effort,' Ben said mildly. 'Apparently, Miss Carlisle is not so prepared to indulge you.'

'Judas,' Dev muttered, scowling as he gave the bottle back to his valet.

With a look of amusement, Ben put it away, closing the traveling box and flipping the brass latches once more. Then he took out a neatly pressed square of white muslin and began the intricate process of folding it for Dev's cravat.

'Obaldeston,' Dev ordered. The knot style was his aunt's favorite.

He bent slightly as Ben slipped the prepared cloth around his neck. Dev studied the white plaster ceiling as his valet worked his careful magic, then shook his head to himself, plagued by the memory of lucid gray eyes and soft charcoal lashes. What a maddening creature she was!

Most women blushed and fluttered and flipped their hair around him, but this one took dead aim at him with her frank, cool gaze and hit him right between the eyes with a wallop of honesty that he was in no mood to hear. Who did she think she was to judge him, to manipulate him, to heap him in guilt – even if he deserved it?

He quite believed he was still in shock. *Nobody* treated Devil Strathmore that way. 'Where did she come from, that she must now plague me?' he wondered aloud as Ben finished tying the cravat and handed him his light-blue silk waistcoat. He slipped it on. 'What the hell does she want?'

'Merely to teach you a lesson, I think.'

'A lesson, eh?' He sauntered away, buttoning his waistcoat and cuff links in front of the mirror. 'Perhaps it's time I taught her a thing or two.'

'What do you mean?' Ben asked uneasily, holding up Dev's black tailcoat for him.

'Nobody makes a fool out of me. And I'll tell you another thing.' He slipped his arm into the impeccably cut garment. 'This little schemer has just thrown down the gauntlet to a foe she should have known better than to challenge.' Pulling on the formal evening jacket, Dev inspected himself in the mirror.

'You intend to have her dismissed?' Ben eyed him warily.

'No.' Dev shook his head. 'She serves her purpose here. Even I can see that. She takes good care of my aunt.' With this begrudging acknowledgment, he considered for a moment. 'No, this is between Lizzie Carlisle and me.'

'What do you mean to do to the girl?'

Dev's eyes gleamed in the reflection as he ran his hand over his still-damp hair, smoothing it. 'She is rather a tasty little thing.'

'Sir!' Ben breathed. 'You mustn't!'

Dev turned elegantly to him, feigning innocence. 'Hm?'

'Oh, no. I know that look. You leave her alone!' Ben took a step toward him. 'She's just a young lady. She meant no harm!'

'Neither do I.' Dev smiled cynically and turned back to the

mirror, making a last adjustment of his cravat. 'It's just a bit of sport, Ben. Teach the chit a lesson.' Giving his reflection a cool, final glance of approval, he ignored Ben's protests and left his chamber. He headed down to the drawing room, where he had been instructed to meet the ladies before dinner. Hands in pockets, he was sauntering down the hallway toward the grand staircase, assuring his stung male pride that he would very soon even the score, when suddenly, he stopped in his tracks – and stared.

Coming down the hallway from the opposite direction was Miss Carlisle. For a heartbeat, he almost did not recognize her.

The floppy white house cap was gone, its owner quite transformed.

He watched her dazedly. Her silky hair shone in the candlelight, a rich and lovely shade of warm, walnut brown; it was curled and pinned in an elegant topknot that showed off the clean line of her jaw and the graceful arc of her white neck. Her frumpy beige day-dress had been replaced by a charming, high-waisted dinner gown of rose-pink satin. The low candlelight from the wall sconces played over her pearlescent complexion and the rich fabric of her dress, giving the material a liquid shimmer as she strode toward him, her ankle-length skirts belling slightly over her matching pink slippers.

His entranced stare feasted on the expanse of creamy skin that the wide-scooped neckline of her dress displayed, the tempting hint of womanly cleavage. The girl was well made, he thought in admiration as she came nearer. Beautifully well made, with soft, generous curves ripe for his skilled seduction.

He lowered his chin a bit to continue holding her gaze as she joined him at the top of the stairs. She stopped a foot or so from him, hanging back at a wary distance.

In spite of himself, he offered her a rueful half-smile; it smoldered with approval. She regarded him in trepidation, but the blush that bloomed in her cheeks was almost as pink as her gown. He thrilled to the way her dove-gray eyes darkened to a smoky deep blue as her gaze skimmed him, in turn.

His desire to get her alone quickened apace, but suddenly it was not so much for the sake of teaching her a lesson as it was for his own sensual enjoyment.

'Well,' she said, veiling the sparkle of interest in her eyes behind her demure long lashes, 'I trust you are in a better humor, my lord.'

'I am now,' he agreed in a caressing tone. 'You, my dear Miss Carlisle, are a very rose in this dark winter.' He stole her hand gently from her side and lifted it to his lips, bending his head to place a courtly kiss on her knuckles.

'Don't even try,' she advised softly, and at the smile of chiding amusement she sent him, Dev felt her feminine power with every fiber of his being. Withdrawing her hand from his light grasp, she turned away, daintily lifted the hem of her skirts, and started down the staircase.

'Try what?' he countered, pouncing down a couple of steps to land in front of her.

The move allowed him to block her path and put them on eye level, since she stood two steps above him. He rested his foot on the step beside her, edging nearer. Near enough to kiss her.

Or to get slapped. She did neither, inspecting him with a skeptical stare.

'Look here,' she said briskly, taking the situation in hand with a businesslike air that he found thoroughly adorable. 'We seem to have started off on the wrong foot, you and I. I think it's safe to say we both acted badly in the parlor, but it does not signify. All that matters is your aunt.'

He gazed at her lips as she spoke. 'On that, we are in perfect union.'

She blushed at the silken innuendo and pretended not to understand his meaning. 'Good. Then let us both do our best to be agreeable at dinner, hm? After that, you stay out of my way and I shall stay out of yours.'

'Not a chance,' he whispered.

She gave him a look and then went around him, as steady as his weatherly little brigantine in an Atlantic gale.

Dev's eyes flickered hungrily at the challenge as she flounced off ahead of him. His Cherokee friends had taught him that there were certain beasts in the forest from whom one must never run. Flight only triggered the predator's instincts to chase.

Somebody should have warned Miss Carlisle.

With another pantherlike jump, he landed agilely in her path and leaned on the banister with a pleasantly flirtatious smile. 'As it happens, I have a proposition for you, my dear.'

'Oh, I'm sure you have a whole repertoire of them, my lord.'

'I speak in earnest. Hear me out.'

She gave a bored sigh, but her eyes sparkled as she met his playful gaze. 'Very well.'

'I propose a truce,' he said. 'I shall concede that you sent your *deceitful* letter with admirable intentions if you admit, in turn, that I indeed care for my aunt, not just her money, as evidenced by the speed of my arrival. What say you?'

'Hmm.' She feigned indecision, holding his stare. 'I suppose we ought to at least try to get along, for it would upset Her Ladyship if we were cross with each other at table.'

'Precisely.'

'But under the terms of this truce, am I still in danger of losing my job?'

He gave her a sardonic smile. 'I never had any intention of getting you sacked, *chérie*. Pity, though, how you make me show mercy. I'm sure I could have used the threat to wrest any number of interesting favors from you.'

'Hmm, no doubt.' Gazing at him for a moment, she lifted her hand to his cheek and inspected his cut in fretful sympathy. 'Your poor face. This is all my fault,' she murmured. 'Does it hurt very much?'

For a moment, Dev could not breathe let alone speak, electrified by her feather-light caress. 'No,' he managed to force out, his voice gone a trifle hoarse. Her innocence ravished his defenses; his whole being begged her in a silent whisper, *Take me*.

'I'm glad it wasn't worse.'

He flinched at the denial when she took her touch away, lowering her hand again to her side, but the artless smile she gave him was nearly his undoing. It dimpled both her glowing cheeks and lit her gray-blue eyes like silver sun-shafts piercing through a dark cloud-lattice. He could not tear his gaze away. It was the most generous, radiant smile he'd ever seen, and the kindest. He had the strange feeling he was out of his depth as a thousand questions about her exploded through his mind, fireworks on a midsummer's night. Who was this angel? Where had she come from? He suddenly wanted to know everything about her.

'Very well,' she resumed brightly, 'I shall accept your truce, Lord Strathmore. And now we really should hurry. Your aunt will be waiting.'

'May I?' He offered her his arm.

She smiled again, flicking a cautious glance over his face as she slipped her hand through the crook of his elbow. Dev sent her his own heated smile, absorbing the sheer lightning when they touched like a jolt from a Leyden jar. She seemed to feel it, too, quickly looking away with a fiery blush in her cheeks. They exchanged another guarded look full of fascination, but spoke no more as they went down together to dine.

Wistfulness – this maudlin sentimentality – was a most unaccustomed caprice for an old dragon lady who prided herself on her eccentricity and her ability to terrify rude young persons. But as Lady Strathmore gazed into the crackling fireplace, waiting for the others to join her, she was filled with the sense of time slipping away. And so it was. She would not live to see the spring. She could feel it in her tired old bones, no matter what that beardless whelp, Dr. Bell, had to say on the subject. *Tut-tut*, she scolded herself.

Death, after all, did not scare Augusta Strathmore. Any woman who had flouted the Patronesses of Almack's could hardly tremble before the Reaper. In any case, she was not sorry to go, for there had been a woeful lack of amusing conversation for some years now, all her most interesting friends having gone senile or hopped off into the afterlife ahead of her.

What mattered was that she could look back in pride on a long life well lived. The heiress of an iron ore tycoon, she had crowned her ambitious papa's efforts in life by snaring a penniless viscount for a husband, God rest his soul. She had never borne Jacob any children, for the odd duck had foolishly died shortly after their wedding. Ah, but she had led a merry life – had taken the Grand Tour before the war – why, once she had even danced with the now-mad old king, poor fellow. Such days! Oh, yes, she had given the ton a shock or two in her time, she mused as she toyed with her jet beads. She had countless fine memories and no regrets . . .

But one.

He walked in at that moment, tall, dark, and dashing in his black formal clothes – Augusta opted to ignore the earring. The white flash of his grin was as charming as ever, but she knew better than anyone that her beloved nephew was unreachable, locked within himself these twelve years behind fortress walls of pain. After all that he had been through, she shuddered to think of how he would take it when it came her time to go. She could not bear to think of leaving him so all alone.

To her surprise, however, he came in escorting Lizzie. Augusta smiled, charmed to see her shy young companion looking more her age in the pretty pink satin. Why, the child could be perfectly lovely when she wasn't trying to blend into the wallpaper. She gave Lizzie a regal nod, discreetly acknowledging her compliance with her request; but, privately, Augusta was bemused to see the two of them together after the mysterious tiff she had overheard in the parlor.

They made a comely pair as they crossed the drawing room to her: Devlin dark and suave, Lizzie fair and sweet. They looked as natural together as if they had known each other all their lives. Soon she was surrounded by the rosy glow of their youthful vitality; Augusta, however, eagle-eyed as always, was quick to note the subtle glances that passed between them.

My, my, she mused. Now here was a curious state of affairs. Come to think of it, there was something altogether mysterious about her nephew's unannounced visit today, bloodied and covered in mud. It was peculiar behavior, even for Dev.

Between his odd visitation and the whispered battle she had heard coming from inside the parlor earlier, Augusta was reminded again of Lizzie's outraged reaction a few days ago to the arrival of Dev's latest gambling IOU.

The girl apparently had some strange aversion to gambling.

When the post-boy had brought the note, the chit had grown so furious in her silent way that she had actually begun shaking. Her lips had turned white, and she'd made an excuse to leave Augusta's side, taking a few minutes alone to becalm her rage. Augusta had marked her reaction closely because it was unlike the steady girl to lose her temper over anything.

Now she began to wonder if tranquil Lizzie had not taken matters into her own hands in bringing Augusta's errant nephew to Bath. The girl was very loyal, after all. What had she done? the dowager wondered with rising curiosity and growing amusement.

Then she noticed Dev gazing at Lizzie with a golden luster in his eyes and a telltale softening of his aquiline features. For her part, Lizzie, the would-be spinster, returned his stare with one of her gentle smiles, blushing a little.

Good heavens! thought Augusta.

It was only a look – just a fleeting glance – ah, but one look was all that a first-rate matchmaker required.

Chapter Four

How did he do it? Maybe by some dark magic he had learned in an exotic land? Lizzie wondered. How did Devil Strathmore fill her mind with the most improper thoughts? The wine at dinner seemed to go straight to Lizzie's head; the evening was a swirl of sensory opulence, and she couldn't take her eyes off him.

Candlelight danced over sparkling silver and fine china plates on a field of snowy white damask; it glittered in golden spangles over crystal wine goblets and was cast back by large gilt-framed mirrors hung from plum-colored walls. The hearth fire crackled cozily beneath a white marble chimney piece, and liveried footmen manned their posts by the wall, ever ready to serve. The table was richly laid, the dining room a setting of luxurious elegance for the unspoken interplay between the two of them.

Lady Strathmore sat at the head of the table, unwittingly giving Devlin and Lizzie an unfettered view of each other through the intimate glow of the candelabra. Though they had based their truce on an agreement that what mattered most was the viscountess, Lizzie feared his aunt would soon notice they were entirely engrossed in each other.

She was stunned to find herself capable of capturing the

notice of such a gorgeous specimen. Dressed to perfection and utterly dashing, he was elegant and savage with his swarthy skin and formal clothes, dangerously seductive. His coal-black hair was tamed back in a sleek queue, but his golden earring and the long, thin scratch on his cheek added to his aura of untamed male power. Every move he made mesmerized her – the slow, sensuous drumming of his fingertips at the base of his wine goblet; the way he stroked his chiseled jaw in thought; his languid pose as he leaned back in his chair, the very picture of lordly leisure, his broad shoulders slouching, his hand tucked contentedly into his waistcoat.

Watching him eat did strange things to her in some deep, primal layer of her being, but his aunt was right – the man had a lusty appetite. He had made short work of the first course of pea-soup, roasted beef, and salmon with smelts. For her part, Lizzie had such butterflies in her stomach that she could only pick at her food, though she felt half-starved. She could barely comprehend her own mood, all eager and trembly. She feared she was a trifle smitten, which she knew was absurd, because men like him flirted with everyone. It meant nothing.

And yet he was wonderful with his aunt, irresistibly charming; he was kind to the servants; and the way he looked at Lizzie made her wonder if any man had ever truly seen her until now.

If there was any doubt that he was flirting with her, he removed it the moment he stretched his long legs out under the table and slowly rested his crossed heels between her slippered feet. Her eyes widened in shock, but he gave no outward sign of his mischief, resting his chin on his hand as he listened to Lady Strathmore telling him the local gossip.

Subtly, oh so subtly, he slid Lizzie a roguish look from under his long, black lashes. She nearly moaned aloud at the banked sensuality in his glance, but she quickly smothered the sound, so all that came out was a small cough.

Though she did her best to hide her desire, she suspected he knew exactly what was going on in her mind – for he was as smooth and worldly as they came – and this thrilled her despite herself.

'I hope you do not mind our country hours, Dev, dear,' his aunt was saying. 'I'm sure you do not dine till ten in Town.'

'Not to worry, ma'am, I can always eat. The question is, will you?'

The dowager pooh-poohed his pointed glance at her thin, frail figure. 'What news of London, darling? Any juicy *on-dits?*'

'Let's see.' With a rakish smile playing at his lips, he took a leisurely sip of his wine. 'Prinny has shaved off his side-whiskers,' he declared, setting his glass down again.

'Has he, indeed?' Lady Strathmore asked with interest. 'And what of Princess Charlotte? Is she breeding yet? Oh, don't blush, Lizzie – if the princess does not bear a child, there will be chaos in the line of succession. I daresay England should get *something* out of that German prince the gel wed last summer, in light of all we've given him.'

'No word yet, ma'am, but I'm sure the newlyweds are doing their best. After all, they say it is a love match.' Devlin sent Lizzie a mirthful look over his wineglass.

'And what of Gloucester's wedding to Princess Mary? I heard they held their first party at home. How was it?'

'Exceeding dull, nor will I discuss the new theater season until you eat something more than a few drops of soup. Really, Aunt Augusta, a good breeze could blow you away. But enough of those royal buffoons. They're not half so interesting as present company. Miss Carlisle, for instance. My dear, you must allow me to improve my acquaintance with your fair self. Where do hail from? Who are your people? What was your last position before you came to be in my aunt's employ?'

'Is this an interview, my lord?'

'Yes,' he declared with a grin. 'A belated one. I must make certain you are a worthy companion for my aunt.'

He sent her a playful wink while the dowager scoffed. 'Oh, Devlin.'

Lizzie smiled back at him, but before she could answer, the second course arrived, slightly lighter fare of game and pastries and stewed fruits. The parade of footmen uncovered silver-domed dishes of woodcocks, hare, and scalloped oysters. There were stewed pippins, a dish of jelly, muffin pudding, and a pear tart with a fine flaky crust.

After refilling their wine from crystal decanters, the servants withdrew.

Devlin regarded her expectantly. 'Well? I am all ears, Miss Carlisle.'

She set down her fork, yielding to the spirit of fun he had cast over the table. 'Well, then, let's see. I was born in Cumberland, where my father served as land steward to the Duke of Hawkscliffe, as did his father before him, and his father's father, and so on. Unfortunately, Papa died when I was four. His heart gave out while overseeing the June haymaking. My mother had preceded him the year before, of yellow fever. But I have little memory of either one.'

'I am so sorry,' he said quickly, looking genuinely taken aback.

She merely shrugged and gave him a hapless smile.

'What became of you after they died?'

'I was made the ward of the present Duke of Hawkscliffe – Robert.'

'I've met him. Excellent chap,' he murmured.

'The best of men,' she agreed with a reverent nod, though she rather doubted the straitlaced Robert would have approved of *him*. 'Upon my joining the ducal household, I was designated as companion to His Grace's young sister, Lady Jacinda Knight.

She was three and I was four, and we have been best friends ever since. We grew up together, had all the same tutors. The family has always been extremely good to me,' she said fondly. 'I accompanied Jacinda into Society from the night of her debut ball, charged by His Grace with the solemn duty of keeping the mischievous creature out of trouble.'

'Did you succeed?'

'For the most part, yes, but then Jacinda met her Billy, and I passed my duties on to him.'

'Who's Billy?' he asked in amusement.

Lizzie chuckled. 'Actually, it's William, Marquess of Truro and Saint Austell. He dotes on her so – it warms my heart. They were married last summer. He just finished building her a villa on Regent's Park. I have not yet seen it, but knowing Jacinda, I am sure all is in the first stare of fashion.'

'I haven't met them, but I have seen them in Town,' he remarked. 'She's very beautiful.'

Lizzie nodded in unstinting agreement. 'More than that, she's smart. Much smarter than she prefers to let on behind all that sparkling vivacity. At any rate, once Jacinda married, I knew it was time for me to move on.' Lizzie opted to leave out the part concerning A Certain Person. 'In August, I came here, where I have had the good fortune of enjoying Lady Strathmore's company ever since.' She glanced affectionately at his aunt, who had been unusually silent throughout the meal, watching and listening to their exchange.

'It sounds like you miss your friend,' he observed.

'A little,' she admitted. 'We write to each other every week. But what of you, my lord? Any further adventures planned?'

He shook his head. 'The *Katie Rose* is up on blocks in a London shipyard, having her barnacles scraped.'

'The *Katie Rose*?' she echoed, charmed.

'The brigantine Aunt Augusta bought me for my twenty-first

birthday,' he explained with a rueful smile. 'I named her for my mother. Her name was Katherine, but that's what my father used to call her when he was trying to talk her down from flying up into the boughs, as she was wont to do. To me, she had only one name, and it was: "Yes, ma'am."'

She laughed softly. 'Temper?'

'An Irish one, he answered with a shadow of a smile.

'I didn't realize you had Irish blood.'

'Half. Don't tell anyone,' he said dryly; then he seemed to notice that his aunt was staring at him.

The two exchanged a wordless look that made Lizzie wonder if she was missing something, but the awkward pause vanished as a nod from Her Ladyship caused the footmen to clear the table for the third course. Plates and trays were whisked away; wineglasses and candelabra held clear while the white damask tablecloth was removed, exposing the rich mahogany table beneath with its silky patina of beeswax polish.

Again glasses were refilled, this time with a sweet dessert wine.

'Tea, coffee, or chocolate, ma'am?' the first footman asked the dowager gravely.

'Coffee,' she clipped out.

Devlin requested the same, but Lizzie declined, content with her glass of Madeira.

The first footman retreated to fetch the freshly brewed coffee while the others marched in with the third course: a small maple-cured ham that all of them were too full to taste, blanched almonds and raisins, an assortment of biscuits, and lastly, set down with great pride in the center of the table, a magnificent floating island.

'You spoil me,' Devlin declared, turning to his aunt.

'Indubitably,' she agreed with a chuckle.

In a silver soup epergne – filled with sweet heavy cream that had been thickened with sack wine, whipped to a froth, and sprinkled with nutmeg and the bright yellow shavings of a lemon rind – floated three French rolls, cut sliver-thin and piled high with colorful layers of jelly, fruit, and sweetmeats. Mrs. Rowland and Cook had truly outdone themselves. The floating island was divine, as were the other delicacies. Savoring the lavish dessert, Lizzie was just reflecting on what a success the evening had been when everything began going wrong.

'Miss Carlisle, I know you mentioned Hawkscliffe is the ducal title, but what was it you said your Lady Jacinda's family name was?' Devlin asked as the footmen brought in the coffee service on a gleaming silver tray. 'Was it Knight?'

'Yes.'

'Hang me, I knew that sounded familiar.' He leaned back in his chair with a broad smile. 'I went to school with her brother.'

'Which one?' The startling news instantly made her a trifle uneasy. 'She has five.'

'Alec,' he said, and then let out a sudden, roguish laugh. 'Of course. Lord Alec Knight, or, pardon, 'Alexander the Great,' as he used to insist on being called in those days.'

'Oh, yes, that sounds just like him,' she uttered faintly, but she felt as though she had just got the wind knocked out of her. Good God, it couldn't be – they were friends!

But of course. Alec knew everyone, and the two were of an age. Devlin only seemed older because he had gone places, done things, while Alec had remained in London playing cards and breaking hearts. She lowered her gaze to hide her shock.

Lord Alec Knight. Her best friend's brother, whom she had worshipped from the age of nine. The youngest of the five Knight brothers. The one she had always dreamed she'd marry. Her blue-eyed darling, who had answered her lifetime's devotion with a humiliating rejection last summer in the coldest possible terms.

'Lord, we used to get into so much trouble together,' Devlin was saying, but she barely heeded his nostalgic chuckle.

Her heart had begun pounding, a knot of bitter hurt forming in the pit of her stomach at the mere mention of her former idol's name. The elegant meal had turned to ashes in her mouth, and the euphoria she had felt all evening rose up to mock her. *God, what am I doing?*

Idiot! Did she intend to make the same mistake twice? Was she mad?

'We were great mates back at Eton – and at Oxford, before I flunked out. God's bones, I haven't seen him in years. How is the blighter?'

Trembling, Lizzie lifted her gaze and stared at him, at a loss. She could not think of a single word to say.

Alec. Her chest felt squeezed in a great vise at the thought of his sunny grin and sapphire eyes, but there were no more tears left in her. Gambling was Alec's first love; she had finally learned that the hard way. He had the beauty of a fallen archangel and had used it last summer to pay off his debts, had whored himself out to a rich baroness so he could go back and gamble some more. Oh, it had been the jest of the Season, how the captain of all London rakes had become the glamorous Lady Campion's kept man for a while.

Only Alec Knight could get away with such a thing and come out gleaming.

A born showman full of dash and style and outrageous charm down to the tips of his elegant fingers, he had made it seem a coup, a blow struck on behalf of all males, the usual financial supporters of women. Congratulated left and right by his hordes of scoundrelly friends for turning the tables on the female race, Alec Knight had made his choice, as far as Lizzie was concerned. He had thrown her love away on a roll of the dice.

She had thought she would never be able to glue all the pieces of her broken heart back together again, but finally, in the peace and quiet of Bath, she had begun to mend. So, what, in God's name did she think she was doing making cow eyes at Devil Strathmore? He and Alec Knight were not the same man, but they were the same breed, a fact underscored by their friendship – and by their gambling debts. The parallel was obvious, though they were night and day – a dark devil and a golden god – both of them too beautiful and too highborn for the likes of her; both dissolute scoundrels obsessed with adventure, addicted to living on the edge. Devlin might be king of the dark forest, but Alec ruled every glittering ballroom he stepped into, which was why she was never going back into Society again.

Devlin set down his fork and furrowed his brow, studying her intently. 'Are you all right, my dear?'

Still mute with emotion, she looked straight into his eyes and thought, *Don't flirt with me. I can't have you. I don't want you. I don't need any man*. She was an independent woman.

A spinster.

A bluestocking and deuced proud of it. She cared only for books. Never again would she place herself at the mercy of his kind. Never again hand her heart over to be broken.

As the excruciating silence stretched thin, Pasha suddenly came to her rescue, jumping up on the table to make a dash for the pigeon pie.

Chaos exploded across the table, much to Lizzie's relief.

'Pasha, no!'

'Get down!'

'*Reeer!*' The cat leaped over the epergne, a tawny streak of fur and insolence.

Wine splashed. Flatware clattered. Devlin yanked his coffee out of the way just in time to avoid wearing it, while Lady Strathmore laughed in delight. Silver lids went spinning. The candelabra tipped over, catching one of the linen napkins on fire.

The shocked footmen stumbled into motion, one quickly dousing the little flame with a heave of melting ice from the wine cooler, while the second leaped to roll the dowager's chair out of the way.

Her nephew was on his feet. 'Get that damned cat out of here!'

Without forethought, Lizzie seized the distraction to effect her escape, purposely knocking over her wineglass in the confusion so that her Madeira spilled all over her best gown. She didn't even care. She just wanted out of there, now. Away from Devlin's all-too-perceptive gaze.

'Oh, no!' she cried, looking down at herself as the footmen chased the cat down the far end of the twenty-foot table. When the Strathmores looked over at her, she glanced up with an innocent expression, hoping she gave no sign of her Jacinda-like ruse.

The eagle-eyed dowager regarded her skeptically, but Devlin let out a mild curse to see what the cat had done to her gown.

'Blazes, Aunt, can't you keep that rat on a leash?'

'But, Devlin, Pasha loves pigeon pie,' Lady Strathmore protested mildly, chuckling as her spoiled pet huffed over to the warm bricks in front of the fireplace and pretended to ignore the scolding, sulking and licking his paw.

Having barely escaped a dousing from his own tumbled glass, Devlin cast about with a look of distress in her behalf, as if he knew she could never afford to replace the gown, a gift from the fantastically wealthy Jacinda. 'That will come out if you hurry,' he offered. 'I'm sure my valet could give it one of his treatments. Ben's a genius, truly. No stain can stand against him.' He got out of the way while the footman quickly mopped up the spreading puddle of coffee.

'You're very kind,' she murmured barely audibly. 'I'm sure I'll manage. If you'll excuse me.'

'Off you go,' the dowager said blithely. 'Do not fret, my dear. Owing it all to Pasha's mischief, I promise your gown shall be replaced with a new one if the valet cannot fix it.'

'Thank you, ma'am, but I'm sure it won't be necessary.' What need did she have for such finery? An estate keeper's daughter had never really had any business going into Society in the first place. Without further ado, she sketched a curtsy and then hurried out of the dining room in a rustle of ruined wet satin.

Dev frowned and sat down slowly again after she had gone. 'Now, that's a shame,' he said, still puzzled by Miss Carlisle's strange reaction of a few moments ago and the stricken look he had glimpsed in her eyes. 'You will replace her gown for her?'

'I said I would.' His aunt observed him with a narrow smile. 'You like her, do you?'

He glanced over, startled by her frank inquiry. *Careful, old boy.* His aunt had a habit of trying to marry him off to every eligible female in England. 'She seems pleasant enough,' he said guardedly.

'To be sure, she is not the sort of idiotic miss you are used to. I confess, I am worried about the gel. Do you know how she spends her nights?'

'I cannot imagine.'

'Translating foreign texts for extra money.'

'Don't you pay her enough, Aunt?' he asked indignantly.

'Of course, I do. She is saving up, you see, to open a bookshop.'

'A *what*?'

'You heard me.' They exchanged a puzzled look. Aunt Augusta shrugged and shook her head at the notion. 'She is quite the bluestocking, our Miss Carlisle. French, Italian, German.'

'Even German?' he echoed, impressed. 'I wonder where she learned that.'

'Why don't you ask her? Or is the great adventurer, like every other man, frightened of a woman with brains?'

'I am not frightened of Elizabeth Carlisle, Aunt. Hang it, old girl, I haven't seen you take to someone this way in years.'

'Well, she is quite worth one's time. Reminds me of myself as a gel, in fact.'

He laughed idly, reaching over to pour himself a glass of port from the crystal decanter, now that his coffee had been spilled. 'You were an heiress with a dowry of thirty thousand pounds and to the best of my knowledge, you've barely a smattering of French.'

'Yes, but I never took any nonsense from blue bloods like you, and neither does Miss Carlisle,' she said with a pointed glance. 'In any case, I'm sure she will soon be whisked away in matrimonial bliss by my very capable young doctor, Andrew Bell.'

'What, Dr. Bell of the Bilious Pills?' he exclaimed.

'Oh, he's quite mad for her. A good match, I should think. Solid, dependable, polite young man. Not bad looking, either.'

'Solid, dependable—?' Dev scoffed, shifting in his chair. 'How relentlessly dull! That's not what a woman like her needs.'

Aunt Augusta raised an eyebrow. 'Well, I do worry about her, now that you mention it. I fear some foolish fellow has made mischief of the poor gel's affections.'

He stopped and stared at her, his goblet halfway to his lips. 'Is that so?'

'She does not speak of it, but I know a broken heart when I see one.'

He set his glass down, narrowing his eyes. 'How very intriguing.'

'Careful, Devlin,' his aunt chided. 'You've left enough of those in your wake.'

And so, Dev thought, had his old friend Alec Knight.

Suddenly, her strange reaction at dinner began to make sense.

His chum had always been a notorious Don Juan. Indeed, Dev recalled how, even as a youth, Alexander the Great could usually be found half-buried under a mound of clamoring girls eagerly covering him in kisses. And then there had been the older women. Married women. Sophisticated seductresses old enough to be the then-teenaged lover's mother. Everywhere Alec went, ladies fell at his feet; it was as though he had some unnatural power over them.

Taking a brooding sip of his port, Dev wondered if the innocent Lizzie Carlisle had succumbed to the rogue's famous charm while growing up with him all those years under her guardian's roof.

His protective instincts disliked the thought of it immensely.

Meanwhile, his aunt shook her head. 'But enough about Lizzie for the moment, darling. Even more than her, I am worried about you,' she declared, taking him off guard.

Here we go again, Dev thought, suppressing a sigh, while her pointed gaze seemed determined to reroute the conversation in a direction where he had no desire to travel.

'I do not like at all what I am hearing about your wild ways in Town. Your drinking, your gambling, your women. These companions you keep of late – I hear they are a very bad sort. I hope you are not returning to your old ways, Devlin. We have been through this before.'

'That was a long time ago, ma'am.'

'Barely long enough to live down your former reputation.'

'My reputation?' he echoed, resting his cheek on his fist with a cynical half-smile. 'When have you ever cared about the world's opinion?'

'I always care where you are concerned. Wild and wicked, a sensualist and slave to pleasure – that is how Society remembers you from your troubled times, and lately, I cannot see that you've done much to show them you've matured.'

He stared at her for a long moment. What she said, of course, was true, but the ton's misjudgment of him aided his pursuit of his enemies. The lads of the Horse and Chariot Club were fast-living hellions who spared no expense on their pleasures, and Dev's past as a lost boy of the ton gave them reason to accept him as one of their own.

Devastated by grief, he had flunked out of Oxford at eighteen, a year after his family's destruction, and had moved to London, where he had quickly sunk into dissipation in an effort to escape his pain. He had earned the nickname *Devil* for his efforts, but by the time he hit rock bottom, Aunt Augusta put an end to all that with her ingenious plan of sending him off to see the world. He had no doubt she had saved his life.

'Oh, what am I to do with you?' she murmured, gazing tenderly at him. 'Running full-tilt down the road to perdition, as always. I do not hold at all with such self-destructiveness. Why can you not form healthier habits?' She eyed his glass of strong port in disapproval. 'Do you know what my father always used to say? "Early to bed, early to rise, makes a man healthy, wealthy, and wise."'

He smiled with a teasing glint in his eyes. 'Your father, dear lady, was middle class,' he drawled. 'We "blue bloods," as you put it, have a fine old tradition of destroying ourselves in the grand style. You wouldn't understand.'

'Scoundrel,' she muttered, smacking his arm lightly. 'Papa was worth ten of you useless aristocrats. Why, if not for our factories, you fine Strathmores would not have had a roof over your heads – except for the half-finished dome of your Uncle Jacob's masterpiece.'

Dev smiled wanly at her. His father's elder brother, Uncle Jacob, the eighth Viscount Strathmore, had driven the family to the verge of bankruptcy sixty years ago with his architectural obsession, building Oakley Park, the magnificent white mansion in Kent. Uncle Jacob had been forced to rectify the situation by marrying the heiress of an industrial magnate – Aunt Augusta. The best Society had viewed the match with pity – so noble a name forced to resort to the great merchant classes for its rescue – but the ton had soon learned that the ironmonger's daughter was not to be trifled with. No, indeed, Dev thought fondly. Even now, at the grand age of eighty-two, old Lady Ironsides could still make the ton tremble in fear and awe of her wrath. Perhaps it was the origins of her fortune – iron ore – that were to blame for her formidable streak, but even he found the nickname amusing. As for Oakley Park, though it now belonged to Dev, he never went there. With his loved ones buried in the little Greek temple-style mausoleum overlooking the ornamental pond, visiting the estate was simply too painful.

Meanwhile, Aunt Augusta was still on about her idolized papa. 'Made himself from nothing, he did, to die a very wealthy man.'

'And left it all to you, lucky lass.'

'And I am to leave it to you, in turn, knowing you are going to squander everything that great man worked for.'

'Nonsense. I shall marry an heiress and squander *her* dowry. Your father's fortune I shall not touch.'

'Oh? And when will you do this thing?'

'Eventually,' he mumbled with a noncommittal shrug.

'You are a pretty liar, aren't you?' Aunt Augusta regarded him shrewdly. 'Why don't you stay for a while? You need rest, darling. I can see it in your eyes.'

'That is what I love about you, old girl. You go straight at a thing, no beating about the bush for you,' he muttered, and took another drink.

'Devlin, I am losing patience. Practice your flatteries and evasions on your London coquettes. They shall never work on your old dragon aunt.'

'Who has been calling you a dragon? I shall issue a challenge at once to anyone who dares suggest such a thing.' He played with the candle in front of him, catching a bead of wax on the flat of his butter knife.

'Oh, I fear this is all my fault,' she said in a tone of quiet distress.

He glanced over, frowning. 'What is?'

'You. I know why you're like this. It is all my doing.' She laid her hand atop his, her lined face softening. 'Darling, you cannot escape your pain over the past in mindless pleasure. I should have done better with you. My methods were all wrong. I had no children of my own. I hadn't the foggiest idea what to do or say to you after the accident.'

His eyes flared with malice at that word – *accident* – but he said nothing. That was, after all, what the official report had stated.

'I was quite terrified, in truth. I tried to think of what Papa would have told you in my place, but of course he was very strict and practical and hardheaded. It seemed logical enough that school was the best place for you – that your life ought to go on in as close to a state of normalcy as possible. Do you remember what I told you?'

He lowered his gaze. 'I truly don't see the point in revisiting all this—'

'"Chin up, lad. Keep a stiff upper lip," I said. "Life must go on. Get good marks in school. That would have made them proud." Good marks in school! As if that mattered when your whole world had fallen apart. What a fool I was,' she whispered mournfully. 'How could any lad concentrate on Greek or calculus when his life had been shattered? I understand now that my thoughtless advice only made you hate yourself more—'

'Stop!' he cried abruptly, an anguished note in his voice which he quickly routed. His heart pounded. 'Please, ma'am. All that is ancient history.'

'Is it? If I had been capable then of simply holding you and letting you mend in your own time, I feel sure you would have settled down long ago, taken a wife—'

'God, please, not that again.'

'And seen to the duties of your rank,' she insisted. 'Unfortunately, loving-kindness was never my forte. It was not how I was raised, you understand.'

'Aunt Augusta, whatever you are blaming yourself for, do stop,' he said impatiently, withdrawing slightly in his chair. 'Really, you gave me the best advice you could at the time, and I am grateful—'

'No, Devlin, it has to be said. I was as hard-nosed as my father, incapable of giving what you really needed. Just simple . . . love.'

He nearly threw down his napkin and bolted from the room at the mention of the hated term, but since it was Aunt Augusta, he forced himself to remain stiffly seated. 'First of all, there is nothing simple about *love*.' He fairly snarled the word. 'It's the most bloody complicated, painful thing there is, and I want none of it. Second, you have always loved me, and I have bloody well always known it. Now, stop talking nonsense, and for God's sake, send Miss Carlisle back to London, if she is to blame for this change in you. I want my scaly old fire-breather back. The chit is softening you up to a degree that is downright alarming.'

'I'm old, boy,' she said with a weary smile. 'It takes too much strength to breathe fire. The best I can manage these days is a lukewarm snort.' She paused, then shook her head, suddenly turning peevish. 'I am tired, Devlin. Go and fetch Lizzie for me. I wish to retire.'

'Yes, ma'am.' Now that she mentioned it, his aunt did look terribly drained. He got up, grateful, in any case, for the reprieve.

'By the way,' she added as he started to walk away, 'Miss Carlisle didn't happen to write to you, did she?'

He froze, then turned slowly, unsure how to answer. He did not wish to lie to his aunt, but he certainly did not want to get the girl into trouble. 'No, ma'am,' he said cautiously. 'Why ever would she write to me?'

'Hmm, never mind,' the old woman answered with a crafty glint in her eyes. 'I noticed you mentioned your parents to her at dinner. You realize you have not spoken of them in years?'

Dev did not answer.

She gazed at him for a long moment, then quickly waved him off. 'Run along, then. Off you go.'

Dev frowned with uncertainty, hoping she had not seen through his well-intentioned lie, but as he turned to go, something made him hesitate. 'I say, is the girl really interested in the good doctor?'

Aunt Augusta chuckled. 'Not in the slightest.'

'Ah.' Dev nodded, absorbing this, then sketched a bow to his aunt and went to do her bidding. When he came across Mrs. Rowland near the kitchens and inquired after his aunt's companion, the housekeeper pointed him in the direction of the laundry. 'Shall I fetch her for you, Master Dev?'

'It's all right, Mrs. Rowland. I don't mind. By the way, the floating island was—' He kissed his fingertips and said with gusto. '*—magnifique!*'

She beamed at him and then bustled on cheerfully about her business. In a more lighthearted mood at the prospect of encountering Miss Carlisle again, Dev continued to the laundry room, which connected through the large, busy kitchens. Approaching the dim space, he heard low-toned voices from within; when he stepped up to the threshold of the dim, flagstone-floored workroom, he observed the fair creature deeply engrossed in conversation with Ben over the large laundry sink.

The nerve of this girl, he thought in idle amusement. Having procured his forgiveness for her ruse, she did not quit while she was ahead. Oh, no. Now it seemed the intrepid E. Carlisle was busy cultivating his valet for information about Dev's past. The fact that she was here, though, asking questions about him, frankly interested, was flattering enough in itself to make his pulse quicken.

Dev folded his arms across his chest with a sardonic smile and leaned in the shadowed doorway, eavesdropping, unnoticed. Clad once more in the drab muslin dress – though the silly house cap was mercifully absent – the girl had rested her elbows on the edge of the tub. With her lovely face propped in her hands, she listened in rapt attention as Ben regaled her with tales of their adventures while treating the injured satin of her gown. Dev was taken aback, however, when Ben mentioned his years of bondage in America, for it was not a tale the man often shared. The expert valet preferred to be known for the excellence of his cravats, not for the color of his skin. Dev supposed Ben sensed, as he did, the air of trustworthiness the girl radiated and thus found it possible to open up to her.

'Mama was the midwife on the plantation,' Ben was saying, 'and since that's a position of respect, I was set from an early age to attend the master's son as valet. I was treated fairly well, but then, I never was one to make trouble. The mistress even trusted me enough to let me learn how to read and write. Most black folks are kept in ignorance, you see. Most of the time, you have to hide what you know.'

She shook her head sympathetically. 'For what it's worth, girls are advised to do the same.'

'I know that's true,' he agreed, his long-buried Southern accent emerging slightly as he spoke about the past. 'Mama was the one who taught me the use of the medicinal herbs for healin' and treatin' wounds – and it's a good thing she did, too, the way His Lordship's always gettin' into scrapes.'

Dev raised an eyebrow as they shared a fond chuckle on this point, but then Ben's tone turned ominous.

'That summer, lightnin' set the crops on fire, and the plantation burned. Master was ruined, said he had to sell us all. Those were bad days, Miss Lizzie. Bad days.' He shook his head. Even now, years later, the pain and anger of his ordeal were evident in his kind, scholarly face. 'Families were broken up, all of us to be uprooted, and the final humiliation – we were delivered to the slave mart in Charleston to be put on the auction block in the mornin'.'

'How horrible,' she said softly.

'That night, we shared a cell with some poor, wild souls who had just been brought over from Africa. You see, there was a deadline in 1806. After that, no more slaves could be brought into the country. Well, you can bet that terrible business was boomin' right up to the end. Those poor tribesmen – men, women, children, too – they were terrified, just off the ship. Some of them were hurt, sick. Mama and I helped the ones we could, but we couldn't understand a word they said, nor they us.'

'They were to be sold in the morning, too?'

He nodded. 'But it didn't work out like that. No, ma'am.' Ben sent her a charming smile. 'What we didn't know was that Lord Strathmore was sailin' into the Charleston harbor aboard the *Katie Rose*. You see, he'd been following that slaver all the way up from the West Indies. Just a young captain, barely twenty-two, but ain't nothin' scares him, especially when he's worked up in a temper over somethin'. Fact is, he had seen a terrible thing while crossin' the Caribbean.'

'What was it?' she murmured, visibly engrossed in the tale.

Ben hesitated, uncertain, Dev guessed, about how much to say to a young lady, and then lowered his voice. 'When that slaver passed off the bow of the *Katie Rose*, he saw them throw a man overboard – still alive. Shackled in chains. Probably caught a fever and the crew didn't want it to spread. Master Dev and his men tried to reach the poor fellow to save him, but they were too late. It affected him somethin' fierce.' Ben paused, musing. 'That's when he made up his mind to follow that slave ship and find a way to rescue those poor wild Africans.'

'Ohh,' she murmured in a dreamy tone, her eyes wide.

'That night,' Ben continued, 'in the wee hours, he took his twelve-man crew and stormed the slave mart in Charleston, breakin' the lot of us out of there – forty in all! We didn't know what was happenin' at first. We thought they were pirates.'

'With the earring, I can understand your error,' she agreed earnestly.

Dev smirked.

'He and his sailors rushed us into the jolly boats, then rowed us out to the ship, but, lo and behold, he sailed us way on up north to New York, where no bounty hunters could ever find us. Instead of stealin' us and sellin' us off for his own profit, as Mama and I both expected, he took us by canal to Philadelphia, where we were taken in by the free black community there. You see, the slave laws in Pennsylvania are a good deal less cruel than the rest, on account of the Quakers in the state congress. Lord Strathmore gave us money to start a new life. He made us free.'

'What a beautiful gesture,' she whispered. 'It's more than that – heroic.'

'Yes, ma'am, it was.' Ben nodded solemnly, but Lizzie's admiring words had sent a frisson of pleasure through Dev's veins – and embarrassed him a little, truth be told. He was sure any feeling man would have done the same. Besides, after his family had been broken up by the cruelty of fate, helping Ben keep his mother, brothers, and sisters together had been reward enough in itself.

'He saved our lives,' Ben continued. 'Not just mine, but my whole family, as well. That's why Mama said, "Bennett, my boy, that plantation was always too small a place for you. You done gave yourself the name Freeman, so go on, be free. Go with that crazy Englishman and see the world." So, I went.'

She smiled at him.

'Clear on through the wide state of Pennsylvania, to the high forests where it's still wild,' Ben went on, his tone brightening. 'Into the mountains of the Iroquois tribes, who rule the northern lakes, and south to the realm of the Cherokees. Why, once, goin' over the Appalachians, Master Dev even fought a mountain lion! It was stalkin' us for days before it sprang. You should have seen that battle—'

'But the savages, Mr. Freeman?' she asked in amazement. 'Did you actually get to see these primitive peoples?'

'See any?' Ben exclaimed. 'Why, we wintered with the Cherokees when we came to the Cumberland Pass and found it snowed over. We would have frozen to death, but they saved our lives, taught us their customs. They're kind folk, hardly savages at all once you get to know 'em – unless, of course, you join them on a raiding party – but I should think young ladies don't want to hear about that.'

'Oh, Mr. Freeman, did you go on an Indian raid?' she whispered, wide eyed.

'Not me, ma'am, certainly! But one time His Lordship went—'

'Ahem,' Dev interrupted before his servant related anything too incriminating.

'Well, uh, ahem, good evenin', sir,' Ben coughed, turning sheepish. 'I was just, er, helpin' Miss Lizzie get the wine marks out of this fine gown. That cat is quite a devil, I hear.'

'Indeed,' he said dryly. 'Miss Carlisle?'

'Yes, my lord?' She tucked her chin in demure mortification, knowing she was caught at her prying, but when she peeked bashfully at him from beneath her lashes, Dev noticed at once that she looked at him differently. A newfound respect glimmered in the morning-gray depths of her eyes.

He was pleased.

He clasped his hands politely behind his back. 'My aunt requests your presence, Miss Carlisle. She wishes to retire.'

'Oh – yes, of course.' She lowered her gaze, then sent Ben a nervous glance. 'Thank you very much for your help, Mr. Freeman. If you have everything you need, then?'

'Yes, ma'am,' Ben said quickly, giving her a polite bow.

'Very well. Good evening, Mr. Freeman.' As she hurried past him on her way out, Dev cocked his eyebrow dubiously at his servant.

Ben shrugged. 'Well, it's all true, ain't it? You're welcome,' he called after him with a mirthful grin as Dev pivoted and followed his quarry.

Chapter Five

Her skirts swishing in her haste to flee him, Lizzie whisked through the adjoining kitchens, red-faced at having been caught snooping into Devil Strathmore's past with an all-too-avid interest. Coming out the other side, she sped down the corridor while his footfalls echoed a few paces behind hers.

'Oh, Miss Carlisle . . .'

She ignored his beguiling call with its hint of amusement in the vain hope that if she pretended not to hear him, maybe he would go away. Ugh, she felt like such a cake! If only she had heard him come into the laundry room! But the man moved with the stealth of a hunter – a fact he proved yet again by suddenly capturing her wrist, stopping her forward momentum.

'Elizabeth, wait.'

She turned to him reluctantly, fighting the feverish thrill that traveled all the way up her arm from his light grasp.

'Don't be embarrassed, *chérie*,' he murmured so gently that she quivered.

Her cheeks turned redder at his silken endearment and at the way his crystalline blue-green eyes glowed with pleasure at his discovery of her interest.

She looked away, struggling to lay hold of any remaining shred of her dignity. 'Er, Lord Strathmore—'

'Devlin,' he corrected in a tone like a caress. He made no move to release her hand.

She cleared her throat a bit. 'Please do not be angry at Mr. Freeman for telling me about your travels, my lord. It was my fault. I was curious. Y-you've had an exciting life. Unlike mine.'

'Well, you needn't go to Ben if there's aught you want to know,' he offered in an intimate tone. 'I'd be happy to answer all of your questions . . . personally. Why don't you meet me in the library after you attend my aunt, and I'll tell you all about it?'

She looked up quickly, wide-eyed.

He smiled. 'We'll open a bottle of champagne. Say, ten o'clock?'

Her heart quaked. 'I don't know . . .'

'Yes, you do,' he whispered.

She stared at him, tongue-tied and taken off guard. Lord, he was bold! Lady Strathmore had been right – there was probably nothing he would not dare. The fact was a trifle worrisome now that his single-minded gaze was fixed on her, full of amorous intent. Utterly confounded, she just yanked her hand from his velvety hold and sped away again on legs that shook beneath her. Good gracious, she was out of her depth!

He was right behind her, striding fast. 'I didn't catch your answer, sweet.'

'No! No, no, no.'

'Why not?' he asked in amusement, no doubt thinking her a typical nervous virgin. 'My aunt told me of your interest in languages. I could teach you some words in Arabic or Algonquian – a few useful curses, at least.'

'No, thank you.'

'Spoilsport.'

She stopped and turned to him, her chin coming up a notch. Alec used to call her that on occasion. 'Am not.'

'Good. Then I'll see you there.' A wicked smile crept over his lips – it seemed to suggest if she went to the library to meet him, talking was the last thing they'd be doing.

In any language.

'No, thank you,' she forced out a tad breathlessly. Heart pounding, she spun around and whisked off to carry out her nightly duties.

'I'll be waiting in the library if you should change your mind,' he called after her, but she dared not look back.

Going through the entrance hall, Lizzie found Lady Strathmore waiting for her at the bottom of the staircase in her Bath chair. She masked her confusion from that rogue's advances and assisted the frail old woman to her feet, letting her lean on her. Together they began the slow and painstaking nightly journey of climbing the stairs. They had gone up only three of the steps, however, when Devlin ambled into the entrance below.

'May I be of assistance?'

Lizzie glanced back as he sprang up the stairs. In another moment, he swept the dowager off her feet with a jolly grin.

'At your service, my lovely.'

His aunt let out a peal of girlish laughter.

'Oh, Devlin, you rogue, put me down this instant!'

'Absolutely not.'

'Careful!' Lizzie warned him, fearful for the old woman's frail bones, but she saw that she needn't have worried.

He was all protective tenderness, conveying the dowager to the upper hallway, where he very gently set her down on her feet. While Lizzie steadied her, he dashed back down and carried up her Bath chair.

'Anything else?' he asked, directing the question to Lizzie.

She shook her head.

'Good night, darling,' his aunt murmured as he bent to kiss her cheek. 'However long you stay, I'm glad you came.'

'Me, too,' he said softly, and sent Lizzie a meaningful stare over her shoulder.

Augusta did not miss the look that passed between them. Oh, yes, there was definitely something *there*.

Heavens, this night had been the best entertainment she'd had in a year, what with her nephew's jealousy of Dr. Bell, and Lizzie's sly stunt of pouring wine on herself to escape the table when Dev's conversation had wandered into dangerous territory. What a lark!

Her heart was light as her young companion helped her into her bedchamber down the hallway and patiently assisted her in changing into her nightclothes. All the while, Augusta mused on how to proceed. Dev and Lizzie were both such cagey creatures when it came to affairs of the heart, she knew that she would have to use caution.

Margaret brought in the hot-water bottles for her bed, then bobbed a curtsy and hurried out, mumbling good night. Before long, Lizzie had helped her into her large, canopied bed.

'There you are, ma'am.' The girl snugged the coverlet around Augusta. 'Shall I read you a few verses from your Bible before you nod off?'

'Sit with me for a moment, dear.' Augusta patted the edge of the bed. 'There is something I wish to say to you.'

Lizzie sent her a look of guilty alarm, but ever obedient, sat down on the edge of her bed and waited.

Augusta fought the urge to smile and instead gave the girl her most dragonly glower. 'Miss Carlisle, am I amiss in my suspicions that my nephew's presence here tonight is no coincidence?'

She lowered her chin and shook her head. 'No, my lady. It is not.' The girl sent her a contrite look from under her lashes. 'I wrote to him.'

'And what exactly did you say?'

'I did not lie. I only implied that . . . if he did not come immediately, he might regret it,' she confessed in dismay.

'You mean you led him to believe I was about to turn up my toes, eh?'

'Oh, I know it was dishonest and very improper, but I've been so worried about you, ma'am! It's not fair, the way he neglects you. If you were my aunt, I would not leave you to sit here alone for months at a time—'

'I am not alone, child,' she interrupted gently. 'I have you.'

The girl gave a doe-eyed blink of uncertainty.

'You do count, you know.'

Lizzie searched her face, at a loss.

Augusta smiled and took her companion's youthful hand between her own in a light, grandmotherly hold. 'I have a new tale for you tonight, child. Of all the stories I've told you of my nephew's exploits, there is one chapter about Devlin's life that I have never shared with you. But something tells me that it's time you knew.'

Lizzie tilted her head attentively.

'When my dear, departed Jacob died, his brother, Stephen, Devlin's father, inherited the title. What a lovely man. As the younger son, Stephen would have been quite content to live out his days as plain Mr. Kimball, reading his books, happily peering through his microscope, and walking in the country with his dogs. But the viscountcy fell to him after my husband's death, and through him, passed to Devlin all too soon. You see, Stephen and his wife, Katherine, perished in a terrible hotel fire when Dev was seventeen.'

'Oh, how horribly awful,' she breathed, lifting her fingers to her mouth in shock.

Augusta nodded. 'We also lost his little sister in that fire. Sarah. She was only four years old. Such a beautiful, happy child. Long black ringlets, big blue eyes. They were one of those rarest of finds: a genuinely happy family. His parents wed for love, you see. . . .' Her voice trailed off wistfully as she remembered her own marriage, by contrast, to advance her father's ambitions and to replenish Jacob's fortunes.

'Devlin was at Oxford when it happened, and I will tell you in confidence that he has never fully recovered. In addition to myself, two of his uncles were also appointed as his legal guardians and trustees, but as the only female, it fell to me to provide what motherly influence I could. He became my ward until his twenty-first birthday. The truth is, I knew nothing of raising a young lad, especially not one faced with a tragedy.' She let out a heavy sigh. 'Devlin flunked out of Oxford within a year, ran wild in London for another, and finally, after a stern talking-to, set out to travel the world. Letting him go was the hardest thing I've ever done, but a change of scenery seemed the only way to jar him off his self-destructive path. It seemed to work. He was gone for nearly three years to the West Indies and America, came back only long enough to visit with me, then sailed off again, that time to India.

'I scarcely know where all he went on that second trip,' she continued, 'but he said he journeyed north into the Asian deserts and wound up at Moscow in time to see Napoléon's retreat.' Augusta's gaze turned far-away. 'He has been to the wild and empty places of the world . . . and has brought them back in his eyes. You see, my dear, he has never let anyone close to him again since his family was destroyed. That's why he doesn't come here very often – not because he doesn't care, but because he does, and he is so frightened of the fact that I must leave this earth sometimes.'

'But, my lady, what you're telling me – that letter I sent,

threatening him with a – a change in your condition – oh, what have I done?' the girl whispered with a stricken stare. 'Surely there was nothing I could have done to hurt him worse. I did not know!'

'Now you do.' Augusta smiled fondly at her distress and patted her hand. 'Take heart, my dear. You are made of stern stuff, and for that, I like you well. But whatever heartache you came here hiding from, do not take it out on Dev. As you now know, he is not as invulnerable as he seems. In fact, I would ask a favor of you.'

'Of course, ma'am, what is it?' she murmured. Not yet recovered from her attack of conscience, Lizzie looked startled at the request, for Augusta Strathmore was not one to ask a favor of anybody.

The dowager stared shrewdly into the girl's open, honest face. 'Will you look in on him from time to time when I am gone? Make sure he's all right?'

'My lady, you mustn't talk like that—'

'Will you, yay or nay?'

She cast about helplessly. 'But – how can I? It isn't proper. And with his reputation—? Ma'am, I am sorry – I truly am – but I'm sure I cannot promise any such thing.'

'Does his story not move you?'

'Of course it does—'

'He has no one else.'

'He has you.'

'I will not last long. Surely, Miss Carlisle, you would not deny an old woman her dying wish?'

'Gracious, you are not dying! I forbid it.' She jumped up from Augusta's bedside, looking shaken. 'Of course it pains me to refuse you, my lady. You know how grateful I am for the position you have given me. I'm happier here than I ever expected to feel again, but I will have no more of this grim talk.

By my troth, no one around here is dying for a very long time, and that is final!'

Augusta studied the girl intently, but did not press her. 'You are a very stubborn creature, aren't you?'

'Yes, but I am not one to make promises I cannot keep. Now, you need your rest, ma'am. I will see you in the morning.' She crossed the bedchamber with an anxious little hurry in her step, but stopped at the door and turned around in guilty hesitation, her drab skirts swirling around her. 'It's not that I don't *want* to help. It's just that . . . he would never listen to someone like me, you do understand? If I were pretty or highborn or rich, he might, but I'm me and he's him, and there's an end to it.'

The dowager smiled. *Not quite an end, my dear*. The scoundrel would listen – given the proper motive. Aye, throw them together and let Nature do the rest.

'Take no thought of it, Miss Carlisle. I understand perfectly.' *You'll change your mind*, she thought shrewdly. *I know you, my girl. Your conscience will give you no choice.*

'Thank you, ma'am. I *am* sorry,' she added, looking rather cast down.

'Good night, Miss Carlisle.'

'Ma'am.' The girl curtsied and withdrew respectfully from the room.

In the darkened hallway, Lizzie closed her eyes and leaned against the wall for a moment, feeling slightly ill with her transgression and despising herself for violating her own highest value. As a Christian woman and a helper, a nurturer in the world, it was unthinkable that she could have done something so cruel, threatening an inwardly wounded man with his worst fear. No wonder he had come so quickly. No wonder he stayed away.

Yet as terrible as she felt for hurting him, she was glad she had not let her guilt force her to yield to Lady Strathmore's request. She was a person who took her promises very seriously, and at the moment, she knew that Devil Strathmore was more than she could handle. It would be foolish to agree to take care of him – assuming she could! – when she had only lately broken her habit of fussing over Alec like a mother hen – for all the good it had done her. No, the next time she focused her efforts on a man, it would be someone both willing and able to give to her in return.

There was a time when she would have meekly obeyed the order, but she was stronger now. If nothing else, her break with Alec had taught her to stand up for herself in this life, or else let her heart be continually trampled.

In any case, she had no doubt that if Devil Strathmore knew of the request his aunt had just made of her, his male pride would have been incensed. No man ever thought he needed anyone to take care of him – but of course, they all did. Fortunately, he had the trusty Bennett Freeman to look after his basic needs.

Be that as it may, she still owed him an apology. She opened her eyes slowly and took a deep breath, knowing he was waiting for her in the library, with God-knew-what sort of intentions. It did not matter, she decided. She could hold her own, and he would soon discover the seriousness of her visit.

Pressing heavily away from the wall, she lifted a candle from the wall sconce to light her way, then walked down the hallway, shoulders squared. The night was so still as she glided through the house, the settling winter darkness so deep. As she drifted down the stairs, reflecting back on their fight in the parlor, she marveled at his chivalrous restraint in not throwing it all in her face, as he could easily have done. She had dealt him probably the worst blow possible, but he had remained silent, retreating rather than hurting her the way she had hurt him. She shook her head at herself as she rounded the newel post and walked bravely toward the library. Obviously there was a great deal more to this man than met the eye. Much more substance to be weighed than his mere bills. The candle's flame danced as she let out a sigh of regret. Her wrath at his expenditures seemed so petty to her now. Just because he gambled on occasion did not make him Alec.

Ahead, the library door stood open. She could see the ruddy glow of the dancing hearth fire. Trembling slightly, she forced herself forward. Her heartbeat quickened. Silent in her soft kid slippers, she padded over to the threshold and cautiously peered inside.

He was there, reclining on the brown leather couch, though he was too long for it. He lay with one knee bent, the other foot sprawled off the side. One arm pillowed his head; the other rested across his flat belly. Pasha snuggled, curled and purring, by his shoulder. As Lizzie took a few cautious paces into the room, the viscount did not stir. That was when she realized he had fallen asleep waiting for her.

At once, her tensed shoulders dropped in mingled disappointment and relief, but in spite of herself, a tender smile spread across her face. The poor thing, she mused, the sight of him tugging at her heartstrings. After his eighteen-hour ride from London through last night's blizzard, no wonder he was exhausted. For a moment, her gaze lingered over his sleeping male beauty, licked by shadows from the cheerful blaze in the fireplace. *Magnificent man.* His hard mouth had softened; his lips looked plump and lusciously inviting. His inky lashes fanned across his high-boned cheeks. His lovely chest rose and fell peacefully, his breathing deep and slow.

Her gaze homed in on his throat, a rare and most intriguing sight in a world of starched cravats. The noble curve of his neck was golden-bronzed. He had also removed his tailcoat, affording her a fine view of the way the paper-thin cambric of his elegant white shirt draped his broad shoulders and bulged at the level of his biceps. His waistcoat hung unbuttoned.

Gliding silently across the library, she collected the quilt that sat folded in the window nook and covered him with it. As she spread the blanket lightly over him, Pasha's whiskers at his cheek tickled him to stir drowsily. Lizzie straightened up to leave, but her heart skipped a beat as his long-lashed eyes swept open.

'Hey,' he murmured, starting to sit up. He swatted the cat away with a shove of his hand, but Lizzie bent down and pressed his shoulder gently.

'Go back to sleep,' she whispered. 'You need it.'

'Stay.' He sent her a roguish but sleepy smile, clutching lightly at her skirts with one hand.

Lizzie paused and gazed down at him for a long moment. He tilted his head and stared back at her with a slightly astonished look, perhaps surprised that she had actually come down to meet him. Before he got the wrong idea, she lowered herself to her knees beside the couch and held him in a sober gaze as she searched for words.

'Thanks for the blanket. That was very sweet of you.' When she said nothing, he studied her distraught face and then frowned. 'What's wrong, sweeting?' he murmured, cupping her cheek.

'Oh, Devlin,' she whispered. She wrapped her hands around his forearm and pressed her cheek harder against his palm, squeezing her eyes shut while she cringed with remorse at his tenderness. 'I'm so sorry.'

He was silent. When she flicked her eyes open again, there were tears in them. He had sat up on the couch, the blanket still loosely draped over his lower half, but his expression was unreadable, his serious gaze fixed on her with swordlike intensity.

She stared at him, clinging to his hand still cradling her cheek. 'I didn't mean to hurt you so badly – I swear it. Lady

Strathmore just now told me about your family. If I had known, I would never have written that letter. I would never have done it. Not like that.'

'Hush.' He caught her tear on the pad of his thumb. 'It's all right.'

'No, it's not,' she cried. 'You didn't deserve that, nor had I any right to judge you. I acted like a – a self-righteous prig! It's just that I never thought – I didn't know.'

'I know you didn't.' He shook his head, looking mystified by such remorse. 'It's all right, sweeting. You didn't do anything wrong.'

'I don't want you to hate me,' she choked out.

'Hate you?' He gave her a chiding half-smile, trying to coax a smile from her in answer. 'I thought you were an expert on "my kind," but I'm afraid you know nothing about men if you think I could ever hate you. Look at this beautiful face.' He caressed her cheek with one knuckle, smiling wistfully at her. 'No, my dear E. Carlisle, I could never be angry at you.'

Fresh tears filled her eyes at his tender words. Without warning, she launched at him, hugging him hard around his neck. A small sob escaped her.

'There, there.' He slid his arms around her with a paternal chuckle, but she shut her eyes tightly, her heart clenching at his manly strength and generosity of spirit.

After all he had been through, she could barely believe how kind and gentle he was. Most people in his place would surely have turned bitter and cold long ago.

'Hush, sweet, no more tears,' he crooned softly in her ear as he held her in a comforting embrace, his large, warm hand stroking her hair. 'All's forgotten. We made a truce. Remember?'

She sniffled. 'I'm sorry.'

'You have nothing to be sorry for. It wasn't your fault. Besides, you didn't know. I'm the one who should apologize.

It's my neglect that drove you to this action. The truth is, I'm grateful.'

'Grateful?' she whispered, bringing her tears in check, though she did not release him from her embrace.

'Of course. You risked yourself, your job, to get my aunt what you thought she needed. Do you know how rare it is to find someone who really cares that much? Never mind your wages – I've been around long enough to know that it's not possible to pay someone to give of themselves from the heart the way that you do. You went above and beyond the call of duty simply because you love my aunt, and for that, I shall be always in your debt.'

She moved back slowly a small space and peered into his eyes. He dropped his gaze after a second, looking a trifle chagrined.

'It's not that I don't want to come and see her. It's just – so difficult. You lost your parents, too – you said so at dinner. You know how it is. At least I have memories of mine. Too many memories,' he added, then shook his head in brooding frustration. 'I know that's no excuse. The fact that my family was taken from me *ought* to make me come here even more. I should be here while I still have time with her, as you said, and I know that, but the more I spend time with her – the more I let myself care – the more it's going to hurt when—' His voice broke off, as if he could not even bring himself to say the words.

'Your aunt knows you love her, Devlin,' she told him softly, running a comforting caress up and down his muscled arm. 'It's not a question of that. But if you don't spend time with her while you still can, how will you ever be able to forgive yourself once she's gone?'

He glanced darkly into her eyes.

'I know it hurts to see her getting weaker and to know the day draws nearer when you must say good-bye, but avoiding the situation will not stop that day from coming.'

'You're right, of course. I know that.' He shook his head. 'It's just – hard.'

'Then I will help you,' she whispered, taking his hand. 'Stay and make her happy, and somehow we'll get through it together.'

He stared down at their joined hands. 'I get the feeling you're good at helping people.'

She smiled wanly and shrugged; her deceitful letter had obviously not helped much. 'Well, it's all out in the open now if you wish to speak to her about it. Somehow she suspected that I had written to you. She questioned me, and I confessed.'

'You confessed?' he echoed, glancing at her in surprise.

'Of course. I would not lie to her.'

'Wonderful,' he muttered, shoving his other hand through his hair with a rueful smile. 'She asked me the same thing, but I told her I had no idea what she was talking about.'

'*You* lied?' she asked, lifting her eyebrows.

'I didn't want you to lose your job, sweeting.'

'Oh,' she murmured; then they both laughed at their faux pas as they gazed at each other. Lizzie blushed at the intimate warmth in his smile. She lowered her lashes, suddenly feeling shy. 'Who ever would have thought you and I could have something in common?'

'Yes,' he murmured. 'We're both alone.'

She lifted her glance slowly and found him watching her.

Words failed her. The smoldering glow she had glimpsed in his eyes at dinner was back; indeed, there was something almost possessive in his stare as he studied her, desire gentling the hard, angular precision of his face. With a measured balance of boldness and caution, he lifted his hand once more to touch her, running his knuckle lightly along the line of her jaw.

She trembled at the contact, a tingling spark of sheer thrill rushing down her spine and searing along every nerve ending from her fingertips down to her toes. Staring into her eyes, Devlin slid his hand beneath her hair, clasping her nape, drawing her to him. She went willingly, leaning toward him, as eager as he. So close that she could feel the warmth of his breath, Devlin tilted his head; Lizzie's eyes drifted closed at the first gliding caress of his lips on hers – smooth, satin bliss. He brushed his hungry kiss back and forth across her mouth, entrancing her. She could feel her lips swelling, growing acutely sensitized beneath the tender stroking of his mouth, his hand cradling her head all the while.

Her senses a-swirl with dizzying pleasure, it was all she could do to brace herself with a hand on his thigh, the other at his chest, clinging to the open front of his unbuttoned waistcoat. Then Devlin let his lips wander slowly away from her mouth, dusting her face with light, heated kisses, while his other hand clasped her waist. Lizzie smiled in sensual delight at his playful seduction, trailing little kisses over her cheeks, her brow. Then he bent lower, pressing a kiss full of hotter intent to her throat.

She tilted her head back with a catch in her breath, her lips parting. She draped her arm over his broad shoulder, drawing him closer, all her awareness fixed on his open-mouthed kiss on the curve of her neck. The man would drive her mad.

When he came back and claimed her mouth with electrifying demand, Lizzie felt her heart would surely burst, it was pounding so hard.

Devlin cupped her face, his thumb caressing the corner of her lips. 'Open your mouth for me, angel. Let me taste you,' he begged in a panting whisper.

Hesitantly, she yielded, afire with enthralled fascination as his tongue glided into her mouth, an exploratory stroking. He moaned low and gathered her closer, his deepening kiss consuming her. She had heard about French-style kisses like this – hot, wet, deep, erotic. But when she responded boldly in kind, licking

Devlin's tongue slowly as his mouth slanted over hers, nothing could have prepared her for his explosive lust. He lifted her astride his lap, both his hands gripping her backside almost roughly through her gown. He pressed her against his body, kissing her more hungrily still. In his fierce eagerness, his teeth bruised her lip, but Lizzie didn't even care. With her arms wrapped tightly around his neck, the feel of his hard, lean hips between her thighs was too much. Though layers of clothing stood between them, the lock-and-key fit of their bodies ignited such a surge of wild need in her blood that she tore her mouth away from his by some superhuman effort.

'God, no more,' she gasped.

'Wait,' he pleaded.

'No, Devlin. We have to stop.'

He flinched and closed his eyes as if she had struck him, but he let her go without argument, steadying her by her elbow as she climbed off his lap.

'Have I upset you?' he whispered when she stood before him on shaky limbs.

'No.' Would that she could claim to be upset, insulted, scandalized, instead of craving more of him – much more. 'It's late. My duties start early.'

He sent her a cynical half-smile, his eyes still glittering and heavy-lidded with passion. 'Good girl.'

'You don't make it easy.'

He reached for her hand and held it gently. 'You're all right?'

'Oh, yes,' she assured him with a breathless laugh, for she was feeling a good deal better than merely 'all right.'

'Good,' he whispered, caressing her hand with his thumb.

She gave his fingers a fond squeeze. 'Good night, Devlin.'

'Good night, Lizzie.'

'See you in the morning?' she asked meaningfully.

He seemed to think it over for a second. 'I'll be here.'

She nodded in approval and let her hand slide free of his light hold, walking resolutely across the library. She hesitated at the doorway, however, and glanced back, stealing one last look at him. Beautiful in the firelight as a visiting god, he was still sitting lazily on the couch, flushed and tousled and so tempting. His inviting gaze snared hers with magnetic power. Staring at the magnificent man, hers for the taking – at least for tonight – she let out a yearning sigh of virtuous self-denial; it roused a throaty chuckle from him.

'I am leaving now,' she announced firmly.

'Come back,' he called in soft beguilement.

'Devil,' she whispered, and shook her head at him with an arch smile. Before his silken charm could weaken her any further, she forced herself out of the room and hurried up to her bedchamber, still grinning from ear to ear.

Over the next few days, Lady Strathmore did what she could to nurse the spark between her nephew and companion into a scintillating little flame. She gave them ample opportunity to be together, requiring both of them to attend her the next day on a visit into Bath. They sampled the waters at the Pump Room, where she showed her handsome nephew off to all her aged friends and busied herself catching up on the local gossip, leaving Dev and Lizzie to join the other onlookers at the great window, watching the bathers sink into the healing pools. Afterwards, they went to Sally Lunn's and bought a few dozen of the famous Bath cakes sold there to bring back for the servants: Dev said he had to repay Mrs. Rowland for the floating island.

On the first evening, they played chess, bantering their way through the game, much to Augusta's amusement. Each seemed surprised by how well matched they were; no one ever beat Lizzie at chess unless she was letting one win, but Devlin had learned the game from his keenwitted father as a boy. The following afternoon it snowed again. Augusta looked out the parlor window in response to a tapping on the pane and laughed aloud to see the fat Napoléon snowman the two of them had built outside her window, complete with bicorne hat. Lizzie waved at her, pink cheeked in the cold, and then went on scattering seeds across the snow for the hungry birds.

That evening, over warm, mulled wine, her nephew had both women in such fits of laughter over a game of charades that tears rolled down their cheeks. No one in Society ever got to see this side of him. He felt at home here, she knew, and like a great lion at play, rolling in the tall grass, he left the dark jungles behind for now. Lizzie and she teased him for his ineptitude at the game, both secretly loving him for rising to the occasion when most males would rather not have risked their dignity to make an old lady laugh.

'What is *that* supposed to be?' Lizzie exclaimed, barely catching her breath from gales of laughter as he continued making some throwing gesture, his growing frustration apparent. 'Throw?'

He tugged his ear with a look of exasperation.

'All right, sounds like *throw*. Go? Know? Show?'

He glared at her expectantly, hands on hips, but they eventually guessed his selection, *Le Nozze di Figaro*. Next it was Lizzie's turn, and Augusta smiled to herself at how Dev watched the girl's every silly move with a look of quiet delight.

The evening passed merrily.

On the third day, the sky was clear and blue, so Dev took the ladies out for a drive, intent on getting his aunt out of the house as much as possible before he was to leave on the morrow – all too soon, Augusta thought, but the past few days, in truth, were more than she had hoped for. She knew better than to ask him to stay.

They watched the snow-kissed countryside pass by while

the silver bells jangled on the harness of his high-stepping horses. They drove through the village past a crowd of playing children and looped back again to the house. The two of them helped Augusta back inside and into her Bath chair, but once Lizzie had helped the dowager get situated in the warmth of the parlor, Dev offered the girl a driving lesson in his flashy black traveling coach.

'I don't dare,' she vowed.

'Oh, come—'

'That thing is enormous! I've barely driven a one-horse gig, let alone a four-in-hand.'

'Then it's time for you to give it a go!' He seized her wrist with a pirate laugh and dragged her back out into the already darkening afternoon.

Sitting at her desk, Augusta watched them out the window for a long while, tapping her lip slowly in thought.

The grooms looked on in varying degrees of amusement and alarm as Devlin cajoled Lizzie into the driver's seat. He climbed up beside her, placed the whip in her right hand, and then showed her how to hold the double reins in her left.

'Let your arm lie loosely against your side. Bend your elbow to make a right angle with your forearm. Sit up nice and straight, there you are. You want to keep your hand even with the lowest button of your waistcoat.'

'My waistcoat?' she teased.

'This looks about right.' He reached over with a quick grin, grasping a waist-level button of her pelisse. 'Use this as your marker. Now, bend your wrist inward slightly, like so.' She tamped down a frisson of awareness at his touch as he arranged her hand in the proper angle. 'Your knuckles should face outward toward the horses. This creates an easy spring, as it were, from which you may keep a good feel on their mouths.

They're very responsive, so there's no need to saw on the reins, but never allow the reins to lie slack, either, or the team won't know what you want them to do. As for the whip, you don't need to worry about it at this stage. A light tap now and then is enough to make sure they're still paying attention. Ready?'

When she gave him a resolute nod, he threw the hand-brake.

The first few yards felt a bit precarious, the tall, stately coach lurching across the courtyard in fits and starts; but when the steady team of black Fresian horses gained the long, flat stretch of drive, the coach's pace became steady, the ride smooth.

'I'm doing it!' she cried as the wind blew back her bonnet.

'Yes, you are,' Devlin murmured fondly to her. 'Watch your pace, now. Easy through the turn.'

Pulling back gently on the reins, she executed a fine halt as they rolled up to the gate, giving no insult to the horses' soft mouths.

'Excellent, my dear. Now turn them to the right.' He coached her through the task, which felt precarious to her, but was old hat to the horses.

She gained confidence as the four black Fresians went steadily clip-clopping along. They were frightfully large beasts, but they seemed agreeable enough, willing to do as she asked – chiefly, she suspected, because they could smell and hear their master up on the driver's box with her. After a brief, easy jaunt of less than a mile down the road, they made use of a packed-dirt roundabout that encircled an ancient elm tree.

Not wishing to press her luck, she relinquished the reins to the expert whip Devlin and rode happily beside him, her bonnet trailing down her back by its ribbons and the cold wind nipping at her nose. In the west, the sun was already setting, though it was barely five; the larger stars began to glitter, brilliant and silver, in the crisp winter air. Rolling back into the cobbled courtyard, the grooms greeted them with broad smiles and teasing congratulations on her success. The team was unhitched; then Devlin and she accompanied the men and horses into the stable.

Hands in her coat pockets, Lizzie followed as the head groom led Devlin over to the stall of the tall, chocolate gelding he had ridden so hard on the last leg of his grueling journey to Bath.

'He favors it less today, my lord. The rest seems to have done him good.'

'Hm.' Devlin went into the gelding's stall and greeted the horse with a gentle scratch on his broad cheek, then made his way back to the animal's hindquarters, where he ran his hand down the left back leg, palpating the horse's hock down to his fetlock.

'Is he all right?' Lizzie asked, wincing guiltily to know that the animal had been injured due more to her lies than to Devlin's rough riding.

'Inflammation seems to have gone down. A bit of strain to the flexor tendon and this suspensory ligament, here,' Devlin murmured. 'Mac, have you got that liniment?'

'Aye, sir.' The groom went into the stall with a small brown bottle of some medicinal ointment and an old, soft rag with which to apply it.

'I'll do it.'

'You needn't trouble yourself—'

'I'm the one who hurt him,' Devlin murmured. He held out his hand for the supplies. The groom gave them to him without further comment, nodded his respects, and left to marshal up his trio of young stableboys to begin the busy process of feeding all the horses in the barn. It was their dinner time.

'Is there anything I can do?' Lizzie inquired, leaning uncertainly against the stall door.

'Pet his head to distract him. He's not sure whether he likes this stuff or not. It feels funny going on, doesn't it, boy? Camphor – hot and cold at the same time. Very strange!'

'I imagine so,' she murmured, smelling the sharp, pungent odor of the ointment when he opened the bottle.

He set the rag aside and took off his thick leather gloves while Lizzie held out her hand, luring the horse over. The chocolate gelding approached, shuffling its hooves through its bedding of fragrant hay.

'Does he have a name?' she asked as the horse investigated her hand with its soft muzzle, lipping at her palm with its velvety mouth.

'If he does, they didn't tell it to me when I bought him. Why don't you name him?'

'All right.' The gelding ambled closer, blowing a puff of breath against Lizzie's cheek. She laughed. 'What would you like to be called, you handsome thing?'

Devlin poured the liniment oil into his hand and crouched down, massaging it into the gelding's hock and fetlock, the animal's knee and ankle joints, respectively. The gelding snuffled and swung his head around to see what Devlin was doing.

'Come here, boy. Let me have a look at you,' Lizzie said, doing her part to distract the animal from the treatment.

While Devlin picked up his back hoof and inspected its motion from the ankle, she got the horse's full attention by scratching behind the ears. It leaned its head into her hand. 'Let's see. We could name you for your color. Chocolate. Brownie. He's got a bit of dappling on the rump there. Shadow?'

'This horse has the heart of a hero,' Devlin remarked, intent upon his task. 'He took me at a full gallop through a snowstorm in the middle of the night. I refuse to let you call such a noble beast Brownie.'

'I'm so sorry, you dear thing,' she told the horse, smoothing his dark floppy forelock off to the side so she could see the expression in his big, soulful eyes. When she brushed the forelock aside, she noticed a small white star in the center of his forehead. 'You are a hero, aren't you? A star! That's it. We'll call him Star, Devlin. See?' The gelding bobbed his refined head and snorted against her cheek a second time. 'He approves!'

'Fine by me.' Devlin glanced at her, his sea-bright eyes twinkling. '*Star* it is.'

They fell into a companionable silence. A moment later, Devlin straightened up and moved to inspect the horse's left foreleg, keeping his hand planted reassuringly on the animal's flank. Pouring more liniment oil into his hand, he crouched down and began massaging it in, while Lizzie leaned on the half-door of the stall and continued petting Star, trying not to stare at the mesmerizing motion of Devlin's able hands gliding over the soft hide of the horse.

Devlin worked with his head down, and a few strands of his long, jet hair escaped the queue and trailed down gracefully alongside his square face, where a rosy flush still lingered in his wind-nipped cheeks. *Such long lashes*, she thought, gazing at him until another wave of sweet, sensual longing made her bite her lip and look away. What was this effect he had on her? It was indecent. She had never reacted this way to a man before. Not even to Alec.

He applied the ointment to Star's other foreleg, then the right hind leg in turn, working more slowly, as though turning something over in his mind. 'I leave tomorrow,' he said after a long moment, as though he had been gathering himself to say it for some time.

'Yes,' she answered softly, leaning her cheek against Star's muzzle for a moment. 'I know.' She had been avoiding the thought all day.

She supposed she ought to be glad he was leaving in the morning before she was tempted to do something rash, but the prospect of life returning to dull normal without him had reduced her to a state of misery. She paused, letting the horse escape her half-hug. 'Will it be another seven months before you're back?'

He smiled. 'Not if you get started soon planning your next ruse. But I warn you, I'm on to you now. . . .' His voice trailed off in chagrin at his own halting attempt at humor. 'Sorry,' he mumbled. Straightening up, he gave a helpless shrug. 'I'm not very good at good-byes.'

'It's all right.' She smiled bravely at him, hiding her dread of how empty the villa would seem once he had gone. 'It's been fun,' she said simply.

'It has.' Dev nodded earnestly and gave her a rueful smile in answer, but wondered, *Fun?*

The word did not begin to approach his experience of the past few . . . magical days. But if that was how she saw it, then he was glad he had managed to keep his craving for her under reasonable control. Perhaps it seemed strange, but he was anxious not to overstep his bounds with her. Somehow over the past few days she had become more to him than just a girl. She had become a *friend* to him in some deep, mysterious sense of the word, and he had so few of those, he was loath to jeopardize it by letting his hunger for her slip the leash. And so he struggled to hide his desire, feeling a little bewildered by it all.

How ironic to think back on how he had schemed to seduce her that first night – teach the chit a lesson, he had vaunted like a fool. Now he was the one seduced – and she wasn't even trying. He was embarrassed by how much he wanted her, frankly. Every time he looked at her, he itched to breed. He could think of nothing else but laying her white body across his bed, spreading her legs, and claiming her again and again by the firelight.

Half blinded by the image, he could not bring himself to meet her innocent gaze at the moment, though her gray eyes smoldered with unconscious invitation as she watched his every move. Never had a woman been so ripe for the taking, he thought in feverish certainty. But with the deadly swirl of intrigue he had left behind in London, and to which he must return in the morning, he could not afford the distraction, nor could he make her the kinds of promises that a girl like her deserved. Though he sensed her willingness, he refused to pluck that particular flower, but God knew the perfume of it was driving him mad.

Lowering his head, he slowly wiped the liniment oil off of his hands with an old rag and cleared his throat in the awkward silence. 'Elizabeth?' he forced out softly.

'Yes, Devlin?' she asked, sounding a trifle faint.

You're such a special girl. You're so different – God, how clumsy that sounded. He lost his nerve, swallowed hard, and forced a smile. 'We should probably go in.'

Before I ravish you.

'Right, yes, of course.'

Resist, he warned himself as he grabbed his gloves off the side of the stall and pulled them back on, doing his best to clear his head with a slow exhalation.

As he turned to leave the stall, she watched him with a smoky stare, but a welcome interruption appeared in the form of a wee stableboy in a tweed cap, lugging a fresh bucket of water for the gelding. The child nearly sloshed it all over himself, for the full bucket probably weighed as much as he did. He looked nine or ten at the most, one of Mrs. Rowland's countless descendants.

Dev smiled at the child. 'Let me help you with that,' he murmured, lifting the pail out of the boy's hands.

'Thank ye, sir!' The boy raced off to fill the next bucket, leaving them alone in the aisle.

Carrying it in one hand, Dev hung the pail on an iron hook in the stall. Star moved over and lipped at the frigid water. He bade farewell to the horse with an affectionate pat on the flank.

Lizzie stepped aside to admit him from the stall, but just

when he thought he was in the clear, he felt her quiver slightly as he brushed past her. His control dissolved.

He stopped, turning to her.

She held his stare. Her cheeks flushed; she did not back away.

In the next moment, he swept her into his arms and drove her back against the stall door, bracing her there with his body and kissing her senseless. She had thrown her arms around his neck and was returning his kisses with eager abandon, neither of them noticing or caring that they had spooked the horse with the suddenness of their passionate embrace.

Dev raked his gloved fingers almost roughly through her long hair while she gripped his lapels as if to pull him even closer, pull him into her. She was an eager partner, caressing him, breathing him in, drinking of his kiss with urgent, thirsty greed. He groaned with delight at her responsiveness and wrapped his arms more tightly around her waist, savoring the soft, moist warmth of her mouth. He grasped her breast, or tried to, through the thick wool of her brown pelisse, and though he noticed she did not protest, he froze at the sound of a throat being cleared somewhere near the end of the stable aisle.

They broke apart, flushed and panting, and both looked over just in time to see Mac, the head groom, leaving discreetly. The warning came mere seconds before the young stableboys turned the corner, bringing the wheelbarrow with the sacks of sweet grain.

Dev stepped back quickly from Lizzie as the youngsters began disbursing the grain into each horse's feed bucket with a metal scoop. His conscience spiraled. Good God, if the stableboys had seen her in his arms, her reputation would have been in tatters by the morning, and by the time she took Aunt Augusta to church on Sunday, she would have been the talk of the village.

They exchanged a frazzled glance; then Dev somehow managed to collect his wits. Damn, she was beautiful, he thought, staring at her tumbled-down hair. Its disarray could be blamed on the wind, he assured himself. While she tugged her pelisse back into place, her cheeks quite crimson, he gestured to her to go ahead of him. 'After you.'

She cleared her throat slightly, and they left the stable, passing the young apprentices, who had no interest in them whatsoever, too busy bickering over who got to feed the horses and who had to wheel the barrow.

Their boyish voices trailed off behind them as Dev and Lizzie left the warm, cozy nest of the stable and walked outside, where full night had descended. The night was frigid, black, and moonless, but he welcomed the cold bite of the winter air. It helped to clear his head as they strode back across the courtyard, side by side.

Both of them were silent with their thoughts. Lizzie folded her arms across her chest, shivering a little; Dev swallowed the urge to warm her and looked away, wondering in despair how he could ever be satisfied with such a fleeting glimpse of bliss. It was torture. The girl put dangerous thoughts in his head, like abandoning vengeance, his duty to his family. She made him want to shake off the chains of the past, give up the awful burden of hate; she made him want to live, and be happy.

Too bad I don't deserve it.

Chapter Six

That night at dinner, Dev and Lizzie forced merriment in their determination to amuse the dowager, but both were excruciatingly aware that tomorrow they were to part. Their last supper together was the most lavish the kitchen had sent up yet, starting with a steaming vermicelli soup with an hors d'oeuvre of oysters, followed by a first course of pork cutlets with sauce, salmon, Scotch collups, prawns, and veal pie. The second course was scarcely less rich, with hare and morels, roast sweetbreads, lobster, artichoke bottoms, pear tarts, and maids of honor.

The wine flowed; the gilt on the china before them and the exquisite Adam ceiling above them glistened as if the whole world flickered in a magic spell; the tongues of flame atop the candles danced like fairies. Lizzie had donned her favorite evening gown, abandoning all her spinsterish protests of a few days ago – it seemed a lifetime ago, and she, a different person. Bold pleasure smoldered in Devlin's pale eyes as his gaze roamed over her, taking in the small, lace-trimmed bodice of her Neptune-blue velvet gown. She knew it looked better on her than anything else she owned. Why it mattered what he thought was not a subject on which she cared to reflect.

After all, he was still a viscount, she a mere land agent's

daughter. If the youngest son of a duke, a mere commoner, had been too far beyond her reach, then a viscount in his own right was ten times more so. She was not about to lose her head over a man she could not have. But she could certainly enjoy his company. *And his kiss.*

The sweet course included a delicate-flavored almond cheesecake, an assortment of flaky pastries, and a splendid trifle constructed from layers of Naples biscuits, macaroons, and ratafia cakes; each striation was laden with wafer-thin slices of fruit and spread with various jellies; then the whole was soaked through with sack and sprinkled on top with colorful nonpareils from the best confectioner's shop in Bath.

They retreated to the drawing room after their feast. Devlin drank port and idly talked politics with his aunt, while Lizzie, half-listening, provided tolerable music on the pianoforte with a few charming airs by the popular Irish composer, John Field. All too soon, however, the clock struck ten. In her reluctance to relinquish her nephew's presence, Lady Strathmore had already stayed up an hour past her usual bedtime. Once more, the two of them cooperated to help the old woman up the stairs.

In the upper hallway, Devlin eased his aunt back into her Bath chair while Lizzie gripped the handles. As Lady Strathmore smoothed her skirts, Lizzie and Devlin exchanged a glance. She forced a haphazard smile, realizing her expression had gone somber now that it had come time to say good-bye. His gaze read her face deeply; then he bent to give his aunt a kiss.

The dowager patted his clean-shaved cheek. 'It's been wonderful having you here, darling. Don't be a stranger.'

'I won't, ma'am. Take care of yourself.' He kissed his aunt's forehead and straightened up, sending Lizzie an uncertain look as he bowed to her. 'Miss Carlisle.'

'Lord Strathmore.' She reached out and offered him her hand. 'Safe journey.'

Instead of shaking her hand, he bent and kissed her knuckles with tender reluctance. 'Well, then, ladies,' he said, releasing her after a long moment, 'I shall bid you adieu.'

'Come along, Lizzie,' his aunt clipped out.

'Yes, ma'am,' she murmured, then turned Lady Strathmore's chair around and began wheeling her toward her chamber. Unable to resist, she glanced back over her shoulder for one more look at him. He was still standing where they had left him, staring after them, the picture of lordly elegance in his black and white evening clothes, his white-gloved hands clasped politely behind his back. She flinched a little, looking forward again with a pang in her heart.

Doing her best to focus her mind on her duties, she helped Lady Strathmore to change into her warm woolen nightclothes. As usual, Margaret came to see if they needed any assistance. She had tucked the hot-water bottles under the covers half an hour ago; by now, the dowager's bed was warm and toasty.

'Send Mrs. Rowland up when you go downstairs, Margaret,' Her Ladyship ordered the chambermaid. 'I have a few instructions for her on tomorrow's meals.'

'I can convey them to her, ma'am. It is no trouble,' Lizzie offered, perhaps looking for an excuse to run into Devlin one last time before he left, but the old woman shook her head.

'No need. I must speak with Mrs. Rowland personally. She may need to make a special trip to market. No doubt the larder is run low after all our excess these few days.'

'Yes, ma'am,' Margaret said. 'I'll send her right up. Good night, ma'am.' The skinny maid bobbed a curtsy and hurried out while Lizzie pulled back the coverlet and assisted the dowager in climbing up the two wooden bed stairs.

At last, the dowager rested snugly atop her thick, high mattress. Her frail body looked tiny under the ceiling-high draperies of the damask canopy.

'Is there anything else, my lady?' Lizzie asked, going over to snuff the oil lamp on the far end of the room.

'No, no, dear. Off you go.'

Thus dismissed, Lizzie curtsied to her employer and let herself out of the chamber, telling herself it was for the best. Even if her soul and body burned for his caress, men like Devil Strathmore could only give her grief. She had not come so far in mending her heart just to have it broken again by a beautiful charmer. She told herself their flirtation was naught but an idle amusement; that, far from London, the notorious rake had probably just needed *some* form of entertainment to help pass the otherwise dull visit he would have spent with his invalid aunt. For Lizzie's part, she assured herself that he meant nothing to her, that his flattering attentions had merely been a sweet salve to soothe the last, lingering hurt of Alec's rejection.

Her heart whispered otherwise, but she ignored it.

Clinging fast to her self-preservation instincts, she stared straight ahead, walking quickly down the hallway to her quarters. She had a feeling that Devlin was waiting for her once again in the library, but, determined to resist temptation, she did not even glance down the staircase as she passed.

The moment her young companion had gone, Lady Strathmore reached for her cane with a mighty effort. 'Come on, old legs, work for once,' she muttered. 'It's now or never.' She struggled out of bed, determination gleaming in her eyes. After easing herself inch by inch down the wooden bed steps, she walked over slowly to her writing table, leaning heavily on her cane.

At last, with a sigh of exertion, she sat down and after resting a moment, took out a piece of her finest ivory linen paper engraved with her family crest. She had never been a meddling woman, but it was astonishing how, even in the eleventh hour, new habits could be formed.

The idea had taken hold, a divine inspiration, and it filled her with devilish glee – the perfect farewell prank of an old eccentric dragon lady – but there was a lifetime's wisdom and a great deal of love behind it. Dev's charm and Lizzie's kindness. His aristocratic fire tempered by her gentry virtue. Miss Carlisle knew the value of a shilling. She would never let Dev squander Papa's hard-earned fortune. More important, both of them had wounded hearts.

Dev would need a great deal of loving-kindness when she was gone, but not from some vapid Society chit who would let the handsome brute walk all over her. No, Lizzie was the only one who could be trusted with the solemn task of making sure the darkness did not claim him.

It would not be easy for her, a girl of ordinary origins marrying into the aristocracy, Augusta knew. As a young bride, she herself had had firsthand experience of the ton's snobbery, but if she could do it, so could Lizzie.

That her nephew and companion had known each other for only a few days did not trouble her. She had eyes. She saw what was happening between them. For another thing, she trusted her matchmaking instincts; besides, her own marriage had been arranged by her father. She had never laid eyes on Jacob until a few days before their wedding. Her formidable mind made up, she dipped her quill pen in ink and wrote out a revised version of her last will and testament.

When a light knock sounded on the door, she looked up from her work. 'Come.'

Mrs. Rowland bustled in. 'Evening, ma'am. Margaret said you wished to discuss tomorrow's meals?'

'No.'

The housekeeper frowned. 'Ma'am?'

'Come in, Mildred. Shut the door.'

She obeyed. 'Is something wrong, ma'am?'

'On the contrary,' she said half to herself. 'Everything at last is going to be all right.' She turned to her befuddled servant. 'My dear Mildred, you have been in my employ these thirty years. There is no one I trust more. That is why I am entrusting you with a task of the utmost importance.'

'Milady?'

'Come and sign this document.'

The housekeeper eyed her skeptically, but approached, wiping her hands on her apron. Augusta handed her the pen.

'What is it?' she asked uncertainly.

'A slight revision to my will. With your signature, you shall vouch as witness that I am of sound mind and that this is indeed my signature.'

'Aye, you are. It is.'

'Then sign here.'

The housekeeper obeyed without further question, carefully scrawling her name at the bottom.

'Excellent. Now, Mildred, you must set out at first light and take this to Charles Beecham, my solicitor in London.'

'London, ma'am?' she exclaimed.

'His offices are in Fleet Street. Oh, I know it is a dreadful inconvenience, but you must do this for me. You're the only one to whom I can possibly entrust such a momentous task. This document must be personally hand-delivered by you to Mr. Beecham, and have Cook sign it, too, before you go. Is that clear?'

'Yes, my lady, but—'

She thrust a pouch of gold coins into Mildred's hands. 'Keep this for your pains, old friend. Run along – and know that your errand is of the greatest possible consequence to the future of this family.'

Mrs. Rowland looked at her in sober awe, then gave a determined nod and trudged off to carry out her mission with no further questions.

Augusta hobbled back to bed, her heart light. When she blew out the candle, her contented sigh hung in the darkness; then a small note of satisfied laughter escaped her.

Papa would have been so pleased.

Dev paced the perimeter of the oak-paneled library, sipping a cordial of cherry brandy and pretending to read a large atlas, which he balanced on one arm. Where the devil was she?

Surely she would come. He had almost suggested a rendezvous, but he had dared not mention it in front of his aunt – and then it was too late. He hoped against hope that she'd come anyway, for he refused to believe she could be any more content with that thoroughly unsatisfying good-bye than he was. He blew a strand of his long hair out of his eyes with growing exasperation. The long-case clock with its painted face of sun and moon soon read eleven, and still there was no sign of her. Suddenly, he froze, hearing footsteps in the hallway. At last.

He pivoted, his heart skipping a beat, but he remembered at the last moment to look casual. The footfalls came closer. He glanced toward the door, lifting his eyebrows in suave inquiry.

Ben's brown face appeared in the doorway. 'My lord?'

Dev cursed and rolled his eyes. 'Yes, Ben, what is it?'

'Everything is prepared for our departure tomorrow. May I advise the driver what time you wish to be under way?'

'Six, I suppose. That should get us into Town by mid-night if the roads are clear.'

'Very good, sir. Is there anything else you require?'

Lizzie, he thought with a crestfallen gaze.

Ben raised a dubious eyebrow at him. 'Sir? Perhaps you'd best retire. Six o'clock comes frightfully early.'

Dev shut the atlas with a massive sigh. 'You're probably right.' He paused, staring absently into the cozy fire crackling in the fireplace, then waved him off with a dismissive gesture. 'You're free to go, Ben. Get some sleep.' *God knows I won't.*

Ben collected Dev's black tailcoat, which he had shed and had tossed over the back of a side chair, then bowed to him and withdrew.

Dev listened very hard in the silence of the house, but all there was to hear was the vague moaning of the wind in the eaves. Beyond the elegant windowpanes lay a deep, black, cold country darkness, and he was very much alone.

He set the atlas he had been restlessly perusing on the library table and ambled over to the seating area, plopping down into the brown, leather club couch. He leaned his head back and slouched low amid the deep cushions, fingering his small crystal cup and staring sullenly into the fire. Not once had she asked him to stay. What was he to make of that?

Women were always asking him to stay, a final step in the mating ritual and one that he despised, but he had to admit that his disgust at their nagging made it all the easier to leave. But Lizzie had not breathed a word of the usual whining, confounding his expectations, as usual.

Maybe she doesn't want *you to stay, you arrogant ass. Did you ever think of that?*

He yanked out the knot of his cravat in annoyance, then smirked at Pasha, who jumped up onto the couch's arm and sat there staring at him, his eyes agleam, his fluffy tail twitching.

'Why do you always look so smug?' he asked the cat after a moment.

'Meow.'

'I figured you'd say that.' He took a drink. 'Bloody hell.'

Silence.

He could not stand the quiet. Pasha walked with delicate steps along the back of the couch and tickled Dev's ear with his whiskers as if telling him a secret.

'I see. Yes. Perhaps I should,' he said more determinedly. He was Devil Strathmore, after all – more than that, he would soon be a full member of the wicked Horse and Chariot Club. Shocking behavior was practically second nature.

He tossed back another swallow of cherry brandy for added courage, his mind made up. The worst he could get was slapped, was it not? He knew full well when a woman wanted him.

'Well, my boy,' he said to the cat as he heaved himself up off the couch, 'it seems the mountain must go to Muhammad.' With that, he left the library and ventured stealthily through the house. The flickering glow from the fireplace in the library reached only as far as the doorway. The marble hallway beyond was dark.

He made his way through the slumbering villa, trailing his fingertips up the cool smooth banister of the staircase. On the third floor, he ambled down the carpeted corridor, his heartbeat quickening as he came to a bed-chamber where light still glimmered under the door.

He ignored the brazen chance that he was taking and grasped the knob. It turned easily. *Unlocked.* He cocked an eyebrow. Practically an invitation, he remarked to himself half in jest. Silently opening the door, he peered in, saw her, and immediately felt his belly quiver with want.

Sitting at her desk on the far end of the room, working on her translations, she was stripped down to a filmy white negligee, silky and sleeveless and cut very low in the back, with naught but blue ribbon shoulder straps to hold it up – a bit of delicious frippery that was not in a hundred years what he would have expected little Miss Sensible to wear to bed. Yet again, the girl continually surprised him.

He was utterly charmed as he took in the sight of her. Her long hair tumbled free about her lovely shoulders, and she was chewing idly on the frame of a pair of wire-rimmed spectacles, her head bent over a large book. She sat at her desk with one dainty foot tucked under her shapely bottom. Seeing her like this brought a sweet, heavy warmth flooding into his loins. It pleased him to imagine she had left her door unlocked for him, but he knew this was delusion.

Genteel, trusting young ladies like Miss Carlisle had perhaps heard but did not fully understand that there were men in the world who were perfectly comfortable ignoring the dictates of propriety. Indeed, there was one in this very house. A narrow smile curved his lips.

One at the very threshold of her chamber . . .

The cheery glow from the ivory candle on her desk danced over her translations, but so far, Lizzie had accomplished little, staring into space and doodling with tiny ink blobs on the margin of her page. Her elbow sprawled on the corner of her desk, her chin rested in her hand, and all that she could think about was Devlin. Her distracted sigh made the candle flicker. She thrust her quill pen back into its holder in defeat and rested her chin on her forearm, watching the little flame tremble and gyrate. Maybe she should have just *checked* to see if Devlin had been waiting for her in the library again. What harm was a bit of dalliance, after all, if no one was the wiser? God's truth, it was awfully boring around here a lot of the time. His visit had been the most excitement they'd had in ages . . . .

She suddenly felt a presence in the room with her. She lifted her head and glanced over her shoulder, then gasped. He was leaning in the doorway, staring at her.

Blast the man's wilderness ways – she had not even heard him open her door!

'Devlin, what are you doing here?' she exclaimed.

He lifted his finger to his lips as he slipped into her chamber.

Her heart pounded like cannon fire as he shut her door

behind him with a quiet click, then leaned against it, keeping to the shadows. Shirtsleeves rolled up loosely over his forearms, he slid his hands down into his black trouser pockets.

Lizzie stared at him, acutely conscious of her state of undress. She did not stand up, but half hid her scantily clad self behind her chair.

'I came to say good-bye.' His gaze traveled over her in vague awe. 'God, you're beautiful.'

A blush filled her skin at his words. She was quite sure no one had ever called her beautiful before. Searching his sculpted face from across her dim chamber, she wondered what had driven this fierce, untamed wolf of a warrior to approach; but then she felt the loneliness that emanated from him, as if in answer to her own. Her initial shock forgotten, she discerned the aching need in the depths of his pale eyes.

Everything within her longed to fill it.

Slowly, she stood, showing herself to him.

He flinched slightly, his face etched with yearning as his stare traveled over her. 'If you tell me to go, I will,' he said in a hoarse whisper.

She shook her head, unable to fight the pull of her desire. She didn't even want to try. There was only this moment, this night. Only him. *Just this once*, her body begged. She was so lonely, as he was, so hungry for a man deep in the core of her. Whatever his faults, she knew Devil Strathmore could give her a night of pleasure the likes of which she would surely never have the chance to experience again.

She lifted her arms to welcome him.

His eyes caught fire. He locked the door and crossed the room to her in four swift strides, sweeping her off her feet. She twined her arms around his neck as he took her mouth with his own and carried her toward her bed.

Chapter Seven

The hunger in his openmouthed kiss reverberated through her reeling senses. She could do naught but cling to him as he laid her on her bed and reclined beside her, caressing her body. His kiss seduced and ravished her; her skin caught fire, her breasts, her whole body rising toward him.

Surely he felt the drumlike pounding of her heart, she thought as his left hand stroked across the bare expanse of her chest; then it slipped inside her silk negligee. She gasped against his mouth as his large, warm hand cupped her breast snugly in his palm. Her chest heaved. He ended the kiss slowly, but did not remove his hand from her breast. Holding her gaze, he watched her reaction as his thumb circled her nipple. His eyes darkened at the way she shuddered in response.

'I won't do anything you don't want me to do,' he breathed.

'I know, Devlin. I trust you.' She laid her hand gently on his square jaw and drew him back down to kiss her.

With smooth expertise, he untied the blue shoulder ribbons holding up her negligee, kissing her all the while. His finesse confirmed her suspicions that he was surely one of the most skilled seducers in England as he peeled the slinky garment down her quivering body, baring her to the waist. For a moment, he stroked her breasts, then pulled back a small space to gaze at them. When his glance climbed to meet hers once more, his eyes glittered with hunger. He bent his head and claimed her mouth again, harder now, easing partly atop her.

With an eager growl, his pace gathering speed, he kissed his way down her neck and captured her nipple in his mouth. His rhythmic sucking filled her senses with a sweet, heavy languor, bringing to life a wantonness in her that she had not known existed.

She pushed his waistcoat off his broad shoulders. He shrugged out of the elegant garment, casting it off smoothly behind him; as his touch returned to caress her, the small lace ruffle of his shirtsleeve trailed intoxicatingly over her skin.

He bent his head again to lavish her other breast with the same attentions. Watching him with a smoky gaze, she stroked his head, then freed the queue that held back his long, black hair, running her fingers through its silky waves.

She was a little astonished by how natural it felt to be with him this way. His golden earring winked in the candle's secretive glow. After several more minutes of his play at her breasts, his ardent attentions had her fairly squirming beneath him, but when he started to work her negligee lower, she stopped him.

'Not fair,' she chided in a coy whisper. 'Your turn, my lord. Why don't you do away with this?' She plucked at his white shirt.

He answered with a smoldering half-smile. She came up onto her elbows, watching as he pressed up to a kneeling position and lifted his fine white shirt over his head.

At once, Lizzie's jaw dropped at the sight of him. Just when she thought the man couldn't get any more beautiful, the chiseled splendor of his body towered before her, bathed in golden, flickering candlelight. As he tossed the shirt carelessly onto the floor, she caught the wafting scent of clean, inviting cologne on his warm skin. Her dazed stare traveled over him in helpless admiration.

Around his neck, suspended from a thin strip of worn, brown leather, hung the ferocious-looking fang of some awful predator. Startled by the savage trophy, yet fascinated, she sat up and hooked her finger through the leathern necklace, examining the yellowed fang.

'Mountain lion,' he informed her in a husky murmur.

She lifted her gaze slowly to his, awed anew by his size, prowess, and power. He was – what did the poets call it? – *sublime.* Yes.

Beautiful and terrible.

And she wanted him.

'Give me your mouth,' he whispered, leaning closer. He captured her chin between his thumb and forefinger, tilting her head back.

He kissed her again. Her heart pounded madly, her finger slipping free of the leather strip to slip down his lovely chest in a slow, exploratory caress. How strange it was to do this with him – to participate in something so dangerous, and yet to feel so safe in his arms.

'May I kiss you . . . here . . . as you did me?' she asked after a moment, running her fingertips boldly over his small, taut nipple.

'My dear Miss Carlisle, you have my permission do with me whatever you please.'

'I like that answer,' she told him with a sultry smile. 'Lie back.'

He obeyed, offering himself up for her enjoyment. Caressing his glorious body, she lowered her head and kissed his chest, studying with her lips and fingertips the mesmerizing sculpture of his chiseled abdomen, before chastely kissing his nipple. Growing bolder by the second, she touched the tip of her tongue to it, and to her delight, felt the little nub harden beneath her delicate licking. He wrapped his arm around her in a loose half-embrace, watching her and merely letting her play.

She moved lower, easing onto her knees between his legs to nuzzle and taste the rippling muscles of his rock-hard belly. She caressed his steely thigh, but after a moment, he groaned low in his throat, his hand tangling almost roughly in her hair.

He brought her back up to devour her mouth, pulling her into his arms. She simply melted at the feel of his naked chest against hers and returned his kisses, certain she would never get enough of the man. He lay back slowly on the bed, pulling her with him. Her hair swung down around him, veiling them both from the candle's feeble glow. It was then that she felt something hard jutting against her belly.

Daft man, was he carrying a pistol in his pocket? she wondered, startled, for lusty London rakes were ever ready for a duel. 'Devlin, what is this?' she started before one of them ended up accidentally getting shot. But when she rolled back and poked it with her finger, her eyes widened. 'Gracious!'

He laughed at her scandalized gasp. 'See what you do to me?'

'I – I'm sorry.'

'Don't be, *chérie*. Don't be.'

'Is that your—?' She could not bring herself to complete the sentence.

He looked at her with a sardonic arch of his eyebrow. 'Well, it's not my folding telescope.'

His jest jarred her out of her initial shock. She smacked him lightly on the biceps.

As he chuckled at her blush, she bit her lower lip, eyeing him in wicked speculation. 'May I see it? After all, you know . . . one wonders.'

'Does one, indeed?' he whispered, his eyes dancing. But he obliged her without further teasing, climbing out of the bed to stand before her. He unhitched his trousers with a bold stare and a justifiably proud lift of his chin.

'You're shameless,' she remarked.

'You're staring. Go on,' he whispered in a taunting challenge. 'Touch it.'

She considered refusing, but could tell by his tone that he didn't think she had the nerve to continue. Well, then.

Telling herself it was merely in the spirit of scientific inquiry, she reached out ever so cautiously and ventured an experimental contact of her fingertips. Immediately, she thrilled to the way the slight caress made his big body flinch with pleasure.

'Interesting,' she murmured. She had yanked her hand back, but now, emboldened, she touched him again.

'Like this,' he whispered, showing her. He wrapped her fingers around the hard silken flesh. 'And stroke it.' He watched her every move. 'Go on. It won't bite you.'

'Like this?'

'Yes, just like that,' he forced out, panting slightly.

His dimensions swelled, his angle rising farther, like a clock that read five minutes to midnight. He stopped her hand with a gentle touch.

'What now?' she queried in genuine curiosity.

'Now kiss it,' he whispered.

Was he serious? she wondered, glancing up at his shadowed facc.

'Like this.' He leaned down and kissed her mouth, his tongue richly stroking hers. He kissed her so deeply and so well that when he pulled away, she could have cried out at the denial. His flaming eyes pleaded with her, urged her on. With an understanding of his need born of pure instinct, she grasped his throbbing member and gave in to his desire.

The second her mouth touched him, she comprehended the profound pleasurc thc act gave him. He reached out to brace his hand against the bedpost, playing with her hair as she tested out her brand-new skill.

The pleasure they shared shimmered in her veins with all the brilliance of an intricately cut diamond, each facet a scintillating, very earthy joy: The first pleasure was in the secrecy of their scandalous rendezvous. The second, as her heart beat faster, was that of feeling him under her power. But the third pleasure was the act itself. The more she tasted him, the more she wanted, and soon, she was in a trance of outrageous desire, her tongue sliding up and down him, her lips – moist and hot, acutely sensitized – feeling every fevered throb of his response.

He stopped her without warning, flattening her back onto the bed. He pinned her hands over her head against the mattress, swooped down on her and took her mouth in a wild, claiming kiss, thrusting his tongue into her mouth with such total dominance that she was sure there would be nothing left of her by the time he was done, and she didn't even care. She could feel his heart pounding against her body and his candied length rubbing deliciously against the place where she most longed for him.

She tried to put her arms around his shoulders, but he held her wrists pinned down, and perhaps it was perverse, but she found that this excited her enormously.

He ended the kiss and gazed down at her for a moment with a look of newfound respect in his eyes, as though he thought her a woman to be reckoned with, indeed. His eyes burned with lust, but he said nothing. Releasing her hands, he slid down slowly over her body, kissing as he went. She shifted under his nuzzling mouth, her chest heaving, a dreamy smile on her lips as he played at her neck, her breasts, her belly. As he trailed his hands down to her hips, moving lower, she swirled her stockinged foot around his raging member in a dainty flirtation. He gave a low, husky laugh at her teasing and glanced up to flash her a wicked smile.

Holding her gaze, he kissed her thigh; then his eyes swept closed and he lowered his head. What came next, she never could have imagined.

'Oh, *grrracious*,' she moaned in a sort of purr as his clever tongue cultivated a center of pure physical sensation there that she had not known she possessed. This he adored with generous care in an act that paralleled what she had done to him. But oh, to be the recipient of such pagan worship was almost more than she could bear.

In moments, she was prepared to beg if need be, aye, to sell her very soul to him so long as he did not stop. She arched into his open mouth; she squirmed and clawed at the coverlet and fought not to scream out with crazed pleasure as he consumed her. Every breath was a soul-deep gasp as he worked her into a lather; every time she was sure her wits could not withstand another second, he drove her on to new heights.

Reality was far behind; the two of them were out among the stars in the velvet blackness of the night. What had become of prim Lizzie Carlisle, the shy bluestocking, she had no idea. This madwoman he had brought to life was a seething cauldron of hot, desperate lust, riding his kiss while his fingers stroked deep within her. God, it was too much. It had to stop. She was out of control; she suspected they both were. With the best of intentions, though her limbs were weak with desire, she laid her hand on his shoulder. His skin was steamy hot to the touch, but even as she tried to gather her strength to curb the unbearable ecstasy, he dragged her relentlessly to the brink of some shimmering, endless canyon and threw her into it before she could protest.

She fell and fell in sheer surrender. Rapturous convulsions racked her body and had barely slackened when his mouth left her. He rose over her, dark and magnificent, his eyes aglow. As he leaned over her, planting his hands on the bed on either side of her, she thought he would simply ravish what was left of her, but he gathered her hand in his shaking grasp and placed it on his tortured hardness. It throbbed against her mound.

'Touch me,' he rasped. She obeyed, and felt the thrill of him stirring her anew to find him huge and straining and shockingly wet with her. Between her swollen flesh and her obedient palm, he rubbed himself in the slick cascade of her release, finding his rhythm with a few quick thrusts before exploding with a groan and a mighty pulsation that loosed a volley of his seed across her belly and all the way up to her breasts.

He collapsed onto his elbows above her, caressed her mouth with a quaking kiss, and leaned his forehead against hers, panting. 'Oh, my God,' he whispered.

'Oh, Devlin.'

They glanced at each other in dazed exhaustion and then both started laughing softly, careful in the intimate quiet to keep their voices down.

A short while later, they lay together entwined in the sheets, holding and touching in the sated afterglow of passion. Dev felt so strange. His fair young virgin could not know, of course, how amazed he was at the way she had made his body respond. He had burst in her hand like a callow youth, but even more unheard-of was the way he stayed with her now, letting her nestle her head in the crook of his neck while her fingertip drew little figures on his bare chest.

He felt . . . dazed. Happy.

Tranquil and tender. Heavy-limbed with contentment. He could not recall the last time he had felt so deeply connected to any lover. He ignored the slightly alarming thought and tickled her cheek with a lock of her hair.

She brushed it away with a velvety chuckle. The soft sound of it thrilled him, so rich with womanly satisfaction. God, if he were half as bad as his reputation, he would mount her and rend her maidenhead even now, consequences be damned. The fierce impulses that shot through his mind were so foreign to him that they almost amused him: He wanted to shelter her, take such care of her, build her a fortress and keep her safely inside where no harm could ever come to her.

Instead, he hugged her a little closer and kissed her head and ignored the fact that he was not the doting type.

She'll get to you if you're not careful, his mind warned, but he couldn't seem to help himself. She was so different from the women he was used to, so kind and giving and warm. He loved her thick, brown hair with its lavender scent, her dove-gray eyes and shy smile, her milky-white skin . . .

'Devlin?' she asked softly, breaking into his absurd smitten musings.

'Hmm?'

'What are you thinking of?'

'You.'

'Flatterer.' She hugged him a little harder and snuggled closer. 'What about me?'

'There's still so much I don't know about you,' he mused aloud. 'I still have many questions, Miss Carlisle. For example, where did you learn to speak German?'

'I'll give you one guess,' she whispered, biting her lip with suppressed mirth.

'Saucy little baggage.' He squeezed her side to tickle her. 'You've been to Germany?'

She nodded, grinning and pleased with herself.

'Explain,' he commanded.

'All the most important thought comes out of Germany these days. I was lucky. The Knight family tutor, Mr. Whitby, taught me the rudiments of the language as a child. He had studied at Gottingen.' She brushed a long tendril of her hair out of her face. 'Three years ago, my interest in German literature was revived when Robert – the duke, I mean – was assigned to the delegation to the Congress of Vienna.'

'Was he?'

She nodded. 'Jacinda and I went to Austria with Robert and Bel to 'broaden our horizons.' We had the most marvelous grand tour. Fortunately, we had already returned to England when the cursed war broke out again.'

'Very well. Second question: What's this I hear about you and some bookshop?'

'Your aunt told you about that?' she asked indignantly.

'Yes, and I do not at all approve, I'll have you know.'

She tweaked his nose in answer.

'Stop that,' he scolded, swatting her hand away.

'I can jolly well open a bookshop in Russell Square if I want,' she informed him with an adorable thrust of her chin, 'and why should I not? You men get to do whatever you please. Go on, laugh.'

'I would never dream of laughing at you, *chérie*.' The corners of his mouth twitched, but he managed a look of mock sobriety. 'But I must know – why Russell Square?'

'Supply and demand, *obviously*. It's right by the museum. Think.' She tapped her temple and stared up at him from her pillow. 'Who buys books? There are coffee shops all around there where the intellectuals like to gather to discuss philosophy and politics, where they go for refreshments after the scientific lectures and such – but I don't suppose you ever set foot out of Mayfair. After all, I hear you are *terribly* fashionable.'

'Well, I hear you are a bluestocking, and now I am beginning to believe it.'

'You asked,' she said with a one-shouldered shrug. 'I try not to inflict my eccentricities on others. Brains in a woman?' She shook her head at him with a wry smile. 'Most unfeminine.'

'Not to me,' he murmured, cradling her in his arms for a moment. 'I find you fascinating, Miss Carlisle. Extremely feminine . . . and altogether unique—'

'Go on!' she scoffed, trying to pull away.

'Why do you doubt me? I shall lavish you with compliments until you believe,' he declared, preventing her from wriggling away. Holding her naked body against him, he pressed a kiss to the crook of her shoulder. 'You're charming, witty, kind,' he whispered. 'And very . . . very beautiful.'

She stopped struggling. Her gray eyes were wary and full of youthful vulnerability as she slowly turned her gaze to his. 'You really think I'm . . . beautiful?'

''Tis not my mere opinion, Miss Carlisle. It is an obvious fact.'

She smiled shyly at him. He pressed a lingering kiss to her forehead. They both fell silent for a long moment.

'What will you do when she – dies?' he asked hesitantly.

'Get another job, I suppose.'

'In London?'

'Why? Do you want to give me a reference, Lord Strathmore?' she asked, sending him a roguish glance over her delicate shoulder.

Laughing softly, he slipped his arms around her waist. 'I'll give you more than that, you hoyden. You know,' he said cautiously, petting her hair for a measured pause, 'once she's gone, you wouldn't really have to work if you didn't want to.'

'Yes, I do,' she said with a sigh.

'No. I could take care of you.' He couldn't believe he had just said it, but there it was. 'I stand to inherit a lot of money. You could come under my protection.'

'Devlin James Kimball.' She sat up swiftly. 'You did *not* just ask me to become your mistress.'

'Why not? It's good between us, isn't it? You could have servants, your own house and carriage. Whatever you want—'

'Stop it.' She pulled away from him. 'It's out of the question. Please do not speak of it again. The thought is disgusting to me. What we did tonight, I gave freely, not for any kind of gain. For heaven's sake, I've never done anything like this before in my life—'

'I know that. Lizzie – I'm sorry. It came out wrong.' He reached for her as she turned her back to him. 'Don't be angry. I'm a fool.'

'Well, I suppose you can hardly be blamed for assuming I'm that sort of girl after I allowed this to happen,' she huffed, half burying her face in the pillow.

'Do you really think you "allowed" this to happen?' he asked, pausing. 'Do you really think you could have stopped me?'

Warily, she glanced over her shoulder at him.

'Don't you know who I am?' His eyes gleamed. 'The abandoned, the wicked, the cursed Devil Strathmore? Dear little thing, you didn't stand a chance.'

'Is that supposed to make me feel better?' she scoffed.

'Yes.' He sat up, leaning behind her. 'Don't be angry, Lizzie. Not at me, nor at yourself. This night was a beautiful thing.' He caressed her arm. 'Promise me you won't regret it.'

In spite of herself, she turned and gazed at him with her heart in her eyes, then cupped his cheek. 'Oh, Devlin, how could I?'

'That's better,' he whispered, staring at her. 'Come here, you.' He gathered her into his arms once more and leaned back against the headboard.

'So, how does this sort of thing work, then?' She nuzzled in the crook of his neck. 'Will it be awkward when we see each other next?'

'Don't know. Come to London, and we'll find out. After all—' He ducked his head to kiss the tip of her nose. 'Who else is going to show me these famous coffee shops I've heard about in Russell Square? You know I can't find my way out of Mayfair all by myself.'

She laughed, rolling onto her side with a sinuous, inviting stretch. Dev slid down and fitted his body behind hers. He reveled in the tempting feel of her backside curving snugly against his groin but managed to keep his libido in check. 'You know, I still have one more question,' he murmured, deciding to chance it.

'Do you, my curious fellow? All right, I will take one more question. What is it?'

He paused, his lips lingering against her shoulder. 'What happened, exactly, between you and Alec Knight?'

She went very still.

He waited with intense alertness, for by now, he had a fair idea of what *hadn't* happened between Alec and her; the girl was as pure as the driven snow. She hadn't even known how to receive a proper kiss that first night in the library, which made his suspicions about the great Don Juan even harder to explain.

'How did you figure it out?'

'I saw the look on your face the other night at dinner when I mentioned I knew him. Then my aunt told me you came here hiding from a broken heart. I can put two and two together.' Sliding his arm around her waist, he tugged softly, rolling her onto her back so that she was forced to meet his gaze. Studying her vulnerable expression, he caressed her cheek. 'What did he do to you?'

With ill-concealed distress, she looked away, twining a length of her long hair around her finger.

'Lizzie?' He grasped her chin very gently and turned her face to him. 'I told you my troubles, didn't I? Don't you trust me?'

'It's not that. It's just – a little humiliating.'

'He hurt you.'

'Don't look like that. It's frightens me.'

He lowered his lashes to veil the quick spark of vengeance in his eyes. 'If the man hurt you, Lizzie, he will answer for it.'

'Heavens, Devlin, it wasn't a dueling offense! We were close, I'll admit, but we had a – a falling out.'

'Why? What happened?'

'Nothing happened,' she said flatly. 'Nothing at all.'

'I see,' he murmured, studying her. 'You wanted something to happen and it didn't.'

'Oh, Devlin.' She let out a wistful sigh and cast her forearm over her brow, studying the white ceiling. 'Did you ever have a wonderful idea of someone in your mind, only to find out they weren't really who you thought they were at all?'

He didn't answer, only listening.

She cast him a wan smile askance. 'Alec Knight seemed the stuff of dreams to me for . . . years. I loved him so – at least I thought I did. But when I finally let him know it, he ran away. And now what I thought was love appears nothing more to me than a lonely little orphan girl's hope of finding somewhere to belong. I thought if I married Alec, I would finally be a *real* part of the family. The Knight family, I mean.' She shrugged and let out a wistful sigh. 'My position in life is a bit confusing at times, I'm afraid. I'm not a servant, but I'm certainly not a blue blood like you or Jacinda. It's precarious, trying to exist in between these two worlds, below-stairs and above. One feels there is never a place where one truly belongs. I thought that if I took perfect care of Alec, the way I had taken care of Jacinda all those years, that he'd love me, and marry me, and then I wouldn't have to worry anymore, because then I'd have a home and a family of my own, and I would always know just where I belonged.'

He stared at her, his heart clenching.

'But I was deluding myself,' she added quietly. 'For Alec never had the slightest interest in me.'

'I find that hard to believe.'

'It's true. Whatever the nature of the bond we shared, it never went beyond platonic. Ah, well, I guess you might as well hear the whole story.' She came up onto her side and propped her elbow on the mattress, resting her cheek on her hand. 'Alec hit a losing streak at the tables last summer and got into a great deal of debt. Usually, he lives off a generous allowance from his eldest brother, the duke. But Robert had warned him repeatedly about his gaming, and by June, the whole family was at their wits' end with him. Well, Alec is very proud. Rather than scale back his fashionable mode of life – and thus jeopardize his exalted place in Society – he sought out one of the low, cutthroat moneylenders that inhabit the most dangerous regions of the City and, despite the most appalling terms of interest, arranged for himself a generous financial rescue.'

'Not wise,' Dev murmured.

'Yes, and Alec knew it, but opted cheerfully to ignore that fact. He was sure his luck would turn around, but in the meantime, he had to pay his IOUs or he wouldn't be able to show himself at White's and Brooke's again. So, he used the loan to pay off his IOUs, and all was well at the clubs. But by the time the first few payments on the loan came due, his luck had still not turned around, which meant he was in even worse trouble than before.

'The moneylender sent out a trio of giant street thugs to demand payment, but there was nothing Alec could do. He put them off for as long as he could. They wouldn't stop. They finally accosted and attacked him when he was on his way home from some night's revels – alone, quite foxed, I'm afraid, and unable to put up a proper fight. He managed to get away despite a broken ankle from their blows, but it wasn't long before they came after him again. By now he was too angry and humiliated to tell his brothers of his plight. I was there the night these horrid creatures came after him again.

'They said they were going to kill him, Devlin. I heard them threaten so – this man I had worshipped since I was nine years old. I couldn't let them hurt Alec. When I realized the danger he was in, I gave him my inheritance that my father had left for my dowry. It's not much, but Robert had invested it well over the years—'

'*What?*' he whispered, staring at her in awe. 'You offered up your dowry to pay Alec Knight's gambling debts?'

'I tried to, but it didn't work out that way. I'll never forget the look on his face when I gave him the money. He just stared at me as though he were seeing me for the first time, finally grasping my feelings for him after all those years of living under the same roof as chastely as if we were brother and sister. For the first time in his life, I think, he was faced with something serious, something he couldn't charm his way through. He didn't know what to say.' A sheen of tears misted her eyes briefly, but she blinked them away.

'In any case, he took the money as I insisted and left, but his mood was very strange. He was supposed to take it to the moneylender's office and come straight back, but he was gone for hours. Day passed to night; I was scared to death. I thought those brutes had done him a violence in spite of the payment, and, I admit . . . it crossed my mind that he might have gone to White's to try his luck one last time with my money. But when morning came, he strolled back in, quite unharmed. And that's when I found out just how great a fool I had been all those years. He gave me back my money and said that he wouldn't be needing it. That he had found suitable employment by which to pay his own way henceforth. Then he told me where he'd been.'

'Where?'

She bit her lip and looked away. 'I thought everyone knew. Oh, but you've been abroad. Of course.' She closed her eyes and shook her head. 'There is a rich baroness – everyone in London seems to know her – Lady Campion. I'm sure you must have seen her in Town. She's very elegant, sophisticated, worldly. Everything I'm not,' she added with an unhappy little smile.

He took her hand. 'Go on.'

'I'm not quite sure how to put this. It was Lady Campion who paid off Alec's debts in the end. He became – that is, he had made arrangements with her to work off the sum . . . in her bed.'

Dev stared at her in shock. 'Poor sweeting,' he whispered. 'You must have been crushed.'

She nodded, avoiding his tender gaze. 'Billy – Jacinda's husband – has attempted to explain to me that Alec did this only because to take my money would have caused him too much shame. But I cannot see that *his* solution was any less humiliating. He didn't have to do it, after all. He could have swallowed his pride and turned to his elder brothers for help, or even to Billy. If any of them had known he was in danger, they would have helped him in a heartbeat. But, you see, Alec chose his course with Lady Campion to kill two birds with one stone. Not only did he get his debts paid without having to swallow his pride and ask his big brothers for help; he also succeeded in making it crystal clear to me that there was no possibility of a marriage between us – ever. The moment he realized how much I adored him, he took the sharpest possible action to drive me away. And do you know something, Devlin? It worked.'

She fell silent for a moment. 'A part of me will always love Alec, but I could never trust him now. And I could never respect a man who has so little respect for himself.' She paused. 'He actually said I would thank him one day. But he never did explain what it was about me that he found so objectionable. So, I've been left to wonder about that.'

'There's nothing objectionable about you, Elizabeth. Trust me, your friend Billy is dead on. No man with an ounce of self-respect could take a sweet young girl's dowry to pay his gaming debts, and I daresay Alexander the Great has never lacked for pride.'

'You condone what he did?' she exclaimed.

'Of course not, but I think you are too naive to see the meaning of it.'

'Enlighten me, then.'

Dev shrugged. 'Alec's refusal to exploit your devotion suggests to me that you mean more to him than you know.' When she blinked with fawnlike confusion, Dev gathered her closer and kissed her cheek, slowly petting her hair. 'There are some men, *chérie*, who will kiss every girl in town except the one that matters.'

She scowled at him. 'That's just silly. Why would any man do that?'

'Fear, my darling.'

'But Alec's like you: he's not afraid of anything. I mean, he's never fought off a mountain lion, but he's been in countless duels—'

'No, you misunderstand. It's not danger that scares men like Alec and me. It's love.' Dev suddenly snapped his jaw shut – aghast at what had just slipped out of his mouth. *Bloody hell!* It was all well and good to analyze the foibles of another, but what perverse inner devil had compelled him to confess that he, too, fell into this sorry class of men?

It was true, but – God! The old, ingrained fear returned, slapping him back to his senses. With an odd, jarring sensation, it was as if his objective mind swept back for one second to a safe distance of several feet away to view the bed where he lay entwined with his aunt's little paid companion – whom he had half debauched! – consoling her and crooning to her like some lovelorn swain. Reason returned like the searching beam of a lighthouse, blaring out the dreamy, candlelit haze of her chamber, and what Dev saw in himself by its harsh glare appalled him. Just what in the Hell did he think he was doing?

'Is something wrong?' she inquired, while he stared at her, withdrawing steadily by tiny fractions of an inch.

His heart pounded. *I've got to get out of here.* As if his attachment to his aunt were not threatening enough, he obviously had some strange, dangerous weakness for Elizabeth Carlisle. It would not stand. He knew too well that the safety he felt with her was an illusion. *Love equals pain.* Fate had smashed his heart to pieces once. He was never going through that again.

He did not think he could survive it.

She frowned when he forced a suave smile, like a man strangling for air.

'It's late,' he said as carefully as possible, his stiff smile plastered in place. 'I should go.'

Lizzie had sensed the exact moment when Devlin withdrew; he did not move, did not blink, but she felt the change in him like a shift in the wind. At first, she did not understand what was happening. 'Devlin?' she proded when he failed to answer. 'Is something wrong?'

'No, of course not, darling.' He sat up without warning, throwing his long legs off the edge of the bed. He stood up, pulling free of her light embrace, and took a few restless paces away from the bed. 'You need your rest.'

But I'm not tired. Her stare traveled reverently over his warrior's body, glorious in his nakedness. He bent down and retrieved his clothes, pulling them back on, while she began wondering unhappily if she had done something wrong. But then she recalled what his aunt had told her – *'He hasn't let anyone get close to him in twelve years'* – and understanding dawned.

The poor silly thing had scared himself with their closeness tonight.

Finished fastening his black trousers, he returned and sat on the edge of her bed, where he drew on his boots. He was closed up within himself, imprisoned in a cage of his own fears, and with the way he turned his back to her, she might as well have ceased to exist.

But instead of anger or indignation at his sudden urge to bolt, she felt a wave of sadness for him. He had not come by his scars lightly, after all. Very gently, she reached out and laid her hand on his broad, smooth back.

He allowed it with a pause, neither moving closer nor pulling away. She could feel how his big, lean body thrummed with tension under her touch.

Leaning toward him, she tilted her head and studied his patrician profile for a moment, wincing inwardly at the lost look on his chiseled face, so beautiful in the candle glow.

'It's all right,' she whispered.

'You think so?' he asked in a low, cynical tone, but at least he did not attempt to deny what was really going on in his head.

'Devlin.' She came up onto her knees behind him on the bed and draped her arms loosely around his wide shoulders, kissing his cheek. She closed her eyes for a moment and rested her head against his. *I could fall in love with you . . . so easily.* The thought was unsettling. But there was no need for him to be anxious. She stroked his raven hair and soothed him in a teasing murmur: 'Don't be distressed, darling. Alec Knight may be a lost cause, but I'm fairly sure there's hope for you.'

'Oh, really?' His tone was wry.

'Yes. You're much more of a grown-up than he is.'

'Thanks, I think.' He hesitated. 'Lizzie?'

'Yes, Devlin?'

'If you're ever in London—' He stopped himself. 'Ah, never mind,' he whispered, staring at the floor, but the trapped, tangled frustration in his eyes moved her to compassion.

'Come here, sweet.' Before he could pull away, she gave him a loose half-hug and kissed his temple. 'If I'm ever in London and I should see you, I will remember this night and how lovely it was. That is all,' she said in a soft tone, then patiently gathered his long hair back into its loose queue and tied it for him. 'I said I don't expect any promises from you, Devlin. I know the lay of the land. I wanted this as much as you did, and I'm still your friend.' She kissed his left earlobe just above the small golden hoop.

He glanced warily at her from the corner of his eye. 'Are you an angel?'

She smiled at him. 'What do you think?'

'Very possible.' Looking a trifle more relaxed, he got up, retrieved his white shirt, and slipped it back on over his head, but instead of leaving, he came back slowly to the bed and sat down again. His wide shoulders slumped. 'I'm sorry I'm like this,' he said after a long moment, then offered nothing more.

'Oh, you're not so bad, Devil,' she teased gently, and wrapped him in a comforting hug. She kissed his princely brow, resigning herself to the unhappy prospect of sending him on his way. 'Good-bye, my dear Lord Strathmore—,' she started to say, but he turned and stopped her at the first syllable, laying his fingertip over her lips.

'No. Not good-bye,' he murmured. 'What is it the Italians say?'

'*Arrivederci?*'

'Yes.' He smiled faintly in the shadows. 'Until we meet again.'

'Will we, Devlin?' she whispered, searching his crystalline eyes.

'Oh, I think it very likely,' he whispered, then caught her chin between his fingers and, leaning closer, kissed her tenderly one last time.

She wound her arms around him, loath to let him go, but she knew full well that a peer of the realm like him was not hers to hold, nor ever would be. *Let him go*. Best to take this night simply for what it was – two lonely people coming together for warmth on a cold winter's eve. Reluctantly, she released him with one last caress. He nuzzled the corner of her mouth with a final, lingering kiss, then rose and withdrew.

He paused in the doorway, however, and glanced back at her. 'No regrets?'

'No regrets,' she answered softly, nodding.

He blew her a kiss from his two fingertips, then slipped out of her room as silently as the wind that came and went as it willed.

She listened until his stealthy footfalls had also faded down the hallway, then turned onto her side with a slight, fond smile, though her heart hurt a little. *Arrivederci*, my lord, she thought with a sigh.

Until we meet again.

SIX WEEKS LATER

Give the Devil his due.
– sixteenth-century proverb

Chapter Eight

The tolling of cathedral bells resounded over the rooftops of London, disturbing flocks of pigeons that lifted in vexed swirls, drab as the skies, their feathers smudged with the soot of a thousand chimneys. A gray March drizzle drummed the river of black coaches and umbrellas wending their way along Whitehall, falling steadily on the oddly silent crowd of some two thousand mourners and countless more onlookers who had gathered for the state funeral of the Dowager Viscountess Strathmore.

A few policemen were on hand to clear the way to the Abbey. Near the head of the procession, a hearse was drawn by six pitch-black horses with plumes on their heads and fitted blankets of red velvet embroidered with the Strathmore crest. Behind it walked three musicians: a kilt-clad bagpiper, silent for now, and two drummers beating out a slow, dirgelike tattoo.

Every great family of the realm had sent a representative to pay their respects to old Lady Ironsides. The slow-moving line of black coaches stretched nearly to Trafalgar Square, each stately vehicle emblazoned with some noble's coats of arms, and adorned on this somber occasion with black crape and funeral wreaths. Few voices could be heard – only the clip-clopping of countless hooves and the grinding of carriage wheels, and, always, the deep, reverberant clanging of the bells.

On foot, Lizzie struggled through the jostling throng, trying to find Devlin while his aunt's last request echoed in her ears: *'Will you look in on him from time to time when I am gone?'*

The dowager had passed away a fortnight ago, dying peacefully in her sleep a month after Devlin's visit. Mrs. Rowland had found her in the morning; Dr. Bell had been summoned at once, all for naught. Lizzie had penned a tearstained note to Devlin, breaking the sorrowful news.

The viscountess's frail body had been washed and lovingly prepared by the elder female servants, then enclosed in a pine box that would fit inside the magnificent white casket in which she was to be laid to rest; it was then conveyed to London for burial in the vault beside her husband at Westminster Abbey, who had gained that honor through some long-forgotten service to the King. Lizzie had cried her tears for Lady Strathmore at the villa, but her faith was such that she knew the woman had gone to a better place. Now her grief was for Devlin.

'He has no one else . . .'

Though she had denied the dowager's plea at the time, she was unable to refuse the dictates of her own heart. She had thought about Devlin constantly, though she had not seen him since the night of sensual abandon they had shared. But all that mattered now was finding him. Reaching him. Looking into his eyes and letting him know that he was not alone. She was determined to show him that he had her support on this awful day, just as his aunt had had it throughout the last months of her life.

She caught sight of him at last, a tall, stark, solitary figure before the cathedral, his face an emotionless mask. He and the other pallbearers must have carried the coffin in already; now he stood by the huge open doors of the ancient church, stoically greeting the endless line of mourners filing in for the service, his somber, elegant control never faltering as he thanked them for coming. But to Lizzie, he looked dazed, and the fact that he stood alone in the receiving line was unbearable to her.

As she stood beneath an old leafless tree in the churchyard, staring at him with the cold kiss of the rain wetting her face, a terrible sorrow crept through her as the knowledge sank in: he had been through this before. The present loss surely forced him to relive the triple funeral for his mother, father, and little sister years ago. To see him now was heartbreaking, but to think of him enduring this grim ritual as a newly orphaned seventeen-year-old simply shattered her.

Yet Devlin did not flinch. Locked inside himself, his taut control concealed to all but her how deeply he was suffering. With tears in her eyes for him and a lump in her throat, she fought her way blindly to him, pushing her way through the mob without concern. He chanced to look over and saw her coming through the crowd. For a heartbeat, they just stared at each other.

As she advanced, she saw the signs of strain around his hollowed eyes and mouth. The fractured look in his blue-green crystalline eyes would haunt her, she feared, for the rest of her days. She swallowed hard and pressed on to close the space between them.

When she reached him at last, no words came.

They stared at each other for a long moment in silence. All she wanted was to take him into her arms, but there were people everywhere, including a few dissolute-looking rogues who glanced at the two of them with interest. Lizzie ignored them.

'Oh, Devlin,' she whispered with a slow, earnest shake of her head. 'I'm so sorry.'

He dropped his gaze, barely hiding the way his eyes misted. 'Thank you. Thank you for coming,' he forced out, and though he grasped her hand politely, the same as he had everyone else's, his voice broke to a pained whisper as he said it.

'Of course I came,' she murmured, giving his gloved hand a reassuring squeeze. 'I wouldn't leave you to face this alone.'

Dev stared into her dove-gray eyes with the intensity of a man clinging to a lifeline. God, he had thought of her so often since leaving her room that night. From the second he had caught sight of her bravely marching toward him through the crowd, two warring impulses had instantly raged inside of him: He wanted to lay his head on her chest and let her soft arms surround him; at the same time, he wanted her to get the hell away from him – now. Before she made him crumble in front of these thousands of people. He already had a burning sort of lump in his throat that had not been there until he had seen her.

Unaware she was a threat to every last bloody one of his defenses, the girl searched his face with such tender concern that he could feel his brittle control fraying, strand by strand, until it hung by a thread. Somehow her simply being here made it seem as if everything would be all right. But it would not. She was naive. She did not understand the full cruelty of the world.

He did.

His aunt's death had reminded him with fresh, vivid clarity, lest he forget, exactly why he went through life in a state of well-defended solitude. Lizzie Carlisle's touch and coaxing little smile were mere salt in the wound, for he was not letting this into his life. Not now. Not ever. His mind was made up long ago. He was never going through this again.

Besides, he had no certain expectation of surviving the battle when it came time to move against his enemies, loitering nearby, so why should he let her get attached to him, either? He would not wish this grief on anyone.

Raw with pain, feeling utterly lost, Dev longed to accept the healing comfort she was so good at giving, but instead, he looked away and withdrew his hand stiffly from hers. There was still an endless line of mourners to be faced.

With a look of understanding, she followed his glance at the waiting queue. 'We'll talk later, all right?' she murmured, and gave his arm a gentle caress, trying to coax a glimmer of a smile from him. 'I'll buy you a cup of coffee at a café I know in Russell Square.'

'No – Miss Carlisle,' he forced out, fixing his stare above her head at the milling crowd beyond. 'I'm afraid that won't be possible.'

'Why?'

He could not bring himself to answer for a long moment. 'We can't see each other anymore.'

'But you said if I was ever in London—,' she started in a soft tone of wounded confusion.

He just looked at her.

She stared at him, sobering. Then slowly, emphatically, she shook her head at him. 'Don't do this, Devlin. This is no time to push your friends away. You shouldn't be alone at a time like this—'

'I'm used to it.'

'That's just the hurt talking, sweetheart, and I promise, it will pass. It's all right to lean on the people who care about you. I'm here for you. If you need me, just send for me at Knight House—'

'I don't – need you,' he wrenched out in a harsh whisper, grabbing her arm. He yanked her nearer for a second, bending to glare into her face in angry desperation. 'Don't you understand? I don't need anyone. Please go *away*.'

Her innocent eyes flared with hurt surprise; he saw that his sharp vehemence had frightened her. When she blurted out a barely audible, 'I'm sorry,' Dev released her helplessly and turned away, closing his eyes with a surge of self-hatred, his jaw clenched. The girl had nothing to be sorry for, of course, but he dared not say that for fear of her weakening him even more. *Shut her out. That is all.*

The impatient queue began nudging Lizzie aside, crowding her out as it snaked between them; she fell back like the pull of a riptide were carrying her away from him.

'Our condolences, Lord Strathmore.' A lady in a large black hat reached out to grasp his hand with polite formality.

'Thank you for coming, ma'am,' Dev said like an automaton.

'Her Ladyship will be greatly missed.'

'You're very kind. Do come in out of the weather. Take a seat inside.' He turned to the next person in line and repeated the ritual. But as the stream of black-clad mourners widened the gap between them, Dev eyed Lizzie through the crowd in dark, roiling hunger.

She still stood on the far side of the queue, staring at him, looking young and lost and so very fragile. Dev flinched when she turned away abruptly, pressing the backs of her fingers over her lips, and walked off blindly through the crowd.

He watched her hurry away, then closed his eyes in the most exquisite misery he had ever tasted. At that moment, he wished that someone would have run him through.

Oblivious of the false mourners who had come only to bid his aunt farewell because it was the fashionable thing to do, he dragged his eyes open again and watched Lizzie rushing off awkwardly through the crowd, bumping into people as she went, as though she were not quite watching where she was going. The look on her innocent face . . . As if he'd slapped her.

Well, he said brokenly to himself. *That's that, then.*

He told himself that it was for the best. *Love equals pain.* Lizzie Carlisle had come too close to getting under his skin as it was. The only sane thing to do had been to chase her off before her softness became his undoing.

'Who was that little morsel?' murmured Quint, sauntering over to Dev's side from where he had been finishing a cheroot before going into the Abbey.

Dev managed to refrain from sliding the leader of the Horse and Chariot Club a murderous glance. 'That was no one.'

'Ah, well, cheer up, old boy. That half a million pounds that just fell into your lap can buy you plenty more "no ones" to see you through your time of grief. Ha!' Quint clapped him on the back and went to crush out his cigar on the stone side of the Abbey.

Dev eyed his so-called friends with a guarded glance. Big, vulgar Quint was not entirely to blame for thinking that Dev's aunt had meant nothing to him, that he had cared only for her money, and today was only going through the motions. Familial obligations, after all, were but sap and sentimentality to the hardened men of the Horse and Chariot Club.

When Quint had returned to Carstairs and the others, Dev cast one last, furtive look in the direction Lizzie had gone. His swift scan of the crowded churchyard informed him she was gone. Though the realization left him desolate, it was just as well. There was no need for his enemies to know that the brown-haired girl in the olive pelisse was his last remaining Achilles' heel.

With a leaden heart, he went into the yawning darkness of the cathedral.

God, what I fool I am!

Her arms crossed tightly across her middle, Lizzie walked swiftly up the street, fighting not to cry as she stared at the rain-darkened pavement beneath her striding feet. Her head still reeled in hurt confusion and, with every step, she cursed both Devlin and herself. Surely she deserved the pain that now lanced her heart in reward for her ludicrous folly.

How could she have done it again? Once more, she had made more of her liaison with a charming, worldly rake than it had ever meant to him. Fool! What a fantastic imagination she must have, to have somehow fancied there had been something more between them than the awful loneliness of an oddball blue-stocking girl and the temporary boredom of a dissipated nobleman, who had been tricked, after all, into visiting his invalid aunt.

Devil Strathmore had clearly moved on. What else had she expected? If she had ever really meant anything to him, she would have heard from him again after the night they had shared, but he had not visited again nor even written to her, not a line.

Yes, she knew that it was his custom to pull back when he felt threatened, but her deepest doubts and fears supplied reasons aplenty for his coldness, reasons that were so much easier to believe. *Why should he want me? I'm an estate-keeper's daughter. Plain. Boring. Thoroughly ordinary . . .*

She'd had no reason in the world to believe the man had ever thought of her again since that night – and yet, believe, she had. But now the reality of the situation was all too clear: Devil Strathmore did not want her any more than Alec did.

God, she felt like the village idiot for daring to approach him on this most somber day. He probably had to strain to even remember who she was. So much for Lady Strathmore's muddle-headed notion of making Lizzie promise to look after him when she was gone. The dowager had obviously forgotten that the viscount had his fine Society ladies to comfort him now.

Somehow she managed to bring her angst under control by the time she reached Knight House on Green Park, quietly letting herself into the palatial town mansion of the Duke and Duchess of Hawkscliffe. It was here, to the bosom of the Knight family, that she had returned when Lady Strathmore's villa was closed up after her death. With their usual kindness and unstinting generosity, her former guardians had welcomed her back. To her surprise, they had kept her room just the way she liked it from when she had lived here, attending Jacinda during the Season. Yet for all its opulence, she thought with a sigh, her gaze trailing wistfully over the curved white staircase that floated up weightlessly to the upper floors, this was not really her home. It was just another place where she had existed on the fringes of other people's lives.

She had come here with the thought that she could make herself useful helping to care for little Bobby, Robert's two-year-old heir, especially now that Bel, the young duchess, was expecting her second child. Lizzie had quickly seen, however, that between his mother and his nurse, there was little need for her here; worse, at Knight House, she always ran the risk of running into Alec. So far, she had managed to avoid him.

The youngest Knight brother dwelled in first-rate bachelor lodgings at the Albany, but since the family show-place was so close to White's and Brooke's, where he spent so much of his time gambling, he was liable to drop by at any time, especially when seeking a 'loan' from his fabulously wealthy eldest brother. Perhaps the scoundrel could turn to his old chum, Strathmore, the next time he was short a few quid, she thought cynically. Devlin, after all, was about to take possession of the industrial fortune of Lady Ironsides.

Thrusting both men out of her mind, she took off her bonnet, which was half-ruined by the rain, and was unbuttoning her olive pelisse when the duke's supremely dignified butler, Mr. Walsh, strode into the spacious entrance hall.

'Why, Miss Carlisle, I apologize – I did not hear you come in,' he said with considerable warmth, for him.

She smiled at the tall, stately fellow with his meticulously trimmed gray side-whiskers. 'It's all right, Mr. Walsh. I can certainly open a door for myself. Where is everybody?'

He took her coat despite her refusal to stand on ceremony. 'Her Grace is in the music room with Ladies Winterley and—'

'Aunt Lizzie!' a high-pitched voice cried.

'Harry!' She brightened as the five-year-old came barreling at her, arms flung wide.

The five gorgeous children that the Knight clan had so far produced swarmed around her in the next moment, Harry determined to have her attention all to himself, while little Bobby tugged at her skirts with lordly insistence as if he were already beginning to understand he'd be one of the most powerful men in the realm someday.

Lucien's daughter, Pippa, plopped down at Lizzie's feet and began squealing happily for no apparent reason, while Damien's one-year-old twins came zooming across the floor at a speedy crawl, Andrew just a pace ahead of Edward for the moment.

'All of you, come away from the door. It's too drafty,' she protested, but she succeeded only in leading them a few feet into the middle of the entrance hall before they pulled her down to sit on the floor with them.

Her misery was forgotten sooner than she could have hoped, with babies crawling on her and toddlers hanging around her neck, Harry delivering a monologue all the while about the pony he was getting in the spring. How she loved the children. She was in a state of bliss as she played with them, completely ignoring her cares. Their mothers, Bel, Miranda, and Alice, were probably wondering where the wee ones had rushed off to; their nurses, on the other hand, were probably glad for a break.

The one person Lizzie was not expecting to appear at that moment was Alec.

The front door opened, and he strode in, his long, golden hair tousled – looking, in all, like some errant archangel who had just blown in on a passing cloud. Seeing Lizzie, Alec froze, his dark sapphire eyes blinking once in surprise; then he quickly shut the door, noting the children's presence.

As Mr. Walsh waited to take his coat, Alec stared at her surrounded by children, and for one heartbeat, both of them, Lizzie feared, glimpsed the future they might have had together if he had not wrecked it beyond repair. They had not seen each other since Jacinda's wedding last summer and had not spoken privately for even longer than that.

Harry broke the fleeting silence. 'Uncle Alec!' The boy charged his favorite uncle and dived on him. 'Hang me upside down! Please, please?'

'That's enough of you, fish bait,' Alec muttered in a jolly tone, grabbing the kid up in his arms and promptly dangling him by his ankles.

Harry let out a whoop of delight. 'Swing me!'

'Excuse us,' Alec drawled politely to Lizzie, then swung Harry back and forth with each slow step, as he carried him into the anteroom. He deposited the tot gently onto a large, cushy chair, poking a finger into the boy's chubby belly. 'Have at you, sir!'

Harry was on his feet in an instant, chasing Alec with uproarious laughter. 'Again! More!'

'Now you've got him riled up. Harry,' Lizzie chided in a gentle tone.

'Pippa!' Alec exclaimed, staring beyond her in sudden alarm.

Lizzie turned in surprise as he dashed past her and collected his tiny niece, who was just trying out her stair-climbing skills. Lizzie gasped at her own oversight, but Alec was already plucking the tot off the staircase before she climbed any higher. 'Hullo, sweetheart. Where do you think you're going?' Alec gave the baby's downy head a kiss, then carried her with astonishing gentleness against his chest, while Harry leaped onto his back and clung there, hitching a piggyback ride.

Alec played with them for a moment or two, but Lizzie refused to be charmed, never mind the fact that his easy manner with the children had always been one of the qualities she had always secretly found most adorable in him. The world outside might see the Corinthian, the ringleader of London rakehells, the mad chancer who would take any dare, any wager; the ton might quake in fright of his sardonic quips about their clothes; but all of that was largely just an act. His real father had been a handsome Shakespearean player, after all, one of the scandalous eighth duchess's many lovers. Alec was a chameleon like his actor-father, but in the domestic setting, the wee ones flocked to him, instantly sensing him for what he was – one of their own – a jolly playmate with a world of patience and an imagination that climbed to the stars.

A child at heart.

'Hullo, Bits,' he offered, trying out a rueful smile as she stood up, holding Andrew. Or was it Edward? 'It's nice to see you again.'

She flinched slightly at his old nickname for her, then noticed little Pippa studying her too intently by half. Just like her canny father, Lucien, that one. With the odd sensation that the child could detect her roiling emotions, she forced a taut smile. 'Likewise.'

Seeing that no reprisal was imminent – there were, after all, children present – Alec unleashed one of his dazzling reckless grins.

Lizzie looked away, clenching her teeth. Oh, this was harder than she had thought it would be. He was every bit as beautiful as before, only perhaps infinitesimally less sure of himself. She resisted the urge to ask how Lady Campion was treating him and refused to let herself wonder whether his famous luck had finally returned or if his losing streak continued.

The silence turned awkward; they directed their attention to the children; fortunately, the trio of young mothers glided into the entrance hall júst then with light steps and lavish smiles, like the three dancing goddesses from Botticelli's *La Primavera* come magically to life. Each one more beautiful than the next, Bel, Alice, and Miranda collected their stray babes, then greeted Lizzie with the quiet joy beaming in their eyes of women who had found their true places in the world. Their husbands arrived while they were all still convening in the hall – Robert, Lucien, and Damien – tall, handsome, black-haired men who radiated innate power and leadership. As each nuptial pair were affectionately reunited, Lizzie felt her heart sinking lower. Her solo status – and Alec's – had never felt more awkwardly apparent.

She kept a smile plastered on her face by sheer dint of will, but quickly realized that she could not bear to stay here. If seeing Alec were not uncomfortable enough, it hurt too much to be faced with the constant reminder of what she would never have. Besides, it would not be right to stay and drive a wedge between Alec and his family. They were *his* family, after all. They all had been so angry at him for what he'd done last summer, and had felt so sorry for her, that all of them had taken her side after his transgression. Now that she was back, she had no desire to rekindle their displeasure with him. It was best for her to go.

Later that evening, she wrote to Mrs. Hall in the village of Islington just north of London, accepting the teaching position she had been offered at the girls' school that the imperious headmistress had run for decades. Bed and board were included in the pay. The next day, bright and early, she arrived at Mrs. Hall's Academy for Young Ladies with a portmanteau under each arm.

For a long moment after the hackney coach she'd hired had driven away, she just stood in the dirt road, staring at the fine old redbrick manor that housed the school, tucked behind a white picket fence. The same green ivy grew up the walls; the same white columns steadied the portico. The big, old mulberry tree still stood sentry near the corner of the school, while the even older oak leaned over the flagged footpath leading up to the stately entrance.

Jacinda and she had attended here for two years, and while the duke's daughter had been a mischievous rebel and a general headache to Mrs. Hall, Lizzie had soon distinguished herself as a star pupil. She had liked the studies, the schedule, the predictable routine. She had liked finally finding a place where she could shine despite the fact that she had neither wealth nor rank like the other girls.

Yes, she thought, taking a deep breath, she could be reasonably content here in this safe world of women. Not a single London rake in sight. Nothing here had changed, and in an uncertain world, that was a welcome relief. She could belong here, in a fashion. How long she could actually be happy before she grew restless remained to be seen.

She pushed the gnawing thought away, squared her shoulders, went through the squeaky front gate, and walked resolutely toward the school in anticipation of her new life. And yet she felt a vague shame, as though once more, she was running away from something she probably ought to have faced.

Once more, as Lady Strathmore had said, she was hiding.

Repairs to the gaudy pavilion were finished at last. All was ready. The answers he sought were almost in reach. Tonight, if all went according to plan, Dev would gain the inner circle of the Horse and Chariot Club.

No turning back now.

The full moon hung over the marshes, and Dev stood outside the pavilion at the top of the curved double staircase, slowly smoking a cheroot and waiting with brooding patience for his enemies to arrive.

He knew the exact moment that they breached the massive gates, for in the tranquil silence of the black spring night, beneath the undulant song of the frogs in the desolate acres of reeds and mud, he detected the distant thunder of galloping hoofbeats. He felt the deep drumming of it in his chest as the riders swept closer.

'See that all is made ready,' he murmured to a nearby servant, not taking his stare off the long stretch of moonlit drive. 'And shut the doors.'

'Yes, milord.' The majordomo bowed and pulled the fanciful double doors shut, whisking off to make one last check on the chef in the kitchens and the whores in the garish salons.

From somewhere inside, a sharp burst of melody sprang from a nimble bow as one of the hired musicians gave his violin a last-minute tuning.

Dev's vision adjusted quickly to the light of the moon and the few flambeaux burning in the courtyard. In the distance, he could just make out the silver sparkle of the Thames; eerie bog lights flashed across the marshes like tiny lightning storms. His wilderness-honed instincts narrowed in on the first of the riders to burst into view, barreling up the road.

At the head of the pack, the riders were the first to spy the brightly lit pavilion standing alone in the middle of the bog. Behind them streamed the rest of the brotherhood, tearing along at breakneck speed. The wan moonlight glowed on sleek phae tons, gleaming black coaches, racing drags, exquisitely kept cabriolets – all drawn by the finest horses money could buy.

Dev folded up his hatred and hid it away, idly twirling his favorite walking stick with its concealed knife inside as he ambled down the stairs, bracing himself for his hard-won role of master of ceremonies on this crucial night. God knew it had cost him enough.

He had stopped sending his bills to Aunt Augusta's after his visit to her villa all those weeks ago; having realized Miss Carlisle was monitoring his expenses, he had not wanted to damage her opinion of him with his ongoing profligacy. Instead, the bills now sat in a growing mound on the escritoire in his study, awaiting the day that the papers were signed and his aunt's fortune officially became his. The reading of the will was scheduled to take place in a fortnight at tidy little Charles Beecham's office. As far as Dev could tell, the lads of the Horse and Chariot Club were more excited about his inheritance than he was.

Reaching the bottom of the grand staircase, he sprang up with an agile leap onto the wrought-iron handrail and curled his arm jauntily around the lamppost, greeting the arriving men while a score of liveried grooms marched out to attend their horses.

In another moment, the courtyard began filling up with flashy vehicles from which the most notorious rakes of London alighted. They glanced around in wary fascination at their strange surroundings. He lifted his hand to them in a cordial wave.

Over by the mounting block, Julian, Lord Carstairs stepped down from his racing drag and drew off his driving gauntlets, passing a haughty glance over the building. With flaxen hair and sharp, fine features, the elegant earl looked a decade younger than his forty years. He had a neat, lean build, impeccable clothes, and was joined this evening, as he often was, by his handsome young plaything known to the rest of them only as Johnny.

Johnny, Dev had noticed, was a jealously devoted lover. The fiery-eyed young man did not appear to care at all for the speculative way Carstairs often smiled at Dev.

Next, Dog Berkeley, Nigel Waite, and Raskell Bainbridge came tumbling out of a large black coach amid riotous laughter with the thin, emaciated Dr. Eden Sinclair in their midst, his ubiquitous black bag in hand. It appeared the obliging doctor had treated each of them to one of his specially concocted injections in a back room of the gambling hell they had just left.

Dev's sharp gaze swung next to the enormously rotund Sir Tommy Fane, a cutthroat financier who had gained power by making huge donations to the Tory party, then more or less extorted a baronetcy out of his friends in the government. His light carriage tilted dangerously as the man struggled to squeeze his great girth out of the driver's seat, cursing up a storm at the indignity of it. Big Tom was the secretary of the club, and possibly the richest member, though Carstairs was also fabulously wealthy.

The feared duelist, Sir Torquil aka Blood Staines was the next to join them, eyeing everyone mistrustfully and stroking his small devil's beard as he sauntered over. He was joined by the Holy Rotter, the ex-Reverend James Oakes, the disgraced younger son of a marquess, who had recently written his way out of debtor's prison by composing pornographic poems that were all the rage in the gentlemen's clubs of Saint James's. The drunken, zigzag pattern of Oakes's walk nearly got him run over by the handsome curricle that bounded in behind the men, but Staines grabbed him by the collar and yanked him out of the way before he was run down.

The newly arrived curricle had barely stopped when young Dudley, 'the Booby,' leaped out, full of his pupyish, fresh-faced enthusiasm.

'Dev! Hullo, Dev! Cheerio, lads!'

Dev nodded. 'Your Grace.'

The naive young duke was the only one Dev did not consider a possible suspect. Poor empty-headed Dudley hadn't the slightest inkling of just how far out of his depth he was among these men; fortunately, he had his cold-blooded cousin, Alastor Hyde, looking after him, and slowly bilking the cheery young Dudley out of his vast fortune.

Last of all came Quint Barnes, Baron Randall, who leaped out of his phaeton with a style much imitated by the rest. A flask in one hand, the stump of a cigar clamped between his teeth, Quint swaggered toward the pavilion. The others parted to let him pass. Damage Randall, as he enjoyed being called, had a flashing grin and a manly sort of vulgar charisma. He had taken a particular liking to Dev on account of his inheritance and his bold adventures, and this had proved most advantageous, as the others all seemed to do exactly as Quint said.

Dev waited for the rest of them with the patience of a spider, his features schooled into a slight, enigmatic smile.

'Well, Strathmore,' Quint drawled as the others gathered around the bottom of the steps, 'you've got us here. I admit we are intrigued. What is this place?'

Dev paused for effect, letting them wait; then he jumped down abruptly from the railing and into their midst.

'Follow me,' he murmured with a wily smile. He dashed ahead of them up the stairs like the pied piper with so many rats in his thrall. At the top, he strode to the pavilion's double doors and threw them open wide.

The bright illumination from inside spilled out, luring them in. With looks of wonder and puzzlement, the rakes filed into the octagonal foyer with its red-painted ceiling and touches of gilt. Its tall, mirrored walls scattered the brilliance of the lavish chandelier hanging above them, but the interior doors to all the various galleries and salons were firmly closed. The night itself seemed to be holding its breath.

Dev walked in last and pulled the doors shut. As he strode through their midst, he caught a brief glimpse of his reflection in the surrounding mirrors and was secretly bemused at how convincingly he had assimilated his role as a decadent fiend among the damned: the candle glow played over the rich red velvet of his coat; his unbound hair spilled over his collar. He wore no cravat but a black silk neckerchief carelessly knotted around his throat – even the wicked sparkle in his eyes was disturbingly authentic. But it was no wonder. The role he played was merely a reflection of the debauched roué he would indeed have become if Aunt Augusta had not sent him away all those years ago.

That was precisely why they believed it.

Carstairs eyed him appreciatively as he brushed past. Dev sent him a veiled smile, willing to use whatever it took to obtain the answers he sought.

He leaned against the interior double doors of dark mahogany and faced his companions with a devious hint of a smile playing at his lips. 'Gentlemen, my lords, assorted nasty bastards: You have for some time now been apprised of my desire to be found worthy of your esteemed company. Having passed the first round of requirements to your satisfaction, I now submit to you my offering to the club. Exclusively for the members of the old Horse and Chariot, specifically rendered to cater to each of your various . . . needs.' He glanced from man to man with a knowing smile, for he had studied them well. 'I trust you shall find everything within to delight and stimulate whatever – urges may come upon you.'

'Hear, hear,' some murmured, laughing softly, their grins widening as they caught wind of a first-rate orgy brewing.

'And so, gentlemen,' Dev went on smoothly, 'without further ado, allow me to present your new den of delectations, your paradise of pleasures—' He laid it on thick with flamboyant showmanship. 'Esteemed members of the Horse and Chariot, I give you – the new lodgings for your club!' With a sharp, sudden rap from his walking stick, he banged open the mahogany doors.

They stared into the pavilion, slack-jawed.

No one moved or spoke.

Quint was the first to break their spellbound silence, letting out a low, hearty laugh that built and grew in volume. 'Devil, you mad son of a bitch.' Slapping Dev affectionately on his cheek, the brawny baron sauntered past him and through the open doorway, leading the others inside.

They followed warily, gazing all around them at the disorienting swirls of the restored color murals and candycane columns. At once, the orchestra struck up a fast tune that reverberated out across the marshes, but the festivities only began in earnest when the whores flitted out to greet the men, scantily costumed as wood nymphs with silver net wings and crowns of ivy twined around their hair.

The giggling girls pressed glasses of wine to the men's lips, luring them farther into the pavilion. Upstairs, each themed chamber featured women appropriately costumed to suit the setting, be it Egypt, Jungle, or Ancient Rome – a nice touch, he thought, that had been suggested to him by Mother Iniquity, the rakes' favorite London procuress of fine female flesh.

Dev smiled indulgently at the girls. Strolling along after the others, he clasped his hands behind his back in aloof and rather worldly satisfaction. A wan smile curved his mouth when he saw Big Tom's gluttonous joy upon discovering the sumptuous banquet table laden with meats, puddings, plump steaming rolls, exotic cheeses, fruits and cakes, and rich desserts of every description. An entire wall of the dining room was dedicated solely to the selection of ports and sherries.

Quint swaggered into the dining room a while later and greeted Dev with a laugh.

'Ah, there he is, sly fox!' Quint slung his arm around Dev's neck and steered him toward the liquor. 'You know, Strathmore, I must admit, life has become much more interesting since you've been around. Something like this would never even have occurred to the others. They're such a bore. But you, my lad, you are the genuine article.' Quint slapped him on the back. 'Daresay you remind me of me as a younger man.'

'Do I, indeed?' he answered, none too pleased, though he forced a smile.

Quint summoned the uniformed waiter behind the bar to pour them both a drink.

'So, when will I know the club's decision?' Dev prompted.

'Not so fast, old boy,' Quint replied with an immoral gleam in his eyes. 'You haven't yet fulfilled the third requirement.'

'Which is?'

Quint laughed and leered at him.

Dev gave him a shrewd look of question.

'You'll soon find out, won't you? Cheers.'

'Cheers,' Dev murmured a trifle uneasily; then they both tossed back their scotch in one gulp.

An hour later, Quint had gathered the others into the largest salon. The carpet was scarlet, the ceiling draped in swathes of gold silk like a sultan's tent. When all the club members had arrived in the room, Quint swaggered into the center, idly swirling another draught of scotch in his glass. 'Right, then. Shall we call this meeting to order?' he bellowed.

The company let out a raucous cheer and thumped their glasses on the tables.

Grinning, Quint turned to Dev.

He noticed the snickers and sly glances the men were exchanging and began to wonder what he had gotten himself into this time.

'We've had many members over the years,' Quint addressed them. 'And, as you know, one of the constant requirements is a worthy gift to the group. You, Strathmore, have accomplished that tonight in spades. Hear, hear,' he added, offering Dev a toast.

The others held up their glasses, as well.

'Hear, hear! Good man!'

'To Strathmore!'

Dev sketched a sardonic bow.

'And so, having collected the votes,' Quint continued, holding up his hand to quiet the others, 'we have an answer for you, Devil. You're in.'

'Huzzah!' cried young Dudley.

'Well, that is bloody good news,' Dev said, exhaling.

'There is just one more little . . . test,' Carstairs spoke up with a mysterious half-smile.

Quint let out a low, rough laugh and gestured to a couple of the men. They strode out of the room and returned a moment later.

Dev's sardonic smile faded as they dragged in a terrified country lass who could not have been more than fifteen.

She fought and shrieked and tried to pull free of the men's hold, to no avail. Then she gave up and hung her head, crying.

His heart pounded with building wrath.

'Her name is Susannah,' Quint informed him, his lewd gaze running over the youngster. 'We picked her up in Hertfordshire yesterday afternoon taking her little herd of geese to market. Lovely specimen, ain't she? Plump and soft and squirming with fright – just the way I like 'em!' Quint laughed. 'She thought she'd flirt with us a little, but you got more than you bargained for, didn't you, Suzy?'

Their hapless victim sobbed.

'You must be blooded, dear boy,' Carstairs murmured.

Dev looked at him, not entirely able to hide his stunned reaction.

'Take her, Strathmore,' Quint murmured, turning to stare hard at him, a lawless challenge in his eyes. 'Take her maidenhead.'

Dev glanced around at the men's flushed faces and fevered eyes. He could feel the unspoken question hanging over his head like a very sword of Damocles: *Are you one of us or aren't you?*

'How bad are you, Devil?' Carstairs inquired.

Dev looked again at the terrified girl. Little more than a child, really.

Despoiling a virgin.

But of course. He should have known.

Deflowering virgins was as common a hobby to men of his class as attending the races at Ascot, God knew, but usually they were hardened young creatures from the rookery who sold themselves willingly at the launch of a possibly lucrative career servicing the wealthy men of London. This poor creature, bamboozled, abducted, had probably never even seen the great metropolis before, and had surely never dreamed that men like this existed in the world. God, he hated them.

Her chin trembled, but by now the country lass looked too scared to cry. Though pale from her ordeal, she was sturdily built, a farmer's daughter with a disheveled mop of reddish-blonde curls, apple cheeks, and liquid brown eyes that reminded him of a panicked calf that somehow knew it was destined for a veal fricassee.

Damn it. Anger filled his veins, but he drew on all his considerable control to summon up his best finesse, for he knew the only way to get the chit out of here unscathed was to appear to go along with their wishes – in spades. Indeed, there was extreme danger to both of them if he failed to play his role as ravisher convincingly.

'Take her, Dev,' Quint urged in a whisper, smiling slightly, his hard, lustful gaze running over every inch of the girl's body. 'If you don't, you're out. If you don't,' he added, 'I will.'

Susannah let out a cry of fright at this; the men laughed at her terror. The sound jolted Dev out of his frozen rage.

Launching smoothly into action, he let out a wicked-sounding snicker and sauntered toward the girl.

'I daresay I shall enjoy this. You nearly had me worried for a moment, boys, but if this is your idea of a test,' he drawled, 'by all means, set the bar as high as you like.' Dev cupped her chubby face tenderly. 'There, there, little pumpkin,' he said indulgently, 'no one is going to hurt you. You will enjoy this almost as much as I will. I promise.' With a sharp, wolfish glance, he caused the two men holding her arms to release her.

The moment they stepped back, she tried to run. Dev grabbed her around her waist and hauled her in close to his body. He hated scaring her, but he knew he had to give them a show or they would be too suspicious to leave them in privacy.

'Perhaps we'll watch,' Quint suggested.

'Perhaps you'll learn something,' he retorted. A few of them laughed at his insolent quip. 'Never fear, gentlemen,' he assured them. 'I can handle this little dumpling on my own.'

'We shall require proof afterwards that the deed has been done.' Leaning in an elegant pose by the wall, Carstairs studied him in his cold, calculating way, his arms folded across his chest.

'Then you shall have it.' Dev caught the girl's face in his hand, tipping her head back none too gently. 'Shan't he, dearie?' He swooped down and kissed her neck.

Susannah pushed wildly against Dev's chest. Without warning, he heaved her up onto his shoulder amid delighted laughter from the men. They laughed harder as the girl fought with renewed terror.

'Ow! Be still, damn you!' he bellowed in a jovial tone when she kneed him in the ribs. Then he clapped his hand over her round rump and carried her off down the hallway.

'Be quiet!' Dev ordered her as he opened the door to one of the low-lit chambers. He glanced warily into the room. It was painted scarlet and had a large bed piled with black satin pillows. A swath of thick, sable fur served as a coverlet. Good Lord, had he paid good money for such sleazy decor? he wondered, though it was hard to think above Suzy's copious weeping.

'Oh, please, don't hurt me! Please, sir, have pity! I'm a good girl—'

'Calm down, for God's sake! I'm not going to touch you,' he muttered as he stalked into the awful room and dumped young Suzy off his shoulder and onto the bed.

At once, she scuttled across it, fleeing to the other side to escape him. Dev rolled his eyes, stalked back to the door, and locked it. For a moment, he listened to make sure no one was eavesdropping; then he turned around, scowling with fury over the situation the bastards had put him in.

'Oh, please let me go, sir! Don't hurt me! I want to go home—'

'Would you *please* shut up for two seconds so I can think?'

She stopped abruptly, gazing vacantly at him.

'I am not going to touch you. I give you my word.'

'But y-you k-kissed me, and you said—'

'For show, all for show!' he whispered harshly. 'I did it to fool them; otherwise, they would have insisted on watching, and that would have made things a good deal worse.'

'But—'

'I already have a lady, Susannah. Trust me, if I am feeling amorous, I will go to her. You're just a – a child. For God's sake, I had a sister once. I'm not going to touch you. I know you've had a terrible fright, but try to calm down. My name is Lord Strathmore, and I give you my word of honor that I will get you out of here safely and back to your family.'

At the mention of her family, his words finally seemed to sink in.

'They said you're from Hertfordshire. Is this true?'

She gave him a wary nod.

'What is the name of your village?'

'S-Stevenage.'

'Excellent. With any luck, we'll get you home to Stevenage before the rooster crows. But you are going to have to help me.'

'H-How?'

He pursed his mouth and glanced around at the chamber, racking his brains. His gaze homed in on the empty wineglass one of the whores had left in the room, judging by the imprint of rouged lips on the rim. 'Groan,' he said abruptly. 'And shake the bed.'

'What?'

'You heard me.' Wrapping the wineglass in his discarded velvet jacket to muffle the sound, he stepped on it, feeling it crush beneath his foot. This done, he bent down and unfolded the swaddling of his coat, then picked up a large glass shard, studying it for a second. He lifted his shirt off over his head, ignoring the girl's alarmed gasp.

'Lord Strathmore, what are you—?' Her words broke off.

Dev grimaced against the sting as he used the shard of broken glass like a dagger, cutting a small gash in his left side. 'They want blood, Susannah,' he said through gritted teeth. 'I have no intention of giving them yours.'

He only hoped the blackguards believed the ruse, for if they guessed the truth, Dev had a fair idea that Suzy and he might both find themselves buried at the bottom of the swamp.

Chapter Nine

Waiting for Strathmore to complete his initiation, Carstairs paid little mind as Johnny leaned his hip on the wide, scrolled arm of the couch and lounged beside him, stroking his hair and filling his ear with coaxing whispers about what they could do together in the Ancient Rome chamber. He no longer bothered to hide his boredom with his possessive young lover, though God knew he had groomed Johnny from a tender age for the express purpose of giving him pleasure. At the moment, he was more interested in waiting for Strathmore to emerge with the girl. They had gone in nearly an hour ago, and now he could hear them as their voices and the banging crescendoed.

'Yes, yes!'

'That's right, Suzy. Take it all.'

'Oh, Lord *Strath*more, *please*!'

'I say, are you sure the wench was a virgin?' Big Tom asked through a mouthful of food, with much more piled on his plate.

Alastor nodded sagely. 'Mother Iniquity guaranteed it.'

'Never heard a virgin sound like that before,' the Holy Rotter remarked. 'Mine never do, anyway.'

'You're not Devil Strathmore,' Quint interjected from behind the tangled limbs of the wood nymph on his lap.

They laughed.

'By Jove, I guess his reputation with the ladies must be true!' young Dudley declared with a vacant grin from ear to ear.

'You rush them, Oakes. That's your problem,' Quint instructed. 'Take your time, and they'll let you do whatever you please.'

'Since when are you the expert?' Oakes retorted, but Carstairs remained silent, ignoring their banter with all his attention focused on that closed door. He was unbearably aroused.

His errant imagination easily conjured up images of the seduction taking place within, images that excited him infinitely more than did Johnny's subtle but insistent, all-too-familiar touch. His mind wandered back to the night years ago that he had almost seduced young Strathmore himself, though he was sure the man had no memory of it.

A decade ago, Carstairs had done his best to leave the horror of the fire behind, but a year and a half after it had happened, young Strathmore had showed up in Society – nineteen, gorgeous, and utterly lost. His heartbreaking beauty would have been enough to catch the earl's discerning eye, but knowing the terrible pain driving the youth's wild dissipation – knowing that he in part had caused it – had captured Carstairs's undivided attention.

He had felt an immediate bond between himself and young Strathmore, though they had never met. From a cautious distance, he had watched the young rake's every move in guilty fascination, longing to soothe the hurt he'd caused. But having so much to hide, Carstairs had dared not approach him.

Then one night, after a mutual friend's bachelor party, he had found young Dev alone, passed out drunk on the cool tile floor of their host's conservatory, lying like the lovely Narcissus next to a trickling indoor fountain.

After the drunken revelries of that night, the youth had

removed his cravat and unbuttoned his shirt, and had splashed water all over his face and smooth, muscled chest in a half-hearted attempt to sober up. Carstairs saw him and could have wept at the havoc he had wreaked on the beautiful boy, so vulnerable, so alone. He remembered how he had sat down on the stone brim of the fountain, the lad sleeping at his feet.

'Devlin,' he had said softly. 'Do you want me to take you home?'

His amazing blue-green eyes had opened to slits. His voice had been slurred. 'No, thanks, I'll sleep 'ere.'

Carstairs had smiled faintly, longing to touch him. 'Do you know who I am?'

'Should I? No. Sorry. I'm so fuckin' drunk.'

'I know. It's all right. I'm Lord Carstairs,' he had told him in a soothing tone. 'You probably won't remember this tomorrow, but I want you to know that if you ever need . . . help, you can come to me.'

'What?' he had mumbled, then had turned over on the hard tiles and had gone back to sleep.

Carstairs had stayed there for nearly a quarter hour, staring at him, fighting the trembling impulse to reach down and caress that silky-smooth chest. Instead, he had restrained himself to merely grazing the backs of his fingers against the lad's tousle of thick, black hair, for he could not resist.

Then, in an agony of lust, he had stood up and walked away. He had always been a little too fond of taking risks, but back then, he had been so scared of Society learning of his proclivities and banishing him that he had hidden his true nature. Indeed, he had been scared enough to bring down hell on earth to hide it.

Eventually, as the years passed, he had realized everyone had sensed it anyway and didn't care. As it turned out, his title and his wealth had been enough all along to protect him from those fearsome ancient laws that ordered death for men like him. Jaded as he was, not even Carstairs could stomach the irony of it. After the hellish thing he had done, it seemed to him that now his only hope for redemption was Dev. The boy he had wronged so bitterly alone had the power to free him. Now Strathmore was back, and Carstairs hungered for him.

Nor did his desire seem beyond the realm of possibility. Dev's suave smiles seemed to suggest he enjoyed Carstairs's subtle flirtations. His hand trembled slightly as Carstairs lifted his drink to his lips. Johnny muttered some sulky barb all of a sudden and gave up trying to gain his attention. His pretty boy went prowling off in a huff, shooting him a dirty look from across the room as he went and hung on a few of the costumed wood nymphs in a pitiful attempt to make Carstairs jealous.

Handsome as his strapping Johnny was, the harlots were dazzled, but Carstairs merely smirked. At least now the lad had sought his own kind. In disgusted amusement, Carstairs watched his young lover making a fool of himself, when Staines stalked over to him, looking as tense and cagey as ever.

By God, the infamous duelist was a cocked pistol that could go off at any time, he thought wearily, but over the years, Carstairs had learned how to manage him. Indeed, he had learned how to manage them all.

'Good evening, Staines,' he drawled, but Staines did not even notice Carstairs's debonair smile. The man glanced back and forth in paranoia. 'What's the matter, Torq?'

'I don't like it,' he growled.

'Like what?'

'This place,' he snarled. 'It don't smell right.'

'What are you talking about?'

'It's a trap. I can feel it.'

'Oh, Staines, don't start that again. We've already discussed it—'

'You're blind, you and Quint both! Strathmore knows, I tell you! He's toying with us. Let me get rid of him before he starts anything. I can do it easily—'

'He doesn't know anything,' Carstairs soothed.

'Yes, he does, Carstairs, and I can prove it. Come on, there's something you need to see. Quint, too.'

'What is it?' Carstairs asked dubiously, loath to walk away with Staines for fear of missing the delicious moment when Dev came out of the room after forcing himself on the girl.

He yearned to see the look on Dev's face – and on the lass's. Himself, he could only wonder what it would be like to be ravished by Devil Strathmore.

'There's a picture in the ballroom of Ginny Highgate,' Staines informed him in a low tone.

This took Carstairs entirely off guard.

He turned to Staines in surprise, then smoothly masked his astonishment. Someone around here had to keep a cool head, after all. 'Really?' he asked in a bored tone.

'Come and see it. I'll get Quint. He'll want to see this, too.'

'No. Trust me – it will only set him off.' Carstairs knew that, obviously, Ginny Highgate had been on Quint's mind since they had walked into this place.

Years ago, most of male London had flocked here to see her, and poor, thick-headed Quint, as far as Carstairs knew, had never missed a show. Fortunately, the baron had been able to distract himself from the memories tonight in the same way he always did – with women and drink.

Across the gaudy red salon, Quint sat with a lithe young wood nymph straddling his lap, her arms twined around him. Naturally, she was a redhead. Quint and his goddamned redheads.

Carstairs sighed and shook his head. 'Leave the poor clod alone for now,' he murmured.

Staines gave him a wary nod; then they went to see the portrait.

Irish *bitch*, Carstairs thought as he stared at Ginny Highgate's smug smile in the small painting a few minutes later. But he refused to be convinced that beautiful Dev was leading them into treachery. 'This means nothing,' he declared, rising again.

Staines scoffed. 'Don't you find it a bit coincidental?'

'There are pictures here of all the women who used to star in the shows. So what?'

'So what?' Staines hissed, his intense black eyes flashing. 'You're blind! He's taunting us! Can't you see that?'

'Strathmore doesn't even know who Ginny Highgate is, trust me.'

'Why are you protecting him?' Staines demanded. 'Oh, but of course I know why, you bloody goddamn sod. You're infatuated.'

'How's your daughter?' Carstairs countered softly, staring at him in icy calm.

Staines's eyes flickered dangerously at the question.

'Oh, sorry, I mean your niece,' he corrected himself. 'I forgot she doesn't know who her real papa is. People who live in glass houses, dear. Staines. Tsk, tsk. How is your child's sweet mother doing, by the way? Your mistress . . . your pretty sister?'

'You leave them out of this,' Staines warned him in a vehement whisper.

'Then you do as you're told,' Carstairs snarled back at him, his tone turning ruthless. 'Nobody touches Strathmore *unless* and *until* I say.'

'Something wrong, boys?'

They looked over as Quint swaggered toward them. He looked quite drunk, and for a moment, Carstairs worried. Now that he was growing older, Quint had two modes when in his cups: sloppy sentimentality or rage.

Carstairs preferred sentimentality.

With his size and pugnacity, Quint was transformed by

wrath into a raging bull that trampled everything in his path – just as he had trampled Ginny Highgate. Carstairs had never really meant for it to happen. After Ginny had walked in on him with the boy all those years ago, Carstairs had put the lie in Quint's ear merely to make sure the great brute kept his mistress in line. It was not such an outlandish lie, after all; it might have happened easily enough. Ginny was, after all, just a glorified whore, and Carstairs had far more money, better looks, more brains, and a higher rank than Quint.

He had not foreseen the baron's overreaction to his fiction; but it was certainly not he who had told Quint to beat the poor woman and rape her. To wit, he'd had no reason to suspect that Ginny would run, taking Johnny with her. How close they'd all come to disaster. Not wishing to stir Quint's hot temper with the past, he tried to move discreetly in front of the redhead's portrait on the wall, but was too late.

'What the devil?' Quint murmured, his hazel eyes narrowing. Slowly, he bent down and stared at it. With a look of pain, he ran his fingertips alongside the small painting of his dead love.

'See, Quinty?' Staines urged him. 'Carstairs refuses to believe it, but here's proof that I was right all along. Strathmore is setting us up. He *knows*.'

The baron did not seem to hear, but Staines shot Carstairs a gloating look, for the bruiser Quint had never shrunk from a fight in all his days.

Carstairs saw that if Quint agreed with Staines, it would not be easy for him to block them. Of course, he was smarter than both of them put together and had managed to control them for twelve years as a result, but he never allowed himself to grow complacent. He had gotten roughed up by bigger lads too many times as a boy not to realize that brains, alas, did not always trump brawn.

'Come on, Quint, what do you think?' Staines prodded him.

Quint glanced up uncertainly, his questioning gaze a million miles away. 'Huh?'

'He's on to us, I tell you! He brought us here deliberately to toy with our heads!'

Quint frowned and slowly straightened up to his full height, but Staines was not finished.

'Tell Carstairs we need to solve this problem now, before it starts.'

'No,' Quint said softly, shaking his head. 'I won't do it. I like Strathmore.'

Staines's jaw dropped. 'Not you, too, Quint!'

'He's a good sort. Leave him alone, Torq. He doesn't know anything. How could he? He was only a boy at the time.'

Carstairs folded his arms across his chest and smirked at Staines, who threw up his hands.

'We took a blood oath!' Staines thundered. 'We created this club, got others to hide behind – now you're acting blind! Strathmore's not a boy any longer.'

'I said drop it, Torquil,' Quint repeated.

'I will not! This is absurd! I can't believe you two! Carstairs wants to bend over for him, and you're trying to relive your youth through the man! Am I the only one who can see this bastard's got the whole club in his crosshairs? I am *not* going to the gibbet for you two sons of a bitch. I didn't do it.'

'You helped,' Carstairs coolly reminded him.

Staines turned to the baron. 'Quint—'

Without warning, Quint slammed Staines against the wall with all its myriad smiling portraits and jammed his thick, hairy forearm across the man's throat. 'I said drop it,' he ordered. 'Understand? It's in the past, Torq. As far as I'm concerned, it *never happened*.'

'You haven't got the stomach for it! Both of you have gone soft!'

'Don't push me, Staines,' Quint growled.

'Boys, boys.' Carstairs leaned against the wall beside the spot where Quint dangled Staines up on his toes. He looked from one to the other with another suave smile. It was ever so pleasant having a tame giant of one's own. 'I propose that we agree to leave Strathmore alone for another month or two, continue to watch him, just as we have been doing, then reconsider at that time as to whether or not we have cause to suspect him. If he makes one wrong move, why, then, Torquil, you may have him. Until then, let him be presumed innocent until proven guilty. I daresay he's suffered enough. Agreed?'

'Agreed,' Quint murmured, nodding.

'Innocent? By the time he's proved guilty, we could be on the gallows!' Staines choked out.

Quint smashed his arm harder against the man's throat.

'I'm not worried,' Carstairs said.

'Neither am I,' Quint agreed.

'Fine,' Staines growled at last.

Quint released him. As Staines stalked away from them with a surly look, Quint loosened up his big prize-fighter's shoulders with a restless shrug.

'Well done,' Carstairs said, giving the brute a friendly slap on his bulging arm.

Quint immediately pulled away, bristling. 'Don't touch me.' He shot Carstairs a look of wary contempt, then strutted back to his latest redheaded whore.

Carstairs absorbed the unearned insult in silent chagrin.

How droll it was to think that he could once have wanted an ogre like Quint, years ago, when he had first seen him – a towering, tanned, young barbarian with a body of steel. That was ages ago, when he had been less discriminating in his tastes, well before Quint had developed that saggy paunch around his middle, too. When the baron had first come to London from the wilds of Yorkshire, Carstairs had helped him acquire a bit of polish – Town Bronze – lust, his ulterior motive. But he had never actually attempted to entice the man, realizing all it would get him was a fist in his face, and it would have been a great shame to mar the perfection of Carstairs's handsome nose.

He would have been perfectly happy if he never laid eyes on Quint again, or on Staines, for that matter, but they were bound together by their blood oath of secrecy, tied to each other in guilt and hatred and pain. How Carstairs longed for a new start.

As he ambled back toward the flamboyant tented salon, hands in his impeccable trouser pockets, he heard rude cheering down the hallway and glanced over just as Devil Strathmore emerged from the private chamber with his blushing virgin.

Carstairs smiled. *Ex*-virgin.

Then he shuddered a little, staring at the conquering hero. Strathmore was flushed and sweaty, his shirt hanging open down his muscled chest. His black hair was tousled; holding up his black trousers with one hand, he asked in a scratchy voice if anyone had a cheroot.

The lads laughed at his satyric smile.

Someone handed him a lit cigar and he took a puff, sighing smoke from it as though it was the best thing he had ever tasted in his life. He slung his other arm around the young girl's shoulders and blew the smoke over her head.

She huddled closer to him, slipping her arms around his waist and burying her face against him in embarrassment as the old crone, Mother Iniquity, slipped into the room behind them and certified by the blood on the sheets that the deed had been done.

Carstairs laughed under his breath and shook his head to himself, relieved that Dev had just played right into his hands.

If it turned out he *was* deceiving them, it would be so much easier to keep him under control now that they could hold this misdeed over his head. The club provided the unblemished lamb for the sacrifice, but each aspirant had the privilege of slitting his own throat. It was not a matter of virgin-deflowerment, when it came down to it, but of gaining leverage over every man in their organization, should a test of loyalty or the need for some strong persuasion ever arise.

Who really needed brawn, anyway? Carstairs mused, gloating a little as the newest member of the Horse and Chariot Club led his traumatized victim out of the room. Brains won nine times out of ten, and blackmail was such an efficient solution.

'Do you th-think they believed us?' the frightened girl whispered, clinging to Dev as he walked her outside.

'Oh, yes. I'd say we were fairly convincing.' During the hour they had spent in that bedroom, Dev had taught the girl how to pitch cards until the terror had left her eyes, then had done several dozen push-ups to work up the requisite sweat.

Little Suzy had begun eyeing him as if she were beginning to think ravishment at his hands might not be a fate worse than death, after all, but she definitely didn't like Quint and the rest who had been so cruel to her.

'They're so horrid.'

'I know. Don't think of them anymore,' he murmured. 'We're going to get you out of here, posthaste. Here's my carriage.' His glossy black racing drag rolled to a halt before the curved double stairs. 'My servants will see you back safely to your village. But first—' Reaching the bottom of the steps, he turned her to face him, grasping her firmly by the shoulders. '—I want you to promise me on your most solemn oath that you will never, *ever* take a ride from strangers again.'

She gave him a somber nod. 'I won't – I promise. You're not still bleeding, I hope?' She glanced anxiously at his side, but the wound was concealed by his shirt.

'I'm fine.'

'That's good. Oh, thank you, Lord Strathmore.' She stood on tiptoe and kissed his cheek.

He gave her a stern frown. 'This is Ben,' he said gruffly as his servant joined them. 'He will be escorting you home.'

Ben bowed to the girl. 'Miss.'

She cast him an uncertain glance.

'You can trust him, Susannah,' Dev said softly. 'Ben has been all over the world with me and has saved my life on several occasions.'

'Does he speak English?' she whispered.

'Of course. He's from America, not the moon.'

Ben's eyebrows lifted, but he was too accustomed to odd reactions from white people to let it ruffle his amiable nature. Dev helped the chit into the carriage; then Ben shut the door.

'What's going on?' Ben asked, walking forward to the driver's box with Dev.

Dev waited till they were out of Suzy's earshot. 'The third requirement,' he muttered under his breath, glancing at the pavilion with rage in his eyes.

'The little girl?' Ben exclaimed in shock.

He nodded grimly. 'They picked her up outside a village in Hertfordshire. I finally got her calmed down. See that she gets home safely. Then come back and pick me up so they don't suspect anything. It's not all that far. You should be back by dawn.'

'Be careful.'

Dev smirked. Ben got into the coach with Susannah, Dev directed the coachman to Stevenage, and in another moment, the vehicle rumbled off down the drive.

Susannah blew him a kiss through the carriage window, and Dev scowled. The last deuced thing he needed was an infatuated infant sighing over him. Hands in pockets, he watched his drag go speeding off down the moonlit road through the marshes, then glanced up reluctantly at the pavilion. Steeling himself, he walked back up the curving stairs.

Hard to believe, he mused, but now it was official – he was a 'blooded' member of the notorious Horse and Chariot Club. Now that he had proved himself and had won more of their trust, passing their cursed tests, it would be much easier to press on in his quest, until he had discovered which of the twisted bastards had set that fateful fire twelve years ago.

He could hardly wait to pay the man back in full.

'Now then, girls, the hypotenuse is always the side across from the right angle. It makes no difference what the other two angles are. As long as one of the three is a right angle, then Pythagoras's theorem will work,' Lizzie explained in a firm tone to the roomful of brighteyed sixteen-year-olds as she drew a right triangle on the chalkboard. 'Here is the equation: *A* squared plus *B* squared equals *C* squared.'

As she finished writing out the simple formula, she turned around only to find the whole class staring back at her vacantly.

'Well, don't just sit there, ladies. Write it down.'

'Oh!' In the front row, Daisy Manning, a biddable innocent with big blue eyes and yellow sausage curls instantly obeyed. She glanced up anxiously at the board, copying down the formula on her slate with an air of distress.

Behind her, Annabelle Swanson, the class rebel, made no move to obey. A skeptical and rather cheeky brunette, Annabelle slouched in her chair, furtively reading something that Lizzie feared was another love letter from an unsuitable boy named Tom.

'Annabelle, please pay attention. This equation has been with us since Ancient Greece. It deserves your best efforts,' Lizzie clipped out in her best Lady Strathmore tone. Indeed, she often thought of how much the dowager would have enjoyed talking with the youngsters, or rather, holding forth on how one ought to conduct one's life.

Annabelle huffed and picked up her slate. 'Miss Bamworth never made us learn geometry,' she muttered under her breath.

'I beg your pardon?'

'She does have a point, Miss Carlisle,' Daisy offered, raising her hand in the first row. 'We were told we would only have to learn addition, subtraction, multiplication, and division.'

'Yes, Miss Bamworth never made us do anything this hard,' another student piped up in a plaintive tone.

'Well, I am your new teacher, and I know you girls are much cleverer than that,' Lizzie assured them and drew on all her famous patience to give them a pleasant smile.

'Yes, but, um, M-Miss Carlisle?'

'Yes, Daisy?' she asked in weary amusement.

'What if studying geometry ruins our temperament, so that when we come out next year, nobody wants to marry us?' She glanced back nervously at some of the other girls, who nodded solemnly. 'Papa should be very cross indeed if that were to happen. Papa says gentlemen don't like bluestockings.'

Lizzie managed not to flinch. 'Your papa is quite right, Daisy, but never fear. If I see any adverse effects on your temperaments, I give you my word of honor that we shall desist at once.'

'I still don't see why anybody cares about any silly old triangles,' Annabelle grumbled. 'It's not as if I plan to build a bridge.'

The others dared to titter.

Lizzie swept the class with a sharp look; the tittering stopped. 'It is not a matter of triangles, Annabelle. It is an *exercise* we undertake to develop our brains into keenly honed instruments, the better with which to direct our lives. I'm trying to teach you girls how to reason. She who cannot think for herself will never be the mistress of her own destiny.'

The class stared at her for a moment, absorbing this

revolutionary notion, though the strict headmistress probably would have been appalled by it. Lizzie ignored the thought. Why should they be restricted from learning what was standard fare for their brothers?

'Now, copy the formula please. Then I want you to try applying it to the problems on the board.' Clasping her hands behind her back, she strolled up and down the aisles, looking over her students' work.

When she reached Annabelle's desk, she spied the paper tucked under the girl's slate and took it away with a chiding look. Annabelle sulked, but Lizzie was at least relieved to see it was not another love note. Instead, it was one of the racy scandal sheets that the girls obtained from heaven knew where.

Lizzie frowned at her and brought it back to her desk at the front of the classroom. She barely glanced at the trashy gossip page, but as she started to cast it aside, the first line leaped out at her. She froze, suddenly paling. *Oh, no.*

Not again. Her heart pounding, she sat down slowly at her desk and, with a little piece of her dying inside, furtively skimmed the paragraph while the girls struggled to tackle the first problem. His name had been appearing in such articles more and more frequently in the past few weeks since Lady Strathmore's funeral.

Devil St—m—, the piece began.

She closed her eyes for a second, her conscience twisting with a spasm of remorse as his aunt's last wish once again haunted her mind: '*Will you look in on him from time to time when I am gone? He has no one else . . .*'

Well, no wonder he had no one else! she thought, shoving off guilt with a vengeance. The deuced man pushed away anybody who tried to get close to him!

He had ordered her to go away; she didn't need to be told twice. Perhaps, admittedly, in her heart, she felt somewhat honor-bound to reach out to him – for his aunt's sake, merely – but with scandalous stories like these, she could not fathom how it could even be accomplished. An unmarried young lady – especially a girls'-school governess employed by a high stickler like Mrs. Hall – could hardly take a hackney to the West End and go knocking on the front door of a gazetted rake like Devil Strathmore. Not, anyway, without severe damage to her reputation. Why risk it?

Things were going well for her. The dowager's death had left her saddened, of course, but her new job was a success; she had handed in her German translations on time, and with the publisher's payment, her savings were growing nicely. She enjoyed the proximity to London again, with all its museums and bookshops and learned lectures. She had many friends in Town from all walks of life and was within an hour's ride to Jacinda's villa on Regent's Park. She even received an occasional friendly letter from Dr. Bell, though she could no longer contemplate anything but a platonic relationship with him since that night with Devlin.

Indeed, as she sat at her desk, half listening to the tapping and squeaking of the girls chalking away on their slates, she realized that the only unresolved matter left in her life was Devil Strathmore himself – the thought of whom made her heart ache, her conscience wince, and her body burn.

When the mathematics lesson was over, the girls had only a few minutes to shuffle into the large room down the hallway for their dancing lesson with Miss Agnew, but Lizzie was done for another couple of hours until French class. She was organizing her desk when one of the hall monitors brought her a note from the headmistress, summoning her to the office.

Mrs. Hall was not a woman to be kept waiting. She hurried downstairs with the first bars from Miss Agnew's pianoforte echoing down the corridor after her.

The founder's office was situated off the school's foyer. Arriving there, Lizzie gave a light knock on the door and was promptly called in.

'Do come in, Miss Carlisle,' the headmistress ordered. Mrs. Hall was a large, imposing woman with twin gray side-curls peeking out from under her white muslin house cap, and a prim white betsy laced up to her chin. 'Miss Carlisle used to be a leading student here at the academy, Mrs. Harris. She grew up as lady's companion to the Marchioness of Truro and Saint Austell, who, I might add, also attended our humble establishment. She is also a particular favorite with the Duchess of Hawkscliffe and Lady Winterley, as well, who, I'm sure you know, is wed to our national hero, Colonel Lord Winterley.' Lizzie cringed slightly as Mrs. Hall preened over her exalted connections, determined to impress the two visitors who sat across from her large mahogany desk. 'She is very good with the gels. Miss Carlisle, this is Mrs. Harris of Dublin and her daughter, Sorscha.'

'How do you do?' she murmured, curtsying.

The pair regarded her without expression.

The mother was dressed in a widow's deep mourning. Her elegant silk gown and gloves were jet-black, her face veiled behind a swathe of black lace that draped over her ebony hat. Indeed, the only bit of color to be seen on her person were the ends of her long, coppery-red tresses peeking out from under the edge of her black veil.

'Mrs. Harris has just enrolled the young lady in our fine institution,' Mrs. Hall explained. 'Would you be so kind, Miss Carlisle, as to show our lovely new student to her quarters and familiarize her with the schedule?'

'Yes, ma'am. Welcome, Miss Harris,' Lizzie said to the girl. 'If you'll follow me?'

Sorscha Harris stood. She was a beautiful girl of about

sixteen with the wide-eyed look of a china doll – a pale, round face, a riot of bouncy sable curls pushed back behind a pink ribbon, and big blue eyes filled with youthful uncertainty.

Looking extremely nervous, Sorscha gave her mother's hand a brave squeeze; many of the new students had never been separated from their mothers before, and considering Mrs. Harris's mourning costume, Lizzie realized the poor child must have recently lost her father.

'Are you sure you will be all right without me, Mama?'

'I'll be fine, darlin',' Mrs. Harris murmured softly, her voice tinged with a mild Irish brogue, but behind the lace veil it was impossible to guess her expression. 'Go and enjoy your new school. I'll be back Sunday to take ye to Mass. You will behave yourself.'

'Yes, Mama.'

'Don't worry, Mrs. Harris. I will see that your daughter is well cared for,' Lizzie reassured the woman, then gave Sorscha a warm smile. 'I'm rather new here myself, Miss Harris, so you and I will have to look out for each other.'

A shy smile spread over Sorscha's pretty face.

'Let me help you with that,' she added as the girl attempted to pick up her travelling trunk by herself.

'Thank you, Miss Carlisle.' Sorscha blushed and smiled gratefully as Lizzie took the other handle.

Together, they carried it out of the office, laughing a bit with their exertions as they struggled to heft it up the stairs. Just as they reached the top, Mrs. Hall called up to her, 'Oh, Miss Carlisle! This came for you in the post yesterday.' She held up a letter. 'I do apologize – I forgot to put it in your box.'

They set down the trunk. Dusting off her hands, Lizzie hurried down to get her mail. 'Thank you, ma'am,' she murmured, taking it from her. Lizzie rejoined Sorscha, glancing thoughtfully at the official-looking missive on fine gray stationery. *From the Offices of Charles Beecham, Esquire, Fleet Street*, the envelope read. *URGENT*. Why, that name looked familiar, she thought. Since her new pupil was waiting for her, Lizzie slipped the letter in the pocket of her neat white apron and dutifully took up her half of the traveling trunk.

After helping Sorscha lug it up the stairs into the girls' sunny dormitory on the top floor of the venerable old building, Lizzie assigned the newcomer a bed and dresser, then began helping her unpack her things.

'Aren't you going to open your letter?' Sorscha ventured, glancing at the folded paper peeping out of Lizzie's pocket.

She grinned. 'I was trying not to be rude.'

'I don't mind,' the girl said brightly.

'In that case—' Filled with curiosity, she pulled out her letter and slid her finger underneath the wax seal, breaking it. Eagerly, she unfolded it and scanned the neat lines of script.

Sorscha watched her. 'Good news, I hope?'

'Gracious,' Lizzie said with a small, pained smile. 'It seems Lady Strathmore has left me something in her will.'

'Who's that?'

'A dear old dragon lady I was taking care of before I came here. Her health was poor, and, to my regret, she passed away several weeks ago. I can't believe she troubled herself to remember me in her will.'

'An inheritance! How exciting,' Sorscha exclaimed. 'What did she leave you, do you think?'

'I'm not sure. I've been summoned by her lawyer's office to attend the reading of the will.' Which meant she would see Devlin again. Her gaze turned faraway. 'I suppose I'll find out then . . . I'll bet I know what it is!' she said on a sudden inspiration. 'Some of her books!'

'Books?' Sorscha echoed.

Lizzie sent her a wistful glance. 'She knew I positively envied her excellent library. I often told her I'd like to have my own bookshop someday. She used to say the notion was absurd, but deep down, I think she liked it.' She smiled sadly. 'How kind of her to think of me.' With a pang in her heart, she sighed, refolded the letter, and put it away. 'Now all I have to do is convince Mrs. Hall to give me the morning off,' she told Sorscha in a conspiratorial tone.

'Oh, dear. She does seems a bit – formidable.'

'She's nothing after Lady Strathmore,' Lizzie whispered back, then took the girl's hand and tucked it into the crook of her arm with a bright smile. 'Now, come along, my dear. Let me introduce you to the other girls.'

'I hope they like me,' she said shyly.

'Never fear, Miss Harris.' She patted her hand. 'I suspect you'll all be fast friends by suppertime.'

Gliding like a phantom cloaked in her long black veil of lace, the Widow Harris left Mrs. Hall's office, striding out to her carriage and climbing into it lightly as her large, loyal manservant, Patrick Doyle, held the door for her. His worried glance sought to search Mary's hidden face.

'It's all right, old friend,' she murmured. 'Sorscha will be safe here.'

They no longer called the girl Sarah. Mary had changed the child's name shortly after their escape, for her own protection.

With a resolute nod, the big Irishman closed the door. As they pulled away from the stately brick academy, Mary cast one last, longing look out the carriage window.

It was difficult for her to leave Sorscha, for they had scarcely been separated for twelve years, but she assured herself the young teacher, Miss Carlisle, had seemed most solicitous of her adopted daughter's happiness and well-being. She instinctively trusted the young woman's honest gray eyes and kind smile.

The older lady, Mrs. Hall, on the other hand, struck her as naught but a pompous termagant.

Mary knew her kind all too well, having spent her misguided youth defiantly pretending that she did not feel the sting of such prim ladies' condemnation. What the school's founder would have said if she knew there had never been a Mr. Harris – let alone that the respectable widow had once been the theater diva known as Ginny Highgate – Mary scarcely dared contemplate. But it mattered not, for after all these years, hidden away in Ireland, she had left her old life behind to achieve a veneer of respectability – for Sorscha's sake.

Sorscha was all that mattered.

Her precious foundling was, in truth, the only part of her life that Mary was proud of. The child's presence in her life had filled such an empty hole in her. Her love for the little one had kept Mary alive when she had wanted to die from the sheer hellish pain of her wounds. But now, however much it hurt to give her up, Sorscha Harris – Sarah – deserved the chance to claim her rightful place in life. She owed the girl that.

Doyle drove on to the city and soon halted before the genteel boarding house where Mary had taken rooms. When he came around and opened the door for her, Mary murmured her instructions to him: 'Fetch me at midnight. Have the carriage ready. I don't want to waste any time. Best to get this over with.'

'Aye, ma'am.'

'I shall rest till then. I suggest you do the same,' she added with a smile behind her veil.

'No desire to have a look around at the great city, ma'am?' Doyle asked with a twinkle in his dark eyes, but Mary cast a bitter smile at the countless church spires and smoking chimneys of London.

She shook her head. 'I had my fill of this place long ago.' Gathering her skirts, she strode into the boarding house.

For the next several hours, she did her best to relax; read her Bible; took her meal alone in her room; and lay on her bed, staring up at the ceiling, imagining Sorscha taking the ton by storm. First, there would have to be a glittering coming-out ball. Ah, she could just picture her, a demure debutante in white. She would be awash in suitors who would treat her with the utmost chivalry and reverence – a real lady. There would be dancing and balls. Almack's. If all went well, she might even be invited to make her curtsy to the queen.

With so much advantage for Sorscha to gain, Mary would somehow find the strength for what she must do: She had come back to England to return the long-lost child to her elder brother and rightful guardian, the present Lord Strathmore.

Mary only hoped that when the siblings were reunited, Sorscha's memory might be jarred, for as it stood, the girl had no recollection of her prior life and family, nor had she any memory of the fire. In truth, Mary was grateful for that. Herself, she recalled every detail with horrid clarity.

Soothing her distress by more hopeful imaginings of a better future for Sorscha, she managed to drift off to sleep for several hours, until Doyle's light knock at the door alerted her that the hour was at hand.

She came sharply awake in an instant. Opening the door just a crack, since she wasn't yet wearing her veil, she told Doyle she would be right down. Soon, she glided quietly down the stairs of the boarding house and hurried outside, wrapping her black cloak more securely around her to keep out the chill of the late March night. The street was quiet, Doyle waiting stoically near the carriage by the feeble glow of a street lamp. Moonlight reflected in a silver streak across the vehicle's shiny black top.

'Portman Square,' she reminded him as she stepped once more into the coach.

'Aye, ma'am.'

Her heart pounded with trepidation as they set off, moving northwest toward one of London's most fashionable neighborhoods.

What sort of man would he be? Would he look at all like Sorscha? Would the two bear a family resemblance?

Mary had never stopped following the news from London, though granted, the *Times* took a month to reach her thatched cottage tucked away in the sleepy emerald hills of Tipperary. One day, cynically skimming the gossip column for news of the blackguards she had once known, she had come across the single paragraph that had turned her life upside down:

> *Lord Strathmore is welcomed back to England after several years of journeying about the globe aboard his private vessel, the brig,* Katie Rose. *Most lately come from India and the jungles of Malaysia, His Lordship tells us his adventure was part holiday, part scientific expedition. We are happy to report, however, that this esteemed, handsome, and popular Viscount has no plans for further travel at this time, but seems to exhibit an interest in settling down on England's fair shores. This Season, all Society will be wondering if the noble captain of the* Katie Rose *will next begin to contemplate embarking on a new adventure – of the matrimonial variety?*

Mary had known upon reading it what she must do, though she could hardly bear it. There was so much she had to tell Lord Strathmore about that awful night, what exactly had happened to his parents, but would he be ready to hear it? Would he shrink from what must be done to ensure Sorscha's safety from those who would do her, indeed, both of them harm?

Would he even believe her strange tale? she wondered as she stared up at the face in the large, misshapen moon. It was imperfect, like her own: not round, but an ill-formed gibbous, its ominous dark side pitted and smeared with clouds.

Perhaps she was overly worried that her old lovers might recognize her, she thought with a trace of bitter humor. After the jungles of Malaysia, she at least hoped that her face, scarred by burns, would not scare Lord Strathmore. The first newspaper article reporting his return to England had led Mary to believe that the present viscount might prove as fine a man as his poor gallant father, but upon arriving in London and glancing over fresher issues of the *Times*, Mary had begun to worry. She was no Society insider and could not be sure if Sorscha's adventurous elder brother was the same 'Devil S——' whose rakish misbehavior was gazetted in the gossip columns every other day. She prayed he was not, for he would need to have his wits about him once he knew the sort of creatures he was dealing with.

When her carriage halted in Portman Square, Mary let herself out and sent Doyle a grim nod. From the driver's box, he returned her salute, touching his gloved fingertips to the brim of his hat. He already had his instructions to wait there until she returned.

Her heart pounded and her breath misted around her as Mary slipped away into the darkness and hurried down Portman Street, ducking deeper into the shadows when a carriage went clattering by. The fashionable road was lined with tall, elegant town houses. Some had small, curved, stately white porticoes in front; others had three or four steps leading up to the door. Most had large upper windows, handsome brass lanterns by the door, and black wrought-iron fences in front.

She narrowed her eyes, trying to read the brass house numbers in the darkness, when a second carriage, this time a flashy curricle, went tearing past, hell-for-leather. She turned and watched it pull to a halt before one of the largest homes on the street. She could just make out a servant hurrying out to take the horses' heads.

The silhouette of a man jumped out of the curricle and strode into the house, which sat on the other side of the street several doors down. She took a step in that direction, staring.

When the front door opened to admit the curricle's driver, the sounds of a raucous party tumbled out into the street, and were promptly muffled again when the door closed. With a sinking feeling, she recalled the recent accounts in the gossip pages. Could it be? A glance at the house number implied that, indeed, it was.

Drawn toward the house with a foreboding sense of fascination, she kept to the other side of the street, lingering in the shadow of the spindly plane trees planted at intervals. It was a handsome brown-brick town house with white trim and three bays of windows, a slim wrought-iron balcony lining the upper floor. Against the drawn shades of the front windows, the wild crowd's dark silhouettes played.

She could make out the shape of a curly-headed woman throwing her arm around the neck of a man; a squeal of delight followed as the man swept her up off her feet and playfully tossed her into another man's arms.

Mary stared in astonishment, memories of her own such days flooding with bitter nostalgia back into her mind. Inexorably drawn, she waited as another racing drag tore down the otherwise quiet avenue and more guests leaped out – two men and two drunkenly giggling girls who could not be mistaken for ladies.

When the quartet had rushed into the house, Mary left the shadows beneath the plane tree and darted down the street, slipping around the corner. She ducked into the back alleyway of the mews tucked behind the elegant town houses, where the gardens, stables, and carriage houses were situated.

As she crept up to the wooden fence behind Lord Strathmore's house, it did not surprise her that the back windows and doors were open. She had an unobstructed view into the raucous party; the smell of the young lords' expensive cigars and the whores' cheap perfume floated out to her, unleashing a flood of unwelcome memories.

But then her blood ran cold. For as her searching stare scanned the house, she could see into what appeared to be the dinning room, and that's when she saw Quint.

She drew in her breath in a sudden shock of recognition. Half a dozen men were sitting around the dining room table playing cards.

Carstairs!

Her heart was slamming in her chest, dread unfurling in the core of her heart.

Good God, they've already gotten to him. The younger man sitting between the two of them had black hair and a lazy smile. His gesture to one of the liveried footmen marked him as the host of the evening – none other than Devil Strathmore. The footman stepped forward with a bottle of some sort of liquor, pouring libations into all their glasses.

Mary turned away, feeling sick with panicked confusion. *What am I going to do now?* Silently, she left her hiding place and glided back through the chilly darkness to her waiting carriage in Portman Square, wondering in a daze if she had come all this way for nothing.

Chapter Ten

On the appointed morning, Lizzie set out for the reading of the will in the two-wheeled governess-cart that Mrs. Hall occasionally made available for the teachers' personal use. Though not an experienced driver, she remembered Devlin's instructions from their one driving lesson; thankfully, the staunch little pony in the traces was so docile as they trotted along the road that one of Wellington's cannons firing overhead would probably not have spooked the creature. For her part, she was not feeling quite so steady.

The prospect of facing him again had her tied up in knots. She was still stung by his curt dismissal of her from his life, but there had been another lurid innuendo about his deviltry in the social column of the *Morning Post*, and she was beginning to think that if *someone* did not reach out to him, the man would kill himself for certain. Lady Strathmore had left no doubt as to whom she thought that someone should be. Lizzie shook her head to herself in dismay. Like it or not, she cared enough for that troubled man to try yet again. Perhaps his lashing out at her had been a mere aberration born of grief. If he was prepared to apologize, she decided, she was prepared to accept.

She drove on through the fresh, brightening morning, the

earthy fragrance of fertile fields, new grass, and young plants wafting on the wind and heralding a fine spring day. Here and there a few cows lowed in the pastures that surrounded London's outer borders, but soon, rural simplicity gave way to the hustle and bustle of Town.

The pony remained unflappable, barely breaking stride from his cheerful seesaw trot as Lizzie negotiated the little wood-and-wicker cart down the busy thoroughfare. She passed street vendors belting out their singsong chants, dray carts making their morning deliveries, mail coaches pulling out from the station to fan out to every corner of the realm. There was a hair-raising moment when three rambunctious children darted under the passing horses' hooves, chasing a ball across the street, but at last, her adventure ended when she reached Fleet Street and saw the hanging sign for the law offices of Charles Beecham, Esquire.

The solicitor's name was painted in large gilt letters on a dark green ground. She guided the pony over to the side of the hectic street, looking around in growing distress as she considered the problem of where to put her vehicle. Like an answer to a prayer, Bennett Freeman came out of Mr. Beecham's office, greeting her with an affable grin.

'I see you made it, Miss Lizzie!'

'Yes, in one piece – miraculously. Do you happen to know where I might find the mews, Mr. Freeman?'

'Just around the corner. Would you like me to take your cart there for you? It might be best if you went in straightaway. They're nearly ready to start.'

'Oh, you are an angel! Would you?'

'Glad to.' He laughed at her profuse thanks as she set the brake and climbed down to the pavement, hooking her reticule over her arm. Her knees were a bit wobbly after her ordeal, but she could have hugged the gray pony for being such a stouthearted little soldier. Ben climbed up into the cart and pushed the brake forward. Clapping the reins lightly over the pony's rump, he drove off toward the mews.

Lizzie turned and fixed her gaze on the door to the lawyer's office. Her heart hammered as she gathered her nerve to face Devlin again. Squaring her shoulders, she marched in, pink cheeked and slightly windblown.

Quickly unbuttoning her pelisse, she was greeted by the solicitor's bespectacled clerk, who took her coat and hung it on a peg. She smoothed the skirts of her lavender promenade gown; only her black gloves and black silk fichu tucked into the neckline of her gown signified her mourning. To wear all black when one was not a member of the family would have been, in her view, outrageously presumptuous.

The young clerk showed her into a sober, oak-paneled meeting room. 'This way, miss.'

She followed him, catching a hint of Devlin's familiar clove-and-rosemary cologne on the air. She was unprepared for the pulse of longing his scent instantly aroused in her. Then she saw him. He was standing by the corner bookshelf, conservatively dressed, engaged in a low-toned conversation with the tidy Charles Beecham.

Devlin paused midsentence and stared for a second when she walked in. She gave him a reserved nod of the utmost dignity and sat down as the clerk offered her one of the heavy, carved-wood chairs surrounding the glossy mahogany table. 'Thank you.'

Venturing a discreet glance around, she saw they were not the only two beneficiaries who had been summoned. Mrs. Rowland and Cook nodded to her, both looking nervous and out of place in the stately office. They had chosen chairs against the wall, away from the table. Margaret sat next to them with a pretty ruffled bonnet on her head. Dressed in her Sunday best, the chambermaid sent Lizzie a cheery smile.

Three respectable-looking strangers were also present, two men and a woman. Lizzie guessed these were the distant cousins Lady Strathmore had sometimes mentioned, but they must have been on the middle-class side of the dowager's kin, for they lacked the cool superiority of the only aristocrat in the room.

Presently, he sauntered around the table and took his seat beside Mr. Beecham's chair at the head of the table. He acknowledged her with a guarded nod as he sat down.

Mr. Beecham gestured to his clerk to shut the doors. When this was done, the pudgy little lawyer took his place at the head of the table and spent a few moments busily shuffling some papers and getting his presentation into order. He glanced at his watch at the exact moment that the clock struck nine, and after waiting for the noisy chimes to end, he politely cleared his throat, signaling that the meeting was about to begin.

Lizzie sat up straighter and fixed her gaze on the solicitor, but inwardly, all her awareness was focused on Devlin. He was remote, withdrawn. She could feel the stony wall of his defenses barring out the rest of the world. His arms were folded across his chest, his eyes hooded, careworn lines showing around them. Was he not eating properly? she wondered, noticing that the fine, sharp angles of his high cheekbones seemed more pronounced, as though he had lost a few pounds. With his much-vaunted appetite, this was indeed a bad sign. Lost in his brooding thoughts, his face wore a dark and saturnine look. He did not seem at all like a man moments away from inheriting half a million pounds.

'Ladies and gentlemen, thank you for coming,' Mr. Beecham began. 'Today we remember a grand lady who will live long in our memories, Augusta Kimball, the eighth Lady Strathmore. If no one has questions, we shall proceed with the reading of the will.' Mr. Beecham sent an inquiring glance around the table, but no one spoke up, so he continued with a nod. 'We'll begin with Her Ladyship's charitable endowments, then her retainers, and finally, relatives.'

The solicitor picked up his folio. As he began reading off the very generous donations Lady Strathmore had left to her parish church, the almshouse her father had founded for ironworkers, and an art gallery in Bath, Lizzie glanced at Devlin and found him staring coolly at her.

The wary hunger in his gaze stole her breath. For a moment, they were both oblivious of the proceedings under way. She felt his desire for her running like a lightning bolt down her spine, though he was obviously fighting it. He did not even smile at her. It was as if he was purposely hardening his heart against her, willfully denying the bond between them.

She searched his crystalline, blue-green eyes, trying to understand. If he was grieving, why didn't he seek her help? Why must he push her away?

He lowered his lashes and turned away, forcing his attention back to Mr. Beecham's monotonous reading.

She looked away, shaken and confused by his renewed coldness. If only she knew what she had done to deserve this treatment.

'Her Ladyship designates one hundred pounds to her estimable physician, Andrew Bell, as a token of her thanks for his kindness. Likewise, one hundred pounds to Charles Beecham – myself,' Mr. Beecham added, his pasty face coloring slightly, 'in thanks for many years of skilled, loyal service. Very thoughtful,' he murmured. 'For Mrs. Rowland's twelve grandchildren, one hundred fifty pounds each.'

Dev and Lizzie glanced warily at each other again.

Mr. Beecham moved on to reading the dowager's bequests to her cousins, then laid the document on the table and surveyed all their faces with a brief, businesslike glance. 'We will now move on to Lady Strathmore's instructions for the bulk of her fortune.'

'Charles, you must have missed something.' Devlin's deep voice rumbled through her senses. 'There had to have been some sort of provision for Miss Carlisle in the last section.'

'Er, we are coming to that, sir.'

He raised an eyebrow, then sat back to wait.

Lizzie noticed the cousins staring arrogantly at her, but she paid little mind, still surprised at Devlin's concern that she should receive her share of the inheritance, however slight.

'Ahem,' Mr. Beecham resumed, giving a little cough into his hand. He opened another flap of his leather folio and pulled out a second piece of paper. 'In February, mere weeks before her death, Lady Strathmore made a change to her will. I have verified the viscountess's signature, along with the testimony of the witnesses.' He nodded toward the old, loyal servants seated by the wall, then swallowed hard. 'I shall now read the final instructions, as amended by Lady Strathmore on the night of February the twelfth.'

Across the table, Devlin shifted uneasily in his seat, but his stare was now pinned on his solicitor. For her part, Lizzie resisted the urge to fidget. She had the feeling something strange was going on.

'"Dear Mr. Beecham,"' the lawyer read out, '"I hereby send you my revised will and testament, effective immediately. In August of 1816, I hired a new lady's companion to help me while away the hours. This young woman, Elizabeth Carlisle, has proved herself to me for her kind heart, a responsible nature, and a character of pure sterling. Though I have often teased Miss Carlisle for her eccentric notions, I find myself at this late hour with a few notions of my own, chiefly, a new design for the manner in which I have decided to disburse my fortune."'

Lizzie furrowed her brow, befuddled. *What about the books?*

'"All bequests to my various charitable endowments, my servants, and kin remain unchanged. As to the bulk of my fortune, which was entrusted to me by my most revered Papa—"' Mr. Beecham mopped his brow with his handkerchief, edged away from Devlin, and read on. '"—I do hereby decree that the entire balance of five hundred thousand pounds be split between my beloved nephew, Devlin, and Elizabeth Carlisle."'

Devlin's jaw dropped.

'"The allocation of these funds, however, is contingent upon and only to be granted after the two parties – vis-à-vis, my nephew and Miss Carlisle – have freely and willingly joined together in holy matrimony—"'

Lizzie's mouth fell open. '*What?*'

Chaos erupted, routing the momentary stunned silence.

The cousins were cursing, the servants were arguing, and Devlin leaped to his feet, sending his chair clattering back.

'This is preposterous!' Devlin roared, slamming his mighty fist on the table. 'Damn your eyes, sir! Is this your idea of a prank?'

Everyone was shouting, except for Lizzie, who just sat there in a daze, realizing that, no, it was Lady Strathmore's idea of a prank. *Curse the old girl's matchmaking!*

'Please, ladies and gentlemen, if I may have your attention, there is more.'

'More?' Devlin bellowed.

'"Failing the union of these two young people within three months of these proceedings,"' Mr. Beecham read on in a shaky voice, '"I do hereby bequeath my entire fortune to the Good Hope Society for the Benefit of Ironworkers in Gravel Lane in the parish of Christchurch. This is my last will and testament as witnessed by my faithful retainers of many years, Mildred Rowland and Jane Willis."'

Everyone gasped, turning to stare accusingly at the housekeeper and cook.

Mrs. Willis cowered a bit, but Mrs. Rowland rose to her feet, clutching her cheap reticule in both hands. She glanced around at them with a pugnacious look, but directed her remarks to Devlin. ' 'Tis true, milord, every word. Her Ladyship called me up to her chamber to witness and sign it the night before you left for London. Then she sent me off to bring it 'ere, posthaste. 'Hand it personally to Mr. Beecham,' she says, and that's what I done. On my life, 'tis true – and if you ask me, it's for the best!'

Lizzie's eyebrows shot upward at this declaration, but Devlin looked as though he wanted to strangle someone.

'Leave us,' he fairly snarled at the others.

Lizzie assumed he meant that he wished to speak privately to the lawyer and started to rise to leave with the others, but his predator's stare homed in on her, freezing her midmotion.

'You *stay*,' he ordered.

His harsh tone jolted her out of her astonishment, indignation pricking her to rise from her chair. It helped to lessen the intimidating factor of his greater size as he loomed across the table, bristling at her.

He planted his hands on the table between them, leaning closer. 'Well, Miss Carlisle.' He enunciated each syllable with razor-sharp precision while the lawyer scampered out behind the others. 'I knew you were deviously clever, but, my dear, your latest ruse takes the cake.'

'What?'

Glowering, he scrutinized her face. 'Explain what just happened here.'

'Explain it? I'm as baffled as you! I haven't the foggiest inkling why your aunt would do such a thing—'

'Because she wants me leg-shackled, that's why!' He slammed the heel of his fist on the table between them, then pointed in her face. 'And because you put her up to it! The jig is up, sweet. No one's laughing.'

'What exactly are you accusing me of, you odious fiend?'

'As if you don't know! Now I am going to call Mr. Beecham back in here,' he ground out as he struggled for calm, 'and I expect you to come clean.'

'I don't know what you're talking about!'

'I'll explain it to you, then, my clever Miss Carlisle! You manipulated my aunt into changing her will so I would be *forced* to marry you – admit it!' She gasped aloud, but he charged on recklessly. 'The two of you conspired against me! She's wanted me leg-shackled for years, and you thought to land yourself a title – maybe to get back at Alec!'

Her jaw hung slack, but then she snapped her mouth shut in sheer outrage. 'You utter egotist! I did no such thing. Do you actually think I am that desperate to have you? Do you really think you're such a prize? You? A man who lets his name be dragged through the scandal sheets? Who lives in utter decadence? Marry *you*? My dear Lord Strathmore, I wouldn't have you if you begged me on your *knees*. Good day, sir!'

Her insult took him aback for a second. She pivoted and marched out grandly, but a moment later, he lurched into motion.

'Get back here!' he boomed, striding after her. 'I'm not done with you!'

'Oh, yes, you are,' she muttered, grabbing her coat out of the clerk's hands.

Devlin grabbed her elbow none too gently.

'Don't touch me!' she cried, whirling to face him. 'How dare you accuse me of something so vile? I had nothing to do with your aunt's mad scheme! I knew nothing about it. And I will prove my innocence by walking away. I can do that, you see. It costs me nothing. *You* on the other hand, Devil, my dear – I can hardly wait to see them throw you into debtors' prison!' She yanked her elbow out of his grasp and stalked toward the door.

'Damn, they sound like they're already married,' the clerk remarked under his breath as she passed.

She shot him a scowl and slammed the door behind her, going back out to her pony cart.

Closing his eyes for a second, Dev struggled to leash his wrath, pinching the bridge of his patrician nose for a moment; then he gave up, muttered a curse, and strode outside after her. Short of making a scene in the street, however, there was little he could do. She was marching away swiftly along the pavement, her pretty lavender skirts twitching around her legs with her angry strides. Her spine was very straight, her dainty, black-gloved fists balled at her sides. She glanced over her shoulder as if she could feel his glare. The look she sent him was as sharp as a blow-dart.

Dev bristled, his heart pounding with thwarted lust and fury; then she turned the corner and disappeared into the mews. He suddenly became aware of his aunt's cousins and the clerk watching him out the bow window of Charles's office.

He grumbled wordlessly under his breath and pivoted, stalking back toward the office. 'Get the carriage,' he muttered to Ben, who stood nearby, looking appalled. On the warpath, Dev marched back into the office.

His audience quickly snapped to attention, looking elsewhere and assuming poses of nonchalance.

'Charles!' he bellowed.

Charles gulped. 'Yes, my lord?'

Dev's stare narrowed, predator-like, on the pudgy little man. Beads of sweat popped out instantly on Charles's receding forehead.

The solicitor retreated as Dev advanced.

'This,' he growled, 'cannot be legal.'

'B-but it is, my lord,' the man stammered, nervously mopping his pate. 'Lady Strathmore's fortune was hers to dispose of h-however she wished.'

'Get me out of this, Charles. Find a way.'

'Y-yes, sir. I'll do my best.'

'See that you do.'

'It could t-take some t-time—'

'*I don't have time!*' he thundered, snatching his great-coat angrily out of the clerk's hands. 'Remember the pavilion? The repairs? The house on Portman Street? I have bills, Charles. Bills up to my bloody neck! You will make this go away. Do you understand?'

'Yes, sir.'

'Good.' Dev stormed out, dragging his fine coat after him. In the next moment, he sprang up into his coach. 'Home!' he snarled at his driver.

Ben barely had time to scramble into the chassis with him. Before the coach had even rolled into motion, Dev pulled open the satinwood liquor compartment beneath the opposite seat and poured himself a generous shot of whiskey. The amber spirits sloshed about in the small tumbler with the coach's rocking motion. Dev did not give it a chance to spill but downed it in one swig.

'Perfect,' he spat, marginally steadied as the fiery liquid made its way down to his belly. 'Just – bloody – perfect.' Then he poured himself another.

Ben eyed him apprehensively.

'Blasted women and their ploys.'

'But, sir, by the light of reason, you cannot really think the girl had anything to do with this—'

'I'm talking about my aunt!' After another soothing swallow, Dev sat back against the squabs and stared at his servant. 'The old girl has played me for a fool, Ben. She certainly had the last laugh.' He glanced around at the fancy coach that enclosed them from the dirt and struggle and hubbub of the workaday world, he gazed into his crystal tumbler at the expensive vintage whiskey swirling about, and then he looked at Ben. 'I'm destitute.'

Ben looked glum, knowing it was no exaggeration.

'This throws everything I've worked for into jeopardy. Do you realize how quickly Carstairs and the others will shut me out if they suspect I'm in dun territory? They don't trust me as it is. I'm so close . . . Damn it! That meddling old schemer!' he shouted. 'How could she do this to me? And I swear to God, Ben, if you tell me that I brought it on myself, I'll strangle you.'

Ben shook his head. Gingerly he offered, 'I'm sure that your aunt must've had your best interests at heart.'

'I don't care if she did! I will not be pushed into this! I will not be manipulated from beyond the bloody grave!' he declared, but even greater than his ire at his aunt was Dev's anger at himself. If he had failed to see this coming, what in the name of Hell did he think he was doing taking on the whole lot of the Horse and Chariot bastards single-handedly?

Maybe, just maybe, he was getting in over his head. But he was in too deep to back out now, nor would he. His only exit from this dark tunnel was by going deeper into their evil. Whether or not he'd come out on the other side remained to be seen. Personally, he did not give a damn whether he survived it or not. Either way, no matter what mad scheme his aunt had devised, he had no intention of dragging Lizzie Carlisle down with him.

Yet he hated himself for hurting her, lashing out blindly with his words. Stunned by his aunt's prank, he had accused the finest, most principled woman he'd ever known of the lowest sort of scheming. If she were anyone else, the suspicion would have been reasonable enough, but she was not other people. She was Lizzie.

Warm, gentle Lizzie, he thought with an ache. Honest, loyal, caring Lizzie, who could not lie to save her life. *But damn*, he advised himself, *in the future, never cross a clever woman.* Still smarting from her tongue-lashing, Dev knew not what to do, so he took another drink.

'Is the idea of marrying her really so unpalatable?' Ben asked softly.

'Don't be thick, Ben. That's not it at all,' he mumbled with a sigh, and shook his head.

'What, then? She is not . . . suitable?'

'I care nothing for her birth or station,' he said wearily. 'Look at the circumstances! This is not the time for me to contemplate taking a bride.' His brain half panicked at the thought, utterly refusing what he was being called upon to do.

'Perhaps it is the perfect time.'

Dev snorted. 'Didn't you hear what she said? Not if I begged her on my knees. That, my friend, is a quote.' He downed the rest of his drink, then dropped his head back on the cushioned squab in defeat.

'She didn't feel that way in Bath. Neither, I daresay, did you.'

Dev scowled, blew a skeptical snort from his nostrils, then gazed out the carriage window, at a loss. *Marry Lizzie?* . . .

He shuddered with mingled fear and longing. It would be so easy to fall into her arms and forget all the bitter lessons that life had scarred across his soul, but he would not give in to that traitorous desire. He was not letting that girl into his heart so fate could shatter him again. He had barely put himself back together once already.

'What are you going to do?' Ben asked.

He shook his head. 'I'll think of something.'

When they pulled into Portman Street, he saw that apparently word had gotten out amongst his creditors that today was the day he would be receiving his inheritance. A small crowd of the duns had formed a picket outside his home and stood awaiting his return.

As soon as his carriage came into view, they rushed the vehicle, spooking the horses as they waved their bills. Forced to stop, the vehicle was swiftly surrounded by the clamoring crowd.

'How dare they?' Dev stared out the window, utterly appalled. But each seemed to fear that unless he were in the first batch of merchants to be paid, there would soon be no money left, given Devil Strathmore's reputation for extravagant living.

'Pardon, milord!' they hollered through the glass. 'A moment of your time—'

'I'm from Locke's—'

'I'm from Tattersall's—'

'About your tab at the Scarlet Slipper, my lord—'

Dev blanched to see one of the thick-necked whores' bullies from the high-class brothel where he had often gambled or pursued other pleasures.

'Stand aside!' the coachman shouted, even threatening them with his whip, to no avail.

'We've been patient! We deserve to be paid!' The duns remained stubbornly blocking the carriage from moving on. 'Well, he's got his inheritance now, ain't he?'

In a wave of fury, Dev started to reach for the door to give the insolent cretins a piece of his mind, but Ben stopped him, spotting one of the scandal-sheet journalists leaning against the wrought-iron fence that girded the area. The jackanapes was smirking as he watched the disgraceful scene, his pencil poised to take notes.

'No, sir,' Ben warned in businesslike outrage, 'don't speak to them. I'll handle this.' Ben flung open the carriage door and stood on the metal step, towering over the rabble, 'Silence!'

They obeyed, looking startled.

Ben tugged at his waistcoat with great pomp. 'Be gone at

once, all of you, or I shall call the constable! How dare you make a spectacle of this house and invade His Lordship's privacy? Do you not know the viscount is still in mourning?'

Some dared to scoff, but Ben flung their disrespect back in their faces.

'For shame, sirs!' he thundered. 'You will be paid in due time, just as you always have in the past! Begone, or His Lordship vows he will not frequent your establishments again!'

Dev was impressed. He sent his valet a discreet look of admiring surprise.

Ben gave him a subtle wink that said, *Not to worry*, before jumping down from the coach and securing the carriage door behind him. Having joined the fray, he now began shooing the bill collectors out of the coach's path. Finally, the vehicle was able to move on. It continued around the corner and down the narrow passage to the mews.

Dev's temples had begun to throb with a five-hundred-thousand-pound headache. But once his driver had managed to remove him from the mortifying scene, he realized grimly that it was only a taste of what was in store if he did not get his hands on that money. As it was, his neighbors would chew over this bit of scandal for a week, for in high Society, the only sin that was truly verboten was poverty. And that, he grasped, still rather reeling, put him squarely at Lizzie Carlisle's mercy.

'Not if you begged me on your knees.'

Bloody hell. She was not the type to make idle threats. He saw now there was little worse he could have done in his fit of anger than to attack her integrity, the very trait on which she prided herself. Not her beauty, not her brains. *You'd better think, old boy, and think fast.*

He had gained much ground with the Horse and Chariot Club by spending freely on them; he could not afford for them to suspect in any way that all was not exactly as it seemed.

When the coach halted, Dev walked into his house a few minutes later, still reeling to discover that he had possessed this vulnerability all along and had barely noticed it. It had never crossed his mind that his aunt might pull such a prank. He had learned to live without his family, God knows, without love, even without the comforts of civilization out trekking in the wild or at sea – but those expeditions had been very well funded. He had never before been forced to consider how to approach his life without his great title and his wealth.

Life the way Lizzie Carlisle lived it.

Mulling over the whole debacle, he marched down the main corridor to his study at the back of the house, needing a place where he could simply sit and think for a moment. Upon striding into the room, however, he suddenly stopped in his tracks.

Pasha sat atop his desk, batting at the feather quill-pen with his front paw, a pool of spilled indigo ink spreading across his papers and dripping on the Wilton carpet.

'Pasha!'

The hellcat instantly leaped off the desk and darted under the wing chair, leaving a trail of indigo paw prints.

'Damn it!' Dev stalked over to inspect the damage. His correspondence was covered in ink. The cat had clearly investigated his silver snuffbox, as well, for it, too, was toppled. Fine loose tobacco floated atop the wet pool of ink like sawdust. 'That does it.'

It was bad enough having the little monster here, for every time he looked at the animal, it reminded him painfully of his aunt. But for weeks, Pasha had roamed the house, breaking things, sleeping in Dev's dresser drawers, getting cat hairs all over his neck cloths and shirts, sticking his head in the soup epergne, and making all manner of mischief throughout the house. Enough was enough. Dev reached under the wing chair and pulled the cat out by the scruff of his maned neck.

'Reeer!'

'I don't want to hear it. You had your chance. Tell the driver not to unhitch the horses, Ben,' he ordered as his valet walked in through the front door just then, having made short work of the bill collectors. 'We're leaving again. Well done, by the way.'

'Where to?' Ben asked, his eyebrows lifting to see the haughtiest cat in Christendom hanging in such an undignified fashion from Dev's grasp, fluffy tail twitching.

'Knight House. I've got an idea.'

'Knight House?'

'I expect it is where I may find the intrepid E. Carlisle.'

'Actually, she has taken a post at a girls' school in Islington, sir. I got the address from Beecham's clerk. I figured you might need it.'

Dev harrumphed at his valet's cheeky grin. 'Get this little monster's cage, would you?'

Ben obeyed. A moment later, Dev dropped the cat into the sturdy cane box.

'The little brute should make a perfect peace offering, don't you think?' he drawled, closing the lid. 'Girls love cats.'

Ben eyed him dubiously, but followed Dev as he carried Pasha's cage outside. They got back into the coach.

'What do you mean to do?'

'She's an intelligent woman. I'm sure we can work something out.'

'A bribe?' Ben asked with a worried frown.

Dev smiled cynically. 'Everyone's got their price.'

Chapter Eleven

Oh, that man. Lizzie was still fuming when she returned to her duties at Mrs. Hall's. *What a waste of time!* And to think, she had risked her neck driving into the city and had lost pay for requesting the morning off, only to be insulted to her face! The only consolation was the oh-so-satisfying image of Devil Strathmore locked up in one of London's grimmest debtors' prisons. He deserved it!

By noon, the warm April sunshine had routed the chill of morning, so the young ladies were allowed to spend some leisure time outdoors on the parklike commons across from the school. Now it was a pleasant scene of laughing girls in pastel dresses, their sashes and hat ribbons billowing on the playful breeze. Some fed the ducks on the pond; others played a dainty round of pall-mall.

Pleased to note that Daisy Manning had befriended the new student, Sorscha Harris, Lizzie sat on the bench overseeing the girls' activities and enjoying the warm caress of the sun on her face. She had removed her bonnet in disregard of the risk of ruining her complexion with freckles, though she had occasionally been told that her flawless white skin was her best feature. It didn't matter, because she was never caring a whit again what any male thought of her looks.

As she sat in the sun, playing chaperon to her charges, she ignored the observation that the blue-green pond, glittering with sunlight, reminded her of Devlin's eyes. Well, he could rot in Fleet Prison, for all she cared. Perhaps she'd bring him a book to while away the hours of his incarceration – a book of sermons on the virtuous life, a Bible! Something he could study.

Just then, she heard a carriage approaching and glanced toward the black ribbon of the road. The girls at pall-mall stopped their game and paused, holding their mallets, turning to look at the elegant town coach that presently drew up to the commons, drawn by a high-stepping quartet of black Fresian horses.

Lizzie's eyes narrowed to dangerous slits. So, he had found her. She rose to her feet, the breeze molding her pale muslin skirts against her legs. She bristled as the grand black coach swept the roundabout and slowed, the Strathmore coat of arms emblazoned on its side. The coach halted; all the girls were watching.

Gracious, when that door opened and the gazetted rake, Devil Strathmore, jumped out, come to harass her, what on earth was Mrs. Hall going to say? she thought. But it seemed she would soon find out, for at that moment, he did just that. Ben climbed out after him, carrying some sort of sturdy square basket with a handle on top.

Warily, Lizzie watched Devlin approaching, then scowled to notice her pupils studying him in wide-eyed admiration, whispering and giggling behind their hands.

His untamed stare was fixed on Lizzie. A cynical twist of a smile curved one corner of his mouth; his earring glinted in the sun. Looking every inch the rogue, he sauntered toward her, swinging his walking stick in a debonair arc. He took an idle swipe at a dandelion globe; white fluff flew. She folded her arms across her chest and braced for the inevitable clash.

'Miss Carlisle!' he called in the most treacherously amiable tone. 'I've brought you and your lovely students a present.' With his walking stick, he pointed at the box Ben carried.

A wave of curious excitement rippled through the group of girls. Ben set his burden down on the nearest bench. Devlin unleashed his most Prince Charming-like smile and gave the young ladies a slight bow. Abandoning their games, the girls gathered around Ben and the box, irresistibly intrigued.

'What is it, sir?'

'What could it be?'

Their high voices carried on the breeze. Lizzie joined them, on her guard, as several of the girls bent down and peered into the box. At that moment, a loud, woeful meow arose from within.

'A kitty!' one of the girls exclaimed.

'Oh, look, he's beautiful!'

'Look, Miss Carlisle! The kind gentleman has brought us the most wonderful present!'

Lizzie stared at Devlin in seething ire for this shameless move. She bent down and glanced skeptically into the box. Sure enough, there sat Pasha, caged behind the slatted wicker door, curled unhappily on a velvet pillow.

The dowager's spoiled darling peered back at her, his whiskered face with its dark triangular mask arranged in an expression of great feline angst. Pasha let out a low, plaintive, *'Reeer'* with an occasional hiss at no one in particular.

Lizzie straightened up again and shaded her eyes against the sun as Devlin came toward her, ducking his chin like a contrite schoolboy, while his eyes danced with amusement.

'You are *not* leaving that cat here,' she informed him.

He laughed as though she had said something charming, but the glint in his eyes was slightly smug, for the girls were in ecstasies over the little monster.

'Look how sweet! It's got a jeweled collar!'

'Oh, thank you for bringing him, sir! How I miss my kitty at home!'

'What's his name, please?'

'Pasha,' Ben informed them.

Lizzie pulled Devlin aside by his coat-sleeve and glared at him. 'I don't know what you think you're doing here,' Lizzie muttered under her breath, 'but I have nothing to say to you, moreover, you are *not* pawning that little hellion off on me. Your aunt gave him to *you*.'

'And I'm giving him to you – as a peace offering, Liz – I mean, Miss Carlisle,' he amended, noticing a few of her students eavesdropping on their exchange.

Others were wheedling Ben: 'May we hold him? Please?'

'You know the rule, ladies.' Lizzie turned back to her pupils. 'We do not accept presents from strangers.' She shot Devlin a look of reproach. 'Pasha is here only for a visit. Mrs. Hall does not allow pets, as you well know.'

'But look how happy he makes the little dears.' Devlin clucked his tongue. 'Pasha needs a home.'

This was, apparently, more than Daisy's tender heart could bear. 'Poor little thing!' the millionaire coal-factor's daughter exclaimed. 'Can't we let him out of there, please, Miss Carlisle?'

No one noticed that Sorscha, beside Daisy, was studying Devlin intently.

'You may pet him through the cage, but do not take him out of there,' Lizzie ordered.

'But Miss Carlisle, he looks so unhappy.'

'He'll only scratch you and run away,' she advised them, shooting Devlin a meaningful look. 'He's very spoiled.'

He stared at her, absorbing this. Then he turned to her students. 'If you ladies do not mind, I should like a moment of your teacher's time. I must speak to her on – family business. Ben will make sure no one falls in the pond,' he assured her before Lizzie could protest. When her students nodded their consent, he turned to her and offered her his arm. 'Shall we?'

Lizzie could see no graceful way out of this. Putting up a fuss would only bring Mrs. Hall out to investigate. Ever mindful that it was her duty to set a ladylike example for her girls, she tamped down the tirade she would have liked to unleash, lifted her chin, and walked past him to the stone footpath that wound around the pond.

Its meandering course still allowed her to keep an eye on her charges but would afford the two of them a bit of privacy. Devlin dropped his rejected arm and followed her with a disgruntled sigh.

'How dare you come here? Are you trying to get me fired?' she demanded in a harsh whisper after they had walked a short distance away from the girls.

'Interesting idea. I hadn't considered it, but if you had no other way of putting food in your belly, perhaps you would be more inclined to hear me out.'

'I daresay I've heard quite enough from you for one day. Your accusations in Mr. Beecham's office were—'

'Inexcusable. I know.' His quick concession startled her. But a man would say anything, she guessed, when half a million pounds hung in the balance. 'I'm sorry, Lizzie. I spoke in anger. Well, you must admit my aunt's scheme came as a shock to us both. Besides, you have made sport of me before, if you'll recall. You can't blame me for having a few momentary suspicions that you might have had something to do with it. Still, I ought not to have said those things. You didn't deserve that.'

'What about the things you said to me the day of your aunt's funeral? Do you remember that – how you told me to just go away? Why, Devlin? How did I possibly offend you? What did I do wrong?'

He stared at her, paling. 'Nothing.'

'I was grieving that day, too, you know.' She searched his stark face, then shook her head at him. 'After what we had done together . . . you made me feel like such a fool.'

He dropped his gaze and stood there mute for a long moment. 'That was a – bad day.'

'Yes, I know, but I only wanted to help. You didn't have to shut me out. In truth, I could have overlooked your cruelty to me at the funeral, but it wasn't just *that* day. Even this morning, when I walked into Mr. Beecham's office, you stared at me so coldly, and then accused me of the most despicable scheming, insulted me to my face—'

'I'm sorry.'

'No doubt – now that your fortune depends on my favor. I'm not stupid, Devlin. I know why you're here, but I'm afraid you're wasting your time.'

'Why is that?'

'Because your motives toward me are about as sincere as Alec's are toward Lady Campion, that's why!' she exclaimed. 'Frankly, under the circumstances, I'd rather see the money go to charity than to you. Send a few of your treasures to the auction house if you wish to avoid spending time in the Fleet. Learn to live within your means. It won't kill you.'

He scratched his temple with his thumb, diplomatically searching the ground at his feet. 'Do you have any idea how much money five hundred thousand pounds really is?'

'Not enough to buy my pride,' she declared. 'You would never have chosen this – or me – of your own accord. Your insults today made that fact abundantly clear, and for my part, I would not in a million years inflict myself on a husband who has no wish to be married to me.'

He clenched his jaw. 'You want to see me grovel, is that it? Will that make you happy?'

'You can grovel if it suits you, I am sure, but it won't make the slightest difference on my decision. You and I could never suit. It would be hell on earth for someone like me to be wed to a man incapable of love.'

'Who ever told you I'm incapable of love?'

'Your actions, your demeanor, everything about you warns the whole world to stay back, though God knows you're as lonely a man as I ever met. You kept your distance from your aunt, you've pushed me away – you won't even let yourself care for a silly cat!' She threw an impatient gesture toward the park bench where the girls still clamored around Pasha's basket. 'Shut me out if you must, Devlin, but you can't go on living your life this way.'

'It wasn't a real marriage I was suggesting, if you'd give me half a chance to talk!' he retorted, his cheeks flushing. 'There's a far simpler solution than that, and I am prepared to make it worth your while if you'll go along with it.'

She lifted her eyebrows with a defiant look of inquiry, and then folded her arms across her chest. 'This should be interesting.'

'It's quite elementary. We marry, as instructed, take possession of the money – a week later, we have the match annulled. Go our separate ways. You can name your price.'

'Ah, so now you would bribe me. And pray tell, on what grounds, my noble lord, would we have our match annulled? That I was forced into marriage? You'd need only choose in what order you'd like to duel against all five of the Knight brothers if they caught wind of such a rumor. Or would you prefer an annulment on the grounds of your failure to consummate our union? Wouldn't that cause a stir in the ton? A lover of your reputation, unable to perform! But, no. You would carry it off somehow. Your kind always does – no doubt at my expense. Somehow I can't help feeling I'm the one who would inevitably end up looking the fool. No thanks.'

She heard him curse under his breath as she walked on.

'All right then – forget the annulment.' He caught up to her again with swift; businesslike strides. 'We'll marry, split the money, then petition for a divorce.'

'And both become pariahs for the rest of our lives? An annulment is better than that,' she scoffed.

'Very well.' He came around the front of her, blocking her path. 'Here is my final offer. We marry and just – keep to ourselves. Live separate lives.'

'Stay married?' she clarified.

He shrugged, his face unreadable. 'You need a husband. I need an heir.'

'An heir?' Oh, what a talent he had for infuriating her! She stared at the man, amazed. 'I do not *need* a husband, I'll have you know, and as for your heir, I cannot fathom how you mean to accomplish it, for I have no intention of ever letting you touch me again!' Cheeks burning, she started to march away, but he captured her elbow.

'Lizzie, wait—'

She shook him off wrathfully. 'Let go of me! You have my answer. I gave it to you at Mr. Beecham's office. My sentiments are unchanged. In fact, your visit has merely solidified my decision, so why don't you take your own advice and go away?'

'Why must you be so stubborn?' he cried, roughly turning her to face him.

'Have you never heard of self-respect? If you think I'm going to allow myself to be *used* just so you can get your hands on your silly inheritance, you're mad!'

'No, you're mad, Lizzie, because you want me as much as I want you, only you're too proud to admit it!'

'Oh, yes, you wanted me – for your mistress!' she hissed, lowering her tone lest her students hear. 'That was the only offer you deemed me worthy of until your aunt's fortune came into play. For that matter, I haven't even *heard* from you since the night we were together! You were perfectly content to forget me after our liaison, so forgive me if I feel less than flattered by your miraculous change of heart.'

'Such stubborn pride,' he marveled. 'Listen to yourself! I am giving you the chance to better your station, offering you a life of undreamed luxury. You would be a viscountess – with servants, jewels, the best modistes. Half the ton would cater to your every whim, and nobody would ever dare look down their noses at you again.'

'You would,' she said. 'If you had married me only for cash, of course you would, in time. You would forever see me as not quite good enough for you.'

'God give me patience, woman. I would not!'

'Well, I would.'

'Yes, that is your problem exactly, Lizzie, but I regret to inform you, you infuriating creature, that the only person who looks down on you – is you! But maybe you deserve it. Because for all your virtue and all your brains, you really are a bit of a coward, aren't you?'

'I beg your pardon?' she uttered.

'You'd rather waste your life hiding out here, living vicariously through these young girls, than dare risk taking a chance, seizing a dream of your own. But one day when you're old and you're still here, hiding, you'll look back on this day with the bitterest regret – someday, twenty years hence, when you end up alone. Just you and your stubborn pride.'

Her face turned pale at his words; her blood ran cold, for his threat had struck a nerve, painting the very picture of her worst fears. She swallowed hard, balled her fists at her sides, and lifted her chin. 'Do not assume that just because I refuse *your* mercenary offer that I might not accept another man's. I've had proposals of marriage before. I'll have them again.'

'And you'll shoot them all down, won't you? Of course you

will. We both know it.' He studied her with his crystalline eyes agleam. 'But why? Because you're still waiting for your precious Alec to grow up? You could be waiting a very long time. But why deliberately choose a man in the first place that you can only love from afar? Maybe I'm not the only one pushing people away, Lizzie. Did you ever think of that?'

Her heart pounded fiercely in her chest. 'Good-bye, Lord Strathmore.'

'Oh, I see. You can't take the truth. You only like doling it out.'

'I said good-bye!'

'Don't you mean arrivederci, my love?' he asked in a dangerous murmur.

'I mean *good-bye*.'

'This isn't over,' he whispered, brushing past her as he obeyed her order to go.

She was trembling as she folded her arms tightly across her chest once more; she did not move from her spot until he was a safe distance away, stalking back to his carriage.

When she rejoined her students at length, Sorscha Harris tugged shyly at her sleeve. 'Who was that gentleman, please, Miss Carlisle?'

'That was nobody,' she said through gritted teeth.

Dev, meanwhile, beckoned Ben after him, so angry that he couldn't even speak. The girls bade Pasha crestfallen good-byes as Ben carried the cat away in his cage.

'I gather it didn't go well?' his valet observed gingerly, falling into step beside him.

Dev stared coldly straight ahead. 'Ben,' he ground out, 'this is war.'

Chapter Twelve

'This is a bad idea!' Ben whispered as he helped Dev carry the ladder across the moonlit commons when they returned to the school late that night.

'I don't recall you offering a better suggestion,' he replied through gritted teeth.

'Woo her!'

'No, Ben. Forget it. I offered her my title, my name, half my fortune. She spat on it.'

'But—'

'Trust me, Ben – she brought it on herself.'

'But to kidnap her? She'll hate you for this!'

'That, I am told, is a normal condition of marriage. At least then I'll have my money.'

'This is *not* what your aunt intended.'

Dev scowled at him; then his gaze homed in on the third-storey window above the mulberry tree, which he had determined by a bit of spying earlier this evening was the location of the young harpy's room. He narrowed his eyes as he noticed a flickering glow in the window through the curtains. Their billowing movement told him the casement was open, an excellent development.

The rest of the school's windows were dark.

'Light. She's awake,' Ben whispered.

Busy little ant. Probably working on her thrice-damned translations. Dev knitted his eyebrows, standing square-jawed and determined in the moonlight.

'What if she hears us?'

'Doesn't matter.'

'If she screams, we'll have to run.'

'She won't be doing any screaming.' Casting him a piratelike glance, Dev held up the clean silk handkerchief he had brought along to use for a gag. 'Come on. Over the fence. Don't use the gate. It squeaks.' He rested his end of the ladder atop the waist-high fence that girded the school's front garden, then braced one hand on the rail and sprang over it. He silently pulled the ladder over the fence while Ben followed him.

He lifted his finger to his lips, reminding Ben to be silent; then both men carried the ladder over to the building and gingerly rested it against the redbrick wall.

Perfect. It reached up to within three feet of her chamber window. As an added advantage, the mulberry tree would provide some cover if anyone should come along.

Dev ignored the fact that he could go to jail for what he was about to do, never mind the certain challenge from her precious Knight brothers. He was headed for debtors' prison as it was, and besides, he was a full-blooded member of the wicked Horse and Chariot Club. Bride-stealing was par for the course.

Moreover, the stubborn wench left him no choice. When his bribes and strategems hadn't worked, he had offered to marry her in earnest, the first such offer he'd made in his life; he did not take kindly to being turned down. He could grovel, of course, but there was only one problem: Devil Strathmore did not grovel. The wind soughed through the mulberry tree and riffled through his loose shirtsleeves and his hair.

With a resolute nod to Ben, he stepped up onto the ladder and began to climb. Full of confidence, he grasped the smooth wood rails, rising quickly, his footing on the rungs firm and sure. His pulse raced as he mounted higher toward his reluctant bride.

Reaching the top of the ladder, he peered carefully over the windowsill, trying to catch a glimpse of his quarry between the slow waving of the curtains. He saw a writing table, then waited intently for the curtains to blow again at the right angle.

It would be difficult to take her by surprise if she was working at her desk, he thought, but with any luck, the little oddball bluestocking would be so engrossed in her translations that she would not be aware of him until he was upon her.

Aha! he thought as he caught another glimpse of her desk. She was not at it. Creeping higher onto the ladder, he saw her humble cot. The curtains revealed a pretty elbow, a quick glimpse of a foot.

She's in bed. Somehow this made his heart pound faster.

Watching for another minute or two, hearing nothing, he decided to advance. He reached in through the open window and pushed one of the curtains aside. When he looked in, his eyes widened. For a second, he was hit with such a jolt of lust at the sight of her that he nearly fell off the ladder.

The candle had burned down to a stub beside her bed; the dog-eared book that lay across her chest informed him that she had fallen asleep while reading. Gone was the overly modest gown, undone was the tight chignon of earlier today.

She slept in silken splendor; the flickering candle illumined her pearly white skin and rich brown mane that spilled across her pillow. Her cheeks were a delicate shade of shell pink, her lashes the soft black of a sooty dove. She lay sprawled in luxurious ease, one arm carelessly strewn above her head, her long legs tangled up in her demure white chemise. She looked so very soft and inviting. Dev could not take his eyes off her. His desire raged into thunderous conquest.

This, ah, *this* was how he remembered her from their delicious night together. He needed more.

His eyes burning in the dim glow, he stepped firmly onto the top rung of the ladder and eased onto the windowsill. Sitting on it briefly, he swung one leg into the room, then the other. Planting both black boots on the wooden floor, he crept over to her bed in predatory silence, staring down at her all the while.

By God, he'd had women all over the globe, but this sleeping princess was a pure English rose. She was the loveliest, sweetest thing he had ever seen. Fierce demand tautened his body; instinct pounded in his blood, possessiveness, craving.

Mine.

His heart hammered in his chest. The game had changed suddenly, drastically, as if some massive earthquake had just rearranged the ground beneath his feet. Because if she was his wife, he could have her whenever he bloody well pleased. The morning. The daytime. The middle of the night. He'd have it all. Not taking his hungry stare off her, he lowered himself to his knees beside her.

Touching his finger and thumb to his tongue, he reached over to the bedside table and pinched out the candle's flame.

The dream stole softly through her sleeping brain, wrapping her in cloud wisps and stars. The west wind came to her softly, blowing warm breath on her cheek, swirling down beside her bed, as delicate as floating mist before taking the shape of a man.

She was too amazed to be afraid, especially when she knew somehow that he had sought her out, of all the women on the globe. He had blown in from halfway round the world, a tousled, dark god from some Classical painting; the scent of frankincense clung in his night-dark hair, the smell of distant spice islands far across the green-blue sea.

When she felt his gentle caress on her hair, stirring her, urging her to join him, she understood, though he did not speak aloud. *You, Elizabeth. Only you*. There was so much he wanted to show her. *Yes, show me*. She longed to fly away with him from this dull earth; she wanted to go up on high with him where she could hear the tinkling music of the stars.

All of this he understood, though the words were only in her mind. Then she felt the thrill of unbound freedom as the god of the west wind gathered her in his arms and gently scooped her up in his embrace. Though he was made only of air and dreams, his strength was solid; she had never felt more safe, protected. *Cherished*.

His warm breath nuzzled her ear with the utmost tenderness, but she knew that the mighty immortal could flatten cities with his wrath of wind and storm if he saw fit.

She could feel him lifting her gently off her bed and struggled to find her voice, needing to tell him he must have her back by dawn or Mrs. Hall would be cross. But when her heavy-lidded eyes fluttered open, the dream changed abruptly, baffling her. She stared in confusion.

'Devlin?'

He froze, sending her a guilty look askance.

A shocked cry left her lips, the spell of sleep breaking as she jolted fully awake in his arms. He reacted before she could fight him, dropping her straight back down onto her bed. She landed flat on her stomach.

She started to turn over to demand an explanation, but he stopped her, setting his knee firmly across her back, holding her down. When she opened her mouth to curse him, she tasted a silky cloth. She felt his nimble fingers tying it behind her head.

'I'm terribly sorry about this, *chérie*, but I regret to say you forced my hand,' he murmured as she choked on her furious indignation.

What the deuce is going on? The next thing she knew, he lifted her up and slung her over his shoulder.

'Don't be alarmed, my little bride. We'll be under way in a moment. Just do me the courtesy of holding very still.' He climbed out the window and onto a ladder.

She would have shrieked if not for the gag as she found herself staring down at the ground three storeys below. Her heart pounding, she jolted instinctively, recoiling from the drop-off in terror.

'Hold still!' he hissed, clamping her harder against his shoulder. 'There's no point in any of this if I drop you!'

Oh, God! she thought, going motionless, her eyes flying open wide as she divined what he was about. He couldn't do this!

The man was utterly mad! She clung to his neck with one hand and clutched a handful of his shirt with the other, for even being carried off by Devil Strathmore, though dire, was not as bad as breaking her neck from a headfirst dive off a ladder. She saw Ben standing below, looking distressed as he held the ladder steady.

The moon looked on in sly complicity as her abductor climbed down with bold confidence, lowering himself smoothly and silently, rung by rung. She willed herself not to kick him – indeed, she barely dared breathe for fear of upsetting his balance – but her eyes were narrowed in rage.

Oh, Devil Strathmore, you are done for when we reach the ground. She ducked her face away from the scraping twigs of the mulberry tree, planning her assault.

The moment that both of his shiny black Hessians sank firmly into the soft-packed turf, she launched her attack with a sharp knee in his stomach.

'Uff!' As he doubled over a little, taken off guard by the

blow, she twisted and jumped down off his shoulder, landing unsteadily on her bare feet.

She quickly caught her balance and whirled around to go dashing back up the ladder, but he grabbed her by her waist and plucked her off it before she had climbed the third rung.

'Ben, get rid of the ladder!' he ordered in a whisper while Lizzie thrashed in his hold, cursing him through the silken gag.

Ben obeyed, pulling the ladder back and tilting it down to the horizontal, then carrying the awkward thing away.

'Stop it!' Dev hissed in her ear as he fought to stop her angry flailing. 'You're coming with me!'

With a single, muffled syllable, she demanded the obvious question.

'Why, Gretna Green, my love.'

Her eyes shot open wide.

'And we shall live happily ever after,' he added in a sarcastic growl.

She stared at him in shock, then fought him again, redoubling her efforts – but this time the brute was ready for her. Her best punch collided with a chest of flexed steel. She looked up slowly at his face, suddenly rethinking her attack. He arched his eyebrow sardonically.

Then he reached for her. Their battle exploded. The patient, the mild, most civilized Miss Carlisle fought like a wild woman, and the most infuriating thing of all was that he barely needed to exert himself, warding off her blows with a cunning laugh when she advanced, stopping her from escaping when she tried to retreat.

Everything she tried was futile. When she reached to untie the knotted gag, he caught her right hand and picked her up, tossing her over his shoulder with a devilish laugh. With her body draped across his neck, her hip and wrist pinioned in his viselike grip, he stalked off like some ogre shepherd who had caught a lamb for his Easter feast.

Gretna Green! she thought in helpless fury. There was nothing she could do but glare at Ben as he opened the garden gate for his master, taking pains not to let it squeak. *Traitor!*

Ben shrugged, looking guilty. Devil Strathmore strode through it. Ben hurried to get the ladder, which he had left leaning against the fence.

They must have looked like a very odd trio: two men, one ladder, and an abducted girls'-school governess in a night rail, hurriedly crossing the moonlit commons that sat in plain view of the school.

She saw that they had hidden Devlin's shiny black coach a safe distance away in a stand of trees. His Fresian horses shifted patiently in their traces, the leader tied to a tree trunk.

This is impossible! she thought, more exasperated than afraid. She was far too sensible to be abducted by a dashing aristocrat. This was Jacinda's sort of thing, not hers at all.

Devil Strathmore did not seem to grasp that fact as he strode over to his carriage, yanked open the door, and tumbled her into the chassis.

'Leave the ladder! Just drive!' he ordered Ben, his tempestuous profile silvered by moonlight as he shot a hurried glance at his servant.

Lizzie righted herself on the soft leather squabs. Barely a minute later, he stepped into the coach, pulling the door shut as the thing started moving. Ben drove the horses out from the cover of the trees and turned the coach down the lane. Devlin locked the carriage door, then pulled down the canvas shades. Her heart pounded; she flattened her back tensely against the seat. The shades blotted out the moonlight, and now she could not see him at all in the darkness, could only hear the rhythm of his breathing, feel him moving closer, sense his heat.

She reached her trembling hands behind her head to untie her gag, then nearly screamed into the breath-moistened silk when his fingers closed around her wrists.

'No, *chérie*. Not yet,' he whispered.

Her pulse beat like native war drums as he captured both her wrists and slowly moved them up slightly over her head. She protested as he slipped her hands through the leather hand loop above the carriage window and used it to bind her wrists together.

Her emotions churned in a flutter of fear, with an edge of terrible excitement. Her bindings were not painful; Devlin's fingertips glided along the line of her bare arms, exquisitely gentle. She remembered the way he had held her down in bed, how wickedly she had enjoyed it. She vowed to herself that she'd die before she'd let him know he aroused her even now, angry as she was at him.

'I do regret that you make these measures necessary, *my lady*.' He emphasized the term. 'But now that I have you suitably restrained, let me make a few things perfectly clear.' He closed the small space between them, moving up behind her.

She tried to jerk away, but he pressed gently on her belly and her thigh, stilling her, his hands resting with casual dominance atop the thin white muslin of her night rail.

'Shh. There's no use fighting me. You know it's meant to be.'

Her heart hammered with mingled fear and thrill, her eyes adjusting gradually to the deeper darkness inside the coach. The warmth of his breath tickled her earlobe.

'Yes, that's better. You listen well, my lady,' he ordered in a whisper as his hand stroked her thigh, up and down, slowly. 'There's not going to be any bookshop in Russell Square. You're going to marry me and be a proper viscountess whether you like it or not, and if your precious Knight brothers want my blood, let them try me. By then you'll already be mine.' His sly touch glided up between her legs. He cupped his hand possessively over her mound. 'After all—' His hand traveled higher, claiming every inch of her for his own, until it came to rest firmly on her stomach. 'You won't think of trying to back out of it when I've planted my babe in your belly.'

She shuddered with desire, but shook her head stubbornly, refusing him with all her strength.

'Yes,' he breathed. 'You can't fight it. You want it. I want it . . . and you should know by now that I always get what I want. Don't I?' He bent his head and kissed the crook of her neck, resuming in a low, wicked whisper. 'Do you know what I want right now, Miss Carlisle?'

She was trembling with passion now, and trying very hard to hide the fact, willing herself to hold perfectly still.

'I want to make you *come*,' he whispered slowly.

She moaned through the gag as he cupped her breasts.

Her skin was fevered, her head reeling as though she had drunk too much wine. She was overwhelmed by the sweet torment of her yearning, ashamed to the core for her wanton response, but glad, ever so glad of the bindings that made her his prisoner, and the length of silk that stopped her from demanding what she did not really want – for him to stop.

'You are going to be my wife, sweet. It's right that you should accustom yourself to my touch. Yes, that's good,' he whispered hoarsely, watching her beginning to take pleasure in his caresses, for she could no longer fight it.

She tilted her head back, clay in his hands as he raked his fingers through her hair.

'My God, you are the rarest pearl, all pure and white . . . with skin like virgin snow.' His shaky whisper trailed off. He slipped the silk gag down from her mouth, moving smoothly to the front of her, but his hand trembled as he grasped her face, and she did not fight him at all when he took her mouth.

He kissed her with drugging depth and held her ardently, running his hand up the curve of her spine, as if he could not gather her close enough to satisfy him. She was not satisfied either, pulling against her restraints with her need to wrap her arms around him.

'Free my hands,' she whispered, panting when he let her come up for air.

'Why? So you can fight me?' he taunted.

'So I can touch you.'

'No,' he breathed, and gave her a darkly sensual smile. He bent his head by degrees, deliberately teasing her. He pulled off his shirt and ran a grazing touch down his chest, inviting her to look at him. Dying to get her hands on him, she pulled against the leather strap, which succeeded only in tightening the knot.

He laughed at her panting frustration, then relented at last, kissing her again with tantalizing slowness.

She whimpered for more when he stopped; as he slipped behind her again, she glanced hungrily at his body and saw what appeared to be a healing gash two or three inches long on his side.

'What happened to you?' she murmured, nodding at it.

'All in a night's work, love. Never you mind.'

'You are an infuriating man.'

'So I'm told.' The hem of her night rail skimmed her thighs as he lifted it, sinking onto his knees behind her on the carriage floor. She was unable to stop him as he lifted the muslin high, exposing her to the cool caress of the night air, while his warm breath tickled against her skin.

Then all thought fled as he trailed sensuous kisses down the small of her back and bent his head lower, nibbling each round cheek of her backside.

Ah, the man was driving her insane. His fingertips explored the cleft of her derriere, bringing the most curious little bursts of delight at the strangeness of his gentle probing. Then she gasped when he slipped his fingers inside her sex; she heard his low growl of pleasure to find her already sopping wet. She dropped her head back, blissfully acquiescent; she was utterly at his mercy as he began pleasuring her with a ruthless determination.

Her breathing came shallow and fast. God, she had needed him for so many weeks, had dreamed of his hands on her body, and now it was real, exceeding her fantasies. She shivered, closed her eyes, and allowed herself to absorb the sensations that began spiraling through her. She rocked her hips in time with his expert stroking, beginning to drown in a flood of blissful sensation. *Harder*.

He responded as though he had read her mind, giving exactly what she craved. *God.*

His hoarse whisper filled her world, urging her toward the cataclysm. 'Give in, sweeting. Let go for me, love.' He bit her hip, and she groaned wildly. Her chemise was tangled about her; her skin slick with a fine mist of sweat. She felt marked by him, smeared with his scent.

Every nerve ending tingled with readiness; her body quivered and strained against her bonds, lifting, arching in needy longing, until suddenly, the shattering climax crashed through her. She flung her head back with a wanton cry, her flesh pulsating with release. Her heart pounded wildly as the fiery bursts racked her body and then faded slowly.

Caught up in sensation, she was barely aware of him gently untying her bonds. He scooped her limp body into his arms and cradled her against his chest, kissing her fevered brow. She could feel his heart pounding, however, and realized the effort he was making to hold his own need in check.

It was beyond her power to help him at the moment, in any case. She rested, spent, in his embrace. 'How are such things possible?' she panted after a long moment.

She felt him smile against her brow. 'I trust that is a rhetorical question.'

She laughed weakly.

'You see?' he murmured. 'Being married to me won't be all bad.'

She considered protesting, but did not have the strength. He reached across the coach for his discarded jacket and covered her with it.

'There, sweeting, I don't want you catching cold.' He tucked the ends around her sides with a tenderness that rather amazed her.

She watched him with a bemused expression. 'I'm impressed,' she said after a moment.

'By?'

'Your restraint.'

He smiled and languidly rested his cheek on his knuckles. 'No wife of mine gets deflowered in the back of a carriage. My viscountess deserves better than that.'

She looked away with a small sigh of mingled yearning and distress. What a rogue he was. Perhaps they were well matched in *some* respects, she admitted to herself. Perhaps she did find him unbearably attractive. Perhaps he challenged her as no man ever had.

But that still did not mean she had agreed to marry him. That still did not mean that a marriage based on money was a good idea, or that she deemed it wise to shackle herself to a gazetted rake.

Really, a man should not be allowed to simply invade a lady's chamber and haul her off like a sack of grain. He had tranquilized her with this delicious haze of sensuality, but his words had pierced her trance with the jarring recollection of the real reason he wanted this 'marriage.'

Five hundred thousand reasons sterling, to be exact.

The coach barreled on toward Scotland. She moved the canvas shade aside, glancing worriedly out the window. Heavens, when had they merged onto the Great North Road? There was a hayrick, an occasional barn. The fields were outlined by thick hedgerows, but the countryside looked unfamiliar.

'What's the matter, sweet?'

She looked over and saw him studying her. She was weakened infinitesimally by the tender look on his chiseled face, sculpted by shadows.

Husband, she thought dazedly. *Husband?*

She turned away from him and forced her gaze out the window again. 'I need to stop.'

He scanned her profile until she glanced impatiently at him, blushing.

'Pardon, but I need the loo. If it's not too much to ask?' she insisted with what she hoped was a guileless expression.

'Very well.' He lowered the window, called his instructions to Ben, and then pulled his shirt back on.

If she had expected him to take her to a roadside inn, she was sadly mistaken. His indulgence for her claim of bodily needs ran upon decidedly more primitive lines.

She stared at him in dismay when he pointed her toward a stand of trees shrouded by tall bushes off by the roadside. 'Surely you jest.'

'No. What did you think I meant?' he asked in surprise as he held the carriage door for her and waited for her to step down.

'A coaching inn!'

'You're not dressed.'

'Thanks to you! Is this the accommodations you provide for your "viscountess"?' she berated him. 'At least a proper outhouse—'

'Do you want to stop or not? I am not taking you to a public inn, because I know you'll try to escape.'

'Fine!' Yanking his black coat more securely around her scantily clad body, she jumped down from the carriage, letting out an expletive as sharp gravel on the road pricked her bare feet. 'I will never forgive you if you look,' she warned as she hobbled across the highway toward the tall grasses waving along the roadside.

His elegant frown was full of reproach. 'Really, what do you take me for?'

'A kidnapper, to start,' she muttered, then ventured cautiously into the nearby field while Ben checked on the horses.

'Don't worry, I'll wait right here,' he called as she climbed over the hedgerow stile.

You do that, Dev dear, she thought, gloating slightly as she embarked on her escape. She stole one look back at him as she climbed down the other side.

He stood tall and proud in the moonlight, but true to his word, he turned around and faced the coach, giving her her privacy.

Heart pounding, she stole off into the field. The knee-high grasses were cool and dry; twigs crackled, but she ignored the small jabs here and there as they broke beneath her running feet. Thankful for his black coat that helped conceal her in the dark, she slipped behind the cover of the tall bushes and kept running, dashing through the grove of trees, past a tranquil farm that slumbered under the silvery moon.

'Everything all right?' he called.

She glanced back over her shoulder but kept running. He was still standing on the road, his back politely turned. She knew her lack of a response would alert his suspicion, but she dared not answer for fear of revealing her whereabouts. She just kept going, scanning the landscape for a hiding place. Her pulse pounded as she realized that in moments he would be after her.

'Lizzie?'

Though the distance she had already put between them muffled his deep voice, she could hear the note of worry in it.

'Lizzie!'

She dropped into a crouching position beside one of the farm's outbuildings. A flurry of low, worried cooing from within told her that the little shed was a dovecote.

'Lizzie!'

He's coming.

His voice grew louder. 'Ben, look sharp! She's run off!'

Nervous fear darted through her. She swallowed hard, wrinkling her nose at the smell of the dovecote. She knew if he caught her, he would not fall for a similar trick again. This was her only opportunity to escape.

'Lizzie, stop this foolishness!' he yelled into the darkness. 'Use your head! You're marrying me, and that's final!'

A flicker of motion caught her eye, drawing her gaze to the white of his shirt. He was stalking toward the bushes that he had actually expected a lady like her to use for an outhouse! Oh, that man. She crept around from the dovecote to survey her exit route. As she edged up to the side of the little shed and peeked around the corner, her eyes flared with sudden hope. A plump sorrel pony stood lazily resting its jowls on the top rail of its paddock. Its tapered ears flicked forward as it listened to Dev's stormy calls with a look of pleasant curiosity.

A bridle hung from the nearby post. She bit her lip, glancing back at Devlin in thrumming indecision. Horse-stealing was a hanging offense, but this was different. She was an abducted young lady of good name and connections on the run from a wicked viscount. Right?

'Damn it, girl, I will turn you over my knee when I've got you! Where are you?'

The devil you will – Devil!

She glided out from the shadows of the dovecote and tiptoed toward the pony, greeting it softly so that she would not spook the animal. 'Hullo, darling. There's a sweet little pony. I wonder if I might . . . borrow you . . .'

She lifted the bridle off the post. The pony picked its head up off the rail and ambled toward her, ears twitching.

She made friends with it at once, feeding it a handful of grass. Her hand trembled as the pony lipped the grass off her palm; then she silently climbed the fence. 'There's a good boy.' She stepped down into the earthen paddock, half in dread of getting her bare feet stepped on under the creature's hoofs, but the pony must have been a large child's mount, for it was as gentle as a lamb. It took the bit agreeably into its mouth.

Murmuring gently to the animal all the while, Lizzie led the pony over to the gate and opened it. She stood on the bottom rail to boost her up onto the stout pony's barrel back. Without a saddle, she had no choice but to ride astride, her night rail tucked about her legs, her bare feet hanging down. She gathered the reins and squeezed the pony's satiny sides with her calves, guiding it out of the paddock.

'Lizzie!'

Devlin burst out of the shadows by the dovecote just as the pony lurched into a bouncy trot. He rushed them. 'Get back here!'

'Go!' She kicked the pony's sides and clung to the animal in alarm, urging her little mount into a brisk canter.

Devlin tried to grab her right off the pony's back as she swept past him, but he missed, his hands clutching only air. 'Damn it, come back here!'

She glanced back and saw him running after them, but even an athletic man like him was no match for her equine ally.

Trailing defiant laughter, Lizzie rode off on the cantering pony, victorious. She had won! She was free – and it felt glorious.

Dev chased her for only a few more strides into the field before he gave up, his pumping legs slowing to a halt. Chest heaving with exertion, he bent forward slightly, planting his hands on his thighs as he caught his breath. He let out a curse, but as he heard her nymphlike laughter and glanced in her direction, he caught one last glimpse of her beaming face before she went racing away astride the plump pony, wrapped in his oversize coat, her long hair flying out behind her.

He just stared, his anger melting.

She looked so happy, so blasted proud of herself. How could he be angry when she was so damned adorable? He felt an ache of inexplicable joy swelling in his heart, and as he watched her gallop off, he began laughing wearily. He stood up straight again, laughing harder, raking both his hands through his hair.

'Look at her, Ben,' he said as his servant rushed up beside him, looking frantic. 'Have you ever seen anything more beautiful in your entire life? Look at her go. By God, what a fool I've been.'

'Sir?' Ben panted.

'She deserves it. The title. The money. And she shall have it. With God as my witness, I'm going to marry that girl. What spirit. What heart,' he whispered.

Ben did not quite seem to absorb his words. 'I'll unhitch the lead horse. If you can ride after her, you can catch her in minutes—'

'No.' Dev shook his head slowly, still smiling. 'Let her have her victory.' He could not take his eyes off her, and they shone even after she had disappeared over the moonlit rise. 'She bested me fair and square. There's no way I could take that away from her.'

'Are you feeling all right?'

'Never better. Come on.' He gave his trusty valet a manly slap on the back. 'Let's get the carriage turned around. She'll keep to the fields to avoid us, but we'll give her an escort back to the school. These roads are not the safest place at night.'

'The Gretna plan is off, then?' Ben asked in confusion as they strode back to the waiting carriage.

'Afraid so,' Dev sighed.

'Well, what now?'

Dev smiled in the direction she had gone. 'Now I do it her way.'

Moving happily through the moonlight, Lizzie followed the Great North Road as her guide home, but stayed off it, keeping to the fields and woods as the pony swung along at a comfortable walk. As it became clear that she had successfully evaded her handsome captor, exhilaration crested through her, an almost giddy triumph after her brash escape.

At last, an adventure of her very own! She felt gloriously alive, free.

The pony swiveled its tapered ears, listening to her as she hummed to pass the time and to allay her nervousness as she ventured onward through the dark. There was plenty of time to reflect on what they had shared inside the coach. Her wonder at it all made the whole moonlit world seem to shimmer as the pony trotted down a small gully, crossed a shallow rivulet, and scrambled up the other side.

She rode on.

Before long, an arrowed road sign pointed her toward Islington. She guided the pony across the road, kicking him into a canter. They hurried into the field across the way, and in another quarter hour, she recognized the sweep of the countryside and knew exactly where she was.

She would have to hurry, she realized. The staff and teachers rose at six.

Sunrise had just begun to tinge the eastern horizon with a pink blush when Lizzie reined the pony to a halt in the same stand of trees where Dev had hidden the coach several hours ago. The ladder still lay there, vaguely outlined in the tall grasses.

Across the green, all the school windows were still dark. Her heart hammered, for she knew it would cost her her position if Mrs. Hall found out what had happened. She slid down off the trusty pony's back, then hugged the gentle creature, slipped off its bridle, and freed it. She threw the bridle atop the ladder, then shrugged off Dev's coat and left it there, as well.

The gray dawn air glided coolly against her bare arms as she stole away from the grove, running silently toward the school. Glancing up, she saw her bedroom window still hanging wide open, just as Dev had left it when he had carried her off. She vaulted the fence, her chemise flying up about her knees, and darted around the back of the building, her heart pounding madly.

Oh, Jacinda was going to die of laughter when she told her about this. If she managed to get through this alive, she would write to her at once and suggest they have tea. She was eager to tell her best friend everything about Devlin and the madcap conditions surrounding Lady Strathmore's will.

Her light humor plunged into dread, however, when she rushed through the garden to the back door only to find it locked. Good Lord, she couldn't get back inside!

Then she remembered the mulberry tree.

Her heart sank as she realized it was her only hope. She hurried back around to the front of the building and approached the towering tree. Even as a child, she had never been a tomboy. Tree-climbing was hardly her forte.

She tilted her head back, dubiously planning her ascent, but when light suddenly shone through the curtains on one of the first-floor rooms, she gasped, flinging herself behind the trunk. Her pulse pounding, she knew there was not a moment to lose. Time to give it a go. Grabbing a sturdy branch, she swung up and thrust a bare foot carefully into the tree's barky groin.

Dev's coach rolled past the green just in time to glimpse a fair white foot disappearing into her bedroom window. Relief poured through him now that her safety was assured. His eyes beamed with some newfound emotion, a narrow smile twisting his lips. The pony grazed on the commons; a few lights burned in the school's windows.

'Should we bring the animal back?' Ben called in a loud whisper from the driver's box.

'Not yet,' Dev answered in worldly amusement. 'We wouldn't want to make it too easy on our little horse-thief, now, would we? Drive on.'

Ben obeyed, slapping the horses' rumps with the reins. The coach glided quietly into motion.

Dev watched her bedroom window until the curve of the road pulled it out of sight, then, smiling to himself in thoughtful amusement, he looked forward again, stroking his jaw.

It appeared he had best start planning his apology.

Chapter Thirteen

The next morning, despite her brush with ruin and a serious lack of sleep, Lizzie taught her classes in a thoroughly cheerful mood, still filled with the glow of her triumph.

Not even Mrs. Hall's disapproving remarks about Devlin's unauthorized visit on the green yesterday had dampened her spirits. Fortunately, when she had explained that he was merely the late Lady Strathmore's nephew, come on 'family business' pertaining to his aunt's will, the headmistress had been mollified. Then at midday, a gift arrived for her – a basket of fine, leather-bound books with a little note that sent her heart soaring anew:

> *My Dear Elizabeth,*
> *Please accept these humble offerings as a token of my most wretched remorse for my abandoned behavior last night. Take pity on a poor sinner. I crave a moment of your time that I may apologize properly. Please write back to say where and when I may see you again. You are all that fills my thoughts.*
>
> *Your humble servant,*
> *Strathmore*

Humble servant, indeed, she thought, smiling in spite of herself. *Laying it on a bit thick, Dev, dear.* Yet her pulse fluttered joyously as she read the note five times over in rapid succession.

Considering her countermove for a moment, she dashed off a quick note of her own while her students tapped away on their slates – but her letter was not to Devlin. No, the scoundrel could cool his heels for a few days waiting for her response. Instead, with a wily smile curving her lips, she wrote to her glamorous best friend:

> *Good Morning, Mrs. Billy!*
> *A favor? If there's a ball, rout, etc. that you plan to attend this Sat. eve, might I tag along, like in the old days? It will be my day off and let's just say a* situation *has arisen regarding a certain Devil of my acquaintance . . .*
>
> *Kisses,*
> *Lizzie*

'Sweetie!' Jacinda cried, arriving promptly on the doorstep of Mrs. Hall's Academy on Saturday afternoon to collect her for their leisurely ritual of dressing and getting ready for the ball, which was to be hosted this night by Lord and Lady Madison.

As always, the nineteen-year-old marchioness was all bubbly vivacity and dressed to elegant perfection in a long-sleeved pelisse of lavender silk over a white muslin walking dress. Her golden curls bounced beneath the brim of her matching lavender hat as she skipped over the threshold of her old school, grasped Lizzie's hands, and swung her around in a half-circle with a peal of girlish laughter. 'Oh, we're going to have such fun!'

Jacinda hugged her tightly for a moment, then began talking a mile a minute. 'Oh, Lizzie, I'm so happy to see you! It's been *monstrous* dull in Society without you, but now that you're coming with me, I can hardly wait for the ball! Everyone's going to be in alt to see you! I daresay it's time you came back into the fold, stubborn thing. Come, let me rescue you from this dull place.' She tucked Lizzie's hand through the crook of her arm with a proprietary air. 'I have a million ideas of what we can do with your hair. I've ordered my jewels taken from the vault, so you can wear whatever you want with your new gown, though I recommend diamonds—'

'New gown?'

Jacinda turned prettily to her. 'Guess what I did?'

'Jas!'

'Oh, hush. I commissioned a gown for you from *the* Mrs. Bell, whom I've engaged exclusively for the rest of the day, and who will be waiting for us at the house to perfect your fitting. Come, we haven't a moment to lose.'

'You shouldn't have.'

She waved off Lizzie's protest without concern. 'Consider it an early birthday present, dearest. It was no trouble, honestly! Mrs. Bell kept our measurements on file from last Season. Now, if you don't like it, not to worry – I've had Anne air out and press a couple of your favorite ball gowns from last year – they were still in your room at Knight House – but I do think you should trust me in this. You said you wanted my expertise. Oh, I'm so pleased someone needs my silly, trivial knowledge for once! It's hardly calculus or German, my dear bluestocking, but it does come in handy now and then,' she teased, and laughing, gave Lizzie a girlish squeeze about the shoulders. 'I'm so happy you called on me! Isn't it droll – *I'm* to be your chaperon tonight? What a lark!'

'Oh, Jas, I've missed you,' Lizzie said, laughing in spite of herself. 'You make everything an *occasion*.'

'Well, this time it *is* an occasion, isn't it, my dear? I think this may be the first time in your entire life that you've ever asked for my help – or anyone else's, for that matter – and after all your innumerable kindnesses to me, well, it's past time you let someone else look after you for a change. Now, come,' she commanded, tugging Lizzie toward the door while twenty awed schoolgirls peered down from the stairs at the famed fashion plate so celebrated in the Society columns. 'I want to know everything about this Devil Strathmore of yours! You wicked creature, keeping secrets from me.'

She hadn't heard the half of it, Lizzie thought, but just when they were about to make a clean getaway, Mrs. Hall bustled out into the foyer.

Judging by the purposeful look on her face, Lizzie instantly guessed the headmistress had once again thought of 'one more task' she must do before she would be allowed to leave for her day off.

Mrs. Hall, however, had not counted on seeing Jacinda.

The headmistress gasped and nearly fell forward in her haste to curtsy to her former problem student. 'Oh, goodness, why, Lady Truro! What an honor to have you visit our humble academy again. May I offer belated well-wishings on your recent nuptials.'

Instantly, Jacinda took charge as she was wont to do, the exuberant mischief-maker vanishing behind the well-honed pomp of the grand marchioness. 'Good afternoon, Mrs. Hall,' Her Ladyship intoned with a generous bow of her head. 'I thank you kindly for sparing Miss Carlisle for the day, but I wonder, could you not find it in your heart to excuse her of her Sunday duties, as well? The Lord's Day, after all, was meant for a day of rest, and I am desperate for my dearest friend to attend me.'

'Well, er, if it would please you, my lady, I'm sure that could – be arranged.'

'How very kind you are, Mrs. Hall. I will be sure to remark upon it much in Society.'

'Oh, thank you, my lady! Thank you!'

Lizzie managed not to roll her eyes and wondered what Mrs. Hall would require of her to make up for it once her high-ranking patroness had gone again. Ah, well, Jacinda had been merrily leading her into mischief all her life. Why stop now?

With a grateful nod to her employer, Lizzie allowed Jacinda to shepherd her outside to her waiting coach, an enormous and showy affair crawling with liveried footmen and drawn by four white horses with plumes on their heads. The footman handed them up into the lavish equipage, and Lizzie sat down on the pale, kid-leather squabs across from her friend. A moment later, the vehicle rolled into motion, whisking them southward toward Town.

'Well?' Jacinda demanded, drawing off her lavender gloves with a businesslike air. 'Now, what is going on between you and Viscount Strathmore?'

By the time they reached Jacinda's newly built Nash villa on the edge of Regent's Park, Lizzie had told her the whole story, from the shocking terms of Lady Strathmore's will, to her escape from Dev's kidnapping attempt on the back of a stolen pony.

Jacinda's reaction alternated between scandalized laughter and shocked delight. 'Oh, Lizzie, he sounds divine!'

'You would say that.'

'At least he doesn't treat you like his sister.'

Lizzie chuckled, for it was an ongoing jest between them. For some reason throughout her girlhood, every young man she had met went panting over Jacinda but treated Lizzie with the same warm, chaste respect he might show his mother or his sister. Not even Alec had ever tried to steal a kiss. It was most tedious.

'Well, do you like him or not?' Jacinda exclaimed.

Blushing helplessly, Lizzie stared at her friend in mingled joy and distress, then shrugged. 'You know I would never do those things with him if I didn't, but of course, he's terribly debauched, if the stories in the paper are true, and secondly, I'm not about to lose my head over a man whose sole interest in me is for the sake of gaining wealth. I have my pride. Besides, I am sure the immediate gain could not outlast the misery of a lifetime married to a man who doesn't love one.'

'Hear, hear,' Jacinda agreed.

'Of course . . .' Lizzie dropped her gaze and toyed shyly with the tassel on the end of her reticule. 'If I could be convinced that he wanted me for myself, not for the money, that he had some genuine feeling for me, I . . . would not be averse to his attentions,' she admitted, peeping bashfully at her friend from under her lashes.

A merry grin spread over Jacinda's face. 'Ah, my dear. Say no more. I understand completely. Trust me,' she murmured, leaning closer with a confidential air. 'When Lord Strathmore sees you tonight, his inheritance money will be the farthest thing from his mind.'

For three days, Dev had waited on edge for Lizzie's answer, then came her letter with its imperious instructions and the scramble to procure a last-minute invitation to the Madison ball on Saturday night. That had been a bit precarious, for his association with the likes of Randall, Carstairs, and Staines had compromised his place on the guest lists of London's first circles. He had prevailed, however, and the appointed evening had come at last.

To his dismay, however, the intrepid E. Carlisle was late.

Indeed, he was beginning to wonder if she had sent him here on a fool's errand, his punishment, perhaps. For all he knew, she had no intention of coming, and was merely teaching him one of her infamous 'lessons.' Waiting for her in a state of nervous uncertainty, he could not help brooding on the unappetizing knowledge that foremost on his agenda this night was a grand grovel. For that reason, all things considered, so far, Dev hated this ball.

It ought to have been pleasant enough. It was a gorgeous May evening. The party was lavish, hosted by Lord and Lady Madison at their summer home – a Thames-side villa by Inigo Jones, built as a neo-Palladian temple in a garden setting. But he was miserable. He looked again at his fob watch and wished that he had thought to bring a gentleman's fan. He could smell the starch in his cravat as the sweat from the back of his neck seeped into it. God, he could not remember being this nervous since his schooldays before a big exam!

Hot, restless, and desperately bored, he eschewed the damask-upholstered benches pushed back to the sides of the room and leaned in one of the window nooks, his stare fixed on the entrance. Here, at least, he could get some air and take refuge from the crush of guests thronging the long gallery being used as a ballroom.

The walls were hung with red silk with white pilasters and a plasterwork frieze, lightly gilded. The chamber had a parquetry floor and a coffered apse at the far end where the brass band sat, determined to murder them all by sheer volume. The acoustics of the narrow space did not suit the blaring, bouncy march to which the company was being subjected. Dev felt a headache coming on fast, aided by the glass of sticky-sweet rum punch he had been given upon walking in.

He longed to dive into the nearby river and rather envied the nudity of the Classical statues posing around the room. With any luck, one of the huge chandeliers might fall on him and put him out of his misery, he mused. Otherwise, he could do naught but wait and go on waiting for the lady whom he feared was bent on bringing him to heel.

Then, like the answer to a prayer, the brass band took a breather just as Dev heard the majordomo announce the Marquess and Marchioness of Truro and Saint Austell.

Aha, so, this was Lizzie's beloved Lady Jacinda and her Billy. His gaze homed in on the couple: a tall, striking man with sandy hair and the dangerous aura of a chap who would cut your throat if you looked at him wrong; by his side, a glittering, little fairy queen of a lady with a mass of golden spiral-curls and dark eyes that sparkled with naughty laughter.

Hmm, he thought. This pair could be trouble. As they passed beneath the heavily pedimented doorcase and proceeded down the few stairs into the gallery, Miss Elizabeth Carlisle was announced behind them.

Dev jerked to attention, emerging from the shelter of the window nook, drawn irresistibly; when she appeared, he could have sworn that the whole ballroom let out an admiring gasp.

Standing in the doorway for a moment, she stepped into the room like a cool breeze. The droning roar of conversation halted for a second. Her white gown, light as air, was pure elegant simplicity; her hair was arranged in smooth, shiny curls that framed her face, with a strand of pearls adorning the upswept arrangement of her coiffure.

Gliding forward, she laid one white-gloved hand on the scrolled metal banister. She kept her chin high, as she descended the red-carpeted stairs with queenly grace, her gauzy gown floating around her limbs.

She was luminous like the moon.

Dev was not a man who was easily amazed, but he could not take his eyes off the woman.

His woman.

With an absurd sense of pride cresting through him, he

went to her, heedless of the two hundred pairs of eyes fixed on her. In the next moment, the room buzzed, the urgent mystery carrying all the way out the garden, where the main party was in progress.

Who is she?

I don't know her—

Is she Someone?

Matrons clustered to gossip. Dandies who had never noticed Lizzie Carlisle's existence before lifted their quizzing glasses to their haughty eyes, which then filled with interest.

Dev shoved his way toward her through the crowd, his frustration mounting when he found his path blocked by the riot of fashionable guests surrounding her and her popular friends. He particularly disliked the mob of young men forming a blockade around her, pouring out compliments and gallantries upon her.

'My dear Miss Carlisle!'

'By Jove, you look smashing!'

'Have you been on holiday? We haven't seen you in Society in ages!'

Lizzie stopped a few steps from the bottom, flattered but a little overwhelmed by the bizarre attentions of the half-dozen young gentlemen she had known for years, Jacinda's former suitors, mostly. They had certainly never made such a fuss over her before. While they clamored for dances, she looked over and saw him – her devil, clad in black.

Her heart leaped. Her blood quickened. He was beautiful enough to steal her breath, just as he always did, she thought, but something was different.

There was a glow in his eyes that she had never seen before. It lit them up like brilliant aquamarines. As he came toward her with an air of unstoppable determination, she felt her heart rising, relief pouring through every vein, for until this moment, she had not been at all sure that he would even come – that her audacity would not fall flat.

But with one look at him coming toward her through the crowd, she forgot the strategems she and Jacinda had so carefully planned out while the ladies' maid did their hair. She had meant to act aloof. But when he came to the bottom of the stairs and held out his white-gloved hand to her, waiting for her to take it with fire in his eyes, risking her rejection in front of the entire ballroom, all games and ruses fled.

She wanted this man – wanted his love. She wanted a chance at the possible future that seemed almost within reach – and so, reaching out to him, she laid her fingers on his offered palm.

His hand closed gently around hers, and he drew her to him, neither of them heeding the dismayed looks of the younger fellows. Lizzie trembled when Devlin lifted her hand to his lips and bent his head to kiss her knuckles in fervent silence.

Jacinda's polite 'Ahem!' interrupted their stare. Lizzie steadied herself and glanced over, coloring a bit. She introduced Devlin to her friends; Billy sized him up with a formidable glance, but Jacinda kept her protective, rebel husband smoothly in check, suggesting they remove to a less crowded spot.

Devlin gestured for Lizzie to go ahead of him. Likewise, Billy cleared a path for Jacinda among the guests. With the chandeliers shining on her golden ringlets, Jacinda strode ahead with a blithe smile, doling out nods here and there, while her fierce husband watched her like a man hypnotized. It took nearly twenty minutes for their party to reach the other side of the crowded ballroom, with all the pleasantries that were exchanged. Devlin stuck by Lizzie's side, a fact that was not lost on the ton's gossips. At the end of their long meander, they came to a drawing room that was hardly occupied at all, as most of the guests were either in the ballroom or outside in the vast gardens.

There were several seating areas with gilt-wood chairs and

settees upholstered in flowery silk brocade. A few guests lounged in them, chatting and languidly waving their fans. Portraits in ornately carved gilded frames hung on the walls; beneath their feet stretched a colorful carpet in a Greek honeysuckle motif.

Devlin showed Lizzie over to an armchair and sat on the matching stool across from her while Jacinda, her watchful chaperon for the evening, stood a few feet away, introducing Billy to more of the ton's elite. Jacinda sent Lizzie an inquiring glance from behind her fan, her dark eyes asking, *Are you all right?* Lizzie responded with a subtle nod, then turned her uncertain gaze to Devlin.

He was staring at her with the most earnest look on his face that she had ever seen.

'You look incredible,' he whispered.

She smiled and dropped her gaze with a blush stealing into her cheeks. It was a good start, she had to admit. 'I received the books you sent. Thanks.'

'Thank you for agreeing to hear me out. I'm not sure I deserve it.'

'Ah, well, my generous nature is legendary,' she said in self-deprecating humor, then looked cautiously into his eyes. 'What was it you wanted to say?'

He stared at her for a long moment. 'That I capitulate.'

She furrowed her brow in question.

'Never ventured into this before,' he said. 'I have no idea how it's done, so you will have to bear with me. I will no doubt try your patience, repeatedly. But I won't play any more games, Lizzie. No more bribes. No abductions. In short, I'm giving you the reins.'

'What does that mean, exactly?' she asked warily, her heart pounding.

He let out a huge sigh. 'It means you made me think long and hard on all that you said. You were right on so many points.

Look, I don't know what the hell I'm doing when it comes to love, but I'm willing to try. Are you?'

Lizzie felt a tremor of awe run through her, but she swallowed hard, refusing to walk into something that seemed too good to be true. 'You're only telling me what you think I want to hear so you can claim your inheritance. This is because of the money. Admit it.'

'Oh, yes, *completely*,' he whispered with a rakish smile spreading over his lips and a deepening smolder coming into his eyes. 'All I could possibly want is the money,' he agreed as his stare inched down her body. 'It has nothing to do with your beauty or brains. Your integrity, the way you care about the people around you. Not your wit, your honesty. And of course it has nothing to do with the fact that I haven't been with a woman since I came to your bed back in February.'

'Devlin!' she forced out in a breathless tone, slightly scandalized by his admission. Fluttering her fan with a nervous air, she glanced around to make sure no one had heard him.

He smiled in faint amusement at her. 'Lizzie. I've wanted us to be together since I met you, and you know it's true, because even in Bath, I offered to make you my mistress. To you, it may have seemed like an insult, but for me, that was a fairly big step. I want to do right by you. You're good for me, and I think I'm good for you.'

'Don't toy with me, Devlin.' She could barely find her voice. 'You could hurt me so badly.'

'I won't.' He leaned nearer. 'I'm not Alec. You've got to trust me, Lizzie. You've at least got to give me a chance. That's only fair.' He took her hand gently between both of his.

She noticed Billy eyeing her with a protective frown, until Jacinda reached up and caught her husband's chin between her fingers, turning his attention back to herself again with tender insistence that seemed to say, *Leave them alone*.

'Here's what I propose,' Devlin murmured, gazing into her eyes. 'Let me court you properly, by the book. Let's try it out, see what happens. We'll take it slowly; do the things that courting couples do, and see if we might actually suit. If, at the end of the three months my aunt's will specified, we feel that we do, then we'll marry. If we don't—'

'Then they'll throw you into the Fleet.'

'That's not your problem,' he soothed. 'Don't worry your pretty head about me, *chérie*. I'll survive.'

She plucked her hand gingerly out of his light hold and scanned his finely chiseled face in suspicion. 'I'm still not sure what to make of all this. Why are you being so nice?'

'Oh, it's really rather simple,' he answered, lounging back on his hands with a worldly smile. 'When you bested me the other night, rode off on that silly pony—' Soft amusement played at his lips at the memory, his gaze faraway. '– I discovered that it is not "winning" for me if it's "losing" for you. Surely you must've realized how easily I could have recaptured you if I had wanted to.'

'But you let me go,' she said softly. 'Why?'

'Because I was wrong in the first place, and because I realized I can't be happy in all this unless you're happy, too.'

'Devlin?' she murmured cautiously, studying him in wonder. 'I think that is the sweetest thing anyone has ever said to me.'

'Well, then.' He sent her a lazy, provoking grin. 'Perhaps I shall prove to have a knack for this love business, after all.'

'Devil,' she whispered, laughing as she blushed and dropped her gaze.

'Dare I hope that pretty smile means you are amenable to my suit, Miss Carlisle? Will you let me court you?'

As if she could say no.

'I was told once you would dare anything, Lord Strathmore,' she answered shyly.

'Really? Me? Such tales people tell,' he replied in a chiding whisper, leaning closer.

Lizzie felt herself swept up in the magnetic pull of his attraction, losing all awareness of the other guests in the room. She longed for his kiss, and he seemed more than willing to oblige her, but her neophyte chaperon suddenly stepped between them.

'Now, then, darlings, shall we take a stroll in the garden?' Jacinda interrupted brightly.

'Absolutely,' Dev replied, sending Lizzie a twinkling glance.

After he helped her gallantly to her feet, the four of them left the house through the French doors that opened onto the grounds. Outside in the balmy spring twilight, Devlin's protective touch at her elbow steered her toward the striped open tents where refreshments had been set up. Jacinda dispatched the men to fetch them each a goblet of champagne punch. The moment their broad backs were turned, Lizzie spun to face her friend with a wide-eyed look.

'Well?' Jacinda prodded.

Lizzie gripped her forearm, trying to contain her crazed joy. 'Oh, Jas,' she whispered. 'He's adorable!'

Jacinda barely suppressed a girlish squeal of excitement. 'Do you love him?'

'A little, I think!' She giggled, her eyes sparkling, cheeks aglow.

'Oh, Lizzie, he really is perfect for you! He's just dev-ine!'

Lizzie elbowed her, fighting laughter. 'Dev-astating!'

'I'll bet you can hardly wait to dev-our him! Good Lord, I thought he was going to kiss you right there in the drawing room!'

'I wouldn't put it past him. He's quite mad.'

'The best lovers always are,' she agreed in a scandalous murmur. 'Dear me, I do hope Billy's not threatening his life – or his manhood.' Jacinda tapped her folded fan against her cheek as she searched the crowd for the two tall, handsome men, then let out an amused yet pitying sigh. 'It'll be bad enough when it comes time to meet my brothers. Poor Billy was lucky to survive the interview.'

'They're not going to care. You're their sister. It's different.'

'Oh, Lizzie, won't you ever learn? You never had to marry Alec to be part of our family. You always were and always will be.'

She turned to her, taken aback by her frank declaration, when suddenly they were interrupted by a pair of Jacinda's shallow Society friends.

'Oh, Lady Truro!'

The two ostentatiously dressed and bejeweled young wives crowded Lizzie out to kiss the air beside Jacinda's cheeks as they greeted her. 'Darling, it's so nice to see you!'

'What a gorgeous gown!'

'You *are* coming to our charity breakfast next week?'

'Of course, my dears. I wouldn't miss it for the world!' Jacinda responded, adroitly deflecting their artificiality back onto them. She had to live in their world, after all, but she did not bother trying to introduce them to Lizzie, who had long since expressed her aversion to such creatures. The ladies failed to notice the deft irony in Jacinda's smiling answers.

Lizzie, being no one of any consequence, was ignored, and was glad of it. She turned from the shower of vapid conversation and took a few steps away, glancing into the crowd in the direction Devlin had gone. She did not spot him, but upon turning around again, suddenly found herself face-to-face with Alec.

The lantern behind him threw a glimmering halo over his golden hair and broad shoulders, but it cast his comely face in shadow. Hands in pockets, he stared at her with a hapless smile and a great air of weariness. 'Hullo, Bits.'

'Lord Alec.' She nodded to him, instantly going on her guard.

'You look wonderful.' His deep voice was as soft as a sigh.

She did not answer, but coming from such a leader of fashion, she supposed dryly that she ought to have swooned at the compliment. His admiring glance traveled over her. 'It's good to see you here tonight. Daresay you're causing quite a stir,' he murmured with a faint smile of pride in her. 'I wasn't sure you were ever coming back into Society.'

'Well, time heals all, they say,' she remarked in a breezy tone.

He lowered his head, contrite as a choirboy. 'I'm glad to hear it.' He paused. 'I've been thinking about you a lot lately, since that day I saw you with the children. I was hoping we could talk sometime soon.'

'I'm not sure there's anything to say.'

'Alec, darling! There you are!'

Just then, Lady Campion suddenly flung herself into their midst, sliding her hands up Alec's broad shoulder. Lizzie flinched at the intrusion.

'Where have you been, my pretty fellow? I will not be neglected,' she said with a playful pout. Ignoring Lizzie even more skillfully than Jacinda's haughty Society friends had, Lady Campion tugged Alec down a few inches to whisper something in his ear.

God, how horrendously awkward. Lizzie folded her arms across her waist and looked away, but the glamorous image of the baroness was stamped upon her mind. Rich, beautiful, widowed, and thus, free as a bird, Lady Campion was a slim brunette with a sophisticated tousle of short, dark curls tamed by a silk bandeau. The thick ribbon's long, jaunty ends trailed down one side to skim her alluring shoulder. She was clad in a lemon-striped open-robe with a white muslin underskirt; the skillful fluttering of her fan spoke volumes to every male in her presence.

Feeling slightly ill as she remembered anew how Alec had let this woman come between them, Lizzie looked away, trying to recall why she had even come. Where was Devlin? He had left her standing here like a fool. Jacinda was busy, too, now inundated by the growing knot of her hen-wit acquaintances.

Lizzie glanced again at Alec and saw he was still staring at her even as Lady Campion hung on him and half made love to him right there in the middle of the party. He was unresponsive to his wealthy mistress and her attempts to monopolize him, just gazing at Lizzie with a look of misery in his eyes and deep, deep regret.

As she watched the baroness's sickening display for a second, she realized Lady Campion had sunk her claws into Alec and had no intention of letting him go free.

Not after all she had paid for him.

Just then, Billy, bless him, returned with two goblets of punch. 'Well, now, where did that daft of mine run off to? Jas!'

'Good evening, Lord Truro,' Lady Campion purred, regarding Billy with a gleam in her eye as she slid her clasped fingers over the top of Alec's muscular shoulder.

Billy sent the woman a frown of distaste and turned to look for his wife. 'Nice of you to run off on Lizzie,' he muttered, and handed Jacinda her drink as she came hurrying over to them.

'I'm so sorry! It couldn't be helped, dearest,' she said apologetically to Lizzie. 'You see why I'm desperate for you to come to these things with me?' Jacinda sipped her punch, then furrowed her brow. 'Where's Lord Strathmore?'

Billy nodded toward the wine tent. 'He said he'd be back in a moment.'

Lizzie followed his glance and spotted Devlin, who she now saw had been detained talking to a large disreputable-looking man with brown hair.

'Did you say Strathmore?' Alec asked in surprise, pulling his face free of Lady Campion's light, possessive hold.

'Indeed. Your old school friend, I understand?' Lizzie challenged him politely.

'Rather,' Alec drawled.

'You don't sound pleased.'

He shrugged. 'It's not a friendship I've chosen to renew.'

'Why ever not?' she asked a trifle indignantly.

'I don't particularly care for the company he keeps since his return to England.'

'What do you mean?'

He started to answer, but at that moment, Lady Madison, their hostess of the evening, came bustling by, inquiring if everyone was enjoying themselves. She stopped to chat for only a moment before moving on to continue mingling among her guests. She had just left their group when Devlin rejoined them, bringing Lizzie a glass of champagne punch, which, she discovered the moment she sipped it, had gone warm.

'Sorry,' he murmured. 'I ran into someone I know and couldn't escape.'

'I noticed.' She wondered if the brawny man he had been talking to was one of the undesirables Alec had been referring to. It had been a strange remark, for Alec rarely had anything bad to say about anyone. She would've liked to have known more, but she was still officially not speaking to Alec. Under the circumstances, she was only glad that it hadn't been one of the high-society harlots like Lady Campion who had tried to divert Devlin's attention.

He bent his head and whispered tenderly in her ear: 'Are you all right? I came as soon as I saw.'

She pulled back a small space and glanced up into his eyes. His concerned expression as he searched her face assured her he had guessed who the woman was with Alec, and knew how difficult this moment was for Lizzie.

She had faltered for a moment there, but now that she had her ally by her side again, she succumbed to a reluctant half-smile. Slipping her hand through the crook of his elbow, she nodded and moved closer to his side, drawing strength from his solidity. *I am now.*

Alec was watching them intently. 'Why, Devil Strathmore,' he drawled, 'as I live and breathe.'

Devlin turned and greeted him with equally guarded savoir faire. 'Why, if it isn't Alexander the Great.'

'I'd heard you were back in Town. How are you?'

'Never better. Yourself?'

'Can't complain.'

The two old friends shook hands, but their reunion was markedly cool, and Lizzie detected a certain suspicious reserve on both sides.

'I did not know that you two were acquainted,' Alec commented, glancing from Devlin to Lizzie.

'Oh, yes, we met in Bath some time ago, didn't we?' he murmured to her, casting Lizzie a purposely besotted smile. 'This sweet pearl brought cheer to the last months of my aunt's life, and for that, I shall be eternally grateful to her.' Devlin lifted Lizzie's hand and kissed it.

Lady Campion smirked.

Alec's stare was like ice. After a moment's startled pause, he abruptly remembered his manners. 'Yes, I had heard about your aunt's passing, old boy. My condolences.'

Dev gave him a gallant nod of thanks.

'Alec, darling, aren't you going to introduce me to your friend?' Lady Campion stepped forward, fixing her speculative stare on Devlin. 'I don't believe we've met.'

Lizzie bristled.

'By all means, my lady.' With a smooth and rather crafty smile, Alec obliged the woman, more than glad, it seemed, to sic her on Dev for a while. 'Allow me to present Devlin Kimball, Viscount Strathmore. Strathmore, this is Lady Campion.'

'Ma'am,' Devlin said, bowing to her with frosty restraint.

'I never stand on formalities with handsome gentlemen, Lord Strathmore. Please,' she purred, 'call me Eva.' Extending her jeweled hand to Devlin, she waited for him to kiss it like a queen granting favors.

Devlin just looked at her; then he abruptly thrust his wine-glass into her waiting hand. 'Would you mind holding this while I dance with Miss Carlisle? Thank you so much. Let's go, sweeting. You promised me a waltz.'

With a startled blink, Lizzie hurried after him as he grasped her hand and tugged her away from them with a relentless stride, leaving Alec's haughty mistress holding the half-empty glass and wearing a look of outraged indignation.

Lizzie could barely stifle her hilarity. 'I can't believe you just did that!' She glanced back as Jacinda and Billy turned away from the furious woman, hiding their laughter.

'No one treats you like that when I'm around,' he growled. 'I am sorry, Lizzie, but I am too vexed to dance. The nerve of that witch!' He turned to her. 'Are you sure you're all right?'

'I'm fine!'

When their gazes met – his tempestuous, hers tickled – she was sure the world stopped turning for a moment, that the moon beamed brighter, and the stars danced.

'Thank you,' she whispered.

He grumbled and looked away, a little abashed.

'Devlin?' She crooked her finger at him. When he leaned down nearer, she murmured in his ear: 'I have a better idea than dancing.'

'You do?' His stormy scowl immediately vanished as he took in the flirtatious smile spreading over her face.

'Mm-hmm.' She sent a frisky glance toward the silken shadows of the moonlit gardens, then raised her eyebrow at him in question.

He smiled wickedly. 'Clever girl. That *is* a better idea. Much better.'

'Let's go.'

They escaped together through the sprawling gardens to a serene spot by the river, a secluded little flagstone terrace with a lichened stone balustrade that overlooked the water. Large stone urns with clouds of showy pinks burgeoning around tall snapdragons and trailing tendrils of fragrant honeysuckle capped the pillared ends of the stone railing, framing the moonlit view of the river in flowers and scenting the night with luxurious perfume.

With the breeze billowing gracefully through Lizzie's white gown and the moonlight glinting on Devlin's gold earring, they crossed the stone landing to the balustrade, gazing out at the rippling water.

Standing side by side, they were silent for a long moment, savoring the night and each other. The river was calm, gently lapping at the banks. A lone swan glided against the current, while, far behind them, the distant orange lights of the house and the lantern-lit garden twinkled. From down by the river's meander, they could hear the charming piece that the string quintet was playing aboard the festooned barge that their host had provided to transport the guests back and forth from the heart of London if they so desired. Then Devlin laid his hand atop hers where it rested on the stone railing. She turned to him slowly, her heart fluttering.

With a tender gaze of ineffable longing, he drew her into his strong embrace; she wrapped her arms around his neck, sighing as he lowered his head and caressed her lips with his own. Leaning into his broad chest, she tilted her head back and parted her lips for his sugar-deep kiss, savoring the taste of his tongue in her mouth. His hands ran slowly up and down her back, her arms. He cupped her face as he plied her with kisses until she felt his marvelous body harden against her.

His groan was as soft as the wind in the trees. 'God, I'm going out of my mind for you.'

'There, there,' she whispered, and hesitantly reached down to stroke him through his elegant formal trousers.

'You'll drive me insane.' He stopped her after several moments, catching her hand up behind her back, just roughly enough to excite her. Then, giving her a roguish smile, his eyes glittering, he lifted her by her waist, sitting her up on the stone railing.

'Ohhh, Devlin,' she sighed, welcoming him as his lean hips slipped between her thighs, bunching her skirts up a little. Her fine gown would wrinkle, but she didn't care at all. She clung to him, kissing him like she had sold him her soul, moving with him as he rocked her body with a sinuous motion. Her groan was soft as he fondled her breast through the fine white silk of her bodice.

Above them, the moon beamed; the music played on, the charming minuet floating over the water. They hurried to learn each other anew before their absence was noted, their eager hands molding every curve and plane and hollow, their lips mingling kisses with urgent whispers. They touched each other as deeply as they dared and yet still hungered for more.

He suddenly tore his mouth away from hers. 'Someone's coming,' he panted.

Startling her out of the haze of passion, she, too, became aware of laughing voices approaching from the direction of the garden. 'Don't leave me,' she pleaded, catching the lapels of his coat in a sensuous grasp.

'If I stay, we'll be caught,' he whispered. 'Then you'll have to marry me. I said on my honor it would be your choice, darling, and I meant it.' Cradling her cheek in his palm, he slowly lowered his hand. Then he walked away, disappearing into the shadows among the trees as the small knot of revelers approached.

Lizzie quickly pasted on a smile and nodded to them, but she was left to ponder the unselfish thing he'd done. He could have solved his money problems merely by staying and she would have been none the wiser. He could have feigned innocence, for she had not heard the other guests coming in time to take evasive action.

I guess he is *serious about me.*

A soft, vulnerable smile curved her lips as she stared at the garden shadows where Devlin had vanished into the night.

Chapter Fourteen

Halfway through the week following the Madison ball, Dev walked into White's with his chums from the Horse and Chariot Club. They had just come from a rough bout at Dick Mace's fashionable boxing studio on Bond Street, where Quint had pummeled them all soundly – including Devlin. With a cigar dangling from his mouth and his barrel-chest swelled with pride at having beaten a strong man ten years his junior, Quint strutted ahead of the others into the august male sanctuary.

The oak-paneled walls and dark carpets of the club created a dim atmosphere in sharp contrast to the glaring sunshine of the warm May afternoon, but Dev's eyes adjusted quickly enough to note that the members of the club politely turned away as their party prowled in.

'First round's on Dev, boys! Ha!' Quint slapped him on the back as Dev approached.

'Ow,' he mumbled, wincing.

Quint laughed heartily. 'You! Get pouring! Ale here!' he ordered one of the waiters.

'Yes, my lord.' The waiter blanched and hurried to do Quint's bidding.

Dev now had firsthand knowledge of exactly how Quint had

earned the nickname Damage Randall. The ring was the one place where the great oaf shone.

The baron had a left hook that could take a man's head off and a two-punch combination that he delivered to his opponent's midsection with fists like the pistons of the newfangled steam engine. Dev's ribs still ached from the blows, but he had not been trying to win.

After a marathon brawl of some twenty-five rounds, Dev had finally thrown the fight, just to keep everyone happy. No one had beaten Quint since 1807, and he did not intend to rouse their suspicions by shattering the baron's record. The waiter returned, and soon the scoundrels of the Horse and Chariot Driving Club were guzzling refreshing tankards of cool golden-brown ale.

Dev put the round on his tab with the house, as ordered, and the next, and the one after that, fully aware that his funds were running out fast, but what else could he do? They had no idea that his inheritance floated in limbo, awaiting Lizzie Carlisle's whim to marry him or not.

Dev had not seen her since the night of the ball, but he had sent her flowers and through an exchange of letters, had procured her agreement to take a drive with him this Sunday. The proper courting had begun. The thought of her kiss brought a private smile to his lips.

The practicalities of his financial survival aside, his deepening attachment to her had decided the matter for him: Whatever happened, he would marry her and see her elevated to a station in life more worthy of her many excellences. How amusing it would be for her to find that she outranked even Lady Campion once she became his bride. The drift of his desires where she was concerned had sharpened his restlessness to be through with his revenge, because he was now prepared to consider a life together with her when it was all over. Until now, he had not allowed himself to care about his own fate in the matter, so long as he did his duty, paid the price he owed the stars for drawing his family to their horrible deaths on that fateful night.

He had not cared whether he lived or died when it was all said and done. But a few nights ago, in one of those moments of inspiration that sometimes struck him while he lounged in his bathing tub, it had come to him all of a sudden that Lizzie would hardly be pleased if her newlywed bridegroom ran off and got himself killed. Her feelings for him were growing, as well; he could see it in her smile, taste it in her kiss. Where his foes were concerned, he knew he was unstoppable when he cared nothing for his fate; but if Lizzie fell in love with him, wouldn't throwing caution to the wind and leaving her widowed inflict on her gentle heart a wound of loss similar to the one he himself had suffered so young?

It was a quandary. But it meant he must proceed with even greater shrewdness and control than before. As their courtship progressed, he knew he would also have to take pains to conceal their relationship from his dangerous companions. If they happened to notice his attentions to the pretty girls'-school governess, Dev was thoroughly prepared to say she was nothing to him but a bit o' muslin, a tasty entertainment; and when the time came for them to wed, he could always claim the Knight brothers had caught him in the seduction and had forced him to marry their little quasi-sister. Lizzie would probably be mortified by such a tale, but she need never know. Dev realized in the next moment, however, that there was only one fly in the ointment regarding this particular strategy for keeping her safe: Lord Alec Knight.

His dashing former school chum presently emerged from the famed bow window of White's, where he had been holding court with his usual pack of imitators and hangers-on.

As Dev watched Alec and his dandyish followers sauntering

across the room to one of the card tables, he mulled over the fact that if he were to claim in male company that the little miss was naught but a bit of fun to him, word was sure to travel back to Alec. The man, after all, knew everyone, and, adored as he was by females, he was privy to all the gossip in London.

Dev could well imagine the man's reaction to such news. First would come the challenge to duel, not to be taken lightly. He'd heard that Alec had proved himself a dozen times on the field of honor. Worse, Alec would surely warn Lizzie that Dev had admitted he was only trifling with her. He could probably explain his way out of it, but she would be hurt all the same, and it was not a scrape he fancied getting into.

As though sensing his scrutiny, Alec glanced across the large hall and saw Dev studying him.

Neither man reacted.

Alec smoothly turned away, and Dev clenched his jaw. *What the hell? He might not like me courting Lizzie, but he's got no cause to act like that.* The man had practically given him the cut direct, and Dev was surprised to find himself a bit hurt by it. They used to be such good friends. Well, he certainly wasn't going to sit here and take it, he decided. Downing his last swallow of ale, he set his empty tankard on the table and excused himself from present company, strolling over to have a go at Alec.

'Something you want to say to me – old friend?' Dev inquired, bracing his hands on the back of the empty chair across from Alec and leaning on it as he held him in an insolent stare.

Alec eyed him in cool wariness. 'Strathmore.' He dismissed his entourage with a glance, then looked again at Dev. 'Seems we have a mutual acquaintance.'

'Yes, indeed.'

'What's your interest in her, Strathmore?' he asked bluntly. 'I never knew your taste to run toward the bluestocking type.'

'Neither does yours, I'm told, so I can't see how it matters to you.'

'Who told you that?' he asked slowly, staring into his glass of brandy.

'Why, Miss Carlisle did. She told me all about your falling-out. How badly you hurt her.'

'I see. So, you intend to get whatever you can from her under the guise of offering comfort. Is that it?'

'Not even close.'

'Dev, we've known each other for a long time. But I swear to God, if you hurt her—'

'Like you did, Alec?' He paused. 'My intentions are pure, as it happens. I've asked Elizabeth to marry me.'

'What?' he breathed, staring at Dev in amazement. 'What was her answer?'

'She's thinking about it,' he replied, a faint, possessive gleam in his eyes.

He sat up straighter. 'You mean she said no.'

'Merely "not yet." But I can live with that for now. A young lady of her quality deserves all the trappings of a proper courtship.'

Hearing this, Alec forced out a clever laugh, but there was fear in his eyes. 'No, no, you see, you've set yourself up for a jilt, old friend. She'll never say yes.'

'What makes you so sure?'

'Because all her life, she's wanted me.'

Dev bristled, hating to admit it, but he knew from the girl's own lips that what Alec said was true. 'Well, what do you expect her to do, live on hope? Wait for your convenience? That was a very foolish oversight on your part. For your information, I have reason to believe that my affections are returned.'

Alec stared at him for a long moment, weighing this; then he shook his head and lifted his eyebrows with an arrogant look.

'Tell yourself that if it makes you feel better, but Lizzie has always been mine.'

'People change, Alec.'

Alec glanced at Quint and the other members of the Horse and Chariot Club seated at the far end of the room, then looked meaningfully at Dev. 'Yes,' he murmured with a slight nod of reproach. 'Apparently they do.'

That evening, the girls were eating supper in the dining hall when one of the maids came and whispered to Lizzie that a gentleman caller had asked to see her and was waiting for her on the front porch of the school. With a frisson of happiness, she hurried to meet Devlin, glancing at her reflection in the foyer's pier glass. She quickly smoothed her hair, took a deep breath, and tried to restrain her eagerness to see him. But when she walked out onto the porch, it was not Devlin who stood, hat in hand, to greet her.

It was Alec.

'Hullo, Bits.' He cast her a smile full of rueful affection, the slanted sun burnishing his golden hair.

'Alec.' She was unable to help the slight stiffening of her manner, but gave him a cordial nod and hoped she somewhat hid her disappointment. 'Do you, er, care for refreshments?' Her tone was polite. 'I could send for lemonade.'

Alec declined with a distracted shake of his head. 'Is there someplace we could talk?'

'For a few minutes, I suppose.' She gestured toward the stone path that led around the building to the garden. He was silent as they walked – no cocky jokes, no teasing, none of his outlandish charm.

He seemed troubled.

'So, this is where you've been hiding,' he remarked as they strolled under the arched trellis.

She glanced sharply at him. 'I'm not hiding.'

'It's just a figure of speech.' He swallowed hard. 'Seems pleasant here. Peaceful.'

'*Boring* is the word I think you mean.'

'No. Not boring at all, with you here.' He smiled again and walked on down the flagstone path in slow graceful strides.

Her suspicion deepening, she said nothing and followed him. In the garden, the mellow light of the gathering sunset stretched long emerald shadows across the grass. A haze of yellow pollen gilded everything – the irregular slate flags beneath their feet, the birdbath, and the bench beneath the pear tree.

Tiny bits of dandelion fluff drifted slowly on the air while insects flitted past them, their swift gossamer wings catching the light.

'Did you and Jas like going to school here?'

She stopped walking and turned to him in frank inquiry. 'Why are you here?'

Mute distress filled his big, blue, heartbreaking eyes, then he glanced away.

She immediately wondered if he'd lost badly again at the tables. 'Alec, is something wrong?'

'No, *everything* is wrong, Lizzie. Everything is just – damned – awful and has been for months. You hate me, and I can't take it anymore.'

'I don't hate you,' she conceded, recovering from her surprise.

'Well, you should. I hate myself for what I did, and God knows I deserve it.'

'Oh, Alec.'

'I came to say I'm sorry.' Again, the lost-puppy stare.

She dropped her forehead into her hand and fought exasperation. 'Very well – I accept your apology.'

'No.' He shook his head. 'That was too easy.'

She sighed and looked away. 'You never made me any

promises, Alec. You were free to do as you wished. I forgive you. It's in the past; it doesn't matter anymore.'

She walked on, but he caught up and stopped her, quickly blocking her path.

'Don't say it doesn't matter, Lizzie. That's the worst thing you could say.' She glanced at him in confusion. 'Look, I've worked up my nerve for this, so at least let me speak my piece before you throw me out.'

'I'm not going to throw you out.'

'I think you already have.' His lonely stare would have surely made her swoon a year ago, but now there was Devlin. 'My life's not right without you, Lizzie. I'm so lost.'

She dropped her gaze, scarcely able to believe what she was hearing.

'I never meant to hurt you. I saw no other way out. Bits, you've got to understand.' He took her hand imploringly. 'I couldn't use your dowry to pay my gaming debts. Not even I could sink so low.' He paused. 'I know I hurt you, but it's nearly a year now, so I was wondering if you might let me back into your life.'

She passed a wary glance over his face.

'I know now I took you for granted, but if you'll give me another chance, I swear I won't let you down again. I'm ready to change now. I need you, Lizzie. Everyone's entitled to a few mistakes, aren't they?'

She gave him a pained look, then turned away, shaking her head. 'Don't do this to me, Alec. I'm not going to let you do this to me. You can't come out of the blue with something like this the moment you realize I've become involved with someone else.'

'Out of the blue? Don't be obtuse. It's always been there between us, unspoken—'

'The way I would prefer it to remain.'

He stared at her in wounded accusation. 'My God, Strathmore's really gotten to you, hasn't he? Christ, I thought you were going to let him ravish you in front of all of us there at the Madison ball. How could you permit him to behave with you in such a familiar manner?'

Her jaw dropped. 'This, from Lady Campion's kept man? How dare you reproach me? Oh, this is most instructive! You don't really want *me*, but you can't stand to see me with anyone else!'

'That's not true. I always meant for us to be together as soon as my fortunes were secured. Look at my situation!' he protested when she scoffed.

'I'm so tired of your excuses, Alec. It was in your power to *change* your situation in a trice, but you didn't want to be tied down, laden with adult responsibilities. All you had to do was give up gaming and accept any one of the opportunities Robert offered you – a seat in the Commons, the running of one of the lesser estates. Instead you ran from me. You ran the minute I told you I loved you.'

Turning away with a curse under his breath, Alec sat down on the nearby bench and stared at his well-groomed hands where they lay on his lap. 'I was a fool.'

'Yes.'

'What am I supposed to do without you? I can't lose you, Lizzie. I'm here now. I'm trying, aren't I? That's got to count for something.'

She sat down beside him with a sigh. 'Oh, Alec. Be truthful – with yourself and with me. Your attachment to me is akin to what your little nephew, Harry, feels for his favorite blue blanket. I need to mean more to a man than mere safety, security. I need – no, I *deserve* – to be loved for myself, hang it!'

'Was it any wonder I ran, with you always trying to change me, save me, fix me?' He scowled. 'I know I'm not perfect, but can't you love me as I am, flaws and all?'

'Alec, if I tried to change you, it was only because I don't want to see you end up ruined by your gambling.'

'For your information, I have not so much as shuffled a deck of cards since what happened between us, and that's the gods' honest truth.'

'What?'

'You might say I lost my taste for it. After that debacle, sitting down at the tables made me physically ill. Every time I picked up the dice, all I could think of was the hurt in your eyes. I just didn't have the heart for it anymore. On my honor, I learned my lesson. I haven't gambled since.'

She stared somberly at him. It really was almost too much to absorb. The Prince Charming of her girlish dreams, her darling Alec, sat here telling her he was ready to make a life with her now. He had even conquered his dangerous penchant for gambling.

She could be a real part of the Knight family at last. All she had to do was hang Devlin out to dry.

She shook her head. *Never*. 'Devlin cares for me, Alec. What's more, he needs me.'

'I need you, too.' He studied her for a long moment. 'Have your whirlwind affair,' he concluded softly. 'I deserve that. But when it comes down to it, we both know it's me you love. Always have. Always will. Don't throw it away, Lizzie.'

'You did that.' She glanced away, her heart pounding. 'Shouldn't you be getting back to Lady Campion?'

His jaded smile did not reach his blue eyes. But as he stood and walked past her, he caressed her face for a moment, trailing his finger gently down her cheek. 'I won't give up without a fight,' he murmured, then kissed her brow and left her standing alone in the garden.

Lizzie's life took such a strange turn after Alec's visit that, within a month, it had become all but unrecognizable. With

Mrs. Hall's begrudging permission, she continued to sample the delights of the Season with Jacinda each Saturday night and many Sundays, too. There were balls, routs, at homes, after-theater dinners, nights at Vauxhall, concerts, drives in the park; and, all the while, she had Alec and Devlin on either side of her, each trying to outdo the other in sheer charm.

The ton took note.

Between Devlin's 'proper' courtship and Alec's determined effort to win back her affections, both men showered her with so much attention and gallantry, flowers, candies, an array of pretty gifts and baubles, and made, in all, such a fuss over her, that at last Lizzie walked into the annual May garden party at Devonshire House and discovered that she had become all the rage. She – Lizzie Carlisle! – bluestocking, spinster, land agent's daughter.

Thanks to Alec and Devlin, all the highborn young rakes who had never noticed her existence when she had been merely Jacinda's quiet companion suddenly caught on to the notion of falling in love with her.

It was all due to the racy glamor of her two leading suitors, but suddenly courting Lizzie Carlisle was *the* fashionable thing to do. Now the girl who a few short months ago could not stand the sight of a London rake was hemmed in by them on all sides. It was absurd enough to make her and Jacinda collapse in gales of laughter.

Dev tolerated his lady's triumph with philosophical good humor, pleased that it was finally her turn to be placed on the pedestal he always knew she deserved. He was unselfish enough to wait patiently, watching with quiet pleasure as she basked in the glow of her admirers' worship.

After all, it kept her safer from his enemies' notice if he appeared to be only one of the gang paying court to the newfound belle of the Season.

He was reasonably certain he was first in her affections, after all. He was the only one with whom she took long drives in Hyde Park, where Dev gave her more lessons on the fine art of handling the ribbons of a coach-and-four; more important, he was the only one she exchanged hungry kisses with whenever they could snatch two minutes alone. Assured of his place as her favorite, he let her have her fun and smiled when Society pronounced his future bride an Original, an Incomparable, a Toast.

He had plenty of time to fulfill the terms of his aunt's will, so why rush the girl? It was too delightful to see her blossom like this, no longer hiding her light beneath the proverbial bushel-basket. And so, biding his time, Dev split his attentions between amour and revenge.

The darker matter progressed apace as the month of May fled by.

Now that he had been accepted as a full-fledged member of the Horse and Chariot Club, he moved forward in a systematic effort to pare down his list of possible suspects by a process of elimination. With the utmost finesse and calculation, he got a number of them drunk and contrived to turn the conversation to a casual topic of discussion: *Where were you when you heard the news about the great Lord Nelson's glorious death at Trafalgar?*

The epic sea battle, after all, had happened on 21 October 1805, but word had not traveled to England until early November, at about the same time as the fire. He watched their dissipated faces closely as they each related their alibis. By the end of the night, he was convinced that neither Dr. Eden Sinclair, Dog Berkeley, Nigel Waite, nor Big Tom had had anything to do with it. He crossed them off his list, then searched for another means by which to jar some more of them into showing their cards.

A few nights later at his gaudy pavilion, he took young

Dudley, 'the Booby,' aside, since he was sure the vapid fop was innocent. Forcing Dudley to concentrate on his words, Dev sought to plant in him a similar, revealing question. He knew he was getting closer to the real killer or killers, so, for the sake of allaying their suspicions, he instructed Dudley to ask their gathered company later that night if anyone had ever seen the shows held years ago at the pavilion.

'Ask them if they remember any of the theater girls depicted on the walls,' he murmured. 'I want to know who was their favorite. But *you* say it as if it's *your* idea.' No one would ever suspect if Dudley asked. 'Will you do that?'

'Cheerio, Dev, will do. But why?'

He flashed the lad a reassuring grin. 'Just for a lark.'

'Should I ask about any of the lasses in particular?'

'I think not,' a voice interrupted.

They both looked over as Dudley's cousin, Alastor Hyde, came slithering into the ballroom where Dev had been showing the young duke the pictures of the long-forgotten actresses.

The pale, balding man pinned Dev in a cold-blooded stare. 'Why do you trifle with His Grace, my lord?'

'It's just a bit of fun, old boy. I had a notion we'd hunt down a few of these faded roses for a lark. If they could be found,' he added. 'Likely, they're all dead of the French disease.'

'The French disease! Oh, Strathmore, that's frightfully funny!' Dudley tittered.

'Shut up,' Alastor snapped at the lad. 'You will not ask the foolish question Lord Strathmore has suggested, Your Grace. Forget all mention of it.'

'Yes, cousin,' Dudley said, contritely swallowing his laughter.

'As for you, Lord Strathmore, you would be well advised to quit asking questions altogether.'

'Why?' he murmured. 'What do you know of it?'

'Only that there is danger for those who would dig into a

past that others have gone to great lengths to bury. Leave it be.'

Dev fell silent as Alastor hurried his young cousin off. Though he seethed with tantalized longing for more knowledge, he dared not press Alastor, lest he drive the unpleasant fellow to tell the others about the questions he'd been asking. For now, he would take Alastor's advice and leave well enough alone.

After waiting a few days to make sure there would be no repercussions from that confrontation, he tried yet a different approach. He showed up one night on Big Tom's doorstep, presented the secretary of the club with the most beautiful and obliging harlot Dev had ever encountered.

'You never call on me anymore,' she complained under her breath while they waited for Sir Tommy's butler to answer the door. 'What's wrong, love? Did it quit workin'?' She eyed his crotch in question. 'I should find that hard to believe.'

Dev smirked. 'I've been busy.'

'I'll bet.'

They were shown in to the dining room, where Sir Tommy was taking his prodigious supper alone. 'Strathmore. Join me?' he asked, spewing crumbs everywhere as he spoke, as usual, through a mouthful of food, but his welcoming gesture halted in midair as the blonde sidled into the room behind Dev, wearing nothing but his greatcoat.

'I've brought you a present, old boy,' Dev drawled. When Tom's servant withdrew, Dev gave the blonde a nod; on his order, the greatcoat dropped to the floor.

Big Tom nearly choked on his food.

'I wonder if I might have a look at the club's books for a moment while you get to know Miss Felicia?'

'Y-y-yes, of course,' the fat man stammered, struggling to his feet. He pointed Dev toward his study while beads of sweat popped out on his eager face.

'Excellent,' Dev murmured. 'I need to certify a bet I made last month in the wager book. I'll just be a moment.'

'Help yourself, old boy. No hurry at all,' Tommy breathed, wide-eyed as the blonde stuck her finger in the jelly he had been eating and smeared it on her breast, sending the baronet a fetching glance.

Clever girl, and not a wee bit squeamish, Dev thought, leaving the dining room as the great glutton scurried around the table to indulge. Once inside the baronet's oak-paneled study, Dev wasted no time on the wager book but dug through the box of old ledgers until he found the earliest one, dated 1805, the year the club had been founded. The handwriting was different from Sir Tommy's big, round scrawl. The earliest books were written in a neat small hand with a left-leaning slant. The first page stated Carstairs as the president and secretary of the club.

Dev scanned the pages as quickly as possible. Most of it was inanity, expenditures for a hire of the Argyle Rooms, for example, sums spent on liquor, food, musicians, whores. Nothing much had changed in twelve years, it seemed. But there was one curious entry in December of 1805: two hundred pounds for passage across the Channel for one Signor Rossi, dancing master.

Dancing master, indeed, Dev thought, remembering the murdered cook who had been on duty that fateful night at the Golden Bull Inn, the man they had tried to pin the start of the fire on, saying the blaze had started in the kitchens. The cook had been found hanged presumably by his own hand in a seeming admission of guilt for the fire that had killed forty-seven people.

Dev wondered now if the 'dancing master' had in fact been a practitioner of a darker art. It was no mean trick sending a man to the Continent in 1805 at the height of the Blockade, after all. And if, indeed, someone had arranged for an Italian assassin to make short work of the cook – the only person who could have successfully disputed the official story of a kitchen fire – Dev had one way of learning who might have hired him.

He reached into his vest pocket and took out a scrap of paper given to him by the coroner who had handled the case all those years ago. It was an anonymous death threat ordering the coroner to conceal his true findings after the fire.

The intimidated coroner had complied.

The ominous note had not been signed, but as Dev compared the handwriting to Carstairs's script in the 1805 logbook, he found an exact match.

It was a long moment before he could absorb it. Then he tucked the scrap back into his waistcoat, put the book away, and drove off in his carriage, leaving the blonde in the fat voluptuary's clutches. Big Tom sweated and grunted over her on the dining table. Dev did not worry about Miss Felicia. She was used to such things, and after all, he had paid her in advance.

His mind was in a whirl. What about Quint? All this time he had thought it was Quint! Now he did not know if old Damage Randall would be cleared of guilt or if he shared it with Carstairs. Was there no way to lay hands on evidence of Quint's whereabouts on the night of the fire?

Half an hour later, he broke into Quint's carriage house.

Easing in through a window of the squat brick stable, Dev smelled alfalfa hay and the ripe odor of manure, heard the gentle snuffling of the horses in their box stalls. Making not a sound – for half a dozen grooms or more were sleeping in the loft above – he crept down the main aisle of the barn, passing drowsing horses on each side. He peered into the silent tack room, but abandoned it, finding the head coachman's office behind the next door.

Here, he let himself in and closed the door behind him. One small, high window let in a little moonlight. By its feeble silvery illumination, he hurried to find the item he had come for.

As driving enthusiasts, the rakish members of the Horse and Chariot took more pride in their vehicles than they took in themselves. Their lives were in disarray, but when it came to their horses, carriages, and, for the dandyish few, their clothes, they were meticulous.

The club preferred highway driving and the long, smooth toll roads outside the city, for London's cobblestone streets and poor byways subjected the carriages – which were often works of art – to considerable wear and tear. As a result, the club members were fanatical, Dev had observed, about keeping their equipages in pristine condition – regular maintenance for wheels and axles, the oiling of springs, the checking of wiffletree joints, the keeping of harness in tiptop shape. The number of miles put on each vehicle served as a marker for when the springs and other parts would need replacing. In order to manage it all efficiently and to help track expenses, every head coachman was responsible for keeping a logbook in which all repairs were marked down along with a notation for each journey the vehicle had made – destination, date, and miles traversed.

It was perhaps a long shot, but he was getting desperate to separate the innocent from the guilty, and at least the coachman's log offered a chance to learn if one of Quint's vehicles had traversed the long, fine Oxford Road in November of 1805.

His pulse pounded, but his hands were steady as his finger trailed across the dusty row of annual logbooks on the shelf. Each book had the year engraved in gilt on the spine. His heart beat faster as he came to the book for 1805. Silently, he pulled it off the dusty shelf and took it over to the window, where he thumbed through the pages, holding his breath. The coachman's neat rows of handwriting fanned across the pages. Dates. Expenses. Repairs after His Lordship had backed the drag into the corner of a house. *August, September, October*. He came to November and turned the page. Then stopped.

It was gone. December was the next month logged. All records for November, '05 had been torn out. His eyes narrowed with fury.

A distant sound snagged his attention. He looked up.

Someone's coming.

The barking of a dog suddenly sounded the alarm; a moment later, a carriage rumbled down the quiet street. The sound of mad, booming laughter and drunken singing confirmed with grim certainty that it was Damage Randall himself rolling homeward, no doubt having just returned from his favorite brothel. Nor was he alone, by the sound of it. A raucous female voice crowed the bawdy lyrics of the alehouse tune right along with him.

In the blink of an eye, Dev had shoved the 1805 logbook back in its slot on the shelf and slipped out of the coachman's office, his heart pounding. He had to get out of here. Two grooms or more would be accompanying the baron. Quint would probably rush his harlot into his bed, but the grooms would be here in a trice to put the horses away.

Sneaking into a docile bay's stall, Dev pressed his back to the wall as the drag clattered past going up the mews alley. He waited, watching through a sliver between the heavy wood shutter and the wall as Quint leaped unsteadily out of the coach, then lifted the drunken girl down and swung her around once.

'Stop it, milord!' she slurred. 'I'll be sick!'

'I'll still kiss ye, m'dear,' Quint boomed with a laugh.

'You brute.' She shoved at him affectionately when he put her down, then lifted her skirts a bit and dashed up the garden steps to his house. 'Catch me if you can!'

Quint laughed heartily and disappeared from Dev's narrow line of vision. Their rowdy voices went quiet when the back door shut with a cheerful bang.

A moment later, he heard the carriage wheels grinding over

the alley again. The pair of grooms exchanged remarks too low for him to hear. Wasting no time, Dev climbed out the stall window and jumped down in the alley. With broad, stealthy strides, he slipped away through the night.

A fog had begun rolling in off the river. It blurred the orange ball of light around the quaint iron lamp-post that stood on the distant corner.

As Dev hugged the shadows, starting in the opposite direction, something triggered his keenly honed instincts with an almost imperceptible warning, naught but a light prickling sensation down his nape. He froze, held his breath, pretended to glance at his pocket watch.

He was being watched. He could feel it with a visceral awareness.

Slowly, furtively, ready to attack anything that moved, he looked out of the corner of his eye.

His hairs stood straight up; his heart leapt into his throat. He had been stalked by that mountain lion for two full miles in the mountains, but even that had not filled him with the horror he felt now. At least a mountain lion was a flesh-and-blood creature.

He saw a ghost.

She was just discernible amid the swirling fog down by the street lamp, a spectral widow all in black. She just stood there, staring at him, like a messenger from beyond the grave.

And he realized she had been watching him for some time.

He did not know whether to run at her or away.

Both of them were motionless. Having never been one to flee from danger, Dev took one chancy step in her direction – and the ghost ran.

Ghost? Damn it, no ghost made such distinct footfalls when it fled. Cursing himself and the moonlight and fog that had made sport of his reason, he plunged into motion, chasing the very mortal woman.

Whoever she was, Dev realized grimly, she had seen him breaking into Quint's property.

Not good.

Mary fled in a panic, bewildered by this sudden reversal. Calling up all her girlhood street smarts from a life-time ago, she hitched up her jet-black skirts and dashed through the winding back alleys.

'Show yourself!' Lord Strathmore bellowed after her, his deep voice bounding off the buildings, echoing oddly in the fog. 'I won't hurt you, dammit! I just want to talk to you!'

She ignored him, cutting through a dark shopping arcade, still cursing herself for letting him see her. Now he would be on his guard – just when things had begun getting interesting!

She had been watching him frequently as he went about Town, had been watching all of them. The last thing she had expected Devil Strathmore to do tonight was to break into his great chum's carriage house. His bizarre break-and-entering had turned the whole equation upside down. All of a sudden, Mary was no longer sure who was manipulating whom. Was the young viscount indeed under Quint's and Carstairs's thumbs, or was there more to it than met the eye?

She could not risk asking him face-to-face. She did not yet know his nature; if he turned out to be an evil man, evil as his companions, then she could not risk speaking to him. She could not risk him finding out about Sorscha.

Mary knew full well it was his right to demand custody of his little sister, as it would be her legal duty, in that case, to hand the girl over to her rightful guardian, her only kin.

She lost him amid the traffic on the first busy street she came to, diving onto the back of a passing dray cart. She kept her head down and went by him, unnoticed.

'Come back!' he howled into the darkness, a furious note of despair in his voice.

Concealed amid crates of produce, she saw him standing in the street in the area she had just vacated. He turned wildly this way and that, then dragged his hand through his hair.

He doesn't look evil, she thought, and heard him bite out a curse, saw him rake his fingers again impatiently through his long, black hair, then watched him grow smaller as he stood in the street while the dray cart carried her off toward safety.

Until she could be sure that he possessed at least an inkling of his father's noble nature, she would tell him nothing.

Chapter Fifteen

'*Hang* these blasted bill collectors!' Ben cried upon hearing the insistent knocking at the front door.

'I'll handle this,' Dev growled as he came stalking down the corridor.

It was Saturday evening, and he was on his way out for the night, bound for Vauxhall and another intoxicating dose of Miss Carlisle's company, which he well could use after the unsettling events of last night. Knowing that his long-suffering valet had already chased off a score of his blasted duns throughout the day, Dev emerged from the corridor, deciding it was time he handled the impertinent vermin personally. 'Now, look here!' he roared, scowling blackly as he threw open the door with a bang. He stopped abruptly, taken aback. 'Charles!'

His little man-of-business had nearly jumped out of his skin at Dev's reception, but he gulped and stuttered a greeting. 'M-m-my lord.'

'I'm so sorry, Charles. Do come in.' He gave his pudgy little lawyer an affectionate slap on the back as Charles Beecham ventured cautiously into the house. 'Beg your pardon, old boy. These scurvy duns have been hounding me.'

'Y-yes, sir. That is what I came to discuss.' Charles tugged at his cravat and struggled to gather his composure after his sudden fright.

'Can I get you a drink? You look a bit pale.'

'No, sir. Thank you very much. I just – need a moment, ah.' He swallowed hard, regaining his composure. 'I've come with some most excellent news, Lord Strathmore.'

'Indeed?'

Charles nodded slowly and emphatically, his mouth pursing into a tight little smile like that of a winning chess player.

'Well?' Since the solicitor looked like he might burst if he did not speak his piece at once, Dev gestured to him to do so.

Charles puffed out his chest and beamed. 'Sir,' he announced proudly, 'after weeks of unceasing work, I have found the means to free you from the outrageous terms of your aunt's will.'

Dev's jaw dropped. 'You *have*?'

'Yes! You ordered me to find a way, and I did – I did it! My lord, you no longer have to marry Miss Carlisle! The money is yours, sir. Yours alone! Er, minus my commission, of course.'

Since Dev could only stare at him in shock, Ben broke the stunned silence.

'How ever did you achieve it, Mr. Beecham?'

' 'Twas simple in the end! For the past month, I have been tearing my legal library apart trying to find a way, as you commanded, but then I suddenly remembered to check – Her Ladyship never submitted a copy of her revised will to Chancery. The old version is the only one on record with the courts, and is, thus, the only one that is legal and binding.' Charles burst into giddy laughter.

Ben and Dev looked on in amazement.

Charles endeavored to explain. 'You see, some ten years ago, my predecessor filed a copy of Her Ladyship's will with Doctors' Commons. It is not required that one do so, merely a prudent measure to protect the rightful beneficiaries and the intentions of the deceased, especially when a sizable fortune is at stake. Well, I am chagrined to admit it, but I had simply assumed that Her Ladyship had sent in a copy of her revised will herself – you know how head-strong she was, savvy in financial matters, and very much in charge of her own affairs.

'I meant to visit her to discuss the addendum to her will, given the oddity of her request, but I had such a backlog of work here in London that I was detained for some weeks from going to Bath, and then she died. But now my oversight has proved your salvation. I am sorry for not waiting until business hours tomorrow, sir, but I could not wait to tell you. I knew you would want to know right away. My lord, you're in the clear!'

Ben looked at Dev, trying to gauge his reaction, but Dev was not sure himself what he thought. His head was reeling.

On the one hand, he was so relieved he could have collapsed into the nearest chair. But on the other, he wondered if Lizzie would now balk again or even refuse to marry him. There was always Alec, and her loyalty, indeed, her very integrity made her vulnerable to that smooth rogue. An ignoble thought and distressing to admit, but if all else failed, Dev had been counting on her pity as a last resort to persuade her to marry him, ostensibly to keep him out of debtors' prison. Without that threat hanging over his head . . .

'All that is left to do,' Charles continued, 'is to notify Miss Carlisle that Her Ladyship's more recent will is null and void.'

'No!' Dev barked, startling them both.

'Sir?'

Dev furrowed his brow and scratched his jaw in thought. 'What other provision did my aunt make for Lizzie in her old will, Charles?'

'Why, none, sir. It was drawn up years ago, before the young lady came into her employ.'

'She gets nothing?' he asked softly.

'No, sir,' Charles informed him. 'It's all yours.'

Dev's brooding gaze fell. He rested his hands on his waist. She was so stubborn, so proud. He was afraid of how she might react when she learned all this.

'Shall I write to inform her of this in the morning, my lord? Or would you prefer me to call on her at Mrs. Hall's Academy and break the news in person? I should think the young lady will be aggrieved to hear that her chance to marry into the peerage is lost. Shall I offer her some monetary compensation for her pains?'

'No, no, no, Charles.' He shook his head at his solicitor. 'I will reveal all to her myself, when the time is right.'

'Sir?'

'Well, hang it all, Charles, if she hears all this, she might, well, she might say – no.'

Charles bowed his head to hide a knowing smile. 'As my lord prefers.'

By midnight, they had spent such a lovely time at festive, noisy Vauxhall that Lizzie was quite dismayed to find it was already time to say good night to Devlin. Whenever she was with him, the clock's hands seemed to whirl past the hours like a spinning wheel revolving; and her heightened status in the ton had also meant more eyes on her and thus more difficulty sneaking away to steal a few moments in his arms. Indeed, all evening, it had seemed as if there was something he wanted to say to her, but there were always droves of people around. In truth, she had much to tell him, as well, for it was a momentous night: after several weeks of his 'proper' courtship, she was ready to give her heart and hand to Devil Strathmore. She could not wait to share the news with him – but the moment must be right.

Now it was nearly time to leave, and they had finally managed to slip away for a rendezvous down one of Vauxhall's infamous dark, graveled walks. As for talking, however, there was no time for words. Her light-green parasol matched her summery dress, and she used it as a screen to hide them from the prying eyes of the world, while behind it, they consumed each other with unbearable desire.

He made her ache with pleasure as he kissed her again and again, both of them oblivious of the Vauxhall fireworks bursting in the black night sky above the river, and the loud brass band playing on the green beneath the colored paper lanterns, the jolly tuba keeping time.

In the leafy shadows of a small lover's nook, they were in their own world.

'Oh, Lizzie,' he whispered in intoxication, his breath warm and moist against her cheek. 'I miss you . . . so desperately.'

'I miss you, too, Devlin. When can we talk?'

'Talk? I can barely put two words together when I see you.' He kneaded her back and nibbled her earlobe, making her shiver with sheer thrill. She ran her hand down his wonderful chest and gripped the lapel of his dark blue tailcoat merely to help keep her balance. 'Let me come to you tonight. Remember, I know just how to get into your room.'

'Yes, yes, Devlin, visit me tonight, will you, please? I've missed you so, and we've so much to discuss. Climb up by the mulberry tree. I'll leave my window open.'

'Will you wait for me in your bed?'

'Yes.'

'Wearing nothing?'

'If you wish it, yes. Though my clothes never seem to stop you, my Devil. You're so very skilled at undressing me.'

'God, I could go raving mad for want of you, woman.'

'Wait a few hours before you come and see me. The girls stay up late on the weekends. Oh, I could eat you,' she growled, giving his elegant jaw a light, lover's bite. She preferred his neck, but his cravat blocked her way – she could not wait to tear the thing off him, and all his clothes. *Soon.* She caressed him feverishly, the wanton look in her eyes telling him in no uncertain terms that tonight she was ready to give him her all. 'Wake me if I've fallen asleep when you arrive.'

His throaty chuckle brimmed velvet promise. 'Believe me, I will. Get your sleep while you can, my girl, because I'll keep you up till the morning.'

'I can't wait—'

'Oh, my God,' drawled a deep, coldly insolent voice from the other side of her parasol, interrupting at that moment. 'I do believe I shall be *sick*.'

Devlin and Lizzie swiftly stopped kissing and stared at each other. He winced and mouthed a curse while Lizzie turned bright red.

Alec.

Bracing herself, she lowered the screen of her parasol and found her former idol standing there, his flawless face frozen in a mask of hard contempt, his eyes filled with stunned pain. He stared at Lizzie as though she had betrayed him and then he shook his head in wordless reproach.

She looked away, but was steadied by Devlin's arm that came up around her waist.

'Do you mind?' he challenged Alec in a gentlemanly tone.

'Yes, actually, I do, old boy.' He looked at her again. 'What do you think you're doing? I'm shocked at you, Lizzie. Have you no care for your reputation?'

She closed her eyes, blushing redder as she realized he had heard every word of their risqué exchange. She supposed she should be glad it was merely Alec who had discovered them rather than one of the ton's matronly gossips. Somehow she had been swept up in the moment, as she was wont to do when Devlin held her in his arms.

'Leave us,' Devlin ordered him softly.

Alec turned to her again. 'I guess you're no better than me, are you? How many years did you tempt me, follow me around – doting on me, hanging round my neck, sitting on my lap? I never touched you! I could have. I wanted to. But you were too pure to me.' Anguish tinged his insolent rebuke. 'Hell, if I had known you were like this—'

'Watch it!' Dev warned him.

'Devlin, please,' Lizzie whispered, holding him back when he started toward Alec. 'Alec, this is not the time or place. You are obviously upset.'

'Upset?' he flung back, then he turned away with a curse, his hands propped on his waist. Glaring at the ground, Alec shook his head one more time, then stalked away with a rude, dismissive gesture.

The moment he had gone, Lizzie leaned against Devlin with a shudder and buried her face in his chest. 'Oh, that was – too awful.'

'He's lucky he quit while he was ahead. Do you still want me to come to you tonight? I'll understand if you've changed your mind—'

'Of course I still want you to come!' She hugged him. 'No one can come between us, darling. Not even him. Kiss me.'

He did, bending his head to press her lips tenderly with his own. The passion between them smoldered at once, but after such a perfectly galling interruption, Lizzie was careful to keep her wild response to him tamely bridled.

'*Arrivederci, mi cara*,' he whispered as he gently drew away from her.

With a smile on her lips and stars in her eyes, she watched him slip away through the shadows.

Swinging her folded parasol idly, she drifted back to rejoin Billy and Jacinda, who were saying their final good-byes to their many friends. She glanced around but saw no Devlin and concluded he was probably bound for his club or some other establishment of male camaraderie until the wee hours of the night, when he would come to her and she would tell him, *Yes, I will marry you, yes, have your children, yes, Lady Strathmore was right, right, right, as always.*

But as she leaned against the carriage, waiting for Billy and Jacinda, she braced her defenses, for Alec returned, prowling toward her with a wary stare.

She pressed away from the vehicle to meet him and lifted her chin.

He stopped a few inches in front of her, his temper better controlled now, but his taut expression showed he was still struggling with his anger and jealousy. 'Well, then, it seems you've made up your mind, but before you do something you'll regret, there's something you should know about your darling Dev.'

'If you have come to malign him to me, you are wasting your time.'

'This is serious, Lizzie. I did not want to resort to this, but my God . . .' He paused. 'Have you ever heard of four-in-hand racing club called the Horse and Chariot?'

'No,' she said, but the mention of the sport instantly called to mind laughter-filled driving lessons in Hyde Park. She hid her fond smile at the memory. 'What about it?'

'Strathmore's a member.'

'So?'

'This club is run by very bad men, Lizzie, and trust me, they associate only with their own kind.'

'What are you talking about?' She was confused and not terribly happy to hear anything bad about the man she loved, but the intensity in Alec's eyes removed all doubt that he was in earnest. She was not ignorant of the fact that he knew everything that went on in Society. If Dev had secrets, Alec was bound to know them, if anyone did.

'God, I don't even know if I can say this to you,' he muttered, looking away.

'Alec?' His expression was so dire that it was beginning to frighten her. 'What is it?'

He breathed a curse again and shook his head. 'Look, Dev's a capital chap for a spree, but to marry him, Lizzie? Even if you don't love me anymore, I don't want to see you hurt. You must pardon the extreme indelicacy of what I am about to tell you.'

Wide-eyed and growing increasingly alarmed, she nodded.

Alec lowered his voice and looked around briefly as if to make sure no one was listening. 'The sport is only a cover for what is nothing more than a depraved society of wealthy, high-born men wholly dedicated to debauchery. To be accepted into the Horse and Chariot Club, a man must surmount three tests. The first lies in devoting one's existence to dissipation, which Dev already proved ten years ago before he went to sea.'

'But he was distraught over his family's deaths. He was little more than a boy!'

Alec shook his head, ignoring her protest. 'The second test calls for the aspirant to make a hefty gift to the other members. For this, rumor has it, Dev spent thousands of pounds buying and refurbishing an old, abandoned pleasure garden south of the city, where he entertains the blackguards.'

'How do you know all this?'

'I've been invited to join – repeatedly – by a gentleman called Lord Carstairs.' Alec's lip curled in mild disgust at the name.

'Very well, what's the third test?'

'Oh, my sweet girl.' Alec sighed and held her in a saddened gaze. 'I am sorry, Bits, but they don't call him Devil for nothing. Whatever happens, I'll always be here for you.'

'Tell me!' she forced out, not sure whether to believe him, though she knew Alec would not lie to her about something like this.

His face turned grim. 'For the third and final test, a prospective member is made to force himself on an abducted virgin. While the others watch.'

With several hours to kill before his rendezvous with Lizzie and too much anticipation to sit still, Dev went to the pavilion where the club was gathering. One by one, the blackguards drifted in, having dutifully put in appearances at the more respectable entertainments of the Season; they walked into their refuge loosening their cravats and full of gusto to give their baser impulses free rein.

Dev took the opportunity to see if he could pare down his list by another name or two. He had drawn the Holy Rotter, James Oakes, into conversation. With the others in a particularly raucous mood – the lads were starting up a food fight in the tent-ceilinged salon – he spoke quietly with the man. Dev pressed him a bit harder than he had the others because Oakes's religious past led him to believe or at least to hope that buried beneath his drunkenness, the former reverend still maintained a glimmer of conscience. He had a suspicion, too, that if any of the men had served as the guilty party's confessor, it would have been the defrocked priest.

They were skirting the main substance of Dev's loss quite closely.

'It must have been terrible for you,' Oakes murmured. 'Yet a man must not allow pain to make him reckless.'

'You're not reckless?' he countered in a pleasant tone.

'Fair enough, but I haven't much reason to fear. You should be careful,' he said after a long moment while the hearty laughter and inanity went on around them. 'I hear you're asking questions.'

'Would you worry about being careful if you were me?'

Oakes brooded on this for what seemed a very long time, as if searching his lost conscience.

'What can you tell me, Oakes? You must know something.'

Oakes smiled at him with great weariness, but shook his head subtly and stared hard at Dev through bleary eyes. 'Don't miss what's right in front of you,' he advised in a low tone, then walked away.

In front of me? Dev wondered. What fact had he over-looked that was right in front of him . . . unless the Holy Rotter had meant it literally?

Dev lifted his perplexed gaze, then homed in on what – or rather who – was right in front of him.

Johnny.

God damn it, now he was talking to Oakes!

By the time that cocky bastard Strathmore strutted into the pavilion that night, Sir Torquil 'Blood' Staines had reached a philosophic stage of drunkenness. Sitting slouched at his table in the corner, his eyes were blood-shot, but his hands were still steady as he flicked a hard, derisive glance over the black-haired pretty boy viscount.

Don't trust that bastard. Not one jot. He took another swallow of gin. He'd heard Big Tom bragging about his adventure with a Miss Felicia that Dev had brought to his door while taking a look at the club's books. Now, why would he want to go digging into the past, eh? Not that there was anything for him to find in the club's papers. They were much too careful for that. *Don't care what Carstairs says. Something's got to be done about him.*

Thanks to the liquor, Staines was beginning to feel he was just the man for the job.

Blood Staines's tortured conscience had not rested easy in

twelve years. No matter how much he drank to ward off the demons, these days he felt ready to crack under the pressure of Strathmore's constant presence, a ceaseless reminder of what he'd done, what he'd helped to do, to all those innocent people. Forty-seven. Horrible deaths. No one deserved to die that way.

Worse, it seemed as though he, Torquil, was the only one who saw through Strathmore. He knew in his gut that the man wasn't near as drunk or dull-witted as he played. Aye, that smiling bastard was up to something.

Torq took another swig and watched Dev conversing with a few of the members. An idea was taking shape in his mind. Quint and Carstairs had said Strathmore was not to be touched, that it was too risky, but they were both getting soft. To be sure, he thought in contempt, they both had their motives for wanting to spare the man. Quint was trying to recapture his misspent youth through the bold young hero, while Carstairs had designs on him of another sort entirely. But bloody hell, sunk as they were in their dissipation, neither of them seemed to grasp the seriousness of the peril they were in. Quint was convinced that Strathmore knew nothing of their involvement in his family's deaths; Torquil was not willing to take that chance.

No, he thought, if Quint and Carstairs weren't going to do anything about Strathmore, maybe someone should. Before it was too late. He had the skills to take care of the problem quickly, easily, and efficiently. Aye, with one bullet.

And why not? he thought bitterly. What was one more body to toss in the charnel house he'd already filled? 'Twas of no consequence to him.

Carstairs wasn't there to stop him at the moment. Johnny-boy slipped out of the room even now to go meet his longtime keeper to do things that Torq didn't care to imagine. Quint was absent, also, having chased his latest underage redhead into the dark recesses of the Egypt Room.

The moment was ripe. All he had to do was lure Strathmore into a duel on the field of honor and then – no more worries.

A food fight was in progress among the drunken lads in the great tent-topped hall, and he noticed as he got up from his chair that one of the lads hurled a dinner roll that hit Strathmore squarely in the back.

'Watch it!' the viscount growled, the drink sloshing in his hand as he turned. 'I'm not in the mood.'

Hearing this, Torq glanced down with an evil smile at the bowl of caviar.

He picked it up, hefted it in his hand, then expertly took aim, and with the force, speed, and accuracy for which he was well known, threw it, bowl and all, straight at Strathmore's head.

He did not know what preternatural instinct made that canny bastard step aside, but the bowl hit Dudley, behind his target, full in the face.

Poor Dudley took it splat in the face, and the deadly intent in Staines's arm was apparent, for it knocked the poor, drunken fop flat on his back with a bloody nose.

'Ow! Ow, ow! What the devil?' Dudley moaned.

Strathmore looked over at Staines in astonishment, then quickly crouched down to see if the lad was all right. He helped him sit up and ordered his blackamoor servant to bring napkins, water to wash the mess off with, and something cold for the swelling that started at once.

When Strathmore looked at Torquil again, a bristling scowl had now darkened his face as he grasped that the blow had been meant for him.

Rising to his full height, Strathmore slowly stalked toward him. 'Is there a problem, Staines?'

Torquil was ready for him. He braced himself, poised to break his bottle of gin against the table if need be and use it as a weapon. 'You're my problem, Strathmore.'

The whole room went silent. The food fight stopped.

'Ever since you came around,' Torq continued, slurring a bit, 'you think you can take over everything. Giving out orders, acting like this is your club. But it ain't. I'm watchin' you.'

'You'd better step back, friend. You're drunk.'

'What are you going to do about it, hey, you Irish whoreson?' Torquil jeered, shoving him.

Without warning, Strathmore hauled back and punched him in the jaw with a blow that sent him hurling back into the arms of his nearby mates, which was lucky – for it was only they who then held Torquil back. 'You're goin' to regret that, boy,' he panted. 'You'll hear from my seconds anon!'

'Are *you* challenging *me* to a duel?'

'Why, no, Lord Strathmore—' Torquil shook off his friends' well-meaning holds with a murderous sneer. '—I'm invitin' you to your funeral.'

As the room erupted into exclamations of shock, Staines marched out to see to the arrangements.

In the wee hours of the morning, Dev banged on Alec Knight's door, scowling at the irony of it all.

Alec finally answered in baggy Cossacks and a dressing gown. The moment he saw Dev, his eyes narrowed. 'What the hell do you want?'

Dev barely knew how to begin.

With an insolent toss of his chin, Alec leaned in the doorway, folding his arms across his chest. 'Shouldn't you be with Miss Carlisle right about now? It's late.'

'I have not yet been to see her and now there is no hope left of doing so tonight. Damn it, Alec, I've been challenged to duel.' Dev swallowed his pride. 'I've come to ask you if you'll second for me.'

'*Me?*'

'I've got nowhere else to turn.' Dev lowered his head.

'What about your great friends from the Horse and Chariot Club?' Alec inquired coolly.

'Oh, come, don't you know me better than that?'

Alec cocked his brow skeptically.

Dev sighed and decided it was time to come clean. Though rivalry stood between them, he trusted Alec as a man, trusted in his honor. In truth, he had spent considerable time in his old friend's company over the past few weeks as they had both competed for Lizzie's favor. Sometimes it had been rather droll. In spite of everything, they still got along, and whatever his faults, he knew Alec was too gallant to behave like a sore loser.

'My sole motive for associating with those bastards, Alec, is because I have good reason to believe they had something to do with my family's deaths. In fact,' Dev told him, 'I'm fairly sure of at least three who were involved.'

Alec stared at him. 'You're jesting.'

'Would that I were. Instead,' he sighed, 'I've been called out by Torquil Staines.'

Alec's eyes widened. 'Blood Staines? Bloody hell, Dev, why did you go and do a thing like that?'

'It couldn't be helped.'

'Oh, very well,' Alec grumbled. 'Come in, you blackguard. What's it to be then, swords or pistols?'

At half past five that morning, Dev sat in his carriage, none to happy to contemplate that instead of deflowering the love of his life, he was sitting here waiting to defend his honor against one of the most feared duelists in London. His hands rested on his thighs; his forward gaze was even and only a little tense. He listened to the bird-song that filled the predawn twilight and breathed the springtime scent of dew-drenched turf.

He was ready.

Meanwhile, his trusty second paced back and forth outside his carriage, pausing only long enough to offer Dev a swig from his flask. 'Bumper for your courage?'

Dev shook his head. 'Don't need it.'

'Well, I do,' Alec muttered, downing a draft before he corked the vessel again with a low curse. 'Where the hell are they? I don't bloody believe this! Ten minutes late! Is it a forfeit, do you think?'

'I doubt it,' Dev murmured, glancing across the green at Torquil's second, Nigel Waite. 'Waite insists Staines will be here.'

'Maybe so, but you don't keep a man waiting for a duel. Really, it's the height of bad form!' Alec continued venting, but Dev's gaze wandered over the assortment of men who had already gathered around the grove to watch the fight.

Faced with the possibility of his own demise, he saw with startling clarity how much he wanted a life with Lizzie. For the first time in twelve years, he felt ready to leave the past behind, release the fears that had kept him from letting love into his heart. If he survived this, he would love her, he vowed, always.

'Well, it's about bloody time,' Alec declared, breaking into his thoughts with a tone that turned grim. 'Here they come.'

Dev looked over as the cavalcade of prime carriages came hurtling up the road, stirring up a sizable dust cloud. He kept his keen tension in check as the rest of the Horse and Chariot Club thundered into the grove. The first rays of the garish red sunrise were beaming through the trees, illuminating the coat of arms depicted on the door of the largest black coach, identifying it as belonging to Carstairs.

Dev looked on, hard eyed and cool headed, as the door opened and three men got out. As they strode toward his drag, he saw that it was Quint and Carstairs, with Staines trudging between them, looking like some surly prisoner.

Alec stopped pacing to plant himself firmly between Dev and the approaching men. 'How kind of you to remember our appointment, Sir Torquil,' he flung out, all princely insolence.

'That will do, Lord Alec,' Carstairs chided. 'Stand aside, if you please. Staines has something he would like to say to Strathmore.'

'Let him say it over pistols,' Alec retorted grandly.

'Alec,' Dev muttered under his breath. He glanced worriedly at his brash friend, admiring his gallant style, but after all, it wasn't his neck on the line. 'I'll hear him out,' Dev told them.

Staines glowered at him, but Dev noticed that Quint loomed just behind the man, as though prepared to stop him with his mighty fists of Staines tried anything.

Carstairs nudged the man. 'Go on.'

Staines's mouth worked angrily, but no sound came out.

'Yes?' Alec demanded. 'We haven't got all day. It'll be light soon, and we can't risk the watchmen noticing our presence.'

Dueling was quite illegal, something Lizzie would have been happy to point out, Dev was sure.

Staines cleared his throat, but held his chin high and refused to meet Dev's gaze. 'I – apologize for the insult I gave you, sir. I crave your pardon. 'Twas the gin to blame.'

Dev stared at him in shock. A forfeit – from the foremost duelist in the ton?

An apology, as well, in front of thirty of Staines's best mates, no less? What the hell was going on? Quint's square, rugged face betrayed nothing, but Carstairs cast Dev a private smile.

In that moment, Dev realized his mistake all this time.

Damage Randall wasn't the leader of the Horse and Chariot Club.

Carstairs was.

The earl was also, he realized, behind Staines's about-face. Indeed, Dev grasped that he was now witnessing a supreme display of Carstairs's deft power over his underlings.

It had been Carstairs all along.

Not daring to question the reprieve, Dev snapped to attention. 'No harm done,' he clipped out.

Staines managed a stilted nod. 'Very well, then. I bid you good day, sir.'

'Good day.'

Alec sputtered with amazement as Torquil pivoted on his spurred boot heel and marched off to rejoin his second. A moment later, he and Nigel leaped into the latter's carriage and tore off in the direction of the city.

Alec turned to Dev, his brow furrowed in confusion. 'What the hell just happened here?'

'A forfeit, dear boy,' Carstairs purred indulgently. 'Quint and I spoke to Staines and, ah, showed him the error of his ways. It really was uncalled for, his display of temper. Most ungentlemanly. I hope it will not cast a shadow over our company in the future.'

'Ho, we are not women to hold our grudges for a year!' Quint said with a short boom of laughter. 'Damn me, wouldn't have fancied buryin' either of you lads!'

Dev forced a wry smile, but he was mystified.

'Well, then, gents, I'm off to bed,' the baron added. 'Big match at Dick Mace's studio this afternoon. Four o'clock. Be there if you can.'

'You boys have a nice day,' Carstairs murmured, glancing hungrily from Alec to Devlin. *Don't forget this, Dev*, his sly smile seemed to say. *You owe me now*. Carstairs sketched a suave bow and followed Quint back to the coach.

Alec turned to him in bewilderment, but Dev could only shrug.

'Well, that was all extremely bizarre,' his second huffed after a moment. 'I have no idea what that was all about, but I suggest we get out of here before they change their minds.'

'Agreed,' Dev replied.

'White's for breakfast?'

Dev shook his head as he leaned against his racing drag. 'There's something I have to take care of.'

'Oh, *really*?' Alec drawled, and stopped to stare knowingly at him before tossing the reins over his horse's neck.

Dev shrugged. 'She was expecting me. I left her waiting all night. Obviously, I have to go and see her.'

'Very well, then,' Alec declared, 'so shall I!'

'Alec, give up. The day is lost—'

'Ha, that's what you think. For your information, Lizzie and I share something you can never understand. We have a history, Dev. We've known each other—'

'All your lives, yes, yes, I know and I'm *so* bloody tired of hearing it. You've *never* really known her, Alec. If you had, you would never have let her slip through your fingers. I don't intend to make the same mistake.'

'It's too late, Dev, old boy. You nearly stole the race from me, but I've pulled ahead in the final furlong. Hate to say it, but you've already lost.'

'What are you talking about?'

Alec patted his horse's neck and prepared to mount up. 'I'm sorry it came to this, Dev, but you should have told her about the Horse and Chariot Club. Especially in light of the third requirement.'

'You didn't,' Dev breathed, the blood draining from his face. He could not catch his wind for a second, feeling as though his old friend had just run him through.

'Sorry, Dev,' Alec said. 'All's fair.' With a defiant glance, he swung up into the saddle, gave his white horse's flanks a squeeze, and went tearing off down the dusty road.

Dev stood there frozen, so horrified, he thought for a second he might be sick all over the dewy grass. *Oh, Jesus*. He had to go to her. Had to explain.

Cursing under his breath, he leaped up onto his racing drag and, scowling blackly, threw the brake. Snapping his whip over the backs of his black Fresians, he wheeled the carriage around in the grove and drove off at breakneck speed.

'What the blazes are those two doing?' Carstairs asked Quint in amusement as the two of them flashed by, Alec's horse naught but a white streak, Dev careening past the coach with the fierce look of a Roman charioteer in the Colosseum. 'Is it a race?'

Quint sent him a dull-witted grin and shrugged.

'Let's find out.' Carstairs rapped on the ceiling with the silver head of his walking stick. 'Johnny!' he called up to the driver's box. 'Follow Strathmore!'

Chapter Sixteen

Alec's sickening revelation about Devlin's involvement in the Horse and Chariot Club had kept Lizzie up all night, leaving her further confounded when he failed to appear, as promised. Her head was in a whirl. She could barely fathom him keeping a secret of such magnitude from her, but as Alec had suggested, maybe she did not know her love as well as she had thought. Devlin would never harm a young girl – of that, she was certain – but whatever he was or was not guilty of himself, his free choice of such evil companions threw her into serious doubt about his character.

Alec had been saying it all along, but she hadn't listened. How horrible to contemplate what he had described. Some poor, illiterate peasant girl subjected to brutality . . .

Even if Devlin had not done it himself, which she simply could not believe he had, was it any less bad if he had even *once* been one of the men watching? The Devlin she knew – or had thought she had known – would have drawn his sword if necessary to come to the victim's defense, not sat there enjoying the spectacle of rape as though it were the latest pantomime at Sadler's Wells.

The drift of her thoughts that morning added a fierce

dimension of protectiveness toward her naive, sheltered young girls as they streamed out to the chapel for Sunday services, two by two, or 'in crocodile,' as it was called. For her part, her only prayer was that none of the innocents ever ran afoul of such men as the lawless fiends of the Horse and Chariot.

Somehow she managed to set aside her outrage and roiling disgust as she conversed in the parlor with the widow Harris, who had come to collect Sorscha for the Catholic Mass. Weary but managing graciousness nevertheless, Lizzie gave Mrs. Harris a warmly approving report on Sorscha's progress in her classes and told her how easily she had made friends with the other girls. Perhaps her temper was short this morning, after a night spent fuming instead of resting, but as they talked, waiting for Sorscha to come down from the girl's dormitory to join her mother, Lizzie found it disconcerting to hold a conversation with a woman whose face she could not see.

She ignored her annoyance and reminded herself that Mrs. Harris had obviously suffered a grievous loss. Fortunately, the lady still had her daughter, and her utter adoration of the sweet girl was palpable. She seemed to like nothing better than hearing about how clever and dedicated Sorscha was in her studies. Even from behind the veil, Lizzie could feel Mrs. Harris beaming with pleasure at her words.

'She really is quite mature for her age,' Lizzie was saying fondly. 'Ah, here they are now!' she exclaimed as the patter of slippered feet came rushing toward the parlor from the wooden stairs in the entrance hall.

'Mama!' Sorscha flung into the parlor doorway, then rushed to embrace her.

'Oh, I missed ye, darlin'.' The woman hugged her; then Sorscha turned, smiling toward the door.

'Look, Mama! I have a new best friend! I brought her to meet you! Miss Manning has been ever so kind to me.' Her bonnet dangling down her back, Sorscha bounded back toward the doorway and drew Daisy Manning into the parlor by her wrist.

They clung to each other's arms and Lizzie smiled to herself, recalling herself and Jacinda as wee girls. Daisy even had the bouncy gold curls, though Miss Manning was the daughter of a coal-mining tycoon rather than a duke. Like old Lady Strathmore, she came from the wealthiest class of merchants and was destined to improve her family's lot in life by marrying into the nobility. Thus her enrollment in the fine finishing school.

'Mama, this is Miss Daisy Manning. Daisy, my dear,' Sorscha said, turning to her boon companion with all her youthful earnestness, 'this is my mother – well, not my real mother, but I never knew *her*—'

'Sorscha!' Mrs. Harris breathed with an appalled gasp at the girl's careless slip.

'Oh! I'm sorry, Mama!' Sorscha whispered, wide-eyed as she blanched.

She could feel Mrs. Harris glaring beneath the veil.

Quickly masking her shock, Lizzie cleared her throat. 'Daisy, you really need to hurry over to the chapel or you'll be late.'

'Yes, Miss Carlisle. Mrs. Harris. Bye, Sorscha.' Daisy curtsied prettily, then walked off with perfect debutante posture to catch up to the line of girls wending toward the church down the lane.

Mrs. Harris stood immobile after Daisy had gone. 'Miss Carlisle, please pay no mind to Sorscha's enthusiasms. It is quite true that I am not her real mother, but adopted her when she was very small—'

'Oh, ma'am, it's not my business,' she assured her. 'Please take no thought of it. I can be discreet.'

'It's quite all right, Miss Carlisle. You see, I was in a terrible

– accident – as a young woman. It left me unable to bear children. Still,' she added stiffly, 'perhaps when Sorscha is older, she'll learn to mind her tongue.'

'I'm so sorry, Mama,' Sorscha offered with sadness in her big, blue eyes.

'Your secret will not leave this room, Mrs. Harris. Never fear. I will speak to young Daisy on this matter to ensure your privacy, if you desire.' She sent the contrite Sorscha an affectionate smile.

The girl brightened slightly.

Mrs. Harris gave Lizzie a regal nod. 'You're very kind.' Taking her errant child by the hand, she drew herself up and started to glide toward the parlor door when, all of a sudden, a ruckus reached them through the windowpane, hoofbeats and clattering wheels coming from the graveled road out in front of the school.

An angry male shout punctuated the noise. 'Get out of the way, damn it!'

Mrs. Harris looked at once toward the window, but Lizzie furrowed her brow. It sounded like Devlin.

Sorscha giggled and rushed to the window. 'Uh-oh, Miss Carlisle, your suitors are here!'

Now it was Lizzie's turn to blush. *Blast.*

When Sorscha pushed the lace curtain aside, Lizzie had a clear view out the parlor window, just as Alec, astride a white horse, come sailing over the school fence, cantering his steed right through the front garden.

Lizzie's jaw dropped.

'Good gracious!' Sorscha cried. 'Did you see that? Well done!'

'Lizzie!' Alec yelled up at the tranquil building, but he had barely slowed his horse when Devlin clattered onto the scene, standing aboard his racing drag.

He hauled his team of high-stepping black Fresians to a skidding stop that sent gravel flying, and leaped down out of the vehicle, throwing back the front gate. He looked incensed.

'Damn it, Alec, I'll kill you for this!'

'Oh, dear,' Lizzie murmured under her breath. It seemed Devlin now knew that Alec had exposed him.

He marched toward him with a wrathful glower as Alec jumped down off his horse. 'Why can't you leave her the hell alone?'

'Bugger off, Dev. I saw her first.'

'*Aaargh!*' With a war cry of pent-up frustration, Devlin charged him, driving Alec back a few feet until they both went tumbling over the dainty wooden bench beside the flower beds.

'Sorscha, come away from the window!' Mrs. Harris hissed.

Aghast at their fighting and foul language in front of her student, not to mention the offended parent, she whirled to Mrs. Harris and stammered an apology. 'I'm so sorry, ma'am. I'd best go and, er, manage this.'

Alec rose up onto his knees and dealt Devlin a blow to the jaw, but Lizzie did not see his response, for she was already dashing out of the parlor and through the entrance hall, flinging open the front door, striding out onto the porch.

'*Stop it!*' she cried. Pounding on each other, they both froze at the sound of her voice. 'The two of you, get up and stop acting like children!' she yelled at them in fury. 'How dare you come here and embarrass me like this?'

With looks of chagrin and scowls at each other, they parted with a small shove and ruefully brushed the mud from the flower beds off their clothes.

Lizzie set her hands on her waist, her heart pounding as she glared at them. 'What on earth are you two doing here? You have no business coming here at this hour!'

Devlin slashed a cold glance at Alec. 'I meant to come alone, but I was followed.'

Alec let out a short, haughty snort of sardonic disdain. 'I was not about to abandon the field to you, Strathmore.'

'Field? It's all a game to you, isn't it, you horse's arse? You ruin my life, and it's all just a bloody game!'

'Devlin!' Lizzie clipped out, for he seemed sorely tempted to launch at Alec again.

Simmering, he turned away from his old school chum and took a step toward her with a fiery expression. 'Lizzie, whatever he told you, you have to let me explain—'

'She doesn't have to let you do anything, Strathmore—'

'Lord Alec, that will do – and both of you, mind your language! There are children about.' Indeed, she could see that Daisy had been distracted by the commotion, and, instead of going on to church, had drifted back to see what was the matter.

'Now, I want you to promise you will stop this foolish fighting and go home,' Lizzie scolded. 'Knowing both of you, I cannot imagine what brings you out at this hour of the morning, for I hardly think you're on your way to church.'

'Actually, Bits, we're on our way home from Strathmore's duel.'

'*What?*' she cried.

'You are a bastard.'

'Devlin!'

'I was his second, you see.' Alec smiled at Devlin. 'Did Lizzie ever tell you how much she hates dueling – old boy?'

'Devlin, how could you?'

He opened his mouth to answer, but nothing came out. He shut it again with a look of dismay and lowered his head. 'It wasn't my fault.'

Alec shook his head. 'Tsk, tsk, tsk.'

Lizzie fumed at both of them. 'I am in no mood to deal with either of you right now. You must leave at once. One of the parents already saw your juvenile display, and if Mrs. Hall comes out here, I'm doomed.' But if she had imagined that she had trouble so far, she went very still as a large black coach rolled up behind Devlin's racing drag, next to where Daisy was standing by the front gate.

The brim of Daisy's poke bonnet concealed her face as the girl turned to look at the hulking carriage with an unfamiliar coat of arms emblazoned on the side.

Lizzie saw two dissipated-looking men peer out the carriage window: one flaxen-blond and fine-featured, the other brown-haired with a square, rugged face. She recognized the latter as the same man Devlin had been talking to on the night of the Madison ball.

'Who are they?' she forced out as a prickle of dread ran down her spine.

Devlin and Alec turned around, but somehow she already knew the answer. They were the wicked men Alec had warned her about. Devlin's evil friends, radiating sheer menace.

'Bloody hell,' Devlin whispered.

Lizzie was not sure what made her blood run colder – the icy smile the blond man sent her, or the lecherous look on the larger man's face as he tipped his hat to little Daisy.

'Daisy, come here!' She started down from the porch to run and collect her student, but the grim note in Devlin's voice stopped her in midstride.

'Elizabeth, go back inside. *Now.*'

'Come, Alec. This has gone far enough,' Dev murmured to his rival as they both stared at Quint and Carstairs. 'Neither of us wants those two anywhere near here.'

'Agreed,' he answered under his breath. 'So, how do we get rid of them?'

Standing shoulder to shoulder with his erstwhile rival, Dev

bristled when he saw Quint leering at the little blonde, who couldn't have been more than sixteen.

'Don't know. I'll figure something out. Daisy!' he echoed Lizzie's shout as he and Alec strode toward the girl.

'Mama, there's Daisy!'

'Sorscha, get back here!'

'Perhaps she'll want to go to church with us instead of the others.'

'Don't go out there! Stay by me.' Mary's heart pounded crazily as she grasped her daughter's wrist and pulled her over to her side, holding her near.

'Mama, what is it?' the girl asked in alarm.

Mary did not answer. Her stricken gaze was fixed on the scene playing out beyond the lace curtains.

Holding Sorscha near, she prayed they would both be safe if they stayed hidden in the parlor. As soon as those blackguards moved on, they would leave the school.

They would not be coming back.

Sweet Christ, things had just gone from bad to worse. First Strathmore. Now Quint and Carstairs, but at least Sorscha's little friend was now moving away from the carriage and hurrying back up the path to the school.

Watching the lover's triangle unfold on the lawn a moment ago, Mary had been appalled enough to discover that by some colossal twist of fate, Devil Strathmore had been courting her daughter's favorite teacher. But then matters took an even more virulent turn as Carstairs's coach rolled up to the school like a great black insect landing in search of food. Searching for something it could contaminate.

The way it had contaminated Johnny. He sat up on the driver's box, grown and handsome, still helplessly enthralled with his seducer, it would seem.

To think none of this would have happened and all those people would still be alive if she had not taken it into her head to cross Carstairs in a futile effort to protect that boy. God, she could scarcely believe the tangled nexus of personal ties playing out before her very eyes – but she had known, of course, that Strathmore regularly kept company with Quint and Carstairs.

Now she saw that Strathmore must have made the young teacher his mistress, for fine lords like him had only one use for women below their own class. What a shame, she thought, feeling a bit betrayed. Miss Carlisle had seemed like a decent young woman.

'Mama, we're going to be late for Mass,' Sorscha insisted.

'Shh, it's all right, darlin'.' Mary held the child snugly to her, just as she had all those years ago, when the flames had reached for the black autumn sky and screams had filled the night.

Little Daisy sent Quint a frightened glance over her shoulder as she hurried past Dev and Alec to Lizzie, who had ignored Dev's order to go inside at once, waiting for her student to reach her motherly arms. As Lizzie shepherded Daisy back into the school, Dev turned to Carstairs, his heart pounding with gathered rage.

The earl's cool stare was fixed on Lizzie's retreating figure. Dev heard the school's door shut behind him; only then did Carstairs's knowing gaze swing to meet his.

'Someone,' he murmured, 'has been a very naughty boy.'

Quint's laugh boomed. 'Devil, hang you, you've been holding out on us! Now we know you found the candy jar and didn't mean to share.'

'I say!' Alec retorted, taking a step toward them. 'You leave these girls alone. They're still in the schoolroom!'

'All the better,' Quint rumbled, and took a lusty swig from his flask.

'A governess is always good for a paddling.' Carstairs slipped him a mocking smile. 'Is that what you fancy, Dev, dear? Is she good with the whip?'

Alec let out a huge gasp of affront, but Dev thrust his hand out, blocking his friend's forward surge for the earl's throat.

Control, control. His own temples throbbed with rage, but he could not betray the depth of his attachment to Lizzie.

It would only put her in danger. He could not let them realize that, in fact, she was his Achilles' heel.

He gave Carstairs an arrogant chuckle. 'A whip? Yes, very. Among other things.'

'You bloody god damn *liar*,' Alec lashed out. 'Elizabeth Carlisle is a pure, unsullied lady, and whoever says otherwise will answer to me!'

Dev looked at Alec in bridled rage; only then did the latter seem to realize his mistake. Until now, Dev had managed to keep her beneath their notice, but now, good God, the quick-tempered Hotspur had just told them her name.

'Well, that's another matter, indeed,' Carstairs drawled, regarding Dev in amusement. 'Perhaps our Devil has lost his heart to the little schoolmarm.'

'Don't be absurd,' he answered coolly. 'She means nothing to me.'

'But pure, Dev? Unsullied?'

He tossed them a cocky wink. 'Not for long.'

Alec looked away as though he had been stabbed through the heart, while Quint and Carstairs laughed idly.

Just then, the school door banged open behind them.

'Gentlemen!' bellowed a voice that sounded like that of a female drill sergeant.

'You, there! Halloo! Sirs! Move along, if you please!'

They turned as a tall, strapping matron with gray side curls and a high lace betsy marched out grandly onto the porch and braced her hands on her thick waist.

'Drive on, I say!' She waved her handkerchief menacingly at Carstairs's carriage. 'You have no manner of business here! I am Mrs. Hall, the owner of this establishment, and you gentlemen are trespassing! Now, remove yourselves from the premises at once or I shall send for the constable!'

To Dev's relief, Carstairs snickered and rapped on the ceiling. 'Home, Johnny.'

Quint leaned out the carriage window and waggled his tongue lasciviously at Mrs. Hall as the coach rolled away.

'Oh, you disgusting—!' Mrs. Hall turned red, then fixed her bulldog stare on Dev, who was musing that she would have made a good alehouse bouncer. 'You, too, sirrah! Off with you both! I don't want to see you lurking about here again—'

'Mrs. Hall, may I please talk with Miss Carlisle, just for a moment?' Dev implored her, going toward the formidable woman. 'I must speak with her!'

'Do so at your leisure, my lord. I am sure that I care not. She has just been dismissed from her post!'

'Oh, no. Don't do that, ma'am, I beg you to be fair.' Dev's heart sank. 'This wasn't her fault. It was ours!'

'For your information, sirs, one of our girls' parents is inside and saw your churlish display. The lady is as shocked as I at the scandalous way Miss Carlisle has chosen to carry on with her beaux, and if this is how she behaves on school property, heaven knows what she does off it. No doubt it comes of all that mingling with her betters.' She gave him a sharp look of disapproval that seemed to disparage all 'immoral' aristocrats. 'The student's mother is now removing her daughter from our academy, and that, sirs, *is* Miss Carlisle's fault – and yours. Good day.' Mrs. Hall pivoted and marched back inside.

Dev and Alec exchanged a taut, guilty glance. Going up the path, they slowly filed out of the gate, Alec leading his horse.

'Just to be clear – you lied to them about Lizzie.' He sent Dev a hard look of question.

'Of course.'

'God, man, you cut me to the quick with those words.'

Dev looked askance at him. 'Now you know how she felt when you slept with Lady Campion.'

Alec sobered and fell silent.

They removed to a short distance down the road, waiting for Lizzie to emerge.

She came out nearly half an hour later, weighed down with three large satchels, her face pale, her delicate features etched with anger and humiliation. Maneuvering her bags out of the entrance, she let the door bang shut behind her and trudged up the path. She came through the gate without looking back.

Dev strode toward her to help. 'I'm sure you don't want to see either of our faces right now, but we thought you might need conveyance t-to, er, wherever it is you plan to go,' he finished, stammering under her cold, quelling stare.

'I *have* nowhere to go now, Devlin. That's the whole point of what you and your playmate have done to me.' She glanced from him to Alec in simmering resentment, then continued walking with her bags.

'Lizzie,' Alec attempted, 'you know you are always welcome at Knight House—'

She whirled to face him. 'Don't you see, Alec? Don't you understand anything? I am so sick and tired of being a poor relation – of having to rely on the charity of my friends for my food and shelter! That's why I took this job, why I work so hard. You two don't know what it's like. You, Devlin, with your estate you never even visit and your fine town house – and you, Alec, with your *très* fashionable rooms at the Albany and your innumerable family homes. All I ever wanted in life was a home a-and a place of my own, but I'm never going to have it. I'm always going to be Lizzie the friend, Lizzie the glorified servant, Lizzie the caretaker. Well, I have news for you, boys,' she wrenched out in sarcasm. 'Sometimes I wouldn't mind someone taking care of me for a change!'

Dev's heart clenched as tears of sheer frustration and defeat rose in her gray eyes and streaked down her face. Lugging her bags, she had not a free hand to wipe them away.

They fell faster.

'What I had here might not have seemed much to you, one simple room to call my own, but it was mine, and you've taken it from me. Where am I to go now? What am I to do?' she cried with a sudden little-girl sob.

Dev and Alec stood there, mute with shame for their immature brawling, and cringing with pain at her tears.

She sniffled, bringing her outburst under control. 'It seems I shall have to impose on Jacinda.' When she hauled her satchel of books up higher on her shoulder and resumed walking down the road, Dev and Alec glanced at each other, then sprang into action.

'Lizzie!'

'Come back!'

'Let us help you—'

'I'll carry that for you—'

'No!' she fairly roared, pulling away from them both.

Dev planted himself in her path. 'At least let me give you a ride into Town.' He reached for the crate she was carrying in her arms, but she nearly dropped it on his toes.

'Go away! I don't need your help, Devlin! I don't need either of you! Can't you see that? Go rescue some other damsel, because it so happens I am perfectly capable of taking care of myself!' She bent down and began angrily throwing her belongings back into the crate, but Dev crouched down beside her and helped, lifting a small, floppy gingham dog out of the dust, holding it for a moment in his hand.

An old childhood toy.

He stared at it for a second, then turned to her with renewed dread that he was going to lose her. 'Lizzie, I'm so sorry.'

'Oh, sorry, are you? You know, I might have expected something like this from him, Devlin, but from you? But then again, maybe I don't know you at all. After what Alec told me, I can only wonder – and today you dueled, as well? You could have been killed!'

'The man forfeited,' he mumbled lamely.

'Bits – sorry, I mean Lizzie.' Alec joined them with a tentative stride. 'I wish you wouldn't be so cross. Everything's going to be all right, sweeting. You shouldn't have to work anyway.'

'What, better that I should rely on a man for my livelihood – is that what you mean, Alec, my dear? Ah, but look at the examples I have in front of me! One who squanders at the gambling tables every penny that rolls his way; the other chasing an early grave no doubt for some imagined pinprick to his honor! Trust me, laddies, I would rather grow old and gray alone than put my fate in the hands of such *children*!'

As she shoved her old toy back into her satchel and turned away, Dev wished the earth would crack apart and swallow him.

Someone should have warned him about tangling with outraged bluestockings, he thought, for the cleverer a woman was, it seemed, the greater her wit with which to deflate a man's sense of himself. He still owned the greater physical strength, however, and he used it presently to lift the heavy bag out of her arms, ignoring her protests.

He carried it over to his racing drag and strapped it into the low, flat boot. Alec followed him, carrying her portmanteau.

She regarded both men with a stare devoid of trust, her arms folded tightly across her chest.

'You can hate me,' Dev said. 'Just get in. I'm not letting you walk. It's too far.'

'Fine.' She stalked toward the passenger side of the racing drag, jerking her elbow away when Alec reached to help her up into the seat.

When Dev slapped the reins over his Fresians' backs a moment later and the drag pulled away, Lizzie glanced back at the Academy as though she knew she was leaving her childhood behind forever.

It was a cold, silent ride to Jacinda's elegant villa on Regent's Park. Alec escorted them there on horseback. Nobody spoke the whole way.

When they arrived, Alec was the first to reach the door. He sent one of Jacinda's footmen out to bring in Lizzie's things. The beautiful young marchioness appeared in the doorway and greeted Lizzie with open arms, marveling at her distraught pallor. Dev hung back, grimly realizing that Alec had the clear advantage here. He treated his sister's house like his own. With her best friend's arms around her, Lizzie sent Dev a conflicted gaze from the safety of the doorstep. It was enough of a cue to draw him nearer. She murmured something to Jacinda. He could not hear it, but he deduced she was telling the marchioness what had transpired.

'It's all right, dearest. I'd love to have you here. My home is your home! Billy!' Jacinda called into the house, then turned to face Lizzie's errant suitors. 'Alec, I must ask you to leave,' she said coolly to her brother; then she nodded to Dev. 'You, too, Lord Strathmore. Miss Carlisle is in no mood for company.'

Alec started to argue, but Billy appeared behind the two women.

Sensing the tension, he moved protectively in front of them. 'You heard my wife,' he growled, sending them both a warning glance that was polite, though edged with steel. 'Miss Carlisle is not receiving.'

'Rackford, I just want to talk to her—,' Alec tried, but Billy's flinty green eyes narrowed.

'I suggest you leave before I hurt you, Alec. I let you off easy the last time you made Lizzie cry.' He flicked Dev an equally suspicious glance, then shut the door in their faces.

And locked it.

Chapter Seventeen

On several occasions over the next few days, Quint had driven slowly past Mrs. Hall's Academy looking for a bit of sport, but not until now had he found much luck. It was Thursday afternoon, warm and muggy, with the sky threatening rain. As his coach crept over the rise above the commons across from the school, Quint saw the lovely little thing that had caught his eye the other day sitting alone beside the pond, floating a paper boat on the water and waiting in vain for a puff of wind. There was no one else around.

Gold curls drooping, she lifted her woeful gaze, hearing his carriage approach.

Quint wasn't much of an actor, but this story always worked. He leaned his head out the carriage window. 'Excuse me, miss, have you seen a small brown puppy run by?'

'What?' She perked up slightly but did not get up from the large, flat rock where she was sitting like a lonely little mermaid.

'My new puppy,' Quint said. 'He's run away from home, and I'm desperately worried he'll come to harm. He's only three months old. My servant saw him come this way,' he added with his most earnest look.

The little simpleton frowned, got up, and dusted off her skirts. 'Oh, no. What sort of puppy?'

'Retriever,' he said.

She approached his carriage cautiously. 'What's his name? If I see him, I will call out to him.'

'Why, his name is, er, it's, uh, Fluffy. Poor thing. He must be terrified.' Quint pretended to scan the landscape in distress. 'I so love having something little and soft to stroke. I should hate for him to rush out in the road under the wheels of somebody's carriage. If only I had more pairs of eyes to help me find him!'

She regarded him a trifle skeptically.

How pretty she was. How sheltered, he thought, his heart pounding faster.

'If I see Fluffy, sir, I will try to catch him.'

'Oh, thank you, Miss— Ah, what is your name?' His quick glance calculated the distance at which she was standing, shading her eyes from the overcast glare with a smooth, childlike hand. If he moved quickly, he could almost grab her. Only lure her a little closer. Then drive. He smiled. 'You don't have a name?'

'I recognize you,' she said, taking a backward step, 'and I don't think I like you.'

Quint suppressed laughter. 'Why not, my dear?'

'You were staring at me the other day. It was very rude.'

'I am sorry. Here, have a piece of candy. Friends?'

Daisy eyed it, then shook her head.

Careful, old boy. Don't let her scream out. 'What are you doing out here all by yourself?' he murmured. 'Where are your teachers? The other girls?'

The pretty thing let out a desolate sigh. 'I'm supposed to be taking a nap, but I'm not at all tired.'

'There, there, my pet, what's wrong?' he asked with an indulgent smile at her pouty air. 'Why so glum?'

'I'm having a very bad time of it, if you must know!' she

cried. 'My nicest teacher was dismissed, and my best friend's mama took her away from school. It's so lonely here now. I hate it.'

'You could come with me. To look for Fluffy,' he amended.

She glanced toward the school with a sulk. 'I'm not allowed.'

'No one would know. I could have you back in less than an hour. Don't you care that little Fluffy is in danger, Miss—?'

'Manning,' she supplied as she glanced around with a great sigh to see if she could spy his fictional lost pup. 'I do hope your little doggy's all right.'

Quint blinked. 'As in Manning Mines?'

She nodded absently. 'That's my papa's.'

Quint quickly hid his astonishment. The Manning heiress! Good God! The Manning company mined coal-fields throughout England. His first thought was of Dev's departed aunt, Lady Ironsides, whose industrial fortune had saved the Strathmore family from genteel ruin. Like Quint, most of the nobs needed cash, while the merchants lusted for titles.

It was just the sort of exchange Quint suddenly realized he had needed for years. No more worries! No more loans from Carstairs and Dev and his other rich friends.

Why, it had practically fallen into his lap. When he glanced again at the fair young virgin, his mind leaped past his immediate hunger for an untouched conquest to the fortune the chit's father was worth. God's bones, her dowry was probably worth more than a decade's rents from his rocky, soggy Yorkshire estate.

Think, man, for once in your life! The chit was not yet out of the schoolroom. But if he waited until she entered Society, there would be too much competition. *Must act now.*

Quint decided on the spot he would procure her hand in marriage. Her father would surely receive him, hear his suit. He was a baron, after all, and even a millionaire of the great merchant class would not necessarily know that Quint's title was just a trifle tarnished. He could put on the lordly airs when he needed to. Aye, and if Money-bags Manning tried denying his suit, Quint would put a fist down his throat.

'Daisy!' a woman called suddenly, coming out onto the porch of the school. 'Come away from there at once!' The teacher started toward them.

Daisy let out a longsuffering sigh, then looked at Quint again. 'I hope you find your little doggy, sir.'

'Oh, I will, love. Never fear.'

'You have to go away now.'

'As you wish, little one,' Quint said with a reassuring leer. 'But I'll be back.'

'Are you sure you won't come to the opera with us? There's plenty of room in our box at the theater.' Jacinda crossed the rooftop garden toward Lizzie, adjusting one of her diamond earrings.

'No, thanks.' Reclining on a cushioned chaise beneath the pastel-striped tent, Lizzie smiled with sisterly pride in her friend's lavish beauty.

The young marchioness was formally dressed in a magnificent white gown and diamonds, her guinea-gold curls arranged high on the crown of her head, with spiraling tendrils dangling artfully here and there.

Jacinda lowered herself to the white wrought-iron chair across from her. 'I hate to leave you. Should I cancel? I don't mind—'

'It's all right, Jas. I could use a little time alone. Sort things out.'

She offered her a bolstering smile. 'Something tells me you'll feel better once you've had a talk with a certain viscount of our acquaintance.'

'Am I that transparent?' she asked with a sigh.

Jacinda nodded. 'Always have been. But you're not going to sit here fretting over either of those rogues, are you?' She reached over and patted her hand. 'Come to the opera with Billy and me. You can dress quickly, can't you? It will take your mind off those scoundrels. Cheer you up.'

'I thought you were seeing a tragedy.'

'Oh, well, yes, but one hardly goes for the spectacle on stage,' she declared with a wave of her hand. 'Honestly, the most amusing part to me is watching Billy scowl and twist in his seat and suffer through it so valiantly – for me!'

'He even endures opera for you. Now, that is love.'

'He is well rewarded,' she assured her with a scandalous wink.

'Oh, Jas.' She chuckled in spite of herself as her friend rose, then bent to kiss her forehead.

'Well, I'm off! The butler is on duty if you need anything. You know,' she added in a thoughtful tone, pausing to furl her light evening wrap around her shoulders, 'perhaps it's for the best that Mrs. Hall gave you the sack. The world of that school was too small for you, Lizzie.'

Surprised at her words which nearly echoed something Ben had once said to her, Lizzie sent her friend a wan but grateful smile.

'You'll figure it out,' Jacinda assured her softly; then she left.

For a long while after the sound of the couple's departing town coach had faded, Lizzie sat out on the tented balcony, watching the pink sunset fade between the mountain shapes of some slow-moving purple clouds.

Twilight settled gently over London.

Throughout the nearby park's sprawling acreage, the greens deepened; the boughs whispered; night birds chirped. To the south and west, the city lights glowed gaily with the Season at its peak, but here on the leafy edges of Regent's Park, the only sound was a squawk now and then from the ducks in the canal, an occasional carriage clattering by. All was quiet.

Except in her heart.

Everything felt tangled – yet she knew she could not hide here forever.

Why had Devlin not called on her? He'd made no attempt to see her. He hadn't even sent a note. She had been waiting for several days for an apology on his behavior at the school, and even more keenly for an explanation about his involvement in the Horse and Chariot Club. But there was still no sign of him, and Lizzie was left wondering what his absence meant.

Perhaps the awful tale was all too true, and Devlin could not face her now that Alec had exposed his black heart. But wouldn't the half-million pounds have been incentive enough to make him swallow his pride to come and grovel? Where was he?

The deadline was fast approaching when the terms of his aunt's will would expire. It was as though he'd simply given up.

To her own vast dismay, Lizzie had not.

In the face of his silence and so much conflicting information from Alec, she had finally come to the point of admitting that her reason, her best tool, was of no help in puzzling it out. A choice must be made, and she had nothing to go on but her own blind heart.

With Jacinda's words, the advice that Ben's mother had given him echoed once more through her mind.

'*Bennett, my boy, that plantation was always too small a place for you, so go on, be free. Go with that crazy Englishman and see the world . . .*'

There was no telling where her love for Devlin might lead her. But the longer she stayed away from him, the harder she tried to forget him, the more surely she knew she was already too far gone. Despite the dire warnings of her mind that he was not the man she had come to believe in, that his main interest was still just the money, her intuition whispered that she belonged with Devlin, come what may.

When the butler came up and announced that Lord Alec was at the door, she considered for a somber moment, then agreed to see him, bracing herself as she sat up.

She knew what she had to do.

Soon, Alec sat across from her, gazing into her eyes. 'I want you to marry me.'

She was amazed in spite of herself. There was a time when this moment would have been her girlhood fantasy come true. But now it felt all wrong.

Slowly, sadly, she shook her head.

'No more waiting, no more games,' he forged on bravely, taking her hands in a gentle hold. 'It's always been you and me, hasn't it? Please . . . try.'

'Oh, Alec.' Her heart pounded. Her voice was barely a whisper. 'It's no use. I can't marry you when my heart belongs to another.'

'What about what I told you? The Horse and Chariot Club?' he asked guardedly.

She shook her head slowly. 'I don't know. I'm just going to have to – trust.'

'But you don't trust me.'

'I'm sorry.'

Alec searched her eyes for a moment in silence. 'You really do love him.'

She nodded with tears in her eyes.

'Well.' He dropping his gaze, his eyes misting slightly. 'I'm happy for you. He'll take care of you. No doubt of that. The title. The money. You deserve . . . all that is good. I've been an ass, Lizzie. God, what an ass I've been. I'm sorry for

– everything. Never deserved you anyway. Didn't I tell you one day you'd thank me?' he attempted to joke.

Her heart clenched. 'Oh, Alec.' She gave his hand a caring squeeze and stared at him with tears in her eyes.

'In all fairness, Dev may have another explanation about his involvement in the Horse and Chariot Club. One I am not at liberty to explain.'

She looked at him in question, but he just gave her a sad smile, then leaned nearer and pressed a kiss to her brow. 'Goodbye, Bits, and thanks for everything,' he whispered. Then, rising to his feet, he left her sitting alone in the half-light.

He was gone.

Oh, God, she hoped she wasn't making a mistake. Closing her eyes, she steadied herself with a deep breath. It was done, her decision made. No turning back now. But there was still one more thing to do if she was to see this whole business through cleanly to the end.

A bit shaken but resolute, she left the house and took a hackney coach to Charles Beecham's offices on Fleet Street.

The lawyer was still at work, burning the oil well into the evening when she knocked on the door. He answered it, beckoning her in with ink-stained fingers.

'Why, Miss Carlisle, this is a most unexpected visit.'

'I see you are busy. I crave only a moment of your time.'

'Of course, my dear. Would you care to sit down?'

She shook her head and paced his office, fingering the tassel of her reticule. 'It's about Her Ladyship's will. I've—' She swallowed hard. 'I've come to see if there is any possible way that Dev – I mean Lord Strathmore – can be freed from the terms of his aunt's will.'

He frowned. 'I am not sure what to say, Miss Carlisle.'

'Oh, surely there must be a way. That money is rightfully his. He needs it. I certainly don't. This isn't fair to him.'

Charles looked mystified.

Lizzie decided there was no reason not to divulge the rest. 'You see, his aunt asked me to look after him from time to time when she was gone. But I don't need half her fortune to do that.' She lowered her gaze, a blush rising in her cheeks. 'I certainly don't need him to be forced into marrying me just so he can pay his bills.'

'You are . . . in love with him?' Charles asked in his most delicate lawyerly fashion.

'Very much,' she whispered, avoiding his eyes with a rueful nod. 'I will never know how Devlin really feels about me as long as his fortune hangs in the balance. I'll never know for sure if it's the money or me that he loves.' She lifted her abashed gaze and saw Mr. Beecham studying her with a thoughtful stare. She gave him a hapless smile. 'You must think me very foolish.'

'No, it's not that.'

'What, then?'

Mr. Beecham rose from his desk, slowly walked around it, then drummed his fingers a trifle nervously on the corner of it. He cleared his throat. 'Did you discuss this at all with His Lordship, may I inquire?'

'No, I did not. We had a – tiff.'

'I see. Then perhaps you should speak to him first. I dare not speak out of turn.'

'Out of turn? Sir? I don't understand.'

He pursed his mouth and looked away with an air of distress. 'He was supposed to tell you himself.'

'He hasn't told me anything.' Her alarm climbed. 'Mr. Beecham, please. What is it? You must tell me! If it concerns me, I beg you—'

'Very well,' he soothed. 'You may wish to sit down.'

'Tell me!' she cried, paling.

He cleared his throat with a fist to his mouth, then drew

himself up. 'I'm afraid, Miss Carlisle, that what you ask has already been done. Lady Strathmore's will, which you heard read in this office, has been nullified. Because no copy was submitted to the Chancery, the law provides that the previous will guide the disbursal of the deceased's belongings. The money all belongs to His Lordship, and he has known this fact for several weeks.'

'W-what?' Her heartbeat thundered.

'I am sorry that you must find out this way. He said he would tell you himself – when the time was right.'

'Why didn't he?' she cried, bewildered.

'Why, Miss Carlisle, he said that if you knew that he no longer needed to marry you in order to claim his inheritance, you might say no.'

She stared at him, her head reeling. She could barely find her voice. 'You mean—?' she breathed.

'He loves you, Miss Carlisle. He's loved you all this time.'

'I am sorry, my lord,' the butler intoned, his face blank, for he was very well trained. 'Miss Carlisle is not at home.'

Dev saw red. 'Doubtless that is what you are ordered to say! Damn it, man, let me in! I know she is there. I must see her!'

'My lord—'

'I will not be denied!' Dev went on the offensive, shoved the butler aside and prowling into the house. He threw his head back, howling her name. 'Lizzie! *Lizzie!*'

'Sir!'

'Where is she? Where are you hiding her?'

'She is not here! Sir, you must go.'

'She has gone out?' he demanded warily.

'Yes, as I have already said!'

'With Lord Alec?' he asked in a dangerous tone.

'I know not.'

'Nor would you tell me,' Dev muttered. 'Fine, then. I shall wait.' Jerking his arm away from the butler, he sat down heavily on the stairs, where his bleary gaze searched the polished floor. *I can't be too late.* But somehow it was all too easy to imagine the happy foursome – Lizzie and Alec, Jacinda and her Billy – out celebrating their future kinship. They were probably making wedding plans already, and as usual, he ended up alone.

Elbow resting on his bent knee, Dev shut his eyes in welling despair and propped his forehead in his hand.

He had tried to give up. Had tried to keep his distance. Had tried for four days, nine hours, and seven minutes to relinquish her to what was best for Lizzie, but again and again, he kept coming back to his awful fear, that if he left her to Alec's keeping, Alec would only hurt her again and again for the rest of her life. For if a man strayed once from his lady, he would do it again. It wasn't fair. Not when she was so loyal.

'Sir?' Jacinda's butler bent down and gazed into Dev's care-worn face with a compassion that surprised him. 'Can I fetch you something, my lord? Tea? Brandy? A headache powder, perhaps?'

Dev regarded him ruefully. There was only one thing he wanted, but he was fairly sure it was already lost.

At that moment, she walked in through the front door, halting when she saw him sitting on the staircase in an attitude of defeat. But Alec wasn't with her. She was alone.

Like him.

Dev shot to his feet, trembling suddenly as he held her dazed stare. 'Lizzie.' His voice came out in a whisper.

The butler vanished instinctively, leaving the two of them alone.

Lizzie blinked as though she feared he was a vision.

He stepped down off the stairs.

She walked warily into the foyer and closed the door behind her. 'You're here.'

'Yes.' Dev swallowed hard and took a few more steps toward her, closing the distance between them. 'I've been waiting . . . I need – to talk to you. I have so much to tell you – if you'll listen. I'm sorry for getting you fired. I didn't come before because I was – trying to do the right thing, but without you, everything feels all wrong. I – can't let you go.' His palms sweated as he crumpled the brim of his hat in his hands. *I don't want to lose you.* 'Alec's a good man. No doubt of that. But not for you. He'll only hurt you again the moment he grows restless. I don't want to see you hurt. Please – just listen. It's true I am a member of that club, but I can explain everything if you'll listen, and there's something I need to show you before you decide.'

'What is it?'

His pride crawled, but he was past caring as he stood before her. 'I want to show you what I can give you if you – pick me. You said you never had a home of your own. Well, my Uncle Jacob – Aunt Augusta's husband – was the one who nearly ruined the family, which was why he had to marry her fortune in the first place. The thing he spent it all on was his house, Oakley Park. It's – magnificent, Lizzie. It's yours if you want it. And so am I.'

'Oh, darling,' she whispered, shaking her head at him with tears in her eyes.

'I've been keeping secrets, Lizzie. But now I want to tell you everything. Just tell me that I haven't lost you, because if I have, I no longer want to live—'

'Shh.'

He had not realized they were close enough to touch until she suddenly lifted her hand and laid her finger over his lips, stilling the anguished tumble of his words with a soothing hush.

'I've already told Alec no, Devlin,' she whispered. 'And as to your secrets, I already know the most important thing. You see, I've just come from Mr. Beecham's office. I know about your aunt's will. Oh, Devlin.' Her dove-gray eyes swam with emotion as she searched his gaze. 'I love you, too.'

He gasped at the words, or perhaps it was a sob, but her gentle arms wound around his neck. She drew him down to kiss her, and he surrendered with all his heart, all his being.

With trembling hands, he caught her sweet face between his palms and kissed her with tears burning behind his closed eyelids. He realized she was crying, too, when he felt the hot droplets of her tears fall upon his hands as he held her face so lovingly. She clung to him.

'Marry me,' he choked out, barely pausing long enough to let her whisper, 'Yes, yes,' before kissing her again and again.

'Come away with me. Tonight.'

'Yes.'

'To Oakley Park. I want to show you.'

'Anywhere.'

'We can be there in three hours. I love you.'

'Devlin.' She held him hard, burying her tearstained face against his neck. 'I love you, too, sweet. With all my heart.'

Chapter Eighteen

Euphoria tingled in their veins as they raced through the night, glorious and strong beneath the moonlight, her hair flying as she drove the carriage, his hand resting on her waist as he coached her at the reins and murmured love words in her ear, wicked silken promises that sent shivers of anticipation down every nerve ending and made her drive faster.

With nary a cloud in the sky, a big gibbous moon hung over the blowing trees; its white liquid light lined the black Fresians' supple backs. The fleet cadence of their hoofbeats drummed the dusty road. The deep twilight rang with cricket song, a secret world of silver moon-glow and wan gold globes of light from the carriage lamps.

Her heel firmly braced against the footboard, the leather reins taut in her hands, Lizzie needed nothing more than faith and instinct and Devlin at her side, urging her on; she sped the coach-and-four along with a reckless daring she could only have learned from him.

At the halfway point, they took a break to rest the horses; then Ben took over the driving, and Devlin and Lizzie climbed inside the coach. For the next hour, he told her of his quest, explaining his real motives for associating with the Horse and

Chariot Club and recounting all the steps he had taken to unearth the truth so far, tracing each move as though it were some deadly chess game.

Lizzie marveled at what she heard.

'November 1805. The place was called The Golden Bull. 'Twas a coaching inn on the Oxford Road just below Uxbridge. Between the travelers in the guestrooms, the large staff, and the local people drinking in the pub, it took the coroner weeks to reconstruct a complete list of all the people who were in the place that night. The fire was so fierce that it left several bodies too badly damaged to be identified, and the guest register had burned along with the hotel, so they had to use what records remained from the inn's livery stable, which was untouched, and the way bills of various stagecoach companies whose drivers had traversed their usual route that night. In the end, the number of the dead rose to forty-seven.' His stare was brooding, a dangerous note of hate-filled grief creeping into his voice. 'They never found my little sister's body.'

She caressed his back, trying to give comfort. 'You don't have to tell me all this if it's too painful.'

'No. It all ties back to the Horse and Chariot Club, and I want you to know the reason for my association with such men.' He stared at her for a long moment. 'I mean to prove that some of them were there that night and deliberately set that fire. When my more conventional investigation of my family's deaths ran aground some months ago, I saw no other way to move forward except by joining the club so I could study the bastards.'

'How did you ever realize they might be involved?'

'Through a very long, slow process of meticulous analysis. You forget, my travels were partly scientific expeditions. I am used to the art of observation and objectively collecting facts. My father's influence,' he added softly. 'He was a gifted amateur biologist, forever peering into his microscope. Quite obsessed, I'm afraid, with discovering the mysteries of freshwater eels.'

Lizzie smiled in fond amusement.

'He would have liked you.' Devlin let out a great sigh. 'For two years, I've been gathering evidence, ruling out alternative possibilities. I'm so close to the truth now. I can feel it.'

She frowned thoughtfully. 'Perhaps you'd best start at the beginning, love.'

He smiled. He should have known he could rely on Lady Logic to verify his theorem. 'That's my girl,' he murmured. Suddenly, he was glad he was sharing all of this with her, not just for the sake of harmony between them, but for practical reasons, as well. Intelligent as she was, his little bluestocking might catch something he had overlooked.

'My first step was collecting all the documentation associated with the case – fire inspector's report, coroner's rulings, newspaper clippings, obituaries for each person who died that night in the blaze. The second step was more difficult – trying to track down any survivors. There were only a handful of them, and you may believe my suspicions grew apace when I found that a number of them had died under mysterious circumstances over the course of the year or two after the fire. As if fate was picking them off.

'Of particular interest was the cook's supposed suicide. According to the fire inspector, the blaze at The Golden Bull had started in the kitchen. As the head of the kitchen staff, the cook was responsible for everyone and everything that happened in his domain, including the fire. His "suicide" seemed to acknowledge his guilt for the tragedy.'

'Indeed.'

'But one of the most useful witnesses I was able track down – Tom Doolittle, who had been the kitchen haul-boy at the time – was the cook's nephew. Claims his uncle was a jolly, churchgoing fellow who would never have taken his own life even under those circumstances.'

'Do you mean to say you think the cook was actually – murdered?'

'And his death staged to look like suicide.'

'But why?' she exclaimed.

'Because he was a highly credible man – and that fire never started in his kitchen.'

'Where did it start?' she asked, mystified.

'Outside, around the perimeter of the building. But you won't find that fact written in the fire inspector's official report. It is recorded only in the first version. The version he decided to revise when he began receiving anonymous death threats.'

'Dear Lord.'

'He did not want to talk to me. He is retired now and tried to say he had little memory of the case. But I finally wore him down.'

'Yes, you have a talent for such things, my lord.'

He sent her a pointed glance. 'The official report on record, submitted by this old inspector, states that the fire was accidental and started in the kitchen. Fortunately, being a man of more conscience than courage, he saved a copy of his first report, the version of what happened written immediately after his walk-through of the site. This older version he allowed me to read. In it, he makes the case for arson. His findings were based on the even rate of speed at which the building had burned down on all sides, as though it had been tarred around the edges, or oil poured around the perimeter.'

'So there was no way the poor people trapped inside could run to escape.'

He nodded grimly. 'Even more damning, a few of the iron shutter-latches had been found among the rubble with the teeth still locked together.'

She stared at him in shock. 'My God, that means someone . . . would have to have locked the people in, then intentionally burned the place to the ground. Why? Why would someone do something so evil to scores of strangers?'

'To cover up another crime, I believe – an act that he deemed even worse.' He paused. 'At any rate, whoever was behind the anonymous threats to the fire inspector instructed him to say that it had been a kitchen fire. In fear of his life, the old man falsified his report accordingly. Shortly after the kitchen-fire report came out, the cook was found in an apparent suicide. This seemed very much like an admission of guilt; case closed.'

'So, whoever threatened the fire inspector also got rid of the cook,' Lizzie deduced.

He nodded. 'Back to our kitchen haul-boy. Though he was only nine years old at the time, Tom Doolittle gave me the most significant clue of all. Naturally, it cost me a plum to bribe it out of him,' he added cynically. 'It seems the scullery maid had sent Tom out to fetch water from the pump, and that, he claims, was when he heard the gunshot.'

'Gunshot?' Lizzie whispered, her eyes widening.

'Voices arguing from somewhere up on the second-floor gallery. Tom heard a man yell, "Shut up, you Irish whore!" – then a single gunshot.'

She stared at him in somber amazement.

'Now, if someone had gotten shot that night,' Dev continued, 'it could possibly have shown up in one of the coroner's summaries.'

'That sounds logical.'

'But there was no mention of any bullet anywhere. Of course, one tiny lead ball could have easily been missed. Or—'

'The coroner was receiving death threats, too.'

'Bravo,' he murmured with a grim half-smile. 'A pity he and the fire inspector never saw fit to confide their mental tortures to a living soul, but the killer was surely counting on their terror to keep them silent. The coroner refused to speak with me; you may be interested to know I was unable to break him down. But apparently our conversation preyed on his mind for days after. A week later, I received a file by messenger. When I inquired, the servant told me that his master had packed up and left the country, but at least he had sent me the information that had been suppressed for over a decade. Sure enough, as it turned out, one of the bodies had indeed been found with a gunshot wound to the chest.'

'Whose?' she whispered, not sure she wanted to know.

Dev paused. 'My father's.'

'Oh, sweetheart.' She gazed at him in pain.

He did not speak for a moment, then cleared his throat. 'Someone in the hotel that night shot my father, then – I believe – burned the hotel down to hide the crime.'

'That rude shout about an Irish woman that the haul-boy heard from the upper gallery – you told me your mother was Irish. Do you think both your parents were somehow targeted?'

'That's exactly what I wondered when Tom first told me what he'd heard. My mother was a lady, but I'll tell you, she never backed down from an argument if she saw something she didn't like.'

'But who would do such a thing? Who would burn forty-seven people alive to hide the death of one?'

'Not just any one: A viscount. My father was a quiet, gentle man, but everyone who knew him loved him. The whole aristocracy held him in high esteem. Whoever killed him must have realized who he was, perhaps after the fact. But as far as I knew, it could have been anyone – another guest, an employee, or someone drinking in the pub.'

'What about brigands, highwaymen in the area? The coaching roads are often plagued with them.'

'I thought of that. I checked with the landlords of the other posting inns on that stretch of road, but they had no criminal activity to report. There was only one thing left to do: I started at the top of the list and began looking into the background of every person on it, searching for clues, anything suspicious. Past criminal records. Anything. It was a long, long process of elimination.'

'It must have taken ages.'

'Over a year – and many more bribes. There was one name on the list that I could not make heads or tails of: Mrs. Mary Harris. I could find nothing on this woman. She had come in on one of the stagecoaches. No one knew her; there was no record of her existence that I could locate. Do you have any idea how many women there are in this world named Mary Harris? A lot,' he said flatly.

She smiled. 'I suppose there must be. It was thanks to a Mrs. Harris that I lost my post at the school. That was the outraged parent the headmistress mentioned to you.'

'Ah, yes,' he said in chagrin. 'Well, there you have it. Every Mary Harris I traced was either alive and well, or not a Mrs. I was beginning to think it was a case of mistaken identity. At any rate, I was following a lead on number thirty-two on my long list of the dead, a Mr. James Cox, blacksmith from a nearby village, a regular at The Golden Bull's taproom. He had been drinking there that night and met the same horrible fate as the rest.

'In the course of looking into the blacksmith's life, I was able to track down one of his old drinking mates from the pub and ask him a few questions – an old navvy by the name of Jackson. Earlier that evening, before the fire was set, Jackson was actually in the pub with Cox and the rest of their circle. He left early because he had apparently promised his wife he would lay off the bottle. It was a promise that saved his life.'

'Indeed.'

'As Jackson tells it, the whole pub was abuzz that night because one of their drinking mates called Wiley had spotted a woman in the lobby that he swore was the famous London stage actress, Ginny Highgate. Wiley was sure it was her, even though the woman he saw was wearing a veil. He had seen her in some Extravaganza Water Spectacle at Ranelagh Gardens. He asserted that she was probably trying to disguise herself to hide her fame. Are you still with me?'

She nodded. 'Go on.'

'The name Ginny Highgate was not on my list, so I realized that this Mary Harris might have been an alias the actress was using to avoid being recognized and mobbed by adoring men. Because Miss Highgate had signed in under a false name, to this day, I do not know if her family is even aware that she died in that fire. To them, she would simply have . . . disappeared.'

Lizzie stared at him in intense thought. 'Women who join the theater world are often disowned by their families.'

'Right you are. I figured there had to be someone in London who knew or cared something for Ginny Highgate. I shall now apologize for the next bit of my story, which is rather scandalous.'

She nodded. 'Continue.'

'From the manager at Ranelagh Gardens, I was able to trace Ginny Highgate back to the brothel where she got her start. I had a most enlightening interview with the madam.'

'What did you learn?'

'Two things of note. One, Ginny Highgate was also Irish.'

'Then the insult the haul-boy heard from the gallery could have been directed at her.' She winced. 'She was on the scene. She was Irish. And it would have been literal.'

'Exactly.'

'Isn't that interesting?' she murmured. 'My Mrs. Harris from the school is Irish, too.'

He shrugged. 'It's a common name.'

'What's the second thing you learned?'

'I found out that Ginny Highgate, aka Mary Harris, was a favorite of the Horse and Chariot Club – almost their exclusive property – passed around, rumor has it, among several of the members, who were her protectors in succession. Randall, Carstairs, Staines. Now, I cannot be sure how all of this adds up, but after spending a good deal of time studying the bastards, I have a theory, if you want to hear it.'

She nodded quickly.

'You see, a packet leaves for Ireland every day from the port at Holyhead, and to get there from London, you have to take that same stretch of the Oxford Road. I believe Miss Highgate was on her way there, leaving London, leaving her lover – whichever of them it was. According to the madam, Miss Highgate had made her fortune and talked of going home to Ireland. But what if her protector at the time did not wish to give her up?'

Lizzie stared at him.

'I think Ginny Highgate became the victim that night of a scorned lover's wrath. One of those bastards from the Horse and Chariot Club, perhaps with a few companions in tow, must have chased her all the way to that inn, and there, I believe that my father – gentlemanly, civilized to a fault – stepped into the middle of it, trying to calm the situation down.'

'And they shot him,' she whispered.

He nodded slowly. 'All I can think is that they must have panicked when they realized they had murdered a fellow peer, especially one of my father's popularity.'

'So, you think they set the fire to cover up the crime?'

'And to get rid of the witnesses.'

'Including your mother and sister,' she said softly.

They both fell silent.

'So, what is your next move?' she asked.

'I still require proof,' he said evenly. 'The law won't care what my instincts tell me. I must find evidence damning enough to bring the killer to justice, and that is nigh impossible when we are talking about a member of the aristocracy. Whoever has done this, I want him publicly shamed, disgraced. I want him hanged with a mob to jeer and spit on him. I want him stripped of all he owns. Lands, title if indeed he holds one. I want him to suffer. I want his family to suffer. By God, I want his name obliterated from the book of eternity.'

Lizzie shivered slightly at the leashed wrath that burned in his eyes. She cleared her throat a bit. 'I can see you've given this some thought.'

The ghost of a sardonic smile twisted a corner of his lips. 'Only two years' worth.'

'My poor love.' She gazed across the cramped space of the coach at him, wanting to put her arms around him, but she held herself back, one serious question still left unanswered. She searched his eyes. 'I can't believe you kept all this from me. God, Devlin, if your theory is true, then they *know* who you are. As the son of the man they shot down, they must suspect your intentions against them.'

'I'm sure they do. They watch my every move. That's why I take care to behave like a hellion whose only thought is pleasure and why I spend money like it's water. For the most part, I've convinced them that I have yet to outgrow the wicked ways of my misspent youth.'

'You even had me fooled at the start.' She lowered her head, trying to think how to phrase the question that still nagged at her. 'Devlin, Alec told me of an extremely upsetting practice that is required of any man who would join the Horse and Chariot Club—'

'Lizzie,' he interrupted gently, 'I did not touch her.'

She let out a quiet exhalation of relief. 'I knew in my heart that you would never harm an innocent. But how did you outwit them? Alec said the rule is that the other men must – watch.'

He shook his head. 'Just a myth. Even legends of the Horse and Chariot Club are sometimes exaggerated. Remember the night I stole you away in my carriage? Do you recall the wound on my side? You asked where I'd got it.'

'You never did tell me.'

'I cut myself to provide the required proof that I had "despoiled" the lass. Once the men were satisfied, I spirited her out of there and handed her over to Ben, who drove her back to her village, safe and sound.'

'Oh, darling.' She moved across the carriage and encircled him in her arms, holding him for a long moment. She laid her head on his broad shoulder and closed her eyes. 'Isn't it hard for you to face them, knowing one of them killed your sire? How can you bear it?'

'They rather fascinate me, in some strange way. Hell, I've lived among savages before,' he added wryly. 'A few of them I sometimes almost like. Quint Randall, for instance. He's not half bad. I feel sorry for him. Not sure why. And then the duel. Staines challenged me, but Carstairs talked him out of it and made the man apologize.'

'Hmm, no doubt this Staines will hate you even worse now. Please be careful, Devlin. It's so dangerous. I couldn't bear for anything to happen to you.'

'Because you love me?' he whispered, gathering her closer.

'Exactly,' she purred, straddling his muscular thighs as he pulled her astride his lap.

'I adore hearing you say that.'

'Then I'll say it again. I love you. I love you,' she breathed.

They were kissing heatedly when the coach slowed.

Devlin glanced out the carriage window at the tall wrought-iron gates. 'We're here,' he murmured, then paused. 'I haven't been back here in a long, long time.'

'Are you ready for this, Devlin?' she whispered as she caressed his face. 'I'm sure this place must hold many painful memories.'

'It's all right because you're here now. Come.' Linking his fingers through hers, he lifted her hand and kissed her knuckles, then helped her out of the carriage while his servants opened the gates.

The night wind was fresh and balmy as it blew through the thickly wooded park and played with tendrils of Lizzie's hair.

Hand in hand, they walked up the tree-lined drive. The grounds looked rather overgrown, with weeds sprouting up here and there in the pitted driveway and a tangle of grasses and vines weaving through the wrought-iron gates.

She noticed the outline of a building in amidst the copse of trees to their left. 'What's that?'

'Mulberry Cottage.'

Squinting to see it better in the dark, she could just make out the thatched roof and gingerbread trim of a large cottage orné.

'Why, Devlin, it's adorable! Is it a guesthouse?'

He said nothing.

Glancing from the cottage to him in delight, she was startled to see his face etched with grim remembrance in the silvery moonlight. 'Come on,' he whispered, pulling her hand gently.

They continued up the drive.

Lizzie held Devlin's large, warm hand in hers with a strange, dreamlike feeling settling over her. Perhaps it was the moon and the lulling whisper of the wind in the trees, but she felt as though they had stepped into a fairytale kingdom slumbering under a dark enchantment.

The tension she had sensed in her companion seemed to have eased as they left the vicinity of Mulberry Cottage.

Ahead, through the tunnel-like canopy of trees that lined the drive, she glimpsed the big house, alabaster in the moonlight.

At the end of the drive, she drew in her breath, halting to stare in awe at the splendid Palladian mansion. All gleaming white, the center dome rose, like a scoop of Gunter's vanilla ice cream over a stately front portico with four Ionic columns. Symmetrical wings stretched long on both sides of the entrance, with Wyatt windows all the way down to the ground. There was no sign of life.

'Devlin, it's magnificent,' she whispered.

He swept a courtly gesture. 'For you, my love.'

She looked at him uncertainly, but he slipped her a secretive smile and then led her up to the front door, which he rapped soundly with the lion's mask knocker.

'I have a key, but I don't want the servants to shoot us. As I said, I haven't been here in a while. Aunt Augusta was the last one to live here. When she moved to Bath, the house was closed up. Since then, there's been only a skeleton staff to keep everything clean and well cared for, but they are loyal. You suppose that's enough of a warning?' Without waiting for her answer, he took a key out of his vest pocket and unlocked the door. The hinges creaked loudly when he inched the door open, poking his head in. 'Hullo? Anybody here? Mr. Jeffries!'

'Master?' a weak, elderly voice called. 'Is that you?'

Stepping into the house, still holding Devlin's hand, she saw an ancient butler in a dressing gown and tasseled nightcap shuffling down the hall with a pewter candlestick holder in his hand.

'Oh, my lord, gracious, we are taken quite off guard. I shall wake the others at once—'

'No need. Let them rest,' he soothed. 'We shall need nothing till the morrow.' *Except each other*, his smoldering glance at her added without a word.

The ancient fellow, half-asleep and looking bleary-eyed, was overjoyed when Devlin introduced her. 'This young lady is to be your new mistress, Mr. Jeffries. She is called Elizabeth, and we shall soon be married.'

'Oh! What happy tidings,' he breathed, his sleepy eyes widening, then bowed low. 'Saints be praised, a beautiful young bride for my master. I wish you happy, sir. Most happy!' The old man appeared to be on the brink of tears. 'Heartfelt welcome, Lady Strathmore, and much joy. The staff is at your call. There are only three of us at present, but we will do aught you ask.'

'Thank you, Mr. Jeffries,' Lizzie answered, touched by his sincerity. The old man gazed at her as though she were the eighth wonder of the world.

'Miraculous! There will be life once more at Oakley Park. Perhaps children? Ah, it's been so long.'

She blushed. 'Thank you, Mr. Jeffries. You are very kind. But I see we have disturbed your sleep.'

'Ah, I will to bed!' he exclaimed, taking the hint all of a sudden. 'My lord and lady shall not wish to be disturbed. No, no.'

'Indeed,' Devlin murmured rather wickedly.

Suppressing a chuckle, the old butler lit a candle on the console table for them, then bowed once more. 'Good night, my lady. My lord.' As though he could barely await the arrival of a whole nursery full of Strathmore babies, Mr. Jeffries hobbled back to his quarters.

'I reckon we'd better snap to it girl' Devlin caught her about the waist to haul her up close to his chest with a playful growl. 'You heard the man.'

She tilted her head back, narrowing her eyes at her future husband. 'You really are a rogue, you know.'

'Aren't I, though?' he whispered, and bent his head, claiming her mouth.

She giggled against his lips when he suddenly swept her off her feet, draping her body over his arms. 'Get the candle.'

She reached for it when he carried her over to the console table, then held it up to light their way.

'Now, then, my love,' he murmured, 'you shall have the tour. Mind you, if you see a place where you would like to be deflowered, do speak up.'

'I don't want the tour,' she whispered, nibbling his cheek. 'I want you.'

'My lady is impatient.'

'Yes.'

He quivered when she flicked the tip of her tongue against the corner of his mouth. At once, he turned his face and met her kiss with ardent hunger. His lips entranced her. Holding on tightly around his neck, Lizzie drank of his kiss ever more deeply. Their tongues danced, swirled, mated in delicious anticipation.

He was panting slightly when he tore his mouth away from hers. 'To the bed, then.'

'Yes,' she breathed, thrilling to the words and the white-hot intensity in his eyes.

Her pulse pounded harder in her veins. Holding her stare, he carried her down the corridor, past an impressive staircase framed by towering Corinthian columns, then turned down another hallway while she lit the way with the candle.

He was very strong, she thought, scarcely noticing the rooms they passed and all the furniture shrouded in brown holland to keep off the dust. He carried her easily; she felt quite secure in his muscled arms, even when he stopped not far down the second hallway and braced her bottom on his knee, pausing to reach for a doorknob.

He gave the tall white door a shove. It swung open. As Lizzie held up the light, her eyes widened at the chamber's opulence.

The flickering illumination of her single candle gave her barely a glimpse of the deftly wrought plaster grapevines and ivy that twined around the painted ceiling roundels. A gilded frieze several bands deep enwrapped the walls, which in turn were hung with tapestries on pale green silk. The tapestries depicted a few famed passions from Classical myth: it looked like Venus and Adonis, Psyche and Cupid, Persephone and Hades.

To the right sat an alabaster fireplace, all chiseled white perfection. The room had a private bathing alcove, as well, framed by a profusion of rose velvet curtains. Their rich folds and gathers were looped back with gold-tasseled ties. Four-branched girandoles dripping with teardrop crystals offered more light if they wanted it, but for the night's events, she trusted the intimate glow of the simple taper would suffice.

'It's the state bedchamber,' he remarked as he carried her into it, giving the door a thrust with his boot heel. It swung shut behind them. 'Not all the rooms in the house are this rich. It's supposed to be saved for the royals if they should happen to drop by. But tonight,' he purred with a roguish smile, 'you are my queen. Candle on the table, please.'

She did as ordered.

'Now, kiss me,' he whispered.

She did.

He set her down gently on her feet and, never pausing in kissing her, began to strip away her clothing. Her hands shook as she helped him, her fingers fumbling with her bodice; his hands worked smoothly. She left the task to him and went to work on his waistcoat buttons. He lifted her gown away. He freed her hair, unlaced her stays, made her chemise disappear. Her pulse was wild. She stopped kissing him just long enough to assess the fastenings of his black trousers with a glance. He leaned his head back against the closed door behind him when she reached inside them and wrapped her hand around his steely silken shaft.

'Ahh, I've missed your touch,' he breathed, closing his eyes. His long black lashes fanned his high-boned cheeks.

Going up onto her tiptoes, she kissed his neck and nipped him with a sportive little pinch of her teeth. He let out a sensual purr of laughter in response. Then she pleasured him, breathing in his scent as she nestled her cheek against his chest. She stroked him until he groaned and stopped her.

'Enough,' he rasped.

'Take this off.' She clutched a handful of his fine linen shirt, tugging impatiently at it. He lifted it off over his head and dropped it. His dark jacket and waistcoat already pooled on the floor with her light dress.

She bit back a moan of climbing lust as she ran her hand up his smooth golden torso to his powerful chest, savoring every muscled plane and ridge. Then she pulled back slightly, just gazing at him in admiration. The man was seduction incarnate, naked from his lean waist up. His black trousers hung open a bit, inviting her further explorations.

Her heated stare traveled up his sculpted body to his face. His firm mouth, bee-stung with her kisses, seemed to pout; his sea-bright eyes glittered with desire.

'I can't believe I get to marry you.' The words slipped from her in a soft tone of amazement.

He reached out and cradled her cheek in his palm. 'I was just thinking the exact same thing.'

'I love you,' she said.

Dev stared at her, mesmerized. The only reason he did not say it back was because the love in her gentle gray eyes took his breath away, robbed his voice. He couldn't even speak in the face of such beauty. Nude and white-skinned, she was a pagan goddess, her long brown hair flowing over her shoulders and down her back.

His worshipful gaze trailed down to the twin swells of her breasts, half-cloaked by her hair. Her slender waist was inviting, but the luscious curves of her hips made him blind with want. With his hand still cupping her face, he ran his thumb slowly along her mouth and shivered when she parted her lips to lave it with an erotic kiss.

Who could have known it? His prim bluestocking had the soul of a courtesan.

Removing the pad of his thumb from her kiss, he grazed his hand down her chest to trail the moistness from her mouth to her nipple. She licked her lips and watched him. He brought his hand to her mouth again for another kiss. This time, she moistened his middle finger with her tongue; he then inserted it between her legs, giving pleasure as he probed into the demure mass of tiny curls. She drew in her breath sharply when he found her wetness. He stroked her for a moment as she stood naked before him, arching with pleasure. Then he brought the same middle finger up and tasted it with a wanton gleam in his eyes.

She took a forward step even as he reached for her, lifting her up in his arms. She wrapped her arms around his shoulders, her legs around his waist. With her sweet rump so soft and round in his hands, he carried her over to the elaborately canopied state bed and laid her across it.

Three times with hands and mouth he brought her to the edge of climax until she was frantic, wild with need. Then, when he entered her gently, there was no pain for her. Dev was in heaven, inching deeper into her body by degrees. His heart thundered, his chest heaving. His body trembled with the effort to hold himself in check when he had dreamed of nothing and no one but this night, this woman, for so long.

She cradled his head against her neck as he arched over her, braced on his hands. Every touch, every breath wound a spell of love about their bed. When her long, lovely legs hugged his hips and her body took up a sinuous motion beneath him, Dev glanced down at her rapt face. Delighted by the feathery sweetness of her lashes, he bent his head and kissed the delicate blue-veined skin of her eyelids as she lay with closed eyes, savoring his lovemaking.

'Never leave me,' he whispered as he stroked her hair. 'I feel so close to you now. I never want this to end.'

'It won't. I won't.'

'I love you.'

'Oh, Devlin.' She whispered the sweet words back to him.

Then her breathing quickened, her rising hips drawing him deeper into the rhythm of her need. Her hands crept over his shoulders, traveled slowly down his sides. She stroked his back, then groaned and gripped his derriere, holding him motionless between her thighs. 'Ah, it's too much!'

A seductive smile shadowed his face as he realized she hovered on the very knife edge of release. Hot and quivering beneath him, she was panting for fulfillment, and he intended to give it to her. 'Are you mine?' he whispered.

'Totally.' She fairly sobbed with want when he caught her nipple in his burning palm and teased it with a satyric squeeze. 'Oh, Devlin. You're driving me mad. I can't take anymore.'

'Very well, then,' he said in a husky whisper, clinging hard to the fast-fraying edges of sanity himself.

A few more thrusts and she surrendered, straining and sweating beneath him; at the peak, a shrill little scream of sheer passion tore from her lips. She had been clinging onto his neck for dear life, but her hold already began going weak as the orgasm dazed her. Dev caught her lingering blissful moans on his tongue, clutching her hard in his arms. Driven to the brink by her steamy body's luxurious convulsions, his control broke free. He let go with a wild cry, giving himself to her in a deep, final thrust that sent his hot release flooding into her fertile womb.

For a long moment, they could do nothing but lie there, a

panting mass of sated youth, all tangled limbs, rosy skin, and tousled hair.

She lifted her head and kissed him weakly, then dropped her head back onto the state bed once more. 'I love you, Devlin.'

'My dearest Lizzie,' he whispered softly, drawing her into the circle of his arms. 'I love you, too.'

'Say it again,' she begged him, thrilling to the miraculous words.

He moved his lips close to her ear and breathed his declaration again, whisper-soft. With a small groan of intoxicating desire at the warm tickle of his breath at her ear, she wound her wrists behind his neck and lay atop him.

He pulled the coverlet up to keep her curvy body warm, and when his gaze snagged on the small smear of blood on the flat sheet, he was reminded anew of the lifelong bond they had promised to each other, if not yet before God. He was filled with the sobering knowledge that she was his now – his to love and cherish – his to protect.

With a wave of fierce male instinct in his veins, he pressed her head tenderly to his chest as he held her.

'Is it always that good?' she asked in a drowsy murmur.

He smiled in amusement and kissed her hair. 'Ask me in the morning, and you'll find out.'

When she woke up in the morning, Devlin wasn't there.

Lifting her head from the pillow for a weary glance around, Lizzie started to frown upon finding herself alone, then ruefully decided it was just as well. It was beyond her power to resist that man, and merely sitting up in the great bed called her attention to her body's soreness from last night's exertions.

After a moment, she scratched her head with a drowsy sigh and slid down from the high state bed with the sheet loosely wrapped around her. She crossed the lavish chamber to the bathing alcove. Behind the rose velvet curtains, it was all tiled wall mosaics and gleaming marble, like a miniature Roman bath – quite an unusual luxury even for the grandest houses. She smiled to find that Devlin had filled the bath for her. She knew it had to have been he who had done it because the warrior in him was too protective to let the servants pass through and glimpse her sleeping in the nude. An exploratory splash of her fingertips informed her that the water was still warm. With a fond smile at his thoughtfulness, she let the sheet fall and stepped into the bath.

Refreshed and dressed half an hour later, she went looking for him – and for her breakfast. It was only then, venturing through the gleaming corridors of Oakley Park that the full impact of her decision hit her.

Last night, she had been too shocked by all that he had told her in the carriage and then by her feverish want of him to pay much attention to the house. But now she stared around her, slack-jawed, at the soaring ceilings, the exquisite salons, and the white marble stairs that seemed to float up to the next floor without any support from below, and she could not believe that this masterpiece of a house was to be her home.

No longer just a well-behaved hanger-on of the household, here she would be the wife and mother, the heart of the home. Overwhelmed by the fulfillment of her heart's desire, she walked out slowly into the spacious main gallery and looked up at the inside of the fanciful dome.

How still the whole place was. She suddenly knew in her bones that this was what she had been born for. To love this man, to restore this shattered family to wholeness, and to use all she had learned from the Knight family so that with the elevated rank and wealth she would share with her husband, she could do greater good in the world. Her destiny was at hand.

'Coffee, ma'am?'

Lizzie whirled around to find Mr. Jeffries shuffling toward her with a silver tray on which the coffee service rocked precariously with his unsteady gait. Really, the dear old thing ought to be pensioned off, she thought, hurrying to help him, but he seemed so happy to have someone to wait on.

'Thank you, Mr. Jeffries. You're very kind. I'm afraid I couldn't find the breakfast room.'

He smiled. 'This way, my lady. If you wish, I will show you every room in the house and gladly answer whatever questions you may have. I am sure you will want to see the conservatory, the long gallery, the ballroom, the library—'

She perked up anew. 'Library?'

'Yes, ma'am. But first, no doubt, my lady shall need to be restored by a good breakfast.'

She smiled at him as he beckoned her into a bright, airy dining room where the two other members of the staff waited to meet their new mistress – the aged housekeeper and the cook. Mr. Jeffries introduced her to the old women; then all three gazed at her, marveling at her, as though she were the empress of the known world.

'You must eat, my dear!' the cook advised, and sensing at once that Lizzie was not one to stand on ceremony, they took her under their collective wing like three fairy godparents. They were as solicitous as if they half believed she were already in a 'delicate condition.'

Breakfast was laid out on the sideboard, and though she wanted to find Devlin, she did not have the heart to leave it sitting there growing cold after the aged servants' warm reception and all the trouble they had gone to, to fix it for her. With patient courtesy, she thanked them and helped herself.

They stood by, beaming as they watched her eat. She was tempted to invite them to join her, but they wanted a proper viscountess for their master, and by goodness, she vowed, it was a proper viscountess they would get. She resisted the habit.

As soon as she sat down at the large mahogany table, her gaze came to rest on the portrait of a proud, raven-haired beauty that hung in a gilded frame above the fireplace opposite. 'Who is that?'

'Why, that is your predecessor. Katherine, the ninth Lady Strathmore.'

Katie Rose. She stared at the picture. 'She really was quite beautiful, wasn't she?'

The servants agreed in woeful murmurs, their gray heads bobbing.

Lizzie set her fork down with a sudden sense of uneasiness, but she forced a smile. 'Has anyone seen Lord Strathmore this morning?'

They glanced worriedly at each other; then Mr. Jeffries nodded. 'He has gone down to Mulberry Cottage, madam.'

'The guest house?' she asked, furrowing her brow.

'Oh, it's not a guest house, my lady,' the housekeeper volunteered. 'Mulberry Cottage was where His Lordship was raised.'

Lizzie's eyebrows lifted; then she remembered that Devlin's father, Stephen, had been the younger brother. Jacob had held the title, and this grand mansion was Jacob's masterpiece. The younger brother, Stephen, and his wife must have only warranted Mulberry Cottage as their home. She nearly smacked herself on the forehead. *How silly of me not to realize!* Devlin had been all too easygoing in this grand house last night. No wonder, she thought. He no doubt thought of the grand Oakley Park as Uncle Jacob's house.

Mulberry Cottage was his home.

'Even after his father came into the title, the family preferred the cottage,' the housekeeper volunteered, then nodded again at the portrait. 'My lady Katherine used to say that it was cozier for the children. What a beautiful family they were. Such a loss.'

Lizzie stared at them. Now she understood why Devlin was so down-to-earth. His earliest years had been spent, like her own, not in the manor house, but in a simple thatched cottage.

'Poor Lordship,' the cook sighed, shaking her head. 'When they died, he ordered the cottage sealed up like a tomb. Aye, ma'am, nothing was to be touched. Those were his orders. It was all to be left exactly as it was on the day they died.'

She paled.

In the next instant, she was on her feet, rushing out of the room with barely a murmured, 'Excuse me.' She knew he had gone down to Mulberry Cottage to confront the past.

She did not intend to let him face it alone.

Chapter Nineteen

The path into the thicket where Mulberry Cottage stood was overgrown with wild daisies and Queen Anne's lace, and brambles that caught at Lizzie's skirts as she ran by. The entrance of the cottage came into view with its gingerbread trim and a tangle of climbing roses.

At once, she saw Ben, who came toward her with a desperate look. 'Miss Carlisle, I was just coming to get you! He's inside.'

'Is he all right?'

'I don't know. He won't let me in.'

Lizzie gave him a grim nod and moved past him to the wood-planked door, opening it cautiously. It squeaked, betraying their incursion.

'Leave me alone, Ben!' came her beloved's wounded-lion roar from within.

Lizzie glanced at the valet in trepidation. Ben shrugged and shook his head.

Taking a deep breath to ward off her rising sense of dread, she opened the door wider and slowly poked her head inside. 'It's me, sweeting. Where are you?' She slipped inside and closed the door behind her. 'Devlin?'

No answer.

Venturing deeper into the cottage, she had a vague impression of cheerfully painted walls and simple wooden furniture. Some bookshelves, a pianoforte, homey decorations. An empty birdcage. A table with some porcelain figurines. Pressed flowers hung in small oval frames. The place smelled musty, everything coated in a thick layer of gray dust.

When she stepped around the corner, she saw him in the parlor. He was kneeling on the carpet, immobile, staring down blindly at a child's half-completed puzzle on the floor.

'Oh, Devlin.'

He looked over at her slowly with tears in his eyes.

She crossed the room to him in a hurried rustle of muslin skirts, holding back tears herself. 'Sweetheart.' She laid her hand on his shoulder then petted his head, longing with all her heart to ease the pain in his eyes.

He did not respond at first, not rising from his knees, but then he looked so lost that he wrapped his arms around her hips and buried his face against her waist.

She held him for a long moment, pouring all the tenderness on him that she had to give, soothing him with her touch, whispering the gentlest love words that came to mind to help her comfort him, though she knew no words would ever suffice. Not for this. She could only cradle him against her body and pray that this time, her love would be enough.

He pulled away abruptly and would not meet her gaze. His voice sounded odd and tight when he spoke. 'I have to tell you something. Something so horrible, I don't know if I can even find the words. But before we wed, I want you to know the final secret, Lizzie. The worst one.'

She bent and kissed his head. 'Nothing you could tell me could ever make me stop loving you.'

He rose to his feet, looked at her for a long moment, his angular face taut and pale, his mouth a grim line. Then he looked away, staring toward the stone-cold hearth. He closed his eyes and visibly braced himself. 'Oh, Lizzie,' he breathed. 'It's my fault they're dead.'

She managed to absorb his irrational confession with a show of calm. 'But how can that be, Devlin? You explained to me last night about the men who set the fire.'

He dragged his eyes open and looked at her through a sea of quiet suffering. 'I pulled a prank at school. They were en route to pick me up.' He shook his head bitterly, his brooding stare a million miles away. 'Foolishness. Some other boys and I skipped school to play billiards at a tavern. I was seventeen. We all were getting drunk, toasting Nelson's final hour of glory – the news had just come about Trafalgar.'

Her heart bled. His tone was ineffably heavy. He drifted toward the hearth several paces away.

'Then the proctor's three bulldogs came along – security officers. They made the rounds each day looking for truant boys. Well, they found me and my friends. Tried to haul us back to school. I was just showing off.' He paused for a long moment and dropped his head. 'Several mugs of ale in my belly. I punched one of the officers in the nose. Thought he made a "dishonorable remark" about Lord Nelson.'

'Oh, my darling,' she whispered, tears welling in her eyes as she comprehended at last how he had been torturing himself these twelve years. Now his obsession with revenge made even more sense. Easier to blame those men than to go on carrying all that terrible guilt by himself.

'The next thing I knew, I was in the dean's office under threat of expulsion. They sent for my father to come and fetch me. My parents sent no servant to collect me. Not them. I can imagine the conversation that must have happened here when they received the dean's missive. Mother would have been the first into the carriage, bent on tanning my hide. Father would have been right behind her, trying to soothe her, talk her down out of the boughs, telling her, no doubt, it was naught but boyish mischief, while little Sarah made this puzzle on the floor. If only they hadn't brought her. At least my sister might be alive, but instead, I am responsible for her death, too.'

'Devlin, you are not responsible,' she said fiercely as a pair of tears plunged down her cheeks.

He didn't seem to hear. Pain molded the lines of his face. His wide shoulders sagged in despair.

'Listen to me—' She started toward him, but he put his hand up to ward her off.

'The Golden Bull lies at the halfway point between here and Oxford. They stopped there to dine and rest the horses. Oh, Lizzie, if I had only gone to class that day, they would still be alive.'

'No, Devlin, no,' she whispered as a small sob escaped her. 'It's not your fault, sweetheart.'

'Yes, it is. Don't cry.' His eyes were dry, but their expression was one of emptiness when he gave her his handkerchief.

'How can you be so calm?' she wrenched out.

'It will all be over soon.'

She stopped drying her eyes, her earlier sense of dread returning in a rush. 'What do you mean?'

He ran his knuckles gently along the curve of her cheek. 'Those bastards killed my family,' he whispered, 'but I'll send my soul to hell before I'll let them take you, too.'

The crystallized rage that she read in his eyes sent chills down her spine. 'I–I don't understand.'

'You don't need to,' he said gently, but despite his soft touch, she saw something deadly behind his distracted stare. 'What I've told you,' he murmured. 'Does it change how you feel about me? Will you still marry me?'

She winced that he could doubt her. 'Of course, I'll still marry you, darling. It doesn't change anything.'

At last, he managed a faint smile. 'That's a relief. Right, then. Let's go.' He slipped a folded paper out of his vest pocket and showed it to her. It was a marriage license. 'Are you ready?'

Her eyes widened. Her head was still spinning from his revelations. 'What, go now?'

He shrugged. 'Why not? I have the ring.' He reached into another pocket, took out a shining gold band, and showed it to her. 'Efficient, aren't I?'

'Devlin!' She looked from the ring to his handsome face, not knowing whether to laugh or to strangle him. *Men.* 'Darling, I cannot get married without Jacinda present. She'll never forgive me. Nor will Bel, Alice, Miranda – I want Robert to give me away!'

He stiffened. 'Ah. All of Alec's people.'

'They're my people, too. I'm confused, Devlin. Why the rush?'

He did not answer, slowly folding the special license back up.

Eyeing him with deepening suspicion, Lizzie rested her hands on her waist. 'Tell me what is going on in that head of yours.'

'I just want to get it over with.'

'*Over* with?' she cried.

'Not the wedding, Lizzie. The other part.' He walked away, restless and scowling.

She turned to watch him. '*What* . . . other part, Devlin?'

'You heard what I said. I am not going to let them hurt you.'

She froze, gripped by a sudden uncertainty. 'Oh, Devlin, tell me you don't mean what I think you mean . . . .'

When he looked askance at her, she remembered Lady Strathmore's tales of his many battles – deserts, canyons, seas. And in his fierce stare, she saw the half-savage white man who had gone out on Indian raids. God only knew what he was capable of when the rage and the hatred burned in his wild blood.

She sat down abruptly, fearing she might be ill. 'Oh, Devlin, no.'

'Yes, Lizzie,' he answered softly. 'I'm afraid so.'

'Talk to me,' she ordered in a shaky tone. 'Right now.'

He seemed to debate how much to tell her. 'You are safe for the moment,' he conceded. 'I managed to convince them you were naught but a plaything to me. But once we are wed and they realize you are my love, you'll be fair game.'

'You are being paranoid.'

'They killed my family. I can't risk them coming after you, and they will, if they realize all I know. They'll do anything to cover their tracks, as they've already proved. I tried to let you go to Alec to keep you from all this danger,' he added in a faraway tone. 'But I failed. I couldn't give you up.'

'I don't love Alec. I love *you*. And I don't want you to do this.'

'I love you, too, and that's why I must.' He came over to her and sought to soothe her with a touch. 'We'll marry, and then I shall go and end it. I'll be back in a few days – if all goes well.'

'And if it doesn't?' she wailed, the blood draining from her face.

'If it doesn't . . . you'll have this house, the money, my title and name, and God willing, my babe in your belly.'

'No!' Her pulse was frantic. She shot to her feet. 'No, Devlin! I will not permit you to do this! There are too many of them—'

'I've already worked that out. I own a building. When they are in it – drunk and stumbling – I and my crew from the *Katie Rose* will seal the windows and lock the doors and do to those bastards what they did to my family.'

'All of them?' she breathed. 'The innocent alongside the guilty?'

'To protect you, my love? Without a qualm,' he said.

'No.' She shook her head. 'You will not do this thing in my name.'

He nodded, but behind his gentle gaze, his will was iron. 'Lizzie, I *am* going to do it.'

'Go to the authorities! Tell them what you know!'

'Why should they believe me?'

'You are a lord!'

'So is Carstairs. So is Randall. So is Staines. So are the rest of them, Lizzie. Whatever evidence I can provide is circumstantial only. Besides, this is personal.'

She stared at him in awe. 'You *want* to do it. Sweet Christ.' Covering her lips with her hand, she got up and walked away from him. Her heart pounded with fright.

Devlin said nothing. Folding his arms across his chest, he just watched her with the beast in his eyes biding its time.

Lizzie felt sick as she realized at last the full depth of the darkness in him.

She tried to calm the staccato of her pulse and turned to stare at him. 'Killing those men isn't going to take your pain away, Devlin. All it's going to do is to make you just as bad as them. I can't let you do this.'

His wide shoulders lifted in a shrug. 'No way you can stop me.'

'There's one way.' She swallowed hard. 'I shan't marry you.'

His pale eyes narrowed as he considered her words. 'Don't make that threat,' he chided gently. 'We have been lovers. You will be ruined.'

'So I will. And you'll have to think about that, won't you? You won't let that happen to me, will you, Devlin?'

'*Don't* manipulate me,' he whispered. 'This is not the time or place for one of your schoolgirl ruses.'

'Better that I should be ruined than you should play roulette with your life!'

'To hell with my life!' he roared without warning.

She gasped, taking a step back.

He threw up his hands. 'What right do I have to live happily ever after with you, when my parents' blood, my sister's blood is on my hands? I've got only one possible excuse for the blight of my existence on this earth, and that's revenge.'

'What of love?' she asked softly when the room had finally stopped shaking after his reverberating, jungle roar. 'You said you loved me.'

'I do. That is why I must protect you.'

I must protect you, too, darling, she thought. *From yourself*. 'If we do not marry, I am in no danger, correct? And then you don't need to become a murderer.'

'I already am a murderer,' he said in a hollow tone.

'You were a *boy*!' she wrenched out angrily. Quickly leashing her temper again, she shook her head at him with a resolute glare. 'I'll be in London when you come to your senses.' She walked out.

'Lizzie!'

He followed, reaching for her arm, but she shook him off.

'Lizzie, come back here! You can't leave! *Lizzie!*'

It took all her strength, but she just kept walking, and kept her burning stare fixed straight ahead.

She was gone.

Without rhyme or reason, Dev ran through the thick, shadowed woods as he had as a boy, tearing through the brambles, his heart hammering, his blood seething in his veins. He leaped mossy logs, jumped gullies, and swung a large branch in his path against a tree trunk, shattering it in two with an unreasoned howl.

The satisfying crack of wood barely drained two drops of the near-mindless fury that had come over him with her desertion. But at least he had not let her see him like this, panting and rabid and half-insane with the torment. As a lad, he had turned drunkard to relieve the pain, then traveled far, far around the world. He had seen many things, had distracted himself with adventures, danger, exotic cultures, women – but he had never been happy. Not until Lizzie, and now she was gone.

Truth be told, half of him was glad. If she turned her back on him, there was nothing to live for. Nothing to keep him here. Nothing left to stand between him and an orgy of blood.

He came to the edge of the rise where the woods gave way to meadows, and there he stopped short, his chest heaving, an unhealthy sweat pouring down his face. For there, across the green meadow, overlooking the ornamental lake, was their grave.

He stared at it, his breath sounding jaggedly through his flared nostrils.

It looked so peaceful.

The family mausoleum was built to resemble a small white temple with a triangular pediment and four stout pillars. The torch was burning there, just as he ordered with bitter irony that it must always burn, day and night, in their honor.

Burn.

It should be me in there. Not them.

He had not come to visit them in ten long years, but the pain couldn't get any worse now, so he went forward, walking numbly like a man in a dream. When he reached the crypt, he walked up the three shallows steps and stretched out his hand to touch the sun-warmed marble.

The grief rose from the depths of his being like a whale coming up for air from the bottom of the sea. Dev crumpled against the marble as a low sob tore from him. Wrapping his arms vaguely around himself, he slid slowly down the smooth white wall till he was curled up like a child on the dusty colonnade, racked with the tears he had suppressed for twelve long, lonely years, begging their beloved spirits to forgive him.

* * *

Ben had driven her to the nearest coaching inn, where she had bought a ticket for the London stagecoach. Arriving at Jacinda's villa, Lizzie was plagued with a massive headache from the sheer tension of waiting to see Devlin's next move. Growing increasingly desperate to hear from him, she clung to her faith that she had done the right thing, though she could scarcely wrap her mind around all that she had walked away from.

She'd had no choice.

She was lying on a divan in the sitting room, reading – or rather rereading – the same page of a novel five times over, since she seemed to have no concentration these days, when Jacinda's butler appeared in the doorway and announced she had a visitor.

Never had she moved so fast in her life. In the blink of an eye, she was on her feet, running out to the entrance hall, but instead of Devlin, she skidded to a halt in her satin slippers.

'*Daisy?*'

Her mild-tempered student with the golden sausage curls was standing there, clutching her reticule, no chaperon in sight. The moment she saw Lizzie, Daisy's big blue eyes welled with tears. 'Oh, Miss Carlisle! It's ever so awful! I didn't know where else to turn!' Daisy began crying. 'My life is a shambles! Sorscha wrote me a letter. She told me where to find you. Her mama's taking her back to Ireland in a few days, but she said you would know what to do.'

'There, there, my dear, what on earth is the matter?' Lizzie hurried over and collected her, glad for the chance to turn her thoughts to someone else's problems instead of her own. Soon she had herded the girl into the sitting room and handed her a cup of tea.

'It's all right now, darling. What's happened?'

'Papa has betrothed me to the most horrid old man!'

'He has?'

'Yes! My life is ruined! I shan't get even a single Season!

But Papa says it's just as well, for the ton won't accept me anyway. He says they think we're just a lot of encroaching t-toadstools!'

'My darling dear, you're nothing of the kind.'

'Papa only cares that I should be a b-baroness.'

'Oh, sweeting.' Lizzie hugged her and let Daisy cry on her shoulder a bit, but privately, she scowled with disapproval.

Had the chit's father no compassion? Daisy was a young sixteen. Some girls were quite mature at that age, but she had a trusting, childlike temperament and would not be ready to handle the responsibilities of marriage for several years.

'Papa is such a tyrant! I hate him!'

'Don't say that, Daisy,' she chided gently. 'Perhaps it's not so bad. Do you know the name of the man you are to marry?'

Then Lizzie's blood ran cold at Daisy's answer.

The girl's yellow curls swung sadly as she nodded. 'It's Quentin, Baron Randall. And he's *forty*!' she added in horror.

For two days, Dev had not left the place of their tomb. He took no food, barely a swallow of water. The sun beat down on him by day; by night, the wind sprayed the sudden cloudburst of needling rain against his face, but he did not leave them. He sat unmoving with his back to the hard marble wall, wrestling his demons without a movement or a sound – waiting for something to break. He pondered the stars, recalled the mysteries of sky and sea, and all the beauties of Nature, which had been mother and father to him since their death, and he tended the torch that still burned in their honor.

Through the darkest hours of the night, he stared into the flame, going deeper and deeper into himself, until the fire had somehow purified him.

Only then sleep claimed him.

When he awoke on the third day, the first thing he saw when

his eyes fluttered open was the blue heavens through the white columns of the mausoleum.

Nothing had changed; he heard naught but twittering birdsong. And yet somehow on this new day, he awoke . . . and knew he was forgiven.

After all, if it had been Lizzie who had made a mistake, as he had once done, or a child of his own playing boyish pranks, he would have held no grudge, even if it had resulted in unforeseen tragedy. He could almost feel his parents kiss him in the gentle caress of the breeze and say, *It wasn't your fault.*

He sat up slowly and looked around, realizing that he alone, of the four of them, was still free to leave.

Life was still a promise before him.

He took a deep breath that burned a little, like the first gasp of a newborn babe. But the sun glittered on the ornamental pond before him and a battle-weary smile crept over his lips as he envisioned the memory of his father there, teaching him to fish. A gentle man. A noble man. The man who had taught him that it did not matter what the world might do to you; it mattered only how you then reacted. And suddenly Dev had the answer.

His eyes flared, reflecting the blue-green color of the pond with sudden light.

Immediately, he was on his feet, striding toward Ben, who had been keeping a worried vigil nearby. He shook his trusty valet fondly by the shoulder.

'Wake up. Ben. We've got to go to Hertfordshire.'

Ben came to his senses with a start. 'What, what? Huh?'

'Do you remember that night at the pavilion when I asked you to take that little peasant girl home? Suzy, she was called. Do you remember how to get to her village? Stevenage.'

'Of course. Why?'

'I've had blinders on, Ben,' he murmured. 'I may never be

able to prove to the world what they did to my family, but the girl – God, it's been right in front of me all along! We have to find that girl.'

'Sir?'

'Kidnapping, Ben.' Dev sent him a wily smile. 'That's a hanging crime. She's our star witness.'

As Dev set out for Hertfordshire, meanwhile in London, Lizzie lifted her chin and marched into the hectic city business offices of Daisy Manning's father.

In the anteroom, harried clerks rushed to and fro at the sound of bellowed orders emanating from the coalmining magnate's adjoining study.

'I have an appointment,' she said to the anemic-looking secretary at the counter.

'Name?'

When she told him her name, he bade her wait in one of the nearby chairs. She took a seat, looking on curiously while the great wheels of commerce whirred before her eyes.

'You tell 'im I want that shipment on time, or else!' A fat man with mutton-chop side-whiskers and ruddy jowls shoved upward by a too-tight cravat poked his blustery head out the door of the office and bellowed: '*Next!*'

Lizzie blanched as the secretary gestured to her.

'Dear me,' she said under her breath, but rose and walked into the boss's private office.

'Who are you? Let me check me book,' Mr. Manning grumbled, the stump of a reeking cigar between his chubby fingers. 'Yes, yes, Carlisle. I see that now. Well, what do ye want, then? You are from the ladies' charity, I take it? Shut that door!' he shouted at a passing clerk. 'I already gave to the Foundling Hospital—'

'No, no, sir, I am here about your daughter.'

His impatient blustering paused. 'Wot?'

'I'm here about Daisy. Your daughter?'

'Oh, yes, Daisy, of course. What about the chit?'

'I am – well, was – Daisy's teacher at Mrs. Hall's Academy until recently and I must say, Mr. Manning, your daughter is distraught over her betrothal.'

His bushy eyebrows drew into a line and he leaned to flick the ashes off the end of his cigar. 'Don't see 'ow that's any of your business.'

'Right.' She dropped her gaze and realized politeness was going to get her nowhere. A blunter approach was in order. 'Mr. Manning, the man to whom you are considering allying your child is a lecherous brute with a horrendous reputation.'

'He's a lord,' he grunted. 'Everyone knows the nobs ain't got morals. Besides, Randall's suit has saved me havin' to pay a plum to put the chit through a Season. You know what they say, a bird in the hand is worth two in the bush.' He took a puff on his cigar.

Lizzie stared at him in bewilderment. 'Sir, with all due respect, this is your daughter we are discussing.'

'Aye, she's mine to dispense where I please. Look 'ere, I didn't get to where I am in life bein' a fool, Miss Carlisle. Beggars can't be choosers. Encroaching toadstools – that's what the nobs call the likes o' me. But now I got deep pockets and a pretty daughter – just a foothold's all I need. Do you know how I got started in life?' he asked, cocking his meaty hand on his round waist, in a pose reminiscent of Henry VIII.

'No, sir.'

'Chimney sweep. Ha!' With a look of extreme self-satisfaction, he plunked down into his chair. It groaned. 'Daisy'll wed as her father tells 'er, like a proper lady. No use coddlin' the chit. Life ain't kind to them wot's coddled. Good day. *Next!*'

'Mr. Manning—'

'Miss Carlisle, I'm a busy man.'

'But you are selling yourself short,' she advised in a conspiratorial tone, leaning closer before he took it into his head to throw her out. 'I am well connected in the ton, and I assure you, a lack of cash is positively epidemic amongst the titled. With such a beautiful, charming daughter and an empire such as you have built, why should you settle for a mere baron when you could just as easily snare an earl, a marquess, a duke?'

His eyes narrowed with a speculative gleam. 'Duke?'

'Perhaps.'

He shook his beefy head decidedly after a moment. 'Lord Randall showed me a map of his holdings. His lands straddle one of the richest coalfields in the North Country and the fool doesn't even know it. I could make a fortune there.'

She looked straight into his beady eyes. 'Sir, he will hurt your daughter.'

She dared not reveal any shadow of Devlin's suspicions that Quint Randall might be guilty of murder. It was too dangerous. But she then gave Mr. Manning an earful he would not soon forget about the wicked ways of the Horse and Chariot Club.

When she was through, he sat studying his cigar in thought. He was not thoroughly convinced, but announced that he would hire a private investigator to check into Lord Randall's background and daily life, and once he had the facts, he promised to give the matter more thought.

Lizzie curtsied to him and withdrew.

A couple days later, Dev and Ben rolled into Town with a wide-eyed Suzy peering out the carriage window, bravely willing to lay an information against Quint and Carstairs at Bow Street, as long as Dev backed up her story. She might have been as naive as the day was long, but even Suzy knew that a peasant girl's word was meaningless against peers of the realm.

Fortunately, she had a peer of the realm on her side.

She turned her great cow eyes to Dev, seeking reassurance. 'I hope they believe me, gov.'

He gave her a steadying nod. 'They will.'

Because he was bored and because it amused him, Carstairs accompanied Quint to the business offices of his encroaching toadstool of a father-in-law-to-be.

'I'm glad you agreed to look over the settlement papers for me, Car,' Quint said. 'I got no head for numbers, and that feeder hog is sure to try to cheat me if we're not sharp.'

'Indubitably,' Carstairs murmured as his coach traveled into the mercantile quarter of the city. Normally he would not sully his hands with such grubby dealings, but he was rather curious to see how the other half lived and, more to the point, it would be a blessing to have Quint off his back asking for 'loans' all the time. The great lummox could not even afford a proper solicitor, and it amused Carstairs to assure Quint he didn't need one.

They made a great show of their arrival, the flashy horses prancing to a halt before the dark-green painted storefront of the counting house. Johnny jumped down from the driver's box, his tight livery breeches hugging his muscled bottom as he bent down to unfold the metal carriage step.

Carstairs cast him a well-pleasured glance as he alighted, his silver-handled walking cane gleaming in his hand. Quint jumped out behind him; then they ambled across the pavement to the door.

Carstairs allowed one of his footmen to deal with Mr. Manning's sallow-faced secretary, pursing his mouth in faint distaste at the smell of trade and idly adjusting the fingers of his perfectly fitted gloves. Quint shifted from foot to foot like an impatient schoolboy. Then Carstairs raised his eyebrow as a sort of walrus bellow shook the room.

'*Next!*'

The secretary shot up out of his chair and fled into the adjoining chamber.

'Charming,' Carstairs said, snickering under his breath when Quint's 'feeder hog' poked his pugnacious snout out of his office. The rest of the portly fellow appeared, dressed in an appalling brown suit.

'Er, Lord Randall.' Mr. Manning bobbed a sort of Cockney bow to Quint and then to him. 'Sir.'

'Carstairs, this is Mr. Joseph Manning. Mr. Manning,' Quint said, summoning his best manners, 'allow me to present my great friend, the Earl Carstairs.'

'How do you do, sir,' the upstart coal-factor said.

Carstairs nodded, impressed at how the stalwart fellow resisted the usual urge amongst such folk to grovel. Tough-minded. He liked that.

'Shall we?' Mr. Manning beckoned toward his office.

When Carstairs sauntered after them, Mr. Manning turned and eyed him warily. 'I beg your pardon, sir. I should like to speak to Lord Randall alone for a moment.'

Carstairs gave an idle wave of his hand. 'He's all yours.'

Manning nodded and went into his office. Carstairs sent Quint a pointed look reminding him not to sign anything until he had had a chance to read it, too.

Carstairs paced at his leisure through the counting-house, glancing over the scribblings of frantic clerks, studying this buzzing hive, this world of work of which he knew nothing. He decided within ten minutes that he did not care to know more.

He let out a sigh of vague impatience, awaiting his friend, when suddenly, a curious thud came from the fat man's office.

Work paused.

Then Quint's roar shook the walls: 'What do you mean, *the wedding's off*?'

'Oh, dear,' Carstairs sighed, pinching the bridge of his perfect nose.

A ripple of nervousness moved through the counting-house. Buzz, buzz, the little underfed clerks hurried back to work. Carstairs wondered if he should intervene, hold Quint back as only he could do, but something told him Walrus Manning could look after himself.

There was no need to eavesdrop at the door to hear their shouted conversation clearly.

'Who's been talking to you? These are lies!'

'They ain't lies! I got witnesses.'

'Who? Who is my accuser? I have a right to know!'

'Never you mind. I've done some checkin' up on you, and here's what I say to your suit!' Carstairs heard the sound of ripping paper as Mr. Manning tore up the proposed marriage settlement in Quint's face. 'You, sir, are a blackguard and a cad, and will not be marrying my daughter!'

The second thud which followed, Carstairs realized with a sigh, was Quint's fist slamming into Mr. Manning's beefy face. The anemic secretary and half a dozen clerks rushed to their employer's aid in vain, for Quint was already turning him into meat pie.

'I will not be slandered!'

Slam.

Quint shook off clerks like a bull tossing away a pack of wiry and not particularly brave dogs.

'Give me the name of my accuser, damn you!' Carstairs, as usual, took the more intelligent solution. Rounding the secretary's desk, he ran his fingertips down the list of names in Mr. Manning's appointment book, scanning several days' back, until a name jumped out at him.

Miss Elizabeth Carlisle.

His eyes narrowed, his mind turned. Quint. Daisy. The

school where Quint had first seen Manning's daughter. She was a teacher there . . .

Miss Carlisle.

Dev's little cream-pot love.

But why should Dev's pretty toy come here telling Manning secrets about Quint?

She should not know such things in the first place to be able to relate them to Mr. Manning, nor to anyone else. What exactly had old Dev told the girl about Quint? About all of them? *Good God.*

Could Torquil have been right all along?

Had their great friend Dev been playing them false from the start? For if Strathmore was telling his mistress forbidden secrets of the Horse and Chariot Club, what else might he be doing – planning – behind their backs?

Damn it!

God only knew what Dev's real motives were, but with so much to hide, Carstairs did not intend to wait around to find out. He had been foolishly blinded by lust long enough.

'Quentin, enough!' he clipped out, glancing over as a prickle of fear-tinged excitement shot down his spine.

His terse order stopped Quint's rampage. The baron left Manning in a fleshy heap and came stalking out of the office.

'Let's go,' Carstairs said coldly. 'Are you trying to get arrested, you idiot?' he snarled as they walked back out to the coach.

'What the hell am I going to do for money now? He's rejected my suit for Daisy!'

'We've got bigger problems than that,' he said, eyeing Quint in contempt as the baron took a deep swig from his flask. The coach rolled into motion.

'What kind of problems?' Quint grumbled.

'Dev knows.'

* * *

Lizzie managed to while away the entire afternoon playing with the babies at Knight House, but when the army of nurses came and took her little playmates off to naptime, thoughts of Dev were swift to return. Every day, every hour, she missed him more. She was sure that she would hear from him at any moment. Jacinda was at a meeting for one of her charities, and when Bel decided to lie down, needing plenty of rest in her delicate condition, Lizzie found herself alone.

The day was fine, so she went out. The street was moderately busy, carriages whirring by as she took a stroll down to the bookshop on the corner. Even if she didn't buy anything, the simple fact of being in a bookstore made her feel better.

I wonder if Devlin misses me, too. She could only hope that he was all right.

She stopped before the milliner's shop window and stood admiring the frilly summer hats and bonnets, paying little mind when she heard a carriage halt behind her. There were many shops on this street, after all, with customers coming and going all day.

But then in the window's reflection, she saw two men get out of the coach.

Men did not go to ladies' hat shops.

Her heart skipped a beat and she narrowed her eyes, then horrified recognition made her gasp. She did not waste a second turning around to confirm that they were the two men from the carriage at the school that day – members of the Horse and Chariot Club. She just ran.

'They'll come after you . . .'

'You're being paranoid, Devlin.'

Lizzie fled, but they split up to herd her wherever they wished her to go. When she dodged left, the big brown-haired man blocked her way; when she turned right, the cruelly elegant blond waited to catch her.

'Help!' she shrieked, but the few people nearby merely looked on in startled curiosity.

She whirled around and dashed down her only escape route, the dark, narrow passage between the barbershop and the vintner's, but it quickly dead-ended in a closed courtyard. Lizzie fought and kicked, shouting bloody murder until the brown-haired bruiser clapped his huge paw across her mouth and hauled her against him, half dragging her into their coach.

Chapter Twenty

Dev had spent the afternoon giving his deposition to the officers at Bow Street on the events connected to the abduction of young Suzy. They had many questions about numerous members of the Horse and Chariot Club, all of which Dev had answered as fully as he could. When the grueling interview was finally over, Dev was impatient to go and see Lizzie at last.

Now that he had fulfilled her wishes, he could not wait to tell her what he had done, but first he made the officers swear to warn him before they moved against his enemies so that he could take Lizzie away from Town. That way he could be sure of her safety even if one or more of the villains temporarily eluded arrest.

As his coach rolled through the streets of London toward Lady Jacinda's villa on Regent's Park, Dev mulled over his mixed feelings about having relinquished his obsession with revenge in favor of lawful justice. A small part of him still wanted blood, but the greater portion of his being and chiefly his heart would have paid any price to be with the woman he loved.

When he called at Lady Jacinda's, the butler told him Lizzie had gone to Knight House to play with the children. Undaunted, he got back in the coach and ordered his driver to take him there. It took them half an hour.

At Knight House, the gray-haired butler informed him Miss Carlisle had left two hours ago. To the best of his knowledge, Mr. Walsh said, she had gone down to the bookshop on the corner. Dev thought it a fair chance she might still be there. Two hours in a bookshop was nothing for his fair bluestocking, he thought in affection.

With his hands in his pockets and a musing smile of anticipation playing at his lips, he gestured to his coachman to wait there, then retraced her steps. Upon searching the aisles of the bookshop, however, there was no sign of her.

Blast. Coming back out to stand briefly atop the store's front steps, Dev glanced up and down the street, frowning under the brim of his black top hat. Perhaps she had wandered on to browse in one of the other shops. Or had she hailed a hackney coach back to Jacinda's villa? He heaved a disgruntled sigh at the thought of continually missing her and decided he did not intend to spend the remainder of the day crisscrossing the sprawling metropolis in search of the woman.

Being a man of sense, he walked back up Saint James's Street to wait at White's with a good glass of port. One of them must stay put, after all. He would try again in an hour. His heart was light as he imagined her reaction when he told her that he had found a way to comply with her wishes while still seeing justice served. In truth, he was rather proud of himself.

He sat down by himself at a small round table in a far corner of the club, asked for a newspaper, and prayed he did not see Alec Knight. He was in no mood to face his defeated rival. When the port was brought to him, he toasted Lizzie silently in his thoughts, then let out a satisfied sigh and leaned back in the maroon leather club chair with the *London Times*. Perusing the advertisements, he wondered belatedly if he ought to stop on his way back to Jacinda's to buy a gift. It always helped not to arrive empty-handed when a man had to grovel.

'Ah, Strathmore. I figured you would show up here eventually.'

He looked over the newspaper as Carstairs sat down across the table from him.

'How are you today, Dev?'

'Quite well. Yourself?'

'Splendid.' Carstairs chewed the ivory mouthpiece of his small, stylish pipe, but did not light it. 'I hate to interrupt, but you and I need to have a little talk.'

'What's afoot?' Dev set the paper down, some indefinable note in the earl's cultured voice arresting him.

Carstairs stared at him for a long moment, his expression unreadable. 'I hope you've enjoyed your stay in London, my lord. But it's time for you to leave.'

'Leave? What are you talking about?'

'You know damned well,' Carstairs whispered slowly.

Dev tensed, careful to keep his face expressionless, but he could not have been more shocked if a cannonball had just ripped through his middle. Good God, had they realized he and Suzy had spoken with Bow Street? He had taken care to ensure no one saw him.

'I don't understand,' he said in a measured tone of caution.

'Don't you? Let me see if I can't help.' Carstairs rested his elbow on the chair arm, leaning nearer. 'Do you find yourself missing something valuable of late – or should I say someone?'

Dev felt the earth fall away from its orbit. *Lizzie*. His face turned ashen, and he couldn't seem to breathe. 'What have you done with her?'

Carstairs snickered idly and leaned back in his chair, chewing on his pipe. 'Such a pretty thing. Not to my taste, mind you, but she does have such pretty gray eyes. It would be a shame to put them out.'

Dev launched at him with a garbled cry, going for his throat across the small table.

'Not advisable, Dev!' Carstairs shouted, ducking. 'With a word from me, she dies.'

Dev gripped the man's lapels in fury. 'What have you done with her?'

'Ah, so she does mean something to you. You know, I suspected that,' Carstairs choked out.

'Where is she?'

'Easy.' Carstairs sent a meaningful glance toward some chess-playing clubmen on the other side of the room who had stopped their game to frown in the direction of the commotion. 'I am sure you and I both prefer to conduct ourselves like gentlemen.'

'You don't know the meaning of the word,' Dev snarled, but released him and sat back down, realizing he could do little else, since it seemed his enemy was holding all the cards at the moment.

Carstairs tugged his waistcoat back into order. 'Your little ladybird is safe for the moment. Just a trifle peeved.'

'So help me, Carstairs, if you harm one hair on her *head*—'

'I shouldn't be making threats just now if I were you, old boy. If I were you, I should shut up and listen very carefully to the following instructions.'

His blood boiled. But Dev held his temper in check and waited for the instructions.

Carstairs did not divulge them at once, staring at him for a long moment. He shook his blond head. 'God, I should have let Torquil put a bullet in you weeks ago.'

'Why didn't you?' Dev challenged him.

'I trusted you. It's true,' he said when Dev scoffed in utter contempt. 'I wanted to give you the benefit of the doubt. You know that I was drawn in by your beauty, and,' he admitted, cruelly, deliberately taunting him with only a hint, 'I felt sorry for you after what happened.'

'What did happen, Carstairs?'

'No, Dev. You betrayed me. I'm the only one who can give you the answers you seek, but you stabbed me in the back, so you can go to hell. The only reason I spare you now is because murdering you would call too much attention to the rest of us. Now, here is the plan, and you listen well. You leave London at dawn. You will go to the docks, get on board your little ship and sail away, Strathmore – I scarcely care where, as long as it's far. Do it,' he said slowly, 'or we use your little governess for the village whore before we send her lovely body to the bottom of the Thames.'

'I'll do it. I'll go,' he whispered at once. He felt like he might throw up.

'And never come back.'

'You'll never see me again. It's as good as done. Let her go. I'll take her with me. Neither of us will ever trouble you—'

'Dev, my lad, do you take me for a fool? It's plain to see she's all you care about. If I hand her over, you could write a letter to Bow Street and start all manner of unpleasantness for me.'

So, they didn't know he'd gone to Bow Street. Thank God. But if they somehow found out, he realized with sickening certainty, Lizzie's life was forfeit.

How on earth had they learned of his deception? He had been so careful.

It did not matter now.

He did not even care about the facts Carstairs might have shared regarding the fire. All that mattered was procuring Lizzie's safety. He tried to think clearly above the volcanic pounding of his heart. His mouth was dry with fear, his stomach turning with the half-glass of port he'd drunk.

'The plan is, you leave,' Carstairs reiterated. 'Miss Carlisle stays in England, where we can keep an eye on her. That way, you won't attempt anything rash.'

The full force of his instructions suddenly struck Dev. *I leave. She stays*. Good God, they were to be separated for the rest of their lives! He could barely absorb the shock of it. Live without her?

His mind reeled. He swallowed hard. 'I need to see her again. I need to know she's all right or there's no deal.'

'Do not attempt any pointless heroics, Strathmore. I really do not wish to hurt the girl. It's not in my nature – unless, of course, I am forced.'

'I won't do anything, I swear. Just let me see her. Let me see she is unharmed.'

'I will bring her to the docks, and you can say goodbye,' he drawled in disgust. 'Mind you, come alone. Don't try anything, Dev, or Torquil puts a bullet in that clever head of hers.'

'I will comply fully. Is she all right? For the love of God, man—'

'She is fine. Calm yourself. Now, you tell no one about this, and I'll see you at the docks at five A.M. You see? That wasn't so hard.'

Dev flinched but somehow held himself back from killing the man as Carstairs rose.

'Behave yourself, Dev. We'll be watching you. Oh – and, yes – I almost forgot.' He paused before walking away. 'Quint wants fifty thousand quid. Write him out a draft note before you go. Bon voyage.'

'But, Mama, I don't *want* to go back to Ireland.'

'Sorscha, I've already told you, our packet leaves tomorrow morning from Bristol. We have our tickets. We are going home.' Standing before the dressing table, searching for something in her leather satchel by the light of a single candle, Mary glanced over her shoulder at where her pouting daughter sat atop her packed and locked traveling trunk near the open door of the hotel room, which they were about to vacate.

Her burly manservant, Patrick Doyle, came into the doorway just then, rubbing his hands together. 'May I take that for ye, miss?'

Sorscha gave a sulky nod and sighed as she slid off her traveling trunk so Doyle could carry it down to the coach.

'Hold the candle for Doyle on the stairs, Sorscha,' Mary ordered her daughter. 'It's quite dark in the stairwell.'

'Yes, ma'am.'

The moment the child had gone, Mary pulled her gun out of the satchel and loaded it with cool expertise, dropping a handful of extra bullets into the voluminous pocket of her cape.

Their trip to England need not have been an utter waste.

She blew out the candle and left the hotel room, pulling the door shut behind her. She joined them at the coach a moment later.

'All set, then. In you go. I just need to make one quick stop before we leave the city.' The hard glance she sent Doyle belied her cheerful tone.

He gave her a subtle nod.

Mary climbed into the coach with her daughter. Doyle knew the way to Quint's seedy bachelor house, but when they drove past it, all was dark. They went down to the corner past it, where Mary pulled the check-string to halt her driver.

'What are we doing, Mama?'

'Just a moment, darlin'.' She opened the carriage door and stood to murmur new instructions to her servant. 'We'll try Carstairs.'

The carriage rolled on.

Reaching a much finer quarter of the West End, Mary bade Doyle stop a short distance down the quiet street from Lord Carstairs's large, elegant house.

'Mama, where are you going now?'

'To see an old friend.'

'Why can't I see *my* friend before we go away?'

'This is a special friend, Sorscha. Someone I need to repay.'

The girl huffed. 'No fair.'

'Oh, quit your sulkin', lass.' Mary lifted her veil because it was dark and gave her daughter's rose-petal cheek a teasing kiss. 'I'll be right back, and then we're off to have jolly times in Ireland, like always.'

Sorscha tried to scowl at her, but smiled in spite of herself.

A moment later, Mary was slipping through the darkness, nigh invisible in her all-black clothing, her face concealed by her lace veil. She stole down the mews alley, her feet not making a sound over the uneven cobbles. Carstairs's elegant town house of creamy stuccoed brick was built on the same pattern as the majority of those in London. Mary remembered the layout quite well from the many times she had come to the earl's debauched routs with Quint in her youth. She intended to get in through the walled garden.

Skimming her fingertips along the mews side of the garden wall, Mary waited until she could see the familiar outline of the grape trellis poking above the wall. She had let Quint make love to her once under that trellis.

When she came to it, she reached up and gripped two of the short wrought-iron stakes that lined the top of the shoulder-high brick wall, which was stuccoed and painted to match the house. Moving carefully amid the iron stakes, she heaved herself up to a crouched position atop the wall. From this higher vantage point, shielded by the trellis, she assessed the situation.

At once she heard the lilting fountain in the center of the garden. Nothing had changed except the displays in the meticulously tended flower beds. Twin benches faced the fountain. The trees in the garden's corners had grown bigger, but the same conical shrubs lined the cobblestone drive at intervals a few feet apart.

Her heart pounded with terrible excitement for what she had come to do. She had sailed here to England for justice, but now she was willing to settle for revenge.

Things might have been different if Devil Strathmore had proved a worthy ally, but that hope had come to naught. She had wavered in her view of him after seeing him break into Quint's carriage house, but when she discovered that he had seduced Sorscha's pretty young teacher, Mary had realized the viscount was as thoroughly lost to depravity as his fellow members of the Horse and Chariot Club.

Blood or no, she had no intention of handing Sorscha over to the likes of him. Still, even without Strathmore's help, Quint and Carstairs would not get away with what they had done to her. Before she and Sorscha fled back to Ireland, Mary meant to settle the score.

How to get into the house? She scanned the triple bays of windows on each floor of Carstair's home, but then the smell of smoke distracted her, floating to her on the warm night air. Was someone in the garden? Her alerted glance swept the tranquil green retreat; then a flicker of movement across from her caught her eye.

She had learned that Carstairs housed Johnny in a fine apartment above the carriage house. On the left-hand corner of the balcony there, she saw the earl's handsome young stud lounging against the railing with a rifle in his hands and a cheroot dangling from the corner of his mouth. Outlined against the indigo sky, he appeared to be keeping guard.

What on earth? Only now did Mary abandon her interest in the earl's house, turning her attention to the carriage house. Her gaze traveled to the other end of the long balcony, and her blood ran cold as she spotted Torquil Staines similarly stationed at the other end, keeping watch, a deadly-looking rifle in his hands.

What's going on, boys? she wondered. What dark business were they up to now? A shiver of belated doom ran through her as she realized she would probably be lying dead on the grass already if she hadn't stopped to look first, if she had not smelled the smoke from their cheroots. There was light in the cozy upper window of the carriage house and, thanks to her perch atop the wall, Mary could see straight into the main room of Johnny's apartment, some thirty feet across the garden. She drew in her breath, aghast, at what she beheld.

Quint and Carstairs were framed in the window. They appeared to be in the midst of a heated debate. Between them sat a girl tied up in a chair with her hands bound behind her and a gag across her mouth. Mary stared in shocked recognition. *Miss Carlisle.*

She knew what these men were capable of; she knew she had to help the younger woman.

Mary took out another bullet so she could grab it quickly for a second shot, then she lifted her gun and rested the muzzle on the trellis. She could handle Quint later if it came down to it. Without their leader, they would be in disarray. Taking careful aim, Mary stared through the window and drew a bead on Carstairs's flaxen head.

She held on tight against the gun's expected kick and fired.

Lizzie screamed into her cloth gag when the window shattered and jolted away from it so hard that she toppled the wooden chair she was tied to and landed, wild eyed, on her side upon the floor.

Chaos erupted, a wild rash of shouts both inside and out.

Though barely a moment, it felt like a year as she lay there stranded, unable to right herself. Behind her back, she felt something painful jabbing into her hand. Broken glass from the window. She opened her fingers and clutched the long shard.

Tears of pain filled her eyes, but she blinked them back fiercely. Ignoring the cuts and the trickle of blood across her palm, she used the glass knife to saw away at the rope binding her hands.

'Son of a bitch!' Carstairs screamed, wiping his hand across his temple where the bullet had grazed him, painting his light hair with the mark of a crimson lightning bolt.

Mary reloaded and this time, coolly took aim at Torquil. But as she concentrated on trying to get a clear shot in the dark, she was unaware that Johnny had come down the steps and glided around the perimeter of the garden toward her.

Aiming for Torquil's chest, she was about to pull the trigger when the young man commanded: 'Freeze!'

She whipped her aim down at him, and they stood in a motionless tableau, guns drawn.

'Don't you move!' Johnny warned her. 'Over here, Torq!'

'Hold him!'

'It ain't a *him*,' Johnny yelled back, eyeing her with extreme suspicion.

Torquil was on his way, and Mary knew that when he reached her, she was as good as dead.

'Let me go, Johnny,' she ordered calmly.

'You know me?'

'I tried to help you once. Easy—' Slowly, she pulled back her veil.

His eyes widened. 'Jesus Christ.' His rifle sank.

Mary whirled to fire her shot at Torquil, who was running toward them, but he dived behind the low wall of the fountain.

'Hold your fire!' Johnny yelled, lifting his hand toward Torquil just as Quint banged the apartment door open and came out. 'Hold your fire, I say!'

'Strathmore!' Quint bellowed in fury.

'It isn't Strathmore! Hold your fire!' Johnny abandoned Mary to her escape, jogging toward the carriage house. 'It's Miss Highgate!'

'W-what did you say?' Mary heard Quint utter as she leaped down from the garden wall.

She was already reloading when Quint's thunderous howl floated out across the night. It sent a ripple of fear down her spine.

'Ginny!'

Carstairs let out a disbelieving curse at the hated name, but Lizzie paid no mind, fighting against her bonds. Behind her back, she sawed at them for all she was worth, and she could feel them giving way, strand by strand.

'Get back here, Quint!' Carstairs yelled, but the baron had already gone barreling off into the night. 'God damn it. Johnny!'

'He went with Quint. They're chasing Ginny.' Torquil strode back into the apartment. Lizzie, still toppled onto her side on the floor, eyed his passing boots in fright as they crunched the nearby glass underfoot. 'I can't believe that bitch is alive!'

'Not for long,' Carstairs growled.

'Quint's not gonna let you touch her.'

'He'll have no choice. You know what this means?'

Torquil nodded in cold reproach. 'That she's working with Strathmore.'

'Under the circumstances, sending him away isn't going to be sufficient.'

'Say no more,' Torquil murmured, pausing to poke his gun into Lizzie's ribs. 'Guess we won't be needin' this one anymore.'

She whimpered.

'Go kill Dev,' Carstairs ordered, unsheathing the big knife he had strapped at his side. 'I have a few more questions for her.

Perhaps now she'll be ready to tell me if Dev has been talking to anyone else.'

Torquil sent him a hard-eyed nod askance. 'Bet you wish you would've listened to me now, you bloody sod.'

'Just do it,' he spat.

Torquil growled at him and left.

Lizzie felt another strand of her bonds break, but gave a small shriek into the cloth gag as Carstairs wrenched her chair upright.

He planted his legs wide and bent down to her eye level, giving her a menacing smile. 'Now, then, Miss Carlisle, I regret to say there has been a slight change of plans. You have your lover to thank for your death – for you must die, I'm afraid. Whether it will be slow and messy, or swift and clean is up to you. Let me help you understand your situation. There is no help coming for you. Do you hear me? Your darling Dev will be a corpse within the hour. His adventuring days are over. So you might as well cooperate.'

Oh, I'll cooperate.

'Uff!' he said as she kicked him as hard as she could in the groin. 'Bitch!' he gasped out in an odd, high-pitched wheeze, falling to the floor.

Lizzie burst up from her chair, pulling the last few threads of her bonds apart and ripping off the gag. She dashed out the door, leaving Carstairs balled up and writhing over his privates on the floor. On trembling legs, she rushed down the stairs and out into the night, her heart hammering. Glancing left and right, she was not sure which way to run. A high wall held her trapped in the garden. She saw no gate.

'Miss Carlisle!' a hushed voice whispered. 'Over here!'

She squinted toward the trellis and saw the outline of a veiled woman. *Good gracious – Mrs. Harris?* Her conversation from the carriage that night with Dev came pouring back in her mind.

Then her eyes widened as she realized. Dear God, her Mrs. Harris *was* the same Mary Harris he had been searching for. The actress, Ginny Highgate!

She was alive!

Lizzie was already running toward the widow. Mrs. Harris reached down her hand, helping Lizzie climb.

'Careful of the spikes! Quint and Johnny are just around the corner,' she whispered quickly. 'I managed to elude them for the moment.'

'Mrs. Harris, Carstairs is still inside,' Lizzie warned.

'We'd better get out of here fast – and Mary will do. Come. My carriage is nearby.' The widow whisked her cape around her in a graceful arc as she pivoted and started running.

Lizzie was right behind her, both of them racing up the mews as silently as they could.

'Ginny!' Another half-mad bellow from Quint boomed up the alley.

Mary grabbed Lizzie, and both women flattened themselves against the wall.

'What does he want with you?'

'We used to be lovers.'

'Everyone thought you were dead.'

'I know.'

'We have to warn Devlin. They've sent Staines to kill him!'

'Kill him?' she answered bitterly. 'You are mistaken. He is one of them.'

'No, he's not! It's been a facade all this time! His every effort has been aimed at trying to find out what happened to his family the night of that fire. You have the answers to that, don't you? You must tell him what you know. Come, we have to help him—'

'*Ginny!* Ginny, it's Quint! Let me see you!'

'I don't think you want to see me now, my love,' she

murmured bitterly under her breath, staring into the shadows. 'Come, Miss Carlisle. Devil Strathmore is going to have to take care of himself. You're welcome to come with me, but Sorscha is my first priority. She's in more danger than you know.'

'You brought the girl into this?' she cried in a whisper.

'I would appreciate your help,' Mary said briskly, ignoring her protest. 'Carstairs won't quit until I'm dead. Now they know that I am alive, but they still don't know about Sorscha. The girl has no memory of the fire, but they don't know that, nor will they care. All of Carstairs's witnesses die. If anything should happen to me, you must take Sorscha away on the Irish packet from Bristol. I have the tickets in this satchel. Once she's safe, you can contact her brother from Ireland.'

'Her brother?' Lizzie breathed, turning to her in amazement. 'Good God, you mean – little Sarah?'

'*Ginny!* I just want to talk to you!' They could hear Quint's heavy footfalls clumping down the alleyway along with Johnny's lighter, swifter ones.

'Come, there's no time. This way to my carriage!'

They ran.

Lizzie saw the waiting vehicle ahead, black and shiny, crouched in the moonlight. A coachman in a long carrick-coat stood on the driver's box with a rifle in his hands.

'Doyle will hold them off,' Mary said. 'Let's go!'

As soon as Carstairs could stand, he picked up his shotgun from his selection of weapons and hobbled outside, limping slightly and bent on blood. He heard Quint's lovesick moaning in the alleyway for his goddamned Ginny, so he went in that direction.

He came out of the garden just in time to see both women fleeing together toward the square, Quint and Johnny running after them.

'Move!' he thundered at his friends, cocking the gun. He brought it up as the two bitches plunged into shadow.

He saw the carriage, the driver with a gun.

Boom!

The coachman fell from the driver's box and slammed to earth, and Ginny Highgate screamed. He knew her voice. He'd heard her screams before.

He could hear the hysterical women shouting and began reloading, limping onward down the mews, while Quint and Johnny rushed toward the scene.

'They're coming!' A clearer feminine voice, stronger, sounded over Ginny's sobbing for her manservant. 'Leave him, he's dead! Get in the coach, *now*!'

Carstairs narrowed his eyes as Dev's cream-pot love leaped up into the driver's box and picked up the reins, slapping them over the horses' rumps. The coach pulled away just as Quint grabbed for it with both hands.

His burly arms came away empty. 'After them!' he yowled.

Carstairs smiled coldly as the women's carriage rounded the garden square and took off heading west. *Oh, you want to race against the Horse and Chariot Club, little wench?*

'You're on,' he whispered with a sneer at her fleeing coach, then spun around and marched to his curricle, barking at Quint and Johnny to hurry up.

Chapter Twenty-one

Dev was striding back and forth between his bedchamber and his dressing room, throwing his belongings into several traveling trunks with hands that could not stop shaking, his stomach tied in knots. He was grimly furious and as tense as a blade vibrating after a vicious blow, but behind his tight-lipped silence, he had regrouped and had a plan.

But that didn't make this any easier.

Ben was trying to go about the task of packing his things more calmly, but as for Dev, he had not known what fear was till now. He had never suffered such agonizing worry for another human being in his life. Wherever she was, he knew Lizzie was scared. All he wanted was to hold her in his arms and promise he'd make everything better. And he would.

Carstairs had taken him off guard at White's, but Dev knew that cooperating completely and accepting whatever terms the foe named had been the right thing to do. But pulling back from the moment's horror, he saw that he simply could not live without her for the rest of his life. Nor could he allow them to haunt and control her for the rest of hers. He would end this war at dawn on the docks. Because what Carstairs didn't know was that his once-surly, often drunken, ill-kempt crew from the *Katie Rose* would have fought the armies of hell for Dev.

They looked the part of simple sailors, but tomorrow dawn, when Carstairs brought Lizzie into view, on a cue from Dev, their captain, they would attack; he would rescue her and let his lawless mates of the *Katie Rose* have at the coddled gents of the Horse and Chariot Club.

If it went well, he would explain to Bow Street as soon as he could. If it went badly, he would take Lizzie away on his ship and become an exile from British law, which was why he was collecting his most significant personal effects from the satin-wood box on his dressing table – his signet ring, a miniature portrait of his father, the gold band he still meant to give his bride. She was all that mattered.

It was then that his wilderness-honed senses bristled, sending him their warning, a nameless prickle of danger down his nape. His gaze flicked to the mirror as he felt someone watching him. His eyes flared as he made out the shadowy figure of Torquil Staines on the balcony of his bedchamber, half hidden by the draperies.

He had a gun.

'Get down!' Dev roared, throwing Ben to the floor as the shot cracked into the room.

His valet fell, clattering back against the dressing table; Dev's shaving kit and half a dozen small toilette bottles rained on Ben in a hail as he toppled to the floor, his chocolate-brown face a mask of pain.

Dev charged at Staines, dimly registering the fact that Ben had been hit. Staines swung into the room, drawing his knife from its scabbard. The baronet swung it at him in a blood-thirsty arc.

Dev jumped back, glancing anxiously at his friend. 'Ben!'

'I'm shot, Dev,' Ben answered weakly.

'Hang on, Ben!' Out of the corner of his eye, he could see Ben crawl to a seated position and lean his back weakly against the wall. A crimson stain was spreading across the region of Ben's left front shoulder and chest.

Dev's heart pounded madly while he fended off Staines's attack, his head reeling. Ben couldn't die. He couldn't bear it.

Staines stabbed at him again.

'What the hell are you doing, Staines?' Dev thundered. 'I said I would leave! You can see I'm preparing to go! Stay with me, Ben!' he called to his servant in a shaken tone.

'You're a two-faced double-dealing snake, Dev. That's why.' Staines's blade whizzed through the air and stuck in the carved bedpost when Dev ducked. 'Don't try to play innocent. We know now that you've been working with Ginny Highgate all this time.'

'What are you talking about? Ginny Highgate is long dead!' He saw his jungle machete tucked into the valise that Ben had been packing and dived for it.

'I saw her with my own eyes, Dev. Bitch tried to put a bullet in me.'

'Ginny Highgate is alive? In London?' He parried a savage blow, the memory of the mysterious veiled woman he'd seen spying on him flooding back into his mind.

'As if you don't know! If you haven't noticed, the deal is off.'

'Off? Wait a minute— What about Lizzie?'

He let out a contemptuous laugh. 'Carstairs cut her throat.'

'*What?*' Dev whispered, going perfectly still as horror spiraled through him. He could barely breathe. His voice came out thinly. 'You're lying.'

'Did you think we were going to let you and your bitch send us to the gallows?'

'No . . .' he whispered, as the horror turned faster, spiraling out of control. 'No.' A thousand demons howled in his head, his greatest fears come to fruition.

They had killed Lizzie. Cut her sweet throat. His family was dead. Ben was bleeding his life out on the floor.

All because of him.

Blackness swallowed him; the light went out. '*Noooo!*' The scream that broke from him was a bloodcurdling war cry. He attacked, holding nothing back.

He tore the room apart and set about slashing Staines to ribbons, barely feeling the cuts that he, in turn, sustained. The baronet's expertise was no match for Dev's bloodlust. The murder of Lizzie had unleashed a beast that could never be put back into the cage.

They crashed against one wall, battled across the balcony, nearly flinging each other off it; then Staines threw Dev back inside. Dev picked up a broken chair leg and wielded it in his left hand like a club. It made a useful blocker for Staines's blows.

When Dev saw his opening, he struck with a lightning-fast thrust, and sank his blade into Staines's soft belly, watching without expression as life ebbed from the man.

'Mercy,' Staines croaked out.

Dev snarled and twisted the knife.

Then he dropped the feared duelist to the floor.

He turned away from his bloody work, panting slightly and a little nauseated, but everything in him was cold. There was still more killing to be done.

First, however, he stalked over to his servant and knelt down beside him. 'Ben.'

The man's dark eyes opened slowly.

Thank God for that. Dev swallowed hard. 'Let's have a look.' He moved Ben's waistcoat aside and tore his shirt to see the wound.

'This is a switch,' the black man remarked, attempting a wan smile, but Dev could not respond in kind. All joy and any possibility of happiness had left his life with Staines's incomprehensible words.

Ben gripped his sleeve. 'Dev. Listen to me. Just because he said it doesn't mean it's true. You must *believe*.'

Dev gave him a hard glance and looked away. 'The bullet's in your shoulder. You're going to be all right. I have to go.'

As Dev rose, Ben struggled to his feet.

'What are you doing?'

'Coming with you.'

'The hell you are. Go next door and have the neighbors call the surgeon, Ben. You can't sit a horse with that wound.'

'You've done it. Why can't I?'

Dev shook his head at him and left without further argument, running out to the stable. He threw a bridle on the one horse in his barn that had already proved both its extraordinary speed and endurance – the tall dark gelding he had ridden to Bath months ago when he had thought Aunt Augusta was at death's door, thanks to a certain meddling bluestocking.

She couldn't be dead. So much life, warmth, love. He could not wrap his mind around it. A few minutes later, he charged out of the stable astride the horse she had named Star. *Why didn't I marry her then and take her away from all this?* How could he ever have thought that revenge was more important than love?

He rode full speed to Carstairs's house, but as he galloped into the square, he saw a tight knot of people standing about, looking at something on the ground. *Oh, God.* His dread increased tenfold as he saw that it was a person lying motionless on the ground. *Lizzie!* He flung off the horse and ran into the midst, but when he shoved the murmuring onlookers aside, he saw in relief that the victim was a middle-aged man in a carrick-coat.

'What happened here?' he demanded, for with Carstairs's house a stone's throw away, he knew that it had to be connected.

Five people started babbling, all answering his question at once. All of them had heard a commotion and several shots, but none of them seemed to know much.

'We found this!' one helpful woman offered, holding up a leather satchel.

Dev grabbed it and immediately upended it, spilling the contents onto the pavement. Sundry female accounterments informed him in a glance that the bag had belonged to a woman, but what caught his eye was a pair of papers that fluttered to the ground.

Scanning them by moonlight, he saw that they were travelers' waybills. The tickets secured two places on the Irish packet departing tomorrow morning. They were signed by a Mrs. Mary Harris. His eyes widened.

Ginny Highgate!

'Bristol,' he murmured.

Carstairs would be right behind her.

'What do you make of it, sir? Sir? What about Bristol?' the woman called, but Dev was already leaping back up onto his horse, gathering the reins.

Reeling the animal around, he squeezed its sides with his calves. Star sprang forth at his urging; then they galloped hell-for-leather to the Great West Road.

Lizzie was finding it a tad difficult to concentrate on her driving under the circumstances as she whipped the horses on, barreling down the Great West Road. For one thing, three maniacs in a racing drag were behind them, shooting at them; for another, she had just seen the poor coachman killed before her very eyes. She did not know whether the love of her life was alive or dead; she was driving unfamiliar horses and a vehicle whose dimensions she was not terribly sure of; it was dark; she was scared out of her wits; and they were about to enter a stretch of road known as a favorite haunt of highwaymen.

The cuts all over her hands from using the shard of glass as a knife seemed the least of her worries, though they made the chafing give and take of the leather reins in her left hand hurt worse. She hated to use the whip on the horses, but feared to think what might happen if she allowed their pace to slow.

And yet somehow she was holding her own – for now, anyway. In a few hours' time, who could say? The road was long; Bristol was even farther than Bath.

With any luck, the highwaymen might get them!

She risked another glance behind and noted how the gentle rise of the road now shielded them from Carstairs's guns, then looked forward again, driving the horses relentlessly. It helped to imagine Devlin sitting beside her like that night on the road to Oakley Park, urging her on, helping her. Steadying her. Telling her she could do it. Sharing his great courage and resourcefulness with her.

She had to believe he was safe.

As the coach barreled onward, the one imperative that rang through her brain was to protect and preserve the life of his little sister. When Lizzie recalled the half-finished puzzle on the floor at Mulberry Cottage, it gave her the chills. Sorscha did not yet know her real name and her true birth, but first they had to survive this night. Lizzie clung to her certainty that reuniting Devlin with his long-lost baby sister would have miraculous healing effects on his wounded soul.

'Blazes,' she whispered, spotting a tight, one-lane bridge ahead. It curved on a slight hump over a small river. She was not sure of the angle at which to hit it; she was not entirely sure of her vehicle's width. She knew that she ought to slow down and take it carefully, but if she lost speed, it would be difficult to regain it. The maniacs would be breathing down their necks in a trice, and this time, she might not succeed in outrunning them.

The horses seemed to know what to do. With the reins in one hand, Lizzie reached down and braced herself with the other, gripping the seat-iron. 'Hold on!' she yelled to her passengers as the galloping horses clattered onto the stone bridge, leaving the softer surface of the packed-earth-and-gravel road.

The impact of the front wheels slamming up onto the bridge nearly jarred her teeth out of her head, and the springs groaned in protest, but the coach whooshed through the narrow passage without a scratch on either side.

Lizzie let out a whoop of victory as they crashed back down onto the road, but in a heartbeat, her relief turned to horror. As soon as they left the bridge, she saw a mail coach thundering straight at them, coming dead-on from the opposite direction.

The guard blared the horn, warning her to turn at once, for it could not – the mail coach was larger, had six horses, and was weighted down with all its cargo. Lizzie panicked. The road was too narrow, feeding into the bridge. She was going too fast.

The coaches rushed at each other, reminding her in an aghast, slow-moving second of two knights charging at each other in a joust, the traces of each vehicle ready to collide like lances. With all her strength, she hauled her team to the left. The leader screamed but took her cue. The mail coach thundered by so close she could feel the wind from its passing, but in the terrified blink of an eye, the sudden shift in the horses' direction yanked the coach off balance; it teetered on two wheels.

'Hold on!' she screamed again, but she was unable to do so herself. As the coach tipped over, she saw the crash coming and made a jump for it, even as she was thrown from her high perch atop the driver's seat.

She went sailing, arms out, through the air while the coach skidded on its side for several more yards down the road.

'*Ufff!*' She landed flat on her belly in an alfalfa field at the same moment that the splinter bar shattered, the twisted traces cracking off the chassis with a great wooden crunch. It slid to a halt while the horses kept going.

A terrible silence followed.

Lizzie's heart felt like it would pound right out of her chest. The wind had been knocked out of her, but she took a dazed swallow of air, forcing herself to rise up onto her hands and knees. She looked down at herself and was astonished to see she was not dead. She did not seem to be too badly hurt, except for a jammed right wrist with which she had braced her fall. She could have kissed the ground.

The soft, deep, fresh-tilled soil and its green alfalfa blanket had probably saved her life. But what of the others?

Sorscha. She lurched unsteadily to her feet. Carstairs and his mates would be upon them in minutes.

When she turned and trotted on shaky legs back toward the coach, she saw just how lucky she had been. The alfalfa field was bordered by a squat stone wall; there was also a thick-trunked oak a few feet away, either of which might have easily stopped her midair flight with an outcome she did not want to think about. Rubbing her wrist, she climbed over the stone wall and ran to the coach.

'Sorscha! Mary! Sorscha!' Terrified of what she might find, she approached the overturned vehicle more slowly, when suddenly the carriage door – which now faced the night sky – swung upward and opened.

A curly head emerged. 'M-Miss Carlisle?'

'Oh, Sorscha, darling!' she breathed, moving closer to help pull her out. 'Are you all right? Can you walk?'

'I–I think so. Mama? I think she's hurt!'

'Mary? Mary, wake up!' Quickly helping Sorscha out of the wreckage, Lizzie climbed in, where fortunately, she found the widow Harris stirring back to consciousness with a groan.

'Ugh, I hit my head. Wrenched my shoulder on the hand

loop, too. It's a good thing you called out to warn us. What happened?'

'A mail coach ran us off the road. I'm so sorry! Come, we must go. They shall be upon us in a moment.'

Mary took a deep breath and nodded. Then she glanced around the inside of the coach. 'My satchel! Where is it?'

'Forget it! We must hide!'

'It had the tickets!'

'You can buy more. Come on.'

Lizzie and Sorscha together helped the shaken woman climb out of the overturned carriage. Lizzie scanned the landscape. She could already feel the earth beginning to tremble beneath her feet with Carstairs's carriage approaching in the distance.

'What shall we do?' Sorscha cried.

'There!' Lizzie pointed. 'Amid the trees – an inn! Perhaps we can find help or at least blend into the crowd. Hurry!'

The women kept Sorscha between them as they ran. Lizzie's wrist throbbed with every stride as they fled toward a small wayside inn set back from the road and obscured by some overgrown trees.

The night wind rustled through the twisting boughs above them as the women turned in the gate and rushed up the dusty drive. A single lantern hung above the door, its dim glow offering an uncertain welcome. She glimpsed a dilapidated roof, large patches of peeling paint, a few sagging galleries. Without thinking, she reached for the doorknob and started to twist it, then cried out at the pain in her wrist.

Mary opened the door and stepped through it. Sorscha followed while Lizzie wrapped her hand around her injured wrist, despairing to wonder how she would defend herself without the use of her right hand. She twirled swiftly in a swirl of skirts and bumped the door shut with her hip.

'We need help!' Sorscha cried, her girlish voice gone shrill with fear as she strode into the dark, smoky tap-room, but Lizzie's heart sank as her gaze swept the pub.

There was no crowd to blend into, no one to ask for help but a few doddering old drunks nursing tankards of ale, smoking pipes stuffed with cheap tobacco, and bickering over their chess game. A moldering stag head stared out from the wall; a tainted mirror caught the feeble illumination of a rusty lantern here and there.

The place smelled of greasy pork loin and old tallow.

Behind the bar, an unkempt, potbellied man – the landlord, she presumed – stood drying beer mugs with a rag, sleeves rolled up over his beefy forearms.

'We're closed,' he grumbled.

'The door was open!' Sorscha protested.

'Lock's broken.' He sent them a suspicious look. 'What do ye want?'

Lizzie took an urgent step forward, her heart pounding. 'I'm afraid it's a bit of an emergency. There are men chasing us—'

'They're here,' Mary breathed as the clamor of hoofbeats and heavy wheels grinded into the drive.

'Is there a back exit?' Lizzie demanded of the landlord in a shaky voice, while the old drunks studied them in dim curiosity.

'Why do ye want to know?' he challenged, tossing his rag down on the bar.

Outside, the sound of crisp footfalls marched across the graveled yard. 'Go around the back,' she heard Carstairs order coldly. 'Johnny, you're with me.'

'What the 'ell is going on?' the landlord demanded, but Lizzie ignored him.

'Come.' She grasped Sorscha's wrist with her good hand and pulled her toward the rickety wooden stairs, Mary a step behind them. 'We've got to hide. Now.'

* * *

Johnny kicked open the door and burst in with his specially made blunderbuss trained on the taproom. 'Nobody move!'

Behind him, Carstairs slipped in, both pistols aimed at the ragtag band of startled pensioners gathered around the chessboard.

'God, what a hellhole,' the earl muttered under his breath. His glance darted to the meaty barkeep, who probably kept a musket behind the bar. 'Hands up, unless you want to die!' He strode toward him and confiscated the surprisingly good fowling piece the man had indeed tried to reach for.

Probably used for poaching on the heath, he thought. 'Don't try anything,' he warned the man in an icy tone. He carried the musket over toward Johnny and leaned it by the door behind him. 'This might come in handy.'

'Thanks,' the lad murmured, his fierce stare fixed on his hostages.

'I ain't seen one of those old pieces since the Battle o' Copenhagen,' one of the tipsy old veterans snorted, squinting at the blunderbuss.

'Never fear, old timer, this one's a new model. I had it specially designed,' Johnny warned through gritted teeth, keeping his back to the door. 'The scatter-shot's radius can put you all in your coffins. Keep your hands where I can see them.'

'Where are the women who came in here just a moment ago?' Carstairs demanded.

No one answered.

'Damn you, we saw them come in here. If you want to hide them, it will cost you your miserable lives. You!' Striding over to the bar, he aimed his pistol between the landlord's eyes. 'Where are they?'

Hands above his head as ordered, the landlord pointed a stubby finger toward the stairs. Satisfied that his companion had everything under control in the taproom, Carstairs glided stealthily up the stairs, taking them two at a time.

He came up to a dingy corridor with wavy plaster and a threadbare carpet runner. A row of lanterns hanging at intervals from the beamed ceiling threw off a murky twilight. His gun at the ready, Carstairs crept down the hallway between the closed doors of some twenty guest rooms. By the sound of it, most of them were empty, though from one room he passed, he heard some woman nagging a man named Mortimer to fold his clothes.

Damn it, those two bitches could be anywhere.

Detecting footsteps just ahead where the hall ended, he whipped around the corner, his pistol outstretched in his hand.

'It's me,' Quint grunted.

Carstairs lowered his gun. 'I see you found the back door.'

'Just down the steps.'

'Ah, what a relief I don't have to do everything myself this time,' he drawled in biting humor. 'Did you see them?'

'No. I checked the cloakroom at the bottom of the stairs. Kitchen, too, but saw not hide nor hair of them.'

'Good,' Carstairs purred. 'That means they're here somewhere. Right . . . under our noses.'

Slam! The whole wall shook as their pursuers threw open the door of another empty guest room somewhere down the hallway. The three women huddled together in a pool of moonlight inside one of the musty guest chambers.

'Oh, Miss Carlisle!' the earl's voice sang out. 'Come out, come out, wherever you are!'

'I'm scared,' Sorscha breathed.

Mary wrapped her arms around the girl and kissed her head. 'We'll keep you safe, sweeting.'

'Did you hear what he said? The back door is just down the stairs,' Lizzie whispered. 'We can make it with any luck.'

'No. We'll never reach it without them seeing us.'

'Ginny!' Quint called again in that queer, mournful howl that sounded like an animal calling for its dead mate.

'Why does he keep calling for Ginny?' Sorscha whispered angrily. 'It's all a mistake! We've got to tell them they have the wrong person!'

Lizzie and Mary exchanged a grim look. 'Sorscha, go look out the window over there and see if the coast is clear. Make no noise.'

'Yes, Mama.'

When the girl tiptoed off across the dark guestroom, feeling her way around the furniture, Mary turned to Lizzie.

'I'll hold them off,' she said in a low voice. 'You and Sorscha still have a chance of escaping if I distract them.'

'How?'

'I'll surrender.'

'You mustn't,' Lizzie whispered, paling. 'They'll kill you.'

'Quint won't let Carstairs harm me. The same cannot be said for the two of you. Besides, I've got this.' Mary furtively showed her the small lady's pistol she had brought in addition to the rifle that she had been forced to abandon near Carstairs's town house. Moonlight glimmered along its sleek muzzle, but Mary quickly slipped the weapon into the pocket of her voluminous black cape before Sorscha returned.

Lizzie stared hard at the woman as it dawned on her that Mary meant to kill Quint.

'Don't look so surprised, my dear.' A trace of a cold, cynical smile curved her red lips behind the black lace of her veil. 'It's not as though I happened by Carstairs's house by accident.'

'Whatever your reasons, I'm glad you did,' she murmured. 'Thank you, Mary. I owe you my life. It seems Sorscha does, too. You were there that night. You managed to save her from the fire.'

'She was just a little girl,' she whispered, nodding. 'Her mother begged me to take her.'

'Lady Strathmore was still alive?'

Mary nodded. 'She would not leave her husband, and he was hurt too badly to escape the building as it burned.'

Lizzie stared at her, trying to absorb it all. Then she glanced at the curly-headed innocent silhouetted in the window, and looked at Mary once more. 'Devlin is a good man, Mary. He will help me to protect her.'

'Not if Torquil got to him first. I'm sorry, but I know how these men work. Even if Devlin survived, the others will hunt him down. They won't stop until they've caught him – or you – or Sorscha. You all know too much about their crime. That is why you must go on to Ireland.'

Absorbing Mary's dire words, Lizzie wrestled with herself. How could she possibly leave Devlin behind, knowing that he was in mortal danger? But as Sorscha rejoined them and whispered the all clear, Lizzie gazed at the girl and realized Mary was right. She had to trust that her wild adventurer could take care of himself.

The sheltered schoolgirl could not.

As Mary quickly explained their plan, alarm filled Sorscha's big blue eyes. 'But what about you, Mama?'

Mary pulled her close and kissed her forehead. 'I will see you back in Ireland when I can.'

As they hugged, Lizzie couldn't help but wonder if it was a lie. She rather doubted Quint would ever let his beloved Ginny elude him again.

Reluctantly, Mary released the girl and cupped her cherubic cheeks between her hands. 'Be brave, darlin'. You must trust me now and go with Miss Carlisle. 'Tis the only way.'

'Yes, Mama,' she said woefully.

'Are you sure about this?' Lizzie asked Mary evenly.

She nodded, then Lizzie squared her shoulders, and reached for her pupil's hand.

'Come on, Sorscha, we haven't much time.'

Sorscha held her adopted mother in an imploring stare, but went along trustingly with Lizzie. All three of them walked to the door.

Mary put her ear to it and listened. 'I'll go out first.'

Lizzie's nod was grim but resolute. 'We'll slip down the back stairs.'

Sorscha gripped her hand harder.

Mary opened the door and inched it wider soundlessly.

Around the corner, they could hear Quint and Carstairs opening and closing doors all down the corridor, searching every room for them.

Lizzie led Sorscha out; they stole along the side of the wall. The back stairs were only a few yards away.

Sorscha cast a frantic look back over her shoulder as Mary walked slowly toward the corner of the adjoining hallway to give herself up to her former lover and, Lizzie knew, to kill him with her pistol if she could. Her black lace veil drifted phantom-like behind her, her slender shoulders squared.

Turning away, Lizzie tugged Sorscha forward. As soundlessly as possible, they hurried down the narrow, turning steps.

Chapter Twenty-two

Mary stepped around the corner and faced the creatures of her nightmare squarely. 'Quentin!' Her voice rang out down the hallway, halting both men in their tracks.

Her former lover stopped, turned to her with a look of reverence settling over his square, cruel face.

'Ginny,' he whispered. 'Is it really you?'

'Yes, Quentin. It's me.'

'Then it's true. You're alive. After all this time . . .'

'Alive, yes. But changed.'

'Still a whore, I wager.' Carstairs ignored Quint's warning glance. 'Where is Miss Carlisle?'

Mary said nothing.

Carstairs aimed his gun at her. 'Speak, whore. Where is Strathmore's bit o' muslin?'

Quint reached over and pressed Carstairs's arm down, forcing him with a dark look to lower his weapon. Carstairs gave him a defiant stare, then left them alone with an arrogant huff and continued searching the guest rooms.

'It's all right, Ginny. I won't let him hurt you. I can't believe it. This is a miracle.' Quint took a step closer.

She fingered the gun in her pocket, but she did not intend to kill him until he understood the enormity of his crime. Then he would die.

Staring at her with a glazed look of loss and nostalgia in his eyes, he shook his head. 'Oh, Ginny, why did you leave me?' he whispered. 'We've wasted so much time – but now all that's in the past. Now we can be together. Come back to me. Say you will.'

'But Quentin, you would not want me now.'

'Why not?' he asked with a chiding smile, as if the mere suggestion was absurd.

'Because.' Releasing the pistol, she slid her hand out of her pocket. It was not merely that she wanted to buy time so Miss Carlisle could get Sorscha out. No, she wanted him, both of them, to see what they had done to her. 'As I've told you, I've changed.' She grasped the ends of her black lace veil between her gloved fingertips and slowly, ever so slowly, lifted it away.

His eyes widened as his stare took in the burn scars that had disfigured the left side of her once-flawless face.

'Yes, my love.' Her whisper dripped with venomous reproach as he stared, ashen-faced. 'Behold what you did to me.'

'Oh, God,' he choked out.

Even Carstairs looked unsettled as he stared at her in shock. She sneered faintly at the revulsion she read in their eyes.

'Oh, Ginny,' Quint groaned. 'You never should have run. This need never have happened. Your beautiful face.'

'An improvement, if you ask me.' Quickly regaining his ruthless smirk, Carstairs turned away, but his voice was taut. 'Come on, Quint. We don't have time for this sentimental journey. If we don't find Miss Carlisle and get the hell out of here, we hang. Understand?' Resuming his search, he threw open another door, whereupon a woman let out a piercing scream.

Mary looked over in surprise as Carstairs jumped back.

'What is the meaning of this?' bellowed a male voice from inside the room.

'Mortimer, do something!' the woman shrieked.

'Shut that door, you jackanapes!' A large mustachioed man in footed long drawers appeared in the doorway. Then he saw Carstairs's gun and sobered. 'Put that thing down before you hurt yourself, sirrah.'

Quickly lowering her veil again before the strangers chanced to view her scars, Mary's eyes widened at the fellow's air of self-assurance. *Oh, no*, she thought. *Not another well-meaning Good Samaritan.*

'I'd do as he says if I were you!' The man's wife, appeared behind him in the doorway in a dressing gown and nightcap. 'My Morty was at Waterloo!'

'Ah, a military man,' Carstairs drawled. 'Good, then you're used to taking orders. Now, get back in your room before I blow your damn head off.'

'Why, you little coxcomb! I'll crush you!' Mortimer lunged for Carstairs's pistol, driving the earl's hand upward to point the gun at the ceiling.

Carstairs cursed.

Quint rushed to his aid as they grappled. The screaming wife flapped her arms in the doorway.

For a second, Mary looked on in vexed astonishment, unable to get a clean shot at her former lover, now that two innocent bystanders were absurdly caught in the fray. Suddenly realizing that in the hubbub, she could escape and rejoin the others, she spun around and ran, rushing down the hallway and toward the back stairs.

'Ginny!' Quint roared.

With Mortimer crushing his fingers around the gun, Carstairs lost control of the weapon just then.

The gun went off, the bullet slamming harmlessly into the ceiling.

Lizzie and Sorscha were in the clear. A moment ago, they had found the back door, slipped out of the building, and were now running through the weed-choked kitchen garden, intent on stealing Carstairs's fine carriage to make their getaway.

'My head feels so strange,' Sorscha had just been saying. 'Like right before you swoon.'

'It's just nerves.'

'No, I feel as though all this has happened before. I can't explain it—'

Suddenly, the crisp report of the gunshot ripped through the indigo night, cutting off her words. They both gasped and jerked to a halt, whirling around to stare back at the inn. Lizzie paled. *Mary must have made her kill.* But Sorscha, who knew nothing of her foster mother's pistol, immediately assumed the worst.

'Mama!' she burst out, her young face flooding with horror.

Before Lizzie could even react, Sorscha wrenched her hand free and bolted back toward the inn.

'Sorscha, don't!'

The chit was as stubborn as her brother. In a few wild strides, the girl reached the door and flung inside, vanishing into the blackness.

'Oh, God.' Lizzie raced after her, a shadow of unease darkening her heart like the shifting clouds that now veiled the moon. She shook her head and took off running, following Sorscha back into the place. She had no choice.

Dev followed the sound of the distant gunshot.

The moon went dark, swallowed by a sinuous cloud-dragon, but he did not slow his pace, thundering down the road, gathering power and rage every second, rising to hit like the hammer of a hurricane.

With burning eyes, he stared down the road like a rider of the Apocalypse or some worse fiend loosed from the deepest circle of Hell; they shot through the darkness heedlessly, the dark steed snorting brimstone as his mighty hooves pounded the earth. At this speed, one misstep would kill them both, but it mattered not.

His heart was already dead.

The fire in his soul would lay waste to everything in its path. His mind was fevered, yet numb as ice, unable to digest the image of his beloved lying dead – all his fault. The brief moment of beauty she had shown him had winked out like a candle, the darkness revealing his life to him for what it was – a grotesque, like the frozen stone scream of church gargoyles. He had killed his family, killed his love, and rather feared he had just lost his mind.

It didn't matter.

Clipped free now from the last fragile strand of his humanity, he stared into blackness with the eyes of a demon, the bloodlust of a stalking cougar. His rage was primitive, all consuming. Memories spiraled through his head in time with Star's pounding hoofbeats, war drums beating in his veins as he recalled the fierce Mohawk warriors working themselves into a frenzy before battle. He felt their horrible ecstasy now. *Kill.* Yes, he would kill Quint, Carstairs, take their scalps. There was no fear of death in him now nor any care for consequences. He was filled with the blood-curdling roar of the Bengal tiger, the howl of the wolf, the bellow of the Nile croc; he would tear his prey to pieces.

He slowed his horse to a walk when he came upon the overturned carriage just past the bridge. There was no one there, and the ripped timbers at the front of the chassis informed him the horses had bolted, as well.

He wondered who it belonged to, what had happened. But it didn't really matter. Torquil Staines had told him all he needed to know.

Lizzie was dead.

He swept the darkened landscape with a baleful glance, the moon emerging again from the belly of the beast to illume the smear of blood on Dev's cheek – not his own. His careful glance around revealed a few dim lights glowing amid the trees.

A building.

As the wind teased through the stand of pines and oak trees, he caught sight of Carstairs's racing drag parked outside. His eyes narrowed. The drumming in his veins deepened.

He eased Star off the gravel and onto soft turf to muffle their approach. Stopping amid the trees' cover, he knotted the leather reins so they would not trip the horse if he moved around or bolted; his hands were tacky with dried blood. Sliding down off his horse's bare back, he left the looped reins draped over Star's withers and stalked toward the building, silently unsheathing his big jungle knife.

It proved to be a dejected little coaching inn. There were lights in the high, dirty windows of the first floor, where the taproom was usually located. He glanced around, considering his options. Before approaching the place, he sneaked over to Carstairs's vehicle and freed the earl's horses from their harness. He shooed the quartet of brown mares in the direction of the trees; turf and pine needles muted their skittish hoofbeats. Star whickered to the frightened mares; then the lot of them could be heard cantering off across the road and into the alfalfa field across the way.

Dev glanced back at the building. Now, whatever happened, the bastards could not escape him. As far as he was concerned, none of them were getting out of here alive.

A nightbird gave a lonely warble as Dev crept up to the

building. His sense of danger mounted, the hairs on the back of his neck prickling.

He heard the sound of people fighting somewhere up on the second floor, a shrill woman's voice shrieking, 'Mortimer! Mortimer!'

Mortimer? What the hell?

Holding his knife between his teeth for a moment, Dev swung up onto the balustrade of the first gallery and hung around the corner, peering into the taproom. Through the filth and cobwebs that coated the window, he saw Johnny holding the occupants at bay with a blunderbuss. He saw neither Carstairs nor Quint, but they were here somewhere.

He would have to rely on stealth to retain the advantage of surprise, he saw. Subdue Johnny as quietly as possible and keep the old men in the pub from making a ruckus.

Jumping back down silently to the ground, he caught his knife deftly in his hand, landing with pantherlike agility. Stealing over to the door, he turned the knob soundlessly, easing the hammer back inch by inch.

With a furtive speed that would have made his old Cherokee shaman friend, Yellow Feather, smile, he slipped inside and had his knife pressed to Johnny-boy's throat before the man even realized he was there.

'Put the gun down,' he ordered in a deadened voice.

Johnny froze, eyeballing his big curved knife. Without warning, he ducked to the side and struck Dev in the chin with the sturdy butt of the blunderbuss.

Dev's head snapped back, but he recovered at once and launched at Johnny, more than ready for a brawl.

'Mortimer, behind you!'

'Doesn't she ever shut up?' Quint asked in exasperation.

'Not really,' the mustachioed husband confided; then Quint

managed to pull Mortimer off Carstairs and threw him back into his room, pushing his wife with him. 'Both of you stay in there unless you want to die!'

Quint slammed the door to their room and wedged it shut with a side chair that sat next to a console table in the hallway.

'Much obliged, old boy.' Panting, Carstairs got to his feet and shook the plaster dust out of his hair. It had rained down on him when the bullet had hit the ceiling. A speck had gotten into his eye, burning slightly, but he blinked it away.

'Not convinced we ought to let those bleeders live. They've seen our faces. So did those men in the tavern,' Quint added.

'A handful of old drunks? Forget them,' Carstairs muttered. 'They're no threat to us. We'll come back for "Mortimer" and his wife. First we've got to find Dev's wench.' Carstairs suddenly noticed Quint staring down the empty hallway.

'Ginny!' The baron whirled to him. 'She's gone!'

'Damn it,' Carstairs cursed, reloading his pistol as he followed Quint, who ran ahead of him down the hallway, chasing his Irish whore. The wily bitch had seized Mortimer's distraction to flee – and they still hadn't found Miss Carlisle.

'Ginny!' With heavy footfalls, Quint pounded down the hallway and ducked around the corner. 'Ginny, wait!' He saw her ahead, racing toward the back stairs in a billow of black lace, but she nearly stumbled when someone suddenly came racing up the stairs, nearly colliding with her.

'Mama, you're all right!' cried a high-pitched voice.

Quint stopped, his chest heaving from his sprint, as a beautiful little girl with big blue eyes and dark curls rushed toward Ginny.

'Sorscha, no!' Ginny shrieked. 'Get out of here!'

'Ginny?' Quint queried, his voice turning strange.

Quint heard Carstairs walking up cautiously behind him. 'Well, well, who have we here?' the earl murmured.

Ginny whirled around, hiding the child behind her. 'Leave her alone. She has nothing to do with this. Go, Sorscha. Now!'

The girl clung to her. 'I won't leave you, Mama! You can't make me.'

Quint stared at the child, his eyes glazing over. His memory swam. That last night they'd had together . . .

'Is she – mine?' he choked out, barely able to find his voice.

'Yes,' Ginny answered in a shaky voice. 'Yes, Quint. She's yours. Don't let Carstairs hurt her.'

Quint didn't seem to hear. Staring at the little girl, the life he had not chosen flashed before his eyes. 'Ginny, she's so beautiful.'

At his words, the girl made a small sound of anger and hid her face against Ginny's womanly form.

'Let me see you, sweeting. She's shy? What is your name?' The gentleness in Quint's voice came out foreign, jerky.

Ginny was insistent. 'Let her go, Quentin. I will come with you, I swear. Just let Sorscha go.'

He looked at her in hurt. 'Do you think I would harm my own child? Come here, little one. I am your papa.'

'The brat's not yours, Quint.'

'What?' He glanced over in confusion at Carstairs, who had spoken harshly.

'Look at her. Look closely.' The way Carstairs studied the girl sent a chill of foreboding down Quint's spine.

'W-what do you mean?' he asked uncertainly.

'It's just another of Ginny's desperate tricks. If she had borne you a child, it would be twelve years old. This girl looks to be about sixteen.' Then Carstairs paused, taking a few slow steps toward the pair. 'I know this child. I've heard her screaming in my head for twelve long years.'

Sorscha suddenly lifted her head from the woman's shoulder,

her blue eyes locking with the earl's with a sudden flare of recognition. 'You.'

Quint looked at him, paling. 'You don't mean—'

'The Strathmore brat. Ginny must have rescued her from the fire and raised her all these years. Sorry, Lady Sarah. Nothing personal,' he said, bringing up his pistol. 'Yet again it is merely my unhappy duty to get rid of the evidence.'

'No!' Quint saw Ginny reach for something in her pocket, knocking the girl behind her body: His reaction was too slow.

Boom!

'Mama!' The girl's scream pierced the air, but Quint saw no blood on her clothing.

Ginny fell.

Quint stared, immobile, too stunned to breathe even as Miss Carlisle came rushing up the steps.

From the corner of his eye, he saw Carstairs calmly starting to reload.

The roar that came out of Quint started as a growl somewhere down in his solar plexus. The next thing he knew, he was seizing Carstairs, slamming him with all his might against the wall so that the plaster dented in and Carstairs grimaced with pain.

'Now, Quint—'

'*I'll kill you!*'

'I was aiming for the girl! She jumped in the way! Look, there's Miss Carlisle!' Carstairs pointed down the hallway, but Quint shook his head, his eyes narrowed in disgust. Did Carstairs think him such a beef-brained oaf that he would fall for a schoolyard trick?

'I am so *sick* of you!' Quint hauled back his mighty fist and smashed Carstairs's perfect nose, breaking it with one blow. God, he'd been wanting to do that for years!

* * *

Lizzie had run inside mere seconds behind Sorscha, but had stopped at the landing where the back stairs turned when she had heard Mary's quick-thinking attempt in the corridor above, trying to pass Sorscha off as Quint's daughter in order to buy the girl's safety. She had stayed hidden, knowing that if she showed herself, all hell would break loose and Mary's ploy would fail.

Now that Quint and Carstairs were turning on each other, however, she rushed into the corridor. Her face went ashen as she took in the sight of her fallen ally and hysterical charge.

Lizzie crouched down beside Mary, overwhelmed and fighting wild panic at the blood seeping out of the woman's side. She swallowed hard, but her voice came out shakily. 'I'm so sorry, Mary. She heard the shot and got away from me.'

Mary managed a weak shake of her head. 'It's all right. Just – keep her safe. Go – now, I beg you. Take this.' Furtively, Mary pressed her pistol into Lizzie's hands. 'I never got to – use it. The bullet is still in it.'

Forgetting her sprained wrist again, Lizzie automatically took it in her right hand, then winced. *Wonderful*, she thought in frustration. Unlike her sporting friend, Lady Jacinda, Lizzie had never fired a gun in her life, and now when her life depended on it, she would have to do so using her left hand.

She glanced down the hallway at Carstairs trying to ward off Quint's next titanic punch, then rose. 'Come, Sorscha. Any minute now, they'll be done with each other and they'll come after us.'

'Mama, it's all my fault. I'm so sorry! Why couldn't I listen?'

'It's all right, Sorscha,' Mary forced out with agonized effort, cupping her face. 'I love you, darlin' – and you should know that what Lord Carstairs said is true. There is – noble blood in your veins. I should have told you . . . years ago. Forgive me. That's why I brought you to London. To restore you to your proper place in the world.'

'I don't care about that. I just care about you! Mama, don't leave me!'

'Miss Carlisle,' Mary said, sending her an imploring look heavy with pain.

Lizzie nodded and gathered up the weeping teenager. 'Sorscha, come now!'

As Quint split Carstairs's cheek open with his sledge-hammer fist, Lizzie struggled to drag Sorscha away though the girl's grief nigh broke her heart.

'No!' Sorscha wailed. 'I want to stay with her!'

'You'll die! Listen to me!' Lizzie gripped her shoulders and shook her slightly, staring hard into Sorscha's eyes. 'She fell to save you. If they get you, her sacrifice will have been in vain. Is that what you want?'

Sorscha absorbed this, her chin trembling, face red from crying. Forcing back her sobs, she took one last, longing gaze at Mary, who lay still now in a pool of blood and black silk. With a shattered look, she allowed Lizzie to pull her away once more.

Mary smiled with faint satisfaction when Quint's famed right hook knocked Carstairs out cold. The brute had finally come in use for something, after all.

He left the unconscious earl in a most unfashionably disheveled heap on the floor and ran to her.

She held up a feeble hand to stop him from going after the other two. 'Stay with me,' she whispered. 'Quentin, hold me.'

He fell to his knees beside her, staring at her in misery. 'Oh, my love, I've ruined you,' he groaned, and gathered her tenderly into his arms. 'Ginny.'

She shuddered with the pain of her wound, feeling consciousness slipping away from her. He was kissing her hair, running his thick, tough fingers down her scarred cheek. She was too weak to turn away from his touch.

'Forgive me, my darling. Can you ever forgive me?'

'Quentin, my love,' she murmured just before she blacked out, 'go to hell.'

Johnny had proved surprisingly truculent, but Dev subdued him at about the same moment the second shot had gone off somewhere upstairs. He had heard a girlish scream and thought it must be some guest of the hotel, but he had no doubt that Quint and Carstairs were the cause.

As he pinned Johnny to the grimy flagstones of the pub, a knee in his back, the old fellows in the tavern hurried over with some sturdy hempen twine. They bound Johnny's hands behind his back while the landlord shoved his dirty dishrag into Johnny's mouth to keep him from calling out for his accomplices.

Gesturing at the wide-eyed old fellows in the pub for silence, his finger over his lips, Dev placed the fowling-piece in the landlord's hands. 'If he moves, shoot him,' he ordered in a low tone.

'Let them mind 'im. I'll get them other ones with you,' the big man grunted, nodding toward the stairs.

Dev shook his head with cold murder in his eyes. 'They're mine.'

Satisfied that everything in the taproom was in order, he glided up the stairs as soft as a shadow, taking them two at a time. As he neared the top of the stairs, he noticed that the ruckus with Mortimer had ended.

Sheathing his knife in favor of his pistol, he listened carefully, his back to the wall of the stairwell. Hearing nothing, he emerged from the shadows, pivoting into the upper hallway with the gun cocked and level in his grasp.

The corridor was empty, the dirty lanterns shining dully. Scanning the long row of guest rooms as he moved forward, step by slow, wary step, he wondered about the chair stuck under one doorknob, but passed the chamber for now.

Progressing in this manner, he came to the corner of the hallway. An odd sound reached his ears, a low, mournful crooning. His heartbeat quickened. Gathering himself, he flashed around the corner, legs planted wide in target-shooting stance, and beheld a very strange sight.

He scanned the hallway, narrowing his eyes in skeptical confusion. Carstairs sprawled in a heap against the baseboards, dead or perhaps only unconscious. His back to Dev, Quint was crouched down cradling the limp, black-clad body of a woman in his arms, rocking her slightly.

Ginny Highgate, Dev presumed. He recognized her widow's weeds as those of the woman who had been following him weeks ago. As he sized up the situation, he did not stop to wonder why she had been so interested in watching him; he merely noted in a bitter, final irony that the answers he had chased for so long had just expired with her last breath.

'Wake up, Ginny. Stay with me. Oh, Ginny, we can be together now, like we once were,' Quint whispered, but it was no use.

Her eyes fluttered closed, and he could not be certain whether she still lived or not. Resting her gently on the floor, he pressed his shaking fingertips to her throat, desperately feeling for the pulse.

His guilt was too damning. In this awful moment, there was no way to escape the truth. He had believed Carstairs's lie all those years ago when he should have believed Ginny. She had protested her innocence, denying Carstairs's allegation that she had cheated on Quint, trying to seduce his rich, handsome friend. Why should he not have believed it? Quint knew he was no prize. Carstairs was richer than he, smarter than he, and had always possessed a suave glamour that Quint could never hope to achieve. Carstairs said he had found her waiting for him in his bed . . . all those years ago. Before Quint the country bumpkin finally comprehended that the urbane Carstairs had no real interest in women.

The damage had already been done, and Quint did not know how he had lived with it all these awful, empty years. He had raped the only woman he had ever loved, had shot an innocent, unarmed man in his wrath, and had helped to burn alive a building full of people – all for a lie. If he were half the man Dev's father had been, the stranger he had slain in a moment's fit of rage, he would have turned himself in, or at the very least, snuffed himself out years ago.

Instead, with the heart rotting inside him, Quint had done his best to carry his crime in secret, living hard and fast, surrounding himself with rowdy mates, drinking and whoring like a sailor, cheerfully battering one opponent after another at the boxing studio, always looking for something innocent to ease his pain because, down deep, he knew he was one of the damned. For more than a decade, he had lived on the edge, half-wishing for death.

He did not know how near it was now.

Dev had a clean shot, but though his stare bored into Quint's broad back, he lowered his pistol. *Afraid not, old boy. You're not getting off so easily*. He craved more satisfaction of the man than one fleeting squeeze of the trigger could provide. Besides, he had never shot a man in the back in his life and did not intend to lower himself by doing so now.

With brooding hatred flickering in his eyes, Dev holstered his gun and unsheathed his knife, then alerted Quint of his presence by striking the wall with his blade.

Quint tensed, jarred by the sound. Then a low, deadly voice spoke from a few yards behind him: 'You killed my father. It was you. Wasn't it.'

Strathmore. Holding very still, Quint exhaled slowly. It seemed the time had come. Suicide by Strathmore. The viscount was sure to be obliging.

Quint's fighting anger came easily. One look at Ginny lying motionless was all it took to make his eyes flare with dangerous wrath.

'Get up,' Strathmore ordered.

Quint rose stiffly to his feet. 'You bested Torquil?' he asked, turning around.

'Gutted him, actually,' the viscount said, his cheek smeared with Torquil's blood. 'Just as I shall do to you.'

'I don't advise trying it, old boy.' Quint flexed his fists, cracking his knuckles in warning. 'I've beaten you before.'

'Quentin, you fool.' Dev's eyes burned strangely, ice reflecting fire. 'I *let* you win.'

Quint pulled out his dagger. The man gave him no other choice. 'I'm sorry about your father. He should have known better than to insert himself into the midst of a lover's quarrel.'

'Am I supposed to accept your apology?'

'No,' Quint answered after a moment.

Dev's glance flicked to Ginny lying behind him on the floor. 'You couldn't be happy till you had finished the job, eh?'

'I didn't shoot her. Carstairs did.' Quint shook his head, bringing his knife up in fighting stance. 'I'm warning you, Strathmore, keep your distance. Carstairs has slain the only woman I've ever loved. I've got nothing left to lose.'

'That makes two of us,' he snarled, but as they sized each other up, a cold smile twisted Strathmore's mouth. 'Never fear, Quint. I shall soon put you out of your misery.'

'Allow me to return the favor.'

As their vicious duel exploded, both men knew it was a fight to the death. Both welcomed it.

* * *

The rumble and shake of the earth beneath him roused Carstairs from his stupor. At first, he could not feel his face; then he felt it throbbing. Lifting his chin, he had to struggle to see through his left eye, which was swelling shut. He must look a fright.

The last thing he remembered was Quint's fist coming at him like a cannonball, but somehow, in the interim, Strathmore had arrived. He wondered if Johnny was still alive downstairs, but could not afford to care. His mind cleared with the self-preserving instinct that had never failed him; he shook his head to settle his blurred vision and assessed his situation.

Ginny was dead, he saw. *Good. One less thing to worry about.* Quint would take care of Strathmore – or Strathmore would take care of Quint. It scarcely mattered which. They were so well matched that Carstairs deemed he could safely count on at least one of them killing the other. When the surviving warrior lay wounded, he would simply finish him off with a bullet.

But the Strathmore child had gotten away, and so had Miss Carlisle. He sobered. The former was an eyewitness to the night of the fire, while the latter had nearly become his murder victim earlier tonight, so it was only prudent that he find the pair and silence them forever.

His pistol still nestled snugly in its holster, but he had spent the shot on Ginny, and now he saw his leather ammunition case had flown several feet down the hallway when Quint had attacked him.

He had to retrieve it, but in his current groggy state, he had no desire to flag the attention of the battling titans above him. He glanced up at them, slicing and slashing at each other, feral snarls on their faces.

Barbarians.

They were too busy tearing each other apart to pay him any

mind. Elbow-crawling on his belly, Carstairs inched toward the leather case.

He's here. Lizzie froze on her way out the back door when she heard Devlin's dark cry of rage.

'Come, Miss Carlisle!' Sorscha urged. 'We must hurry!'

She could not answer, turning to gape in amazement at the stairwell they had just left. *He beat Torquil!*

Somehow Devlin had tracked them here.

'Come on!'

'One moment, Sorscha,' she breathed. For all her supposed maturity, Lizzie proved no better able to ignore her emotions than Sorscha had, physically incapable of leaving her love until she had had one glimpse of him to assure herself he was not hurt. His nearness infused her with fresh courage.

When Sorscha took her arm, Lizzie brushed her off. 'I just want to make sure he's all right. Stay here.'

Ignoring the girl's protest, Lizzie glided back to the steps and silently climbed them as far as the small, square landing where the staircase turned. She stared in dread toward the upper hallway, where two huge, grappling shadows twisted and thrashed, one with a long, flying mane of thick hair. They stabbed at each other with dizzying speed, warding off each other's blows with blinding parries, the silhouettes of their knives sweeping at each other in deadly arcs.

She gasped when she saw Quint cut Dev's side, but her lover's answer was the blackest laugh she'd ever heard, all bitter mocking despair.

He fell back against the wall, and for a second, she could see him from her vantage point. One glance told her that something was terribly wrong.

'Is that the best you can do, old boy?'

'Oh, you want to die?' came Quint's labored challenge.

'Carstairs took my love away as well, Quint. I've got nothing left to live for now. Fight harder!' Devlin attacked again, launching out of her line of vision.

Lizzie paled; understanding came in an appalling flash. *He thinks I'm dead.* That explained why he fought so savagely now.

Good God, he would not stop till he got himself killed. Dread gripped her. She knew she must not distract his concentration, but she could not let that happen. She had to show herself so he could see she was alive – stop him from throwing his life away in the fury of despair. Her face hardened.

She knew she was a target, but she still had Mary's gun with which to defend herself. Creeping farther up the stairs, Lizzie kept her shoulder to the wall, the pistol at the ready in her left hand if she should need it.

Inching up over the stairs, she could now see them down the hallway. She felt almost sorry for Quint. The crude baron was as strong as an ox and as big as one, too. He had three inches on Dev and at least twenty pounds, but he had surely never before encountered anything like Devil Strathmore.

She did not know what to make of him herself, but she could not look away. His face looked primal, streaked with blood; his hellish eyes glowed like lava. He was coated in sweat, muscles straining as he drove Quint back before his onslaught. If he felt the gash on his right side, he gave no sign; she stared, aghast, at the crimson bloom where his white shirt clung to the cut. But even more than the wound on his body, Lizzie ached for the suffering inside him.

The stark intensity on his face was at odds with the tortured fury in his eyes; oh, he was somewhere else, somewhere far away, lost and wandering through the desolate badlands of his own scorched soul.

She knew he had never needed her as he did now. How much

time remained for her to call him back softly from the edge of destruction, she did not know, yet she dared not speak for fear of breaking his warrior's concentration. The results could be disastrous. Nor could she shoot at Quint with Dev so close; she dared not trust her untested aim. She could do naught but stand by in helpless frustration until he thrust Quint from him and sent the baron crashing across the hallway.

In the brief reprieve, Dev stole half a second to mop the sweat off his brow, lifting his arm with a quick shrug of one shoulder, when suddenly, he felt someone watching him.

He glanced over – and went motionless. Too caught up in the scarlet exaltation of violence to comprehend for a moment what his eyes beheld, he blinked hard, sweat still trickling down, stinging his eyes. His chest heaved.

Lizzie . . .

He forgot his enemy, staring at the vision in confusion. Reality split, the red haze clearing. Could it be? But—

How?

Something very near to a sob choked from him. Torquil Staines had either lied or been mistaken. It scarcely mattered which.

Alive.

Time stopped.

Light streamed into his darkness as he held her beautiful gaze, some superior force, radiant, awesome in its power casting his demons into oblivion. All in an instant, he was redeemed. He stared in stunned worship.

Alive.

Yes. A second chance.

'Sweeting,' Lizzie whispered, her eyes filling with tears.

Dev's eyes misted in answer as he held her stare, his whole body trembling like a horse that had been run too hard and too fast. Nothing else mattered when he saw her standing there, alive and as beautiful as the dawn. The delicate strain of exquisite joy that pierced his heart was as clean and sharp as a needle. It made him light-headed, not quite able to trust his own eyes. He was so transfixed by the sight of her that he failed to notice that Quint had regrouped.

'Devlin, look out!'

The baron charged him.

Instantly, Dev spun and fell back with a sweeping step that arced under the line of Quint's attack and came back at him with deadly precision; they stood frozen, Dev's dagger rooted deep in the baron's gut.

Quint let out a low rough grunt, absorbing his deathblow.

Dev gripped the man's shoulder, withdrawing the red blade.

Quint reeled back against the opposite wall and leaned there, staring at him for a second in astonishment.

'Ginny,' he rasped, then sank down the dingy plaster wall. He slumped to the floor, his glazed stare fixed on the fallen woman, but Dev was already scanning the floor of the hallway.

His chin snapped up, the color suddenly draining from his face. 'Where's Carstairs?'

He had no sooner uttered the words than a flicker of motion in Lizzie's peripheral vision made her turn her head toward an open guest-room door.

She heard Dev scream at Carstairs as the earl sprang through the jagged opening at her, wielding a dagger.

He swung it at her with a malevolent snarl. She threw herself backwards out of range, falling against the opposite wall of the cramped corridor.

In a heartbeat, she lifted the pistol in her left hand and brought it level, pausing only a second to stare coldly into Carstairs's wild eyes.

She fired; time seemed to slow to a drip. Turning her face away from the flying spatter of blood, she was swallowed up by the earl's deafening roar.

When she dared to look a split-second later, Carstairs was peering down at the bullet hole in his chest, just below his left collarbone. She was fairly sure she had just shot him in the heart, but with the eyes of a demon, he lifted his gaze to hers.

'*Run!*' Dev bellowed.

Her eyes widened in disbelief.

Shot through the chest, Carstairs kept coming.

With a scream, Lizzie whirled clear – but it was not an attack.

Carstairs fell stone dead at her feet, his blue eyes staring blindly.

She let out a jagged gasp, then dropped the empty gun and pressed her hand to her mouth, turning away from the corpse.

Devlin stood frozen with amazement, staring from the slain Carstairs to her.

Lizzie swallowed hard, then looked at Devlin. 'I killed him.'

He nodded slowly with an impressed glance at the body. 'Good shot.'

'Oh, Devlin.' She ran to him.

He met her halfway, and in a heartbeat, they were in each other's arms. He squeezed her hard, holding her and gathering her ever closer, like he would never let her go.

'I love you,' she whispered frantically, pulling back to look up into his eyes. 'Are you all right?' She touched his hair, his cheek, touching him everywhere to assure herself he was more or less unscathed.

He nodded wearily, but his exhaustion from his battle was beginning to show. 'I'm fine – now. I love you, too. Oh, sweeting,' he choked out, 'I thought I'd lost you.'

'Never, my love. Never,' she told him. 'Come, sit. You're hurt.'

'It's just a flesh wound. Oh, Lizzie,' he forced out, shaking his head as he captured her face between his hands. 'I think I need you to kiss me right now, very hard.'

'Gladly,' she whispered, a smile spreading over her face.

He lowered his head and claimed her mouth in needy hunger. She gave him a deep kiss replete with all the tenderness and passion that burned in her soul for this man.

After their kiss, he hugged her again, cupping her head to his chest. She nestled there for a moment with a sigh of soul-deep relief, when suddenly, they heard the muffled clatter of a carriage rumbling up to the inn.

'My lord, where are you?' a familiar voice hollered.

Ben.

They exchanged a heartfelt smile that brimmed with warmth. Then Lizzie sobered. 'Devlin, there's someone I want you to meet.'

He tilted his head in curiosity, but allowed her to lead him by the hand down the back stairs where Lizzie had left Sorscha.

Turning at the landing, Lizzie stopped. Her eyes widened. The area was empty!

'She's gone! Sorscha! Sor—'

'In here!' The high-pitched cry sounded thinly, coming, it seemed, from inside the stairwell wall.

What the blazes? 'Where the devil are you? Are you all right?' Lizzie called in confusion.

'Is it safe now?' Sorscha asked from inside the wall.

'Yes! Please come out.'

'Just a moment.'

Devlin sent Lizzie a puzzled glance. 'Who is it?'

'You'll see.'

From inside the wall, they heard the muffled creaking of rusty pulleys.

'Ah, she's in the dumbwaiter!' Lizzie exclaimed, chuckling as she walked down to the small, cupboard-like door at the bottom of the stairwell. 'Clever girl.'

The creaking grew louder as Sorscha worked the pulleys, lowering herself down the dumbwaiter shaft; then it stopped.

Lizzie leaned down and opened the little door. She beckoned to Devlin over an arch smile. He furrowed his brow and bent down low to peer into the cramped dark space.

Dev was slightly confused as he found himself face-to-face with a young girl who sat folded up on the dumbwaiter.

He thought she looked vaguely familiar. Then he remembered he'd seen her at Lizzie's school. Now, as she stared somberly back at him, he noticed that her hair was black and wavy, much like his own. Her eyes were blue with green in them, like his.

'Hullo,' she said to him in a small voice.

Dev turned to Lizzie and stared, not quite able to believe the miraculous whisper of recognition that teased at his memory. 'It can't be.'

'It is,' Lizzie whispered, tears rushing into her eyes.

Dev turned back dazedly to the little girl. He could barely make his voice work. Her name slipped out uncertainly. 'Sarah?'

'I remember now,' she answered, staring at him. 'I remember everything. And I especially remember you. You're Devlin. You're my big brother.'

'Oh, my God, Sarah,' he breathed, reaching in to lift her out of the dumbwaiter.

She came out with her arms wrapped around his neck. They held each other tightly in joyous reunion, both of them crying. Dev reached for Lizzie and pulled her over to them, kissing her head.

She did not know how long they stayed like that, amazed, weeping and laughing at the same time, but it seemed that at least five minutes passed when Ben's voice suddenly called out to Dev from the hallway above.

'Master Dev, are you there? I could use some assistance!'

Devlin lifted his head with tears of joy still shining in his eyes. 'What is it?' he answered.

'Get the medicine box from the coach!' Ben yelled. 'This woman is still alive!'

'Mama?' Sorscha breathed. She released her brother and bolted for the stairs.

Dev ran to fetch the medical supplies, while Lizzie dashed up to the hallway to see if she could help.

Sorscha was already on her knees beside her foster mother while Ben ripped off his cravat, swiftly using it to bandage Mary's wounded side.

Chapter Twenty-three

'Your father intervened to save my life, Lord Strathmore,' Mary said slowly as they sat in the sunshine a few days later. For once she wasn't wearing her veil, simply enjoying the warm caress of the sun on her ravaged face. Now that she felt strong enough to talk with them, she knew the time had come to give the young viscount the answers he had sought.

For his part, Mary's scars did not bother Dev in the slightest. He owed the heroic woman more than he could ever say. He and Lizzie listened intently to her tale while Ben sat on the porch steps nearby, keeping a protective eye on Sarah and her little friend, Daisy.

The girls were playing with – or rather, tormenting – Pasha at the far end of the garden at Dev's house on Portman Street. Aunt Augusta's haughty cat found himself dressed up in doll's clothes and was not a bit pleased about it. The sound of the girls' giggling laughter, however, softened the edges of Dev's sadness at Mary's account of the fire.

'Quint shot your father in the heat of the moment, all for the great crime of trying to talk sense to him. It was Carstairs who dreamed up the blaze as a means to hide their tracks.'

'But why go to such lengths?' Lizzie asked.

'I do not know,' Mary said. 'Frankly, I think Carstairs panicked.'

Dev saw Lizzie shudder and knew she was remembering all too vividly that moment at the ramshackle inn when she had ended Carstairs's life. He reached over to smooth a comforting caress up and down the tense line of her back. It was fortunate that he had visited Bow Street with Suzy and had warned the authorities that Carstairs, Randall, and Staines posed a threat to him and to Lizzie. This had simplified matters greatly when the time came to explain what had happened at the inn. Johnny had been questioned extensively and remained in custody until his fate would be decided by the courts. In the meantime, 'Mortimer' and his wife had proved excellent witnesses, and the influence of Lizzie's beloved Knight family had helped, as well.

As it turned out, one of the twins, Lord Lucien Knight, had connections in the justice offices. He had assisted in sorting the whole thing out with minimal unpleasantness. Still, Dev and Lizzie had faced the investigators together – just as they would face every challenge for the rest of their lives. She sent him a grateful look askance and relaxed slightly under his touch.

Dev turned his attention back to Mary as she continued her tale.

'As I told Miss Carlisle, your mother refused to leave your father's side when he was hit, not even to save herself from the fire. She kept trying to lift him in the hopes of carrying him out, but she could not.'

Lizzie linked her fingers through his, offering silent reassurance.

'I tried to help, but we were not strong enough, and there was no one else to aid us. Most of the other people on the second floor had already fled downstairs to escape the smoke. Your mother begged me to get the child out safely. To save her, I had no choice but to abandon your parents. The building was already going up in flames. I had Sorscha – Sarah – in my arms,' she corrected herself, 'and finally . . . managed to get out.' She sighed. 'We were among the lucky ones.'

He noticed that Mary's gaze wandered to Ben's as she spoke, as it often had since she had first laid eyes on her soft-spoken rescuer. She seemed to recognize a kindred spirit in him. They were a pair of life's battered survivors, Dev mused, stronger in all the places where they had been scourged. But he lifted his eyebrow, quite sure that Ben had just blushed at Mary's glance. She smiled faintly at him and lowered her gaze.

'I took your sister immediately to Ireland,' she continued, 'and we have lived peacefully there ever since. But when I saw in the newspaper that you had returned from your travels, I knew it was time to bring your sister home.'

'You are a woman of extraordinary valor,' Dev told her softly.

'Hear, hear,' Lizzie murmured with a nod.

'How can I ever repay you? You saved my sister's life.'

'And mine,' Lizzie reminded them.

Mary smiled. 'Just let me remain in Sarah's life – and yours.'

Lizzie reached out and squeezed her hand, then smiled. 'I have something for you.' She reached into her pocket and handed Mary a wedding invitation.

The woman's smile widened as she read it. 'Congratulations.'

'You will be there?' Dev prompted with a lordly stare.

Mary slid a sideward glance at Ben. 'If I can find an escort.'

His valet blinked. 'Would you, er, care to take a turn about the garden, ma'am? I'll push your chair for you.'

'That would be lovely,' she answered softly. Still recovering from her wound, she had resorted to a wheeled Bath chair like Lady Strathmore had used. Ben and Dev carried her, chair and all, down the few porch stairs. As Ben took the handles of the chair and assumed the honor of wheeling Mary through the flowery garden Dev sent him a mirthful glance. *I think she likes you*. Ben scowled at him behind Mary's back, but Dev believed he detected another blush in his friend's brown skin.

'Mama, look at the kitty!' Sarah cried, holding up a disgruntled Pasha.

'*Reeer*.'

They all laughed to see the bonnet the girls had tied on the scowling Persian cat's furry head, but Lizzie laughed the loudest.

'Ah, the little terror has finally reaped what he's sown!'

Dev bounded back up onto the porch and, with everyone else preoccupied, drew his bride into the house with a beguiling stare and a gently insistent hold around her wrist.

'You need another kiss, I presume?' she whispered with a vixenish smile, wrapping her arms around him.

'Deeply,' he murmured.

She obliged with unstinting adoration, but for Dev, a kiss – even two, three, four – was not enough. Whenever he held her, they had the most scandalous habit of getting carried away.

The shades were drawn in the parlor, and soon the door was locked. She straddled his lap on her knees as he sat on the sofa, her skirts hitched up about her slender thighs. They moved together in fevered urgency, making love as swiftly as they could before anyone noticed they had been gone together for a while.

There was only one problem. Dev did not want to hurry. The girl made him insatiable. He wanted to savor every lingering moment. Even the rest of their lives might not be enough for him to get his fill of her. He was in love and had never known such happiness before. His tongue quested into the welcoming softness of her mouth; then she gave herself to him again – gave him heaven. He groaned against her neck, his whole body tingling with bliss as she rose and sank again slowly, taking her pleasure of him, riding the rock-hard length of him at her leisure.

The minx had the nerve to tease him, sliding up to flirt with the tip of his cock, letting it skim the threshold of her body, until he panted for her to take it all. She shook her head with a naughty look. He smiled, let out a playful growl, and dragged her down lower, until his straining rod throbbed within her to the hilt.

'Oh, *Devlin.*' She held very still, merely savoring the satisfying fullness of him inside her; then she pressed a fevered kiss to his brow. 'I love you so much.'

'I love you, Lizzie. Never leave me,' he whispered, and gazed up at her, hopelessly smitten.

'Leave you, sir?' She dragged her beautiful gray eyes open and regarded him with an arch look that smoldered slightly. 'Do you take me for a fool?'

'No, my darling,' he purred, 'I take you for my bride.'

'Fair enough,' she whispered, spilling onto the sofa to pull him atop her. 'As long as you *take* me.'

At this, he let out his most devilish laugh and eagerly obeyed.

Epilogue

24 June, 1817

The bells of the old Norman church pealed their joyous carillon down the sleepy River Medway, resounding through Maidstone town, for a local lord was wed today there in the ancient chancel, like all nine Viscounts Strathmore before him. But none of his esteemed forebears, Dev was sure, could have felt as dazzled as he did on this picture-perfect Sunday morning. He tried to fix his attention on the priest, but could not stop looking at his bride.

The celestial radiance of the sun-ray streaming through the great nave window played upon her creamy satin skin. She was following the vicar's every word with that open, earnest stare of hers that made him tremble inwardly with tenderness. The depth of her beauty could have brought him to his knees, so warm, so pure, so gentle and serene.

As if sensing his stare, she chanced a cautious side-ward glance beneath her lashes. Her eyes told him she loved him – even as they warned him to behave. A faint smile curved his mouth as he returned his gaze obediently to the vicar, lifting his chin.

But good behavior could last only so long.

He chose his moment when the priest informed him he might kiss his bride.

Dearest Lizzie offered him her blushing cheek.

Dev smiled broadly, arching one eyebrow.

The congregation burst out with cheering laughter and thunderous applause as he lifted her up onto her toes and kissed her heartily there on the altar – a full two weeks before the deadline specified in Aunt Augusta's will, not that it mattered now. But it had served the wily old dragon's purpose in the end. Dev knew there was no better gift his aunt could have given him. With a prayer of thanks for the old woman and all her eccentric notions, he deepened the kiss, sliding his hands more firmly around his bride's slim waist.

'Oh, Lord, is that really necessary?' Alec huffed, standing next to Lucien in a pew three rows back on the bride's side of the aisle.

Lucien's answer was a chuckle. 'Don't worry, little brother. The right one will come along soon.'

'Want to bet?' Alec muttered with a cynical glance.

'Incorrigible,' Lucien chided under his breath. 'So, you're back to gambling, are you?'

'We all have our vices.'

'I thought you promised Lizzie you would stop.'

'In light of recent events, I decree that contract null and void,' he said pointedly, but he applauded along with the rest of the congregation, conceding victory to his rival with his usual aplomb.

Lucien smiled at his younger sibling's glum look. 'Someday, little brother, some woman's going to come along and make mincemeat of you, do you know that? And when she does, I want to shake her hand.'

'As long as she's rich,' he drawled.

'Ah, I see. The great losing streak continues?'

'Easy come, easy go. Don't worry, old boy, my luck will turn around. In the meantime – lend me twenty quid?'

Lucien arched an eyebrow at him. 'Not if my wife finds out.'

Alec harrumphed and turned his attention back to the front of the church, where Strathmore finally released Bits from his grasp. 'Your wife. His wife. You're all a lot of dupes in the vicar's mousetrap, if you ask me. He'd better love her,' he added wistfully.

'Are you blind? The man's a goner,' he replied, and as usual, Lucien was right.

Dev and Lizzie beamed as they strode past them, hurrying down the aisle. They were followed by the rest of the bridal party – Jacinda and Billy, and of course, young Sarah, looking as fresh as the dew.

Outside, they plunged into glorious sunshine. The wedding carriage waited, festooned and garlanded, an elegant landau with the top folded down and gold plumes on the four white horses' heads.

As the guests crowded out of the church, Lizzie laughed for sheer happiness and threw her arms around her husband's neck; Dev swept her off her feet, lifting her into the open coach. She kissed him while a confetti of white flower-petals dusted them like swirling snow.

When she opened her eyes, still hugging Dev, her rapt gaze lifted to the fine, gray church tower standing tall against the azure sky. Behind it, fleecy clouds drifted past, their movement as dizzying as her love.

'Are you really mine?' she whispered, gazing at her husband.

'Forever. Come, wife. Let's go home,' he murmured, taking her hand.

She sat beside him and waved to the sea of well-wishers, who soon piled into the long line of stately coaches.

The triumphal parade to Oakley Park wound through the

Kentish fields of white and purple clover, the perfumed breeze rippling through the new wheat in ear.

Come autumn, these rolling acres would turn to gold, Lizzie thought. *Like the ring on her finger*. As Devlin lifted her hand to his lips, she smiled with all her love for him shining in her eyes.

It would be a good harvest.

Turn the page for a sneak preview of the next instalment of the Knights Miscellany series. Available now. . .

Lord of Fire

Chapter One

London, 1814

Shadows sculpted his sharp profile as he watched the crowded ballroom from the dim, high balcony; in the oscillating glow of the draft-buffeted wall candle, he seemed to flicker in and out of materiality like some tall, elegant phantom. Its shifting radiance glimmered over his raven-black hair and caught the Machiavellian glint of cunning in his quicksilver-colored eyes. *Patience*. Everything was in order.

Preparation was all, and he had been meticulous. With a musing expression, Lord Lucien Knight lifted his crystal goblet of burgundy to his lips, pausing to inhale its mellow bouquet before he drank. He did not yet know his enemies' names or faces, but he could feel them inching closer like so many jackals. *No matter*. He was ready. He had laid his trap and baited it well, with all manner of sin and sex and the siren's whisper of subversive political activity that no spy could resist.

There was nothing left to do now but watch and wait.

Twenty years of war had ceased this past spring with Napoleon's defeat, abdication, and exile to the Mediterranean island of Elba. It was autumn now, and the leaders of Europe had gathered in Vienna to draw up the peace accord; *but any man with half a brain could see that until Bonaparte was moved to a more secure location farther out in the Atlantic*, Lucien thought dryly, *the war was not necessarily over*. Elba was but a stone's throw from the Italian mainland, and there were those who opposed the peace – who saw no profit for themselves in the Bourbon King Louis XVIII's return to the throne of France and who wanted Napoleon back. As one of the British Crown's most skilled secret agents, Lucien had orders from the foreign secretary, Viscount Castlereagh, to stand as the watcher at the gate, as it were, until the peace had been ratified – his mission, to stop these shadowy powers from stirring up trouble on English soil.

He took another sip of his wine, his silvery eyes gleaming with mayhem. *Let them come*. When they did, he would find them, snare them, catch and destroy them, just as he had so many others. Indeed, he would make them come to him.

Suddenly, a round of cheers broke out in the ballroom below and rippled through the crowd. *Well, well, the conquering hero*. Lucien leaned forward and rested his elbows on the railing of the balcony, watching with a cynical smirk as his identical twin brother, Colonel Lord Damien Knight, marched into the assembly rooms, resplendent in his scarlet uniform with the stern, high dignity of the Archangel Michael just back from slaying the dragon. The glitter of his dress sword and gold epaulets seemed to throw off a shining halo around him, but the famed colonel's unsmiling demeanor did not discourage the swarm of smitten women, eager aides-de-camp, junior officers, and assorted hero-worshiping toadies who instantly surrounded him. Damien had always been the favorite of the gods.

Lucien shook his head to himself. Though his lips curved in wry amusement, pain flickered behind his haughty stare. If it weren't enough that the colonel had captured the popular imagination with his gallant exploits in battle, as the elder twin, Damien would soon be made an earl by a rather convoluted accident of lineage. It was not jealousy that stung Lucien, however, but an almost childlike sense of having been abandoned by his staunchest ally. Damien was the only person who had ever really understood him. For most of their thirty-one years, the Knight twins had been inseparable. In their rakish youth, their friends had dubbed them Lucifer and Demon, while the alarmed mothers of Society debutantes had warned their daughters about 'that pair of devils.' But those carefree days of laughter and camaraderie were gone, for Lucien had transgressed his brother's soldierly code.

Damien had never quite accepted Lucien's decision to leave the army a little over two years ago for the secret service branch of the Diplomatic Corps. Officers of the line, as a rule, deemed espionage dishonorable, ungentlemanly. To Damien and his ilk, spies were no better than snakes. Damien was a born warrior, to be sure. Anyone who had ever seen him in battle, his face streaked with black powder and blood, knew there was no question of that. But there would not have been quite so many victories without the constant stream of intelligence that Lucien had sent him – against regulation, at the risk of his life – on the enemy's position, strength, numbers, and likeliest plan of attack. How it surely chafed the great commander's pride to know that the fullness of his glory would not have been possible without his spy brother's help.

No matter, Lucien thought cynically. *He still knew better than anyone how to prick the war hero's titanic ego.*

'Lucien!' a breathy voice suddenly called from behind him.

He turned around and saw Caro's voluptuous silhouette framed in the doorway. 'Why, my dear Lady Glenwood,' he purred, holding out his hand to her with a dark smile. *Wasn't Damien going to be cross about this?*

'I've been looking everywhere for you!' Her doll-like side curls swung against her rouged cheeks as she flounced over to him in a rustle of black satin. She smiled slyly, revealing the fetching little gap between her two front teeth as she took his hand and let him pull her up close against his body. 'Damien's here—'

'Who?' he murmured, skimming her lips with his own.

She groaned softly under his kiss and melted against him, the black satin of her gown sliding sensually against the white brocade of his formal waistcoat. Last night it had been skin to skin.

Though the twenty-seven-year-old baroness wore mourning for her late husband, Lucien doubted she had shed a tear. A husband, to a woman like Caro, was merely an impediment to her pursuit of pleasure. Her ebony gown had a tiny bodice that barely contained her burgeoning cleavage. The midnight fabric made her skin look like alabaster, while her crimson lips matched the roses that adorned her upswept, chocolate-brown hair. After a moment, Caro made an effort to end their kiss, bracing her gloved hands on his chest.

When she pulled back slightly, he saw that she was gloating, her cheeks flushed, her raisin-dark eyes glowing with amorous triumph. Lucien masked his insolent smile as Caro coyly lowered her lashes and stroked the lapels of his formal black tailcoat. To be sure, she believed she had done the impossible, what none of her rivals had ever achieved – that she alone had snared *both* Knight twins as her conquests and could now play them off each other for her own vanity. Alas, the lady had a large surprise in store.

He was a bad man, he knew, but he could not resist toying with her a bit. He licked his lips as he stared at her, then glanced suggestively at the nearby wall, cloaked in shadows. 'No one can see us up here, my love. Are you game?'

She let out one of her throaty laughs. 'You wicked devil, I'll give you more later. Right now I want us to see Damien.'

Lucien lifted one eyebrow, playing along with consummate skill. 'Together?'

'Yes. I don't want him to think we have anything to hide.' She gave him a crafty glance from beneath her lashes and smoothed his white silk cravat. 'We must act naturally.'

'I'll try, *ma chérie*,' he murmured.

'Good. Now, come.' She slipped her gloved hand through the crook of his elbow and propelled him toward the small spiral staircase that led down to the ballroom. He went along amiably, which ought to have warned her that he was up to something. 'You swear you didn't tell him?'

'*Mon ange*, I would never say a word.' He did not see fit to add that such was the bond between identical twins that they hardly required *words* for the exchange of information. A glance, a laugh, a look spoke volumes. Appalling, really, to think that this wanton little schemer, for all her beauty, was on the verge of snaring Damien in marriage. Lucky for the war hero, his snake of a spy brother had come to his rescue again with the crucial information: Caro had not passed the test.

Lucien bent his head near her ear. 'I trust you are still coming with me to Revell Court this weekend?'

She slipped him a nervous glance. 'Actually, darling, I'm . . . not sure.'

'What?' He stopped and turned to her with a scowl. 'Why not? I want you there.'

Her lips parted slightly, and she looked like she might climax on the spot in response to his demand. 'Lucien.'

'Caro,' he retorted. It was hardly a lover's devotion that inspired his insistence, but the simple fact that a beautiful woman was a useful thing to have on hand when trying to catch enemy spies.

'You don't understand!' she said with a pout. 'I *want* to go. It's just that I received a letter today from Goody Two-Shoes. She said—'

'From whom?' he demanded, cutting her off with a dubious look. If he recalled correctly, it was a character in a classic children's story by Oliver Goldsmith.

'Alice, my sister-in-law,' she said, waving off the name in irritation. 'I may have to go home to Glenwood Park. She says my baby might be getting sick. If I don't go home and help take care of Harry, Alice will have my head. Not that *I* know what to do with the little creature.' She sniffed. 'All he does for me is scream.'

'Well, he's got a nurse, hasn't he?' he asked in disgust. He knew that Caro had a three-year-old son by her late husband, though most of the time *she* seemed to forget the fact. The child was one of the reasons why Damien was so interested in marrying the woman. Aside from some bizarre fatherly impulse toward a child he had never even seen, Damien wanted a wife with a proven ability to bear him sons. An earl, after all, needed heirs. Unfortunately, Caro had not proved worthy, surrendering wholeheartedly to Lucien's seduction. Damien was going to fume at the blow to his pride, but Lucien refused to allow his brother to marry any woman who did not love him to distraction. Any woman worthy of Damien would have refused Lucien's silken trap.

'Of course he has a nurse, but Alice says he needs, well . . . me,' Caro said in dismay.

'But *I* need you, *chérie*.' He slipped her a coaxing little smile, wondering if his own late mother had occasionally suffered similar pangs of conscience. What a piece of work she had been, the scandalous duchess of Hawkscliffe, making conquests of half the men she met. Indeed, the twins' own father had not been their mother's husband, but her devoted lover of many years, the powerful and mysterious marquess of Carnarthen. The marquess had died recently, leaving Lucien the bulk of his fortune and his infamous villa, Revell Court, situated a dozen miles southwest of Bath.

As Lucien stared at Caro, he realized why he felt so strongly about stopping Damien from marrying her. He could hardly let his brother end up with a wife who was just like their mother. Turning away abruptly, he began walking down the hallway, leaving Caro where she stood. 'Never mind, woman. Go home to your brat,' he muttered. 'I'll find someone else to amuse me.'

'But, Lucien, I want to come!' she protested, hurrying to catch up in a rustle of satin.

He stared straight ahead as he stalked down the hallway. 'Your boy needs you and you know it.'

'No, he doesn't.' Her tone was so bleak that Lucien looked askance at her. 'He doesn't even know me. He only loves Alice.'

'Is that what you think?'

'It's the truth. I am an incompetent mother.'

He shook his head with a vexed sigh. What was it to him if she wanted to lie to herself? 'Come along, then. Damien is waiting.' Tucking her hand in the crook of his arm, he led her to the ballroom to face her fate.

Under the bright glow of the balloon-cut chandeliers, the ballroom looked like a civilized place to those who did not know better; but to Lucien, not for nothing was the marble floor laid out in black and white squares like a giant chessboard. Carefully watching the crowd from behind the facade of the decadent, self-indulged persona he had created, he kept all his senses sharply attuned, on the lookout for anyone or anything that set his instincts jangling. Nothing was ever obvious, which was why he had cultivated an enlightened paranoia and trusted no one. In his experience, it was the most average, ordinary-looking people who harbored the most dangerous treacheries. The strange characters were usually harmless; indeed, he had a fondness for all creatures who refused to be crushed by the iron mold of conformity. This preference was borne out in his acquaintance as, here and there, disreputable persons, odd fellows, outsiders, assorted voluptuaries, rebels, disheveled scientific geniuses from the Royal Society, and freakish eccentrics of every stripe nodded to him, furtively offering their respects.

Ah, his minions were eager to return to Revell Court for the festivities, he thought in jaded amusement, accepting their subtle homage with a narrow smile. He cast a wink to a painted lady who greeted him from behind her spread fan.

'Your Unholiness,' she whispered, giving him a come-hither look.

He bowed his head. *'Bon soir, madame.'* From the corner of his eye, he noticed Caro staring at him in fascination, her lips slightly parted. 'What is it, my dear?'

She glanced at the velvet-clad scoundrels who bowed to him, then met his gaze with a sly look. 'I was just wondering how Miss Goody Two-Shoes would fare with you around. It would be such fun to watch you corrupt her.'

'Drop her by sometime. I'll do my best.'

She smirked. 'She'd probably faint if you even looked at her, the little prude.'

'Young?'

'Not very. She's twenty-one.' Caro paused. 'Actually, I doubt that even *you* could scale her ivory tower, if you take my meaning.'

He frowned askance at her. 'Please.'

Caro shrugged, a mocking smile tugging at her lips. 'I don't know, Lucien. It wouldn't be easy. Alice is as *good* as you are *bad*.'

He lifted his eyebrow and dwelled on this for a moment, then pursued the matter, his curiosity piqued. 'Is she really such a paragon?'

'Ugh, she turns my stomach,' Caro replied under her breath, nodding to people here and there as they ambled through the crowd. 'She won't gossip. She doesn't lie. She doesn't laugh when I make a perfectly witty remark about some woman's ridiculous dress. She cannot be induced to vanity. She never even misses church!'

'My God, you have my sympathies for having to live with such a monster. What did you say her name was again?' he asked mildly.

'Alice.'

'Montague?'

'Yes. She's my poor Glenwood's little sister.'

'Alice Montague,' he echoed in a musing tone. *A baron's daughter*, he thought. Virtuous. Available. Good with the brat. Sounded like a perfect candidate for Damien's bride. 'Is she fair?'

'Tolerable,' Caro said flatly, avoiding his gaze.

'Mm-hmm.' He passed a scrutinizing glance over her face, and his eyes began to dance at the jealousy stamped on the baroness's fine features. 'How tolerable, exactly?'

She gave him a quelling look and refused to answer.

'Come, tell me.'

'Forget about her!'

'I'm only curious. What color are her eyes?'

She ignored him, nodding to a lady in a feathered turban.

'Oh, Caro,' he murmured playfully. 'Are you jealous of little luscious twenty-one?'

'Don't be absurd!'

'Then where's the harm?' he insisted, goading her. 'Tell me what color Alice's eyes are.'

'Blue,' she snapped, 'but they are lackluster.'

'And her hair?'

'Blonde. Red. I don't know. What does it signify?'

'Indulge me.'

'You are an utter pest! Alice's hair is her crowning glory, if you must know. It hangs to her waist, and I suppose you call the color of it strawberry blonde,' she said peevishly, 'but it is always filled with the crumbs of whatever kind of muffin the baby ate for breakfast. Quite disgusting. I have told her a hundred times that long, cascading Rapunzel hair is entirely out of fashion, but Alice ignores me. She likes it. Now are you satisfied?'

'She sounds delicious,' Lucien whispered in her ear. 'Might I bring her to Revell Court instead of you?'

Caro pulled back and smacked him with her black lace fan.

Lucien was still laughing at her ire as they sauntered into the knot of red-coated soldiers. 'Ah, look, Lady Glenwood,' he said in bright irony. 'It is my dear brother. Evening, Demon. I've brought someone to see you.' Sliding his hands into the pockets of his black trousers, he rocked idly on his heels, a cynical smile sporting at his lips as he waited to watch the show unfold.